I0580844

# J.F.R. COATES

Text copyright 2024

Cover by Chromamancer

Fate of Three
978-1-922061-92-8



J.F.R. Coates
Queensland, Australia

# FATE OF THREE

## BOOK 3: THE DESTINY OF DRAGONS

### BY J.F.R. COATES

# Acknowledgements

I don't think I could ever properly thank everyone who has contributed to this series in the ten years since it was first released. So many people have shaped my writing career and skills that I would always risk leaving someone out.

I first have to thank my parents. Not only did they support my choice to become a writer, they also fostered and nurtured my interest in reading as a child. Without that, these stories would almost certainly not exist today.

I also have to thank those other writers who have inspired me over the years. From J.R.R. Tolkien to Philip Pullman, Neil Gaiman to Robin Hobb, my work does not exist in isolation. All of these great writers and more have had some inspiration on the stories I have wanted to tell.

I would also like to thank my husband. His support over the years has provided me with the capability to continue writing these stories.

And then there are my readers. Whether this is your first introduction to the *Destiny of Dragons* series, or you have been with me across the last ten years, thank you all! Without you, the writing process would be a vastly different experience.

And finally, it would be remiss of me not to mention those who supported my Kickstarter campaign to officially launch these 10 Year Anniversary Editions of the trilogy. Your support means the world to me.

Thank you everyone!

# CHAPTER ONE

**Anzig**

I paced nervously around my chamber, pausing every now and then only to look up to Mushussu. The silver statue watched from her perch above the fire, her sinuous neck moving as her head followed my circular progress. Normally, I wanted to keep her out of my head at all times, but now, when I most desired some advice and assistance, she was silent. Not for the first time, I longed for Carlee's voice by my side.

I would never hear her voice again, lost forever. Lost to my own rashness. She had died to protect me, despite knowing that I lived a lie. I was not my father's son. I was not the rightful leader of Laxtal.

I paused again in my pacing and stared at the stubborn paint that still clung to my scales, markings made by Ellian for the wylax. I may have become the ddraig at the ceremony, but that had not settled the unease in my gut. I had spoken the words the clan wanted to hear, but there were too many secrets within me. Magic, lineage, and confidence all worked against me. It would only be a matter of time before someone revealed my lies, ending my rule.

Disapproval simmered through my mind. It was the first contact with Mushussu I had felt since Haeraig Zeena had gone to fetch the ddraig of Nixa. Given what she had seen, what she already knew, there were some secrets that I could no longer hide. She had a right to know. As did her father. My…

The thought died in my head. I couldn't even think it yet. I didn't know how I could possibly say it.

Mushussu finally breached the silence. "I can offer assistance."

I shuddered. My tail curled from the tip. "I would rather you didn't."

I had already felt her assistance once before, words of confidence and strength coming unbidden to my mouth. She had spoken on my behalf at the wylax. I was not keen to repeat the experience again.

The statue sighed. Her magic weakened against my mind, but it did not retreat fully. I could still feel her emotions, bubbling away in the corner of my thoughts. Already I struggled to keep those to myself. Her presence there tugged at the frayed edges of my mental state, blurring the line between what was me and who was nearby. Even without thinking I could sense Ellian and Airil together in the chamber next to mine. Their excitement sent flutters through my heart. Further away was the tortuous roiling of the thousands of Laxtal dragons and the Nixan refugees. So many voices, all clamouring for attention.

And then, much closer, was the darkened spirit of Ddraig Krateos. His steadfast and resolute daughter walked with him.

I lifted my head and turned to the entrance of my chamber a moment before they announced their presence. Mushussu's metallic body fell still as the haeraig entered my chamber, the guardian's magic unable to maintain her ability to move in the presence of a dragon who was not a ddraig. That did nothing to quell her thoughts, however.

Haeraig Zeena bowed her head as she pushed through the dividing veil draped across the entrance. There was a tension in her body, like she braced to fight or flee. I did not need to break into her thoughts to know she had suspicions about me. She had found me holding the Axinstone, something no dragon without magic should be able to survive. She had seen my eyes turn white with magic.

I ran my tongue over my teeth as I waited for the two Nixans to settle, resisting the urge to start pacing. Ddraig Krateos had not looked up once, his eyes staring at his paws. He swayed even as he sat, tail wrapped tightly around his hindlegs. I had not been the only one at the wine overnight. I could scent it on his breath.

"What is this regarding, Ddraig Anzig?" the Nixan ddraig said, words slurring.

I opened my mouth. Hesitated. Closed it again. I quailed under the fierce gaze of Haeraig Zeena. How could I say this? How could I reveal to any dragon that my life was a lie? Saying what I must to a Laxtal dragon would result in expulsion from the clan. This was a ddraig and haeraig of a rival. Nixa may be our allies, but they would still seek to exploit any weakness in Laxtal, and I was presenting to them the greatest gift imaginable.

A quiet voice whispered in my head. *"He deserves to know the truth."*

I suppressed the growl as my eyes flicked up to Mushussu, above and beyond Haeraig Zeena's shoulder. I wasn't sure if Ddraig Krateos could hear the guardian, but the haeraig certainly could not.

I took in a deep breath. Held it. Then slowly exhaled. "I think I can ease some of your pain, Ddraig Krateos. The eggs you could not raise. They didn't die. Two of them, at least, survived."

Only then did the Nixan ddraig look up. His eyes watered, and I had to look away from his shame.

"Don't you dare toy with my father's emotions like this," Haeraig Zeena hissed. She rose to her paws and prowled forward a couple of steps, her fangs bared. Her eyes flashed white and I felt the pressure of her magic against my scales, braced and ready to throw me across the chamber should she wish it.

I held my ground. "I'm telling the truth. You have a daughter and a son. Of the third egg, I'm not sure."

"How can you be sure?" The ddraig's voice cracked. He looked away, the edge of his wing wiping at the tears on his cheek.

"Because I know them." I trembled as I lifted to my paws. The magical pressure against my chest eased slightly as Haeraig Zeena relaxed her guard. "Your daughter is Maznar, the dragon we rescued in Trevena. She was given to the humans as an egg and raised amongst them, twisted by their magic into the monster Nightwings. You saw her in Nixa, but I don't know if she wished to reveal herself to you then."

"And my son?"

I could not keep control of my emotions. My breath caught in my throat, and I felt those hated tears spring in my eyes. I turned my head, but I knew there was no stopping them. Every attempt to speak faded to a whimper. Dimly aware of the ddraig edging closer to me, I pushed my mind out to touch his. *"The son is me."*

The tears now flowed freely down my face, running in rivulets through the narrow cracks between my scales. I bowed my head in a futile attempt to keep the ddraig from seeing them.

The full force of Ddraig Krateos's gaze fell on the back of my neck. "My son?" I heard him say. I felt a touch on my chin, and with one gentle claw, the Nixan ddraig lifted my head to look me in the eyes. His claw gently moved up the side of my face. "Tears? Only a Nixan dragon can cry. Along with our magic, it separates us from the other clans. You are not a Laxtal dragon."

I tried to pull away from Ddraig Krateos, but his hold on me was too strong. I found my throat loosened enough to speak. "Nixan? I didn't know it was a Nixan trait. I cried once when I was young, but my father... Astar. He was furious with me. Told me never to do it again because it was a sign of weakness."

Ddraig Krateos rumbled. His paw fell away. "Then Astar knew you were a Nixan dragon, but he still raised you as his own. I should be grateful to him, but I still don't understand how this is possible."

If anyone from my clan could see me now, openly weeping in front of the Nixan ddraig, then my reputation would crumble. Whether a sign of weakness or a clear indication I was Nixan, it didn't matter. I was a disgrace to my clan. Astar's attempts to hide the truth of who I was were for naught.

"What happens now?" Haeraig Zeena asked into the sudden silence that had swept over us all. I knew what she meant. How could I be ddraig of Laxtal and Ddraig Krateos's son at the same time? My clan hadn't accepted Xital rule – they certainly wouldn't accept a Nixan leader.

My mind was completely devoid of ideas, and it seemed Ddraig Krateos was suffering similarly, as neither of us could answer the haeraig's question. It was an impossible situation, most unlike anything I had ever heard of. With a haeraig who had not yet managed to prove her worth, I risked plunging Laxtal into anarchy and chaos at a time when the clan needed to be strong and united.

It was Ddraig Krateos who finally spoke. "The important thing is to maintain our strength. For all my personal joy, it would only weaken Laxtal should it be known that you are my son, Anzig. For now, at least. You must send your haeraig to the neighbouring clans to gather their support. On her return, we can discuss how to best handle this situation. Until then, though, we must ensure no one else suspects who you truly are."

I hid my face behind a wing. "That will be harder to do when it feels like my mind is fraying. I can't trust my thoughts when I don't know which ones are mine and which come from another dragon. And that's even before..." The words died before I could say them, strangled by another magic I didn't understand. I flicked my tail in the direction of Mushussu and her perch, hoping the ddraig would know what I referred to.

"Then we can train you," Ddraig Krateos said. Through the membrane of my wing, I could see him settle down again. "In secret, do not worry. Our situation with the humans goes beyond clan politics. I would not weaken our alliance when we need every scrap of strength we can muster. Nixa has already lost too much. I would not clip Laxtal's wings when it is your clan that keeps us aloft."

Slowly, I drew my wing back. Anything that would help keep my thoughts my own would be a blessed relief. "I would appreciate that, thank you."

A smile cracked across Ddraig Krateos's muzzle, though it didn't quite reach his eyes. "I would never have thought… I have a son again."

Haeraig Zeena bumped her nose against mine. "Brother," she said, showing her fangs again, but in a smile this time. "I should have suspected. Your horns were never long enough for a Laxtal dragon."

My paw instinctively moved to cover one of my short, blunt horns. I bit down on a growl. She was right. My horns had always been a point of embarrassment, so much shorter than all other dragons in the clan, but no one had ever called me Nixan for them. They had just been a defect, a point of weakness and shame. Now, as my eyes flicked over the heads of the two Nixans in front of me, I recognised them for what they truly were. Evidence of Astar's lies.

"Come," Ddraig Krateos rumbled. "Let us ensure that your haeraig can begin her journey. Then we can start on your training. You have a lot to catch up on."

I bowed my head. "Meet me in the main chamber. I shall be along shortly."

Ddraig Krateos bent his foreleg to sweep down into a lower bow than I had seen from him, the tip of his muzzle bumping against the floor. His daughter repeated the gesture. I doubted he would ever have shown such deference to me before the secrets shared had revealed me as his son.

I was relieved when the two Nixans left me. It would also allow me to get a little more room, away from the dragon who I would somehow have to start calling 'father'. It was too much for my muddled mind to handle right now. I still found it hard to accept that I couldn't turn to Carlee for guidance.

"You have me now," Mushussu reminded me from her perch.

I looked up at the guardian ness. Her silvered body shone in the firelight, but nothing reflected in her scales. Her mind linked with mine, and I was sure that she was aware of the disappointment I felt that she was no match to my old mentor. Carlee had known that I was not Astar's son. She might even have known who my real father was. She certainly would have known I was a Nixan. She had kept that secret from me her whole life. She had looked me in the eye and told me Astar was proud of his son, knowing full well that Astar had no son. I tried to feel anger at her deception, if only to feel some emotion at all, but I felt no emotion but fear.

Drying my eyes off on one of the many thick rugs I had inherited as the Laxtal ddraig, I steeled myself to meet my clan. They didn't yet know my true heritage, so I should have no need to fear them. For the sake of dragonkind, I had to keep the clan strong until Ellian finished her diplomatic journey. She would become the ddraig in my stead, but I could not allow a period of confusion to reign while she secured the necessary alliances for our survival. Ddraig Krateos was right. We needed to keep this hidden until dragonkind could overcome this human threat.

I stared into the reflective surface of my mirror. My eyes lingered on my horns. My muzzle. My tail. They were not weaknesses because of random chance and circumstance. They were indicators of my true heritage. Now that I knew the truth it was impossible to avoid it. I was a Nixan dragon in every way.

Could I really keep the truth hidden?

"No one has noticed yet."

Somehow, Mushussu's words failed to bring me comfort.

A council of dragons had already convened before I arrived in the main chamber. The podium by the great fire was the location of several growling and arguing dragons. Ddraig Krateos and Haeraig Zeena lingered close by, but they did not interact with the squabbling Laxtal dragons. Saya and Marin were unsurprising participants, with Vinzent sat by his mother's side. Yalle and Ellian prowled opposite them.

I growled and snapped my jaws at the disrespect of starting a council without me as I landed, drawing the attention of the five argumentative dragons, bringing their hasty silence. A few interested eyes watched on from around the chamber, but there were not many present. Most would be out hunting or training, I hoped.

"What is the meaning of all this?"

Even Ellian looked cowed as I tucked my wings to my back. I glared towards Saya and Marin, waiting for someone to speak.

Marin was the first to open his mouth. "It is Azlak," he growled. "He has taken two of the Nixans and gone to the forbidden caves deep below the lair."

I snorted. "And that is reason to behave like squabbling dragonets?"

Marin managed to look contrite as he scratched his forepaw against the stone. "It is a continuation of his behaviour since you flew to Xital. He has been favouring Nixan company and ignoring the needs and demands of Laxtal."

From his vantage to the side, Ddraig Krateos scoffed, but he still did not interject himself into the conversation. I shook my head slowly. Whatever the seer was doing in the deep caves was nothing to concern ourselves with. Not yet, at least. There were other, more important matters to deal with.

"We need to focus," I growled, swinging my head around to glare at each of the dragons in turn. Without realising it, I had come to stand in the middle of a loose circle of dragons, with three of Astar's most trusted amongst them. Yalle, Marin, and Saya had both gained significant respect under the rule of Ddraig Astar. I did not think they would offer me the same loyalty as they had to the dragon they believed to be my father.

"What matters would you have us discuss?" Saya asked. Her soft, gentle voice sent a shiver down my spine.

I felt trapped within the circle of dragons. I had no room to pace, but nor did I feel comfortable sitting down. Instead, I remained standing and slowly circled on the spot. "It has been two weeks since Tsona sent out his army from Xital. We do not know where they have gone, but I suspect they flew east to secure alliances and conquer opposition. This gives us a chance to strengthen our position, but we are fast running out of time. We need to act quickly and decisively."

Marin and Saya exchanged a quick glance between them. I was sure something unspoken passed through that look, but I didn't dare cast my mind out to work out what. Until I had better control of my magic, I could not afford to risk losing myself to the thoughts of others. Especially not in such company.

"Haeraig Ellian will fly out immediately, with the intention of securing alliances from our neighbours. Our first target must be Ddraig Aranat of Axaatl." I kept speaking before anyone else could interrupt. I glanced towards Ddraig Krateos, lingering just beyond the circle of dragons. "Our alliance is currently two ruling clans. Bring together three, and we will have an accord that has never been seen before. The minor clans will not be able to deny the show of strength that will present."

"And how much will this weaken Laxtal?" Marin asked.

I stopped to stare at the veteran dragon. He did not look away. "Weaken?" I asked. I tilted my head to the side. "These alliances will only strengthen our position against Xital and the humans."

"And what power will we barter away in order to achieve this… strength." Saya spat at the ground between her forepaws. "Since when has Laxtal ever needed another clan to fly alongside? Do you think so little of us that we cannot win this war by our might?"

I slowly turned on the spot until I faced both Saya and Marin. Vinzent shied back a pace, but the silver dragonet still had a snarl etched on his muzzle.

My claws scratched against the stone. "Ddraig Astar thought as you did to begin with. How many dragons survived his attempts to take the fight to them? And have you forgotten who it was who sent me to the great council at Xital to secure aid? Even Astar recognised that we could not fight this war alone. Had he done so sooner, we may have saved many lives."

Marin sneered. "So, Azlak was right. There is a weakness in your heart, Anzig."

Ellian stomped her paw and snarled, leaping in front of me to snap her teeth at the older dragon. "He is your ddraig, confirmed and chosen by the wylax. Such disrespect to your ddraig should be withdrawn or backed up with a challenge. Which is it to be, Marin?"

The older dragon hesitated. He glanced left, towards Saya. The ness shook her head.

Marin bowed. "My apologies, ddraig. I withdraw my accusation." I did not need my magic to recognise his insincerity.

I bared my teeth at him, but I said nothing and turned away. "We will secure the allies we need to protect ourselves. I will stay here to ensure that the dragons who come to defend our land are trained and ready to fight. With the magic of clan Nixa by our side, we may be able to divine other ways to gather strength. This is not a time for petty feuds and pointless accusations. We must fly together or fall apart. Do I make myself understood?"

Saya simmered in anger, unspoken thoughts at the forefront of her mind, threatening to spill into my head. She moved her paw in preparation to step forward, but before she could do so, her son moved in front of her.

"We understand, Ddraig Anzig," Vinzent said. He held his head up high, with far more height than I could ever manage. He flicked out a wing to block his mother's movement.

I flicked my tail and hesitated. I expected something else from the young dragon, but nothing came. There had to be some other motive, but I didn't dare reach out with my magic to learn what. Instead, I used the unexpected peacekeeping to turn back to Ellian.

"I don't want you going alone. If Ddraig Krateos permits it, I would like you to take someone from Nixa with you," I said, glancing towards the two Nixans who lurked nearby. As I addressed him, Ddraig Krateos took a step forward, ignoring the bristling anger from Saya and Marin.

"I am sure my daughter would be a willing companion for your haeraig," the ddraig said, not once looking back at Haeraig Zeena. The ness frowned, but she said nothing to contradict her father. Our father.

Ellian's wings fluttered. "If I may suggest an alternative, Ddraig Krateos. If I were permitted to take Airil with me, then I would be able to reach Axaatl much sooner. Any hour I can save might make the difference between success and failure."

Haeraig Zeena smiled as she stepped up beside her father. "You speak wisely. I would be happy to concede this opportunity to represent Nixa to Airil. He would make a fine emissary and a dedicated travelling companion to you, Haeraig Ellian."

A deep rumble came from Ddraig Krateos's throat. He said nothing, but after a few moments he nodded in consent.

"Then it is decided," I said. My eyes swept around the small council. Excitement and rage mirrored each other, barely concealed venom coming from Saya's eyes. Only Yalle seemed content with everything that had happened, the albino calmly and placidly watching from Ellian's side. "Go and find Airil and make any preparations for your journey. I shall meet you outside soon."

I waited only for her to agree before I took to wing and flew for my chambers again. I could hear the wingbeats of others as they launched into the air, but they soon faded into the background noise of the chamber, none following me directly.

The silence calmed me, away from the bombardment of thoughts against the edge of my mind. I pushed through the veil into my chamber and let that emptiness fill me, taking a deep breath to push away any lingering tension.

Unfortunately, that silence could never last. I would never truly be alone in my chambers.

"Looking for this?"

I sighed as I looked up to Mushussu. She carried in her paws the jewelled amulet worn by the leader of Laxtal on diplomatic occasions. It had been mine to wear twice before, at the council of Xital and again at the wylax. Now it would be Ellian's.

I took hold of the amulet, letting the golden chain spool across my paw. My claws closed slowly around the azure gem in its centre. "Will you be able to protect her?"

Mushussu barely made a noise as she jumped down from her plinth. "My magic does not extend to her. I cannot warn her of any dangers she may face, nor protect her from whatever may seek to harm her. I can only protect you, and then only when you sleep in this chamber every night. My magic is far from limitless."

I bit down on the immediate response that came to mind. Her power seemed pointless, as well as limited. Judging from the metallic click of her tongue, she heard my thoughts anyway.

"My power was shattered by forces you could never comprehend, young ddraig," the guardian huffed. She turned away and jumped back to her alcove, curling up tight with her head resting on her coiled body. "I do what I can with what little I have left. I hope you will come to understand that, but you do not have time for lectures. Go and see your haeraig away. Your enemies draw close."

Another thing the guardian could not protect me from.

Before I could pick up another annoyed retort from the statue, I fled the chamber with the amulet in paw. I took to wing as soon as I could, sweeping through the lair towards the surface. A few dragons dropped to the floor in deference as I flew by.

Despite the sunlight, the air was still cool as I burst out into the gorge and quickly banked to rise to the grassy hill above the lair. A few clouds raced across the sky, but otherwise the day was a clear one. The approach of winter made itself known in the chill wind that blew down from the distant mountains.

As I had asked, Ellian waited for me on the edge of the cliff overlooking the plains. Though I had not been long in my chambers, she had already found Airil, with the Nixan waiting eagerly by her side. Ddraig Krateos and Haeraig Zeena had come to see her and their Nixan clanmate off, as had Yalle and Vinzent. I could not see the others from the small council, but I was glad of that.

Ellian spread her wings, ready for flight, but before she could depart in haste, I put the amulet over her head. The azure stone rested against the base of her neck, the colour perfectly complementing her lilac scales as though it had been crafted solely for her.

"With this amulet you are representing Laxtal. I fully trust that you will do your clan proud," I said, repeating the words Astar had told me when sending me to Xital. They were very nearly the last words he ever spoke to me.

Ellian's wings quivered in her excitement. Her claws gripped the grass like it was an effort to keep herself on the ground. "I will. You can trust me."

I smiled, seeing in my cousin the same thrilled dragon I had been when I had first flown out with the Laxtal stone around my neck. "Your actions reflect on me now." My smile turned sour as I remembered the might of the ddraig whose pawprints I followed, and those I opposed. "I need all the help I can get."

"Oh Ziggy, you're too hard on yourself," Ellian whispered; her informal words weren't for Airil or any of the others who watched on, but even so, I felt a fragment of her thoughts. *"Maybe Astar was right about him."* I tensed in shock and fear. What had Astar said about me to Ellian? Did she know the truth; that he was not my father? I couldn't ask, for she would question how I had known her thoughts. It was all I could do to slowly nod my head and pretend I had heard nothing.

"Fly safe, Ellian. Don't let anything happen to you," I whispered.

She rested her head on my shoulder. "Airil will look after me. He will keep me safe."

I looked towards the Nixan. Perhaps he would make a better protector than Mushussu. The guardian had shown little ability outside of my chamber.

Ellian finally let her spread wings lift her into the air. With powerful downstrokes she began to soar, Airil following close behind. Yalle also took to wing, but he ventured back towards the lair.

Silver scales sidled close. I didn't take my eyes from my haeraig as she left, but I could feel Vinzent's thoughts simmering by my side.

"My mother wanted you to know," the dragonet said, falling into a brief silence as though waiting for a response from me. I didn't give him one. He cleared his throat, scratching at the grass Ellian had just vacated. "She wanted you to know that she understands who hold the real power between you both. And I understand it, too."

My eyes snapped to the young dragon. "Speak plainly, Vinzent."

The dragonet's eyes flicked upwards. "She is your strength. You have sent her away. That is all."

I spluttered with indignant rage, but Vinzent didn't give me the chance to form a proper response. He fled towards the lair, leaving me alone with the Nixan ddraig and haeraig, but they were too far away to have heard our exchange. Though Ddraig Krateos, my father, looked towards me with curiosity, I did not feel like explaining anything to him.

I returned to my vigil of the sky, trying to keep my discomfort out of my posture. I could not let Vinzent's words upset me. He was just an upstart dragonet guided by the poisoned words of his mother. He was not a true threat to me.

I sat alone at the top of the hill and watched the two dragons fly away. It wasn't long before Ellian and Airil were nothing more than two dark specks in the eastern sky. I held my wings tight against my body, shielding myself from the strong wind that was blowing down from the mountains behind me. I pawed at the ground as I looked to the east. Beyond the distant horizon lay Axaatl and our hopes for defeating the human invaders.

Tsona had been working on building his alliances for a long time now. We couldn't know how many clans had already allied to his cause, but we needed to work hard to catch up. As Ellian disappeared into the distance, I felt comfort in the fact that we were now making progress; we had taken the first steps in forming a great alliance with the western clans.

All I needed to do was keep control of Laxtal and hope that we were not already too late.

# CHAPTER TWO

**Azlak**

I didn't know how many hours had passed, standing vigil over Esperance as she recovered her strength. The strange human had spent much of that time sleeping, her body knitting together the deep wound left by the obsidian blade I had pulled from her heart. Kaz and Inilta kept guard with me, the latter keeping his magical flame alight so we had a small circle of visibility.

I doubted we needed to remain alert. I had heard nothing move outside Inilta's light. The wind carried no scents, but I still did not want to leave Esperance alone, and nor did Kaz. We were the vigilant guardians, while Inilta spent most of the time sleeping close by, his magic still flowing consistently despite his slumber.

Esperance had said little since she had first woken, simply speaking her requirement to rest and recover. I had spent much of the time watching over her to wonder what exactly she was, for she was most unlike any human I had seen before. There was an incredible power radiating from her body with such a force that I was afraid to touch her.

"What do you think she is?"

I glanced up as Kaz padded close, walking on the heel of his paws so his claws didn't click against the stone floor. We were far enough from Esperance and Inilta that I didn't think it mattered too much, but the Nixan kept his voice hushed anyway.

"She's not like any of the humans I've ever met," I said, matching Kaz's quiet tone.

"There's something else to her." Kaz didn't look back to the human and sleeping dragon. Instead, his eyes drifted towards the cavernous archway that opened not far away, beyond which nothing of Inilta's magic reached. I had done my best to ignore that yawning darkness. The Nixan had done no such thing. "There's something else about here, too. Can you feel it?"

I shivered. "I've always felt it. I thought the magic down here might have been Esperance, but I don't think it is. Whatever it is, it's coming from in there." I flicked my tail in the direction of the darkness. I put a paw on Kaz's before he could think about moving. "I don't think we should leave Esperance yet. We don't know what's in there. It might be related to what hurt her."

Kaz huffed, but he settled down by my side, making no attempt to avoid any physical contact. I tensed as his head rested against my shoulder, then slowly relaxed and let my wing drape over his back.

We lay together like that for a long time, the cave almost silent and still, with only Inilta's light to see by. His breathing was soft and regular beside me, descending into a sound that was almost a purr. Never before had a dragon other than Kaz willingly settled so close to me. The constant touch sent a sensation almost like an itch through my scales, but I resisted the urge to move. He was comfortable. I wanted to be.

No one had courted me before. No ness or drake had ever taken an interest in me. But then there was this Nixan. Just thinking about him that way sent heat flooding down my neck. I barely dared to think about the possibility that he truly wished to become my mate.

Instead, I closed my eyes, keeping my ears alert, but letting my mind wander towards the magic deep within me. My visions had led us to Esperance. Was that enough, or would we need more to help defeat the humans? Anything further my magic could give me would be helpful.

Golden threads of light flickered against the inside of my eyelids as I settled into the magic. My paw squeezed around the sharp edges of the shard of stone, almost like the Axinstone but inert of power. So many possible futures threatened to pull my magic away from my control. My tenuous hold on my abilities strained to the limit, testing my mind as I gripped tighter onto the leopard-head rune.

Scattered images started to flash, too quickly for me to understand or comprehend. Each one was a different future, no clear way to know what led to them or whether they resulted in our success. I saw Ddraig Anzig there, many times, sometimes standing in victory and other times in defeat. Haeraig Ellian accompanied him. Always she was by his side. In success and death.

I needed something different. It was no great revelation to know that the ddraig and his haeraig would be important together.

My eyes twitched back and forth as I followed the threads of magic that led into the future. I gripped tighter around the rune in my paw, but it did not give me the strength I needed and desired. My mind cast out for the Axinstone, surely close enough through the rock and stone between me and the lair, but I could not find it.

Magic swelled against my tenuous control. Its golden light bathed over me, diffusing through my mind and ripping away my thoughts like a branch tossed over a tempestuous river. Visions splintered into a terrifying noise of futures.

*Anzig screamed into the darkness...*

*...from the centre of the crater rose a small temple, oddly simple despite its importance...*

*A strange creature of feathers and fur screeched in rage...*

*...a dragon made of purest silver approached a great statue, a dragon reared on hindlegs and screaming in silent pain...*

*Vinzent circled a dragon who walked on his wings, both adversaries covered in blood...*

*...snarls filled the dawn, the bloodshed having already begun...*

*...George ripped the Axinstone from a dragon's paw...*

*...lightning crackled across the sky...*

*...a wolf rose onto its hindlegs and howled to the full moon...*

*Visions flashed.*

*Too many. So quick.*

*A paw closed around mine. Magic cocooned around my mind, different to my own. Healing magic. It calmed the storm that raged around my mind, easing the waters and giving me the opportunity to regain control over the flood that had overwhelmed me.*

*One last vision remained. Focused and clear.*

*A golden dragon sat with his tail curled around his hindlegs. He looked out over a great demesne of farms and fields, dotted with small villages. A great city rose from the horizon, alongside a sparkling ribbon of a river than snaked through the hills.*

*Several people walked close to the dragon, but their forms never came into clear sight. They all walked on two legs, but not all of them were human. Their silhouettes were not black. Instead, they shone with radiant light. One of the figures broke away from the others and approached.*

*Green light danced around the figure's form, obscuring his true shape. Hints of emerald eyes peered through the light. When he spoke, his voice was deep and full of music. "Three dragons to save the fate of all the others. It has a certain poetry to it, does it not, Azlak? The beginnings of a great story that still has not been fully told."*

*The golden dragon looked up. "I don't understand what you mean."*

*"Now? No." The deep voice rumbled with laughter. "But I am not speaking to the you of now. I am speaking to the you of years past. The you who has not yet tread any paw on this saga."*

*The golden dragon bowed his head. "Now that you say it, I think I remember..."*

*The green eyes of the future moved from the golden dragon, gripping magic for his own ends and sweeping away the rest of the vision. "Three dragons, Azlak. For this future to become possible you must find them. You are one, but that is all I can say. The destiny of all dragonkind falls on your wings. Should you succeed, your path will lead to me, and we can discuss what will happen next, but first you must gather the other two dragons whose fate is to save you in the weeks to come."*

*The vision began to fade into darkness. "Answers may be closer than you realise."*

My eyes snapped open. I was out of breath, as though I had been flying hard for hours without rest. Kaz's paw squeezed around mine as my mind slowly resurfaced from beneath the waves of magic.

"That seemed different to usual," the healer said softly.

I took in a deep breath and tried to hold it for a few seconds. I struggled even to do that, and the air escaped my lungs in a drawn-out whimper. "I don't think I Saw something. I think someone Showed it to me. Does that make sense?"

Kaz slowly shook his head. "I've never known anyone to take over magic like that. Not even with the Axinstone can any dragon steal someone's magic."

I turned over the strange rune in my paw to stare at the fiery leopard's head. "It was less like my magic was stolen and more... guided. Like this person in the future knew I would See him there, and so he could tell me something."

"It must be important then." Kaz nudged against my neck.

"He said I had to find two more dragons. Between us three we would save dragonkind, but he couldn't tell me what from, or who these dragons are," I said. My heart thundered away inside my chest, head spinning. Even just repeating the words felt ridiculous. How could I be the dragon to save everyone? I had never been important. My task had only ever been to save those who were to become important, to guide their futures into what needed to be.

Another voice surprised us. "Who did you speak to?"

I looked up, then quickly scrambled to my paws as I realised Esperance was awake. I bowed my head towards her, Kaz doing the same by my side. I stuttered as I tried to answer her question. "I don't know who they were, but I got a sense of the same power I get from you."

"Tell me everything you saw."

I did not think I could refuse her command, even if I wanted to. I found myself telling her about the vision, of everything that had come before it. I left nothing out, taking care to repeat the stranger's words exactly.

As I spoke, the mysterious human slowly approached. She held one hand to her chest, covering the healing stab wound. She still swayed with weakness, but she was stronger than she had appeared earlier.

"You spoke to Ha'Ti," she explained, once I had finished speaking. She offered no clarification for the strange name. "If this is true, then you have given me something to consider. I would like somewhere more comfortable to think. Where can you take me?"

"Do you think you can walk far?" I asked. "There are caves above us that we can make comfortable. Some dragons might not like you up there, but we can keep them away."

Esperance dipped her head. Her eyes sparked bright yellow. "Then take me there. I will deal with any dragons who protest my presence if I must."

Kaz bounded away to wake Inilta, leaving me alone with the strange human. I looked down to her unsteady feet, and then up to the narrow path we would have to follow into the darkness. I didn't want to question her ability, but I doubted that she would make the long climb. After all, she had no wings, and while she possessed a power few of her species could wield, she was still human.

"I have recovered my strength enough," Esperance said, answering my unspoken question with enough clarity that she might have broken into my thoughts.

I startled and took a step back, eyes wide as I looked up to her. "You can read minds?"

She shook her head. "It was not hard to deduce what you were thinking, little dragon. I appreciate your concern, but it is not necessary. I am perfectly capable of this."

I looked away, somewhat chastised, but relieved that she could not read my thoughts. I worried enough when I was close to Ddraig Anzig that he might pick up on my innermost secrets, concerns that I knew I never wanted to share with him. His magic scared me more than any other magic I had come across.

Was Ddraig Anzig one of the two dragons I needed to find? He was certainly powerful enough to alter the future of dragonkind. I had already done that once in trying to save his life, dooming his father in the process. Ddraig Astar had died so that Anzig could live. That had to be for a reason. But why would I be alongside him?

"Do you really think this Ha'Ti spoke the truth?" I asked, the words spilling from my mouth before I could hold them back. Esperance lifted an eyebrow, but she did not command me to stop speaking. "Am I really important in what is to come?"

Esperance didn't answer at first. She limped towards the path that led up the side of the cave, almost vanishing into shadows but lighting the way with the golden tattoos of light that wound over her flesh. "You are the one with the gift of the future, dragon. I can get a sense for it, on occasion, but visions are beyond me. Yet I do know that Ha'Ti is rarely wrong. He has a particular way of judging people and knowing who is important. If he says that you are to be the salvation for dragonkind, then I would be inclined to believe him. As for who your companions on this might be, well, I might be able to assist. First, though, I need somewhere comfortable with food and warmth. I trust you will be able to bring me to those."

With a grumbling Inilta and Kaz not far behind, I started to lead the way. Back towards the lair, towards Laxtal and the dragons who would not appreciate a human in their caves, no matter how powerful an ally she would be. I got the feeling Esperance did not need protection, but I still wondered how to keep her safe from an entire clan.

I wondered if she was the source of magic we needed. How could this strange human help us win the war against the army of George and Tsona. Had my visions been misleading?

A heavy weight settled on my wings. The pressure of the future threatened to push me into the ground. Both my visions and the words of Ha'Ti warned me that dangerous and uncertain times were coming. Could dragonkind really need me to save them? What was it that made me so special?

One paw in front of the other. That was all I could do for now.

The answers would come in time.

Esperance slowly recovered in the deep, dark caves at the far reaches of the lair. She had fallen back into silence, eyes closed as she sat with her back against the wall, hands clasped in front of her face.

I sat guard with Kaz, both of us as silent as the strange human. We were unmoving, doing our best to ignore Inilta, who paced impatiently. The sound of pawsteps occasionally reached my ears, but no one came close enough to disturb us. We were close enough to the cold caverns that it was probably just a regular delivery of salted and preserved meat to get the clan through the winter. No one had any reason to come much deeper than that, so we were alone.

In my paw, I played idly with the leopard-head rune. The fiery outline of the feline looked as bright as the dragon head on the Axinstone, fooling a casual glance several times that what I really held was the Nixan artefact, but no matter how hard I tried I could never get the feeling of any magic from the stone.

Esperance sucked in her breath sharply. I turned in alarm, thinking she was in pain, but the human showed no sign of that. If anything, she looked stronger than she had since she had awoken. There was more colour to the tattoos of light that wound over her skin, and she did not wince in pain with every movement, even if she had been trying to hide it before.

The human clicked her fingers and pointed to Inilta. "I would like to speak to a dragon who represents your species. A leader, whatever you call them now."

Inilta stared at Esperance for a moment, mouth hanging open. He then bowed his head. "I will fetch the ddraig." He scampered away quickly, his magical light guiding the way through the dark caverns. A single, flickering torch illuminated our cave, further shadows cast by the golden light radiating from Esperance.

The human fixed her powerful gaze on me. "He is not the third dragon you will need to seek out."

I looked up to her, then across to Kaz. "The third? Does that mean… are we…?"

Esperance nodded. "Everything I can understand of the future indicates that Kaz will be the second dragon. I am unable to divine the identity of the third dragon, but I believe it will be better if you do not put too much focus into seeking them out."

"Not seek them out?" I choked on my surprise, pawing at the ground. "Is this dragon not important to our survival? Why would I leave that up to fate?"

"Because you should know as well as any, little seer, that knowing too much about the future can result in it changing," Esperance explained. She leaned forward and reached out with one hand to gently touch the side of my head. Her skin was hot, far hotter than any human I had known. Her magic tingled my scales.

I leaned into that touch. "You're saying that by seeking out this dragon, I could accidentally keep them away from what we need to do?"

"Exactly." Esperance moved her hand away, taking with her the heat of her magic. I felt cold without it. She reached for her pocket and put her hand inside, grasping hold of something, but hesitated before she pulled anything out. "It is rare I do this so soon, but circumstances are different, knowing your potential fates. I would ask something of you both."

Kaz stepped forward. "Yes, of course, anything." I echoed his words. Anything this human asked of me I would do, without question.

Esperance pulled her hand from her pocket. In her palm was two squares of a hard, black material. They looked like angular pebbles, with a small border of every colour imaginable. "Hold out your paw."

I obeyed without question, extending my right forepaw to the human. By my side, Kaz mimicked my movement.

Esperance placed one of the small squares on my paw. She did the same with Kaz. For a moment, it did nothing more than shrink to fit my paw. A sudden burst of light and heat surprised me, the pebble vanishing in an instant. I yelped in shock, looking to the floor, sure I must have dropped it.

"It's not there," Esperance said.

"Then where did it go?" Kaz asked, similarly searching for the pebble that had been on his paw.

"It's a part of you now," Esperance said. She leaned forward and took hold of my paw, tracing her finger across a narrow ridge of scales that had not been there moments before. "We call them slates, though they have changed a lot since we first made them. You can use them to communicate with each other, and with me. In the future, you will be able to use them to speak with all my envoys, but until you meet them, I will restrict that. Should you wish to use them, squeeze your paw and think of me, or of each other."

Kaz clenched his paw. "Your envoys?"

"That is what you are now," Esperance explained. "You are to be my eyes, ears, and voice through the world, but right now, I wish to know what is happening here. It has been a long time since the world has given dragons any attention. I wish to change this."

I flicked my tail and stepped back. "You won't be staying here? We need your help in defeating the humans," I said, a whine coming into my voice.

Esperance smiled, sadness in her eyes. "I wish I could, but I am bound by magic greater than anything else on Farenar, restricting how I can interfere in the conflicts of the world. I can guide and give advice. I can empower you as my envoys, but that is all. I will speak to your leader, and then I will return home to Ehran. I feel like I have been away too long."

I hung my head, saying nothing. I knew not to argue with Esperance, not after she had given a great gift in the slate. I clenched my paw, feeling the small ridge there, not too dissimilar to a scar. I was tempted to squeeze and feel the magic of the slate in use, but I resisted the urge.

It did not take long for Inilta to return. I struggled to hide my disappointment that Esperance would soon be leaving as I turned to face the Nixan. He brought with him not one, but two ddraigs. Both Ddraig Anzig and Ddraig Krateos stepped into the small cave. The Nixan ddraig let out a shocked hiss when his eyes fell on Esperance.

The human was the first to say anything. "Which of you has the authority to speak with me?"

"I am ddraig of Laxtal," Anzig said, stepping forward.

"And I of Nixa," Krateos said, joining the smaller dragon in approaching the human.

Esperance regarded them both. "And you speak for all dragons?"

"We speak for our clans," Ddraig Anzig replied.

Esperance pursed her lips. She glanced down to me, and then across to Kaz, before she looked Ddraig Anzig in the eye. "I will speak only to the dragon who commands all of your kind."

The two ddraigs looked to each other, neither able to hold Esperance's gaze for very long. "We are as close to a leader of dragonkind as you will get," Ddraig Krateos said uncertainly. "We have no one true leader anymore, not since Tsona betrayed us all."

A growl came from Ddraig Anzig. "I must ask, who are you, and why are you in Laxtal? Normally we do not allow humans to enter our lair." The ddraig's eyes narrowed as he glared towards me.

I stepped forward and met the ddraig's eye, refusing to look away. If I were to be a voice for this powerful human, then I needed to act like it. "She is Esperance of Ehran. We found her in the caves by the river."

"And what were you doing down there?" Ddraig Krateos asked. His eyes didn't lift high enough to meet the human's gaze. Instead, he stared at somewhere closer to her legs, even as she remained sat down.

Ddraig Anzig clawed at the stone. "Ehran? I know that name."

I looked to the ddraig, my eyes wide. I realised I recognised the name as well, though I hadn't known it when Esperance had first uttered it. I struggled to recall where I had heard the name before, and the thought lanced into my mind as though placed there by another. In the expansive cave we sheltered in after crossing the mountains, where we had found the trove of mysterious artefacts and the strange Nightwings-like statue. I had read the name off a stone slab, though only Maznar had recognised the place. What was it that message had said?

"The Eight thank the dragons of Sxinix for their assistance in reclaiming Kyte's rune. You will always find a powerful ally in Mount Ehran," Ddraig Anzig recited.

Esperance's eyes widened in shock and the tattoos of light that wound through her skin brightened. "That promise was made a long time ago, in another age, to a dragon who is long dead."

"Will you honour it?" Ddraig Anzig pressed.

Esperance lifted a hand. She furrowed her brow. "I told Azlak that I cannot interfere with your affairs except in very specific circumstances. Aid offered in return for aid given allows me to act, though still not directly. I cannot honour this agreement, though I will provide someone who can. That will cover the debt and provide you with the means to win this upcoming war. Azlak knows the importance of victory. You will do well to trust his guidance."

Heat flared beneath my scales as the attentions of both ddraigs fell on me. I pawed lightly at the ground and resisted the urge to wrap my tail around my hindlegs. I could feel a pressure against my mind. I tensed, unsure if I wanted Ddraig Anzig and his magic to learn what Esperance had told me, but I had no way to keep him out. The pressure retreated.

"How soon can we expect your aid?" Ddraig Krateos said, his deep voice rumbling through the air.

"Soon. I will make arrangements as soon as I depart," the human replied. She waved her hand at the two ddraigs. "Leave us now. I would speak to Azlak and Kaz alone before I make my departure."

The two ddraigs did not look happy at the dismissal, but neither of them protested the human's command. They shared a quick glance towards each other, before making their exit from the small cave. Inilta hurried out with them, leaving Kaz and me alone with Esperance.

The human smiled. "You got my assistance after all, my voices. I will send another of my envoys to you. He will bring an army with him, you have my word."

"Who will you send? Are they a human? Or a dragon?" Kaz asked.

Esperance laughed, shaking her head. "So much better than either of those. It is best to let him explain everything, but he will know to ask for you. Be alert for my message and remember to inform me of anything important. You are my voice, but also my eyes. I must know what happens across all Farenar. You must understand the honour and expectations I have given you."

"We will try our best," Kaz said, speaking the words on my tongue as well. I knew we would give our all for Esperance, and to live up to the challenges she had put before our paws. It felt a mighty task, to find this third dragon who would help to save dragonkind. I hardly dared to believe that she had chosen me correctly.

Esperance rose to her feet. She no longer swayed or winced in pain. As she stretched her arms above her head, her tattoos burned with a bright light. "I am glad to have met you both. I hope you will live up to the trust I have placed on you."

I stepped back, unwilling to admit that she was about to leave. As I moved, the edge of the leopard-head rune dug into my scales. I stared down at it, then lifted it towards the human. "Did you wish to take this?"

To my surprise, the human leaped back as though burned, pressing herself against the far wall. "No," she hissed. "Do not give me that. Nor must you lose track of it. Hold onto it for me and protect it with everything you can. The fewer dragons who know about that rune, the better. I will arrange for it to be collected later."

I closed my paw around the rune, confused by her reaction. It was as though it scared her, but why? As far as I could tell it was an inert stone with none of the power of the Axinstone.

Esperance warily moved around the chamber, keeping her distance from me and the rune. "Come. Show me the way out. I long to feel the sun on my skin and to start my journey home."

Taking care to keep my distance from the human, I took the lead with Kaz to guide Esperance through the lair. There was a lot to think about, both on the tasks she had given us, and the fear about the reaction she would surely get in the lair above. Even if the ddraigs warned the Laxtal dragons about her presence, they would not like seeing anyone human. The few dragons we came across in the lower tunnels fled before I could reassure them.

Esperance ignored the dragons entirely. She showed little of the weakness that she had struggled with, though she did keep one hand outstretched against the wall of the cave as she walked.

We met no resistance until we finally reached the main chamber. Word must have spread about Esperance's presence, whether through the ddraigs or those who had fled before us. Several dragons were waiting for us. Amongst them was my father, and the look of fury on his face almost made me quail in terror, but then I remembered who walked with me. Esperance would not let me come to any harm.

"Then it is true," my father hissed, stepping forward from the throng of dragons. "The ddraig has allowed a human into our lair."

"I am no mere human, dragon," Esperance replied. A few wings shuffled uncomfortably as she spoke. Some were already entranced by the music of her voice, stepping away and shedding their aggression like an unwanted skin. Even Saya averted her eyes. By her side was Vinzent, and the dragonet took his mother's place beside my father.

"I don't care what you say you are," my father growled. "You look like a human and that's enough for me. I want you gone from this place immediately. As for you, Azlak, we need to have words."

"Should that not be Ddraig Anzig's decision to make?" I replied. I stomped my paw as I stepped forward, trying to force my father back. He did not move.

"The ddraig is with his Nixan ally," my father said, twisting every word into an insult. He showed his teeth, pulling his lips back into a fierce snarl. "It would appear you and your human have poisoned his mind into ignoring the needs of his clan."

Esperance clicked her tongue. "Cease this bickering. I know I'm not welcome here, even if the army I will provide will be your ally."

"Your army? Who said we wanted your army, human?" my father snapped, turning his ire on Esperance and showing none of the deference the ddraigs had given her.

"Father, she's trying to help us," I said, trying to diffuse the situation before Esperance retracted her offer of assistance. The clan could have no complaints if she did, such was the reaction she was receiving from Marin. I could tell he spoke the mind of the few dragons around him, including Saya and Vinzent. I could see nothing of the ddraig, nor of Yalle and any of the other dragons who held authority within Laxtal.

"You are not my son!" Marin shrieked, and for a moment all was silent. There was nothing in the chamber but for Marin and his words.

"I… I don't understand."

"Astar found your egg in the wild, abandoned," Marin spat. "He knew my mate was barren, so he gifted the egg to us. You were never my son, and I should have told you long ago, rather than keep up this ridiculous pretence. I disown you, Azlak. You were never mine to begin with."

The words were cruel. I should have been devastated, but as I looked up to Esperance, I felt none of that. I felt only cold scorn towards Marin. He had never been a supportive father. I could not feel loss at something I had never truly had.

"Let us get by," I growled, ignoring Marin and glaring at Saya. "Next time you have issue with the ddraig, you should challenge him directly, instead of this cowardly behaviour."

Saya snarled, but she stepped aside without saying anything. I pushed past her, clearing the way for Esperance to follow. The gathered dragons quickly fled as the human approached. Muttered whispers followed us. No one dared to speak their mind louder than that.

It was an awkward climb out of the central chamber for Esperance, but despite her recent injuries she managed it with relative ease. Kaz and I only needed to wait for a couple of minutes for her to reach us as we waited by the tunnel leading outside. There was barely any sweat on her brow. We met no further resistance as we passed through the upper areas of the lair, though there were plenty of curious eyes looking out from the shadows.

Another climb faced Esperance in the gorge outside the lair, which she also managed with ease. She hauled herself up almost as fast as we could fly, an inhuman strength and agility aiding her climb. A couple of dragons followed us out. Others who had been out hunting also joined our procession.

"Which way is south?" Esperance asked once she had reached the summit. She shielded her eyes from the sun with a hand as she peered out across the plains, the mountains at her back. I pointed her in the right direction with my wing, and she placed her hand on my head again. "Tell your ddraig his army will be here soon. I will inform you through the slate when I know more specifically than that. Until next time, little dragons."

Before I even had the chance to utter a farewell, she was gone. She bounded away to the south with a pace I would never have thought possible. She moved so much faster than any other human and had vanished from view within barely a minute.

I gently rubbed my paw, not hard enough to activate the slate, but enough to know it was there, that Esperance hadn't been a dream I had imagined. Already, my heart ached to see her again.

I glanced across at Kaz. Together, we would need to find a way to save dragonkind. Along with a third dragon who would help us succeed, a dragon we had no way of knowing the identity of. There was a lot of work to do if we had any hope of achieving this impossible task.

It was time to begin.

# CHAPTER THREE

**Ellian**

After settling down into a steady flight, I couldn't stop glancing back towards Laxtal. Was I right in flying out to Axaatl? My heart was telling me I needed to be staying at home, helping Anzig to control the clan. I recognised the importance of my task, and my paw kept moving to the azure stone that hung around my neck, but I feared what might happen to Anzig without me by his side.

"He'll be fine," Airil said, drifting close enough so our wingtips brushed against each other. I hoped I was able to hide the tingle of excitement that ran up from my wingtip and right through my spine. I couldn't allow Airil to know how I reacted every time he was close. He made me feel like Vinzent had made me feel, before the dragonet had split my heart in two. But even as I stole a glance over at the Nixan, I could see the corner of his mouth upturned in a small smile; I wondered if he already knew.

He reached out with his paw. "We can get there a lot quicker," he said. I grasped his paw in mine. His smile widened, showing every one of his teeth. I knew what was coming, and that thrilled me even further. It was the closest I would ever get to experience what controlling magic felt like. That it was something I got to share with Airil made it special to me.

"Shall we go?" he asked.

Without hesitation, I nodded my head and tightened my grip on his paw. Then the world turned inside out. Bursts of fractured light accosted my eyes even with my eyelids squeezed shut. Fearsome shapes grew out of the shadows between the light as prickles of heat jabbed at my scales, but Airil's paw in mine was a constant source of calming energy. I knew that so long as I kept hold of his paw I would be safe, no matter what I saw. A whooping cry reached my ears, and it took me a few moments to realise that it was my voice I heard. It was my overjoyed cries that filled the void. And then, as quickly as the magic had come, sunlight warmed my wings.

With a startled gasp I opened my eyes as a strong wind buffeted my wings from a wholly unexpected direction. Unable to catch my flight in time, my right wing collided with Airil's left, both fragile membranes crumpling under the pressure.

Crying out in shock and a little fear, we both spiralled down to the fast-approaching ground. I increased my grip on the Nixan's paw, trying to manoeuvre myself into a position where I could spread my wings again, and Airil tried to do the same opposite me. His hind paws scrabbled against my chest as he tried to right himself, but that movement gave me all the room I needed. I flared my wings and grabbed hold of his other forepaw. My wings and forelegs screamed in agony as they bore the full force of Airil's weight, but I refused to let go.

I had done this so many times with Anzig in the past, with his wings pinned beneath my body in our mock fights, but then my flight had been under control. This was a wild tumble through turbulent air, and as the ground got ever closer, I gritted my teeth and braced for the impact.

We were fortunate that the grass was long and springy as it absorbed most of the force from our fall. We rolled several times before coming to a rest, Airil on top of me with his legs tightly wrapped around my body. I could feel his heart hammering inside his chest, and I was sure he could feel the wild beat of mine that wasn't entirely caused by our sudden plunge from the sky.

"Are you hurt?" Airil gasped, not moving from where he lay.

"No. You?"

"No."

I tried to hold back an overjoyed giggle but couldn't hold it for long. Soon I was rolling through the grass again with Airil, both of us whooping and laughing as the fear of our fall subsided. I was sensitive to the Nixan's every touch – the way his paws clenched at the scales of my belly and sides, the way his wings brushed against mine, and how he would lower his head next to mine and nuzzle against my cheek. I struggled to recall a moment that had filled me with so much joy before.

It couldn't last though, and after a while I reluctantly pushed Airil off me and rose to my haunches. The Nixan quickly sat by my side and, after a moment's hesitation and a furtive peek towards me, wrapped his wing around my body.

Together we looked over the landscape that stretched out before us. It didn't look too much different from Laxtal, but a quick glance back told me we were no longer in my home. The Sxinix Mountains were no longer on the horizon. A gently undulating plain spread out as far as I could see in all directions, broken only by a few rocky crags and small patches of forest. High overhead I could see five dark shapes against the clear blue sky. They were heading right for us.

It seemed we had chanced upon a Clan Axaatl patrol, for they would not have known we were coming. Axaatl dragons were typically much larger than any other, and these five were no exception. Even the smallest of the five was larger than any dragon in Laxtal. They must have been close to four feet in height.

"I am Hyantl, commander of the armies of Axaatl. Speak," the largest of the five said, touching down on the grass with a deftness that defied his size. War paint covered most of his green scales.

"I am Haeraig Ellian of Laxtal. My companion and escort is Airil of Nixa. We wish to speak with Ddraig Aranat," I said, taking a step forward into the shadow of the taller dragon and lifting the azure stone around my neck, trying not to feel intimidated. I was a haeraig now. I needed to act it.

The Axaatl dragon grunted. "A Nixan escort for the Laxtal haeraig? These are strange times, with strange happenings all around, but this is one of the strangest I have witnessed," he said. He turned back to his companions, focusing on a red-scaled ness. Whatever guidance Hyantl was seeking, he found it in the eyes of the other dragon. "Very well, Haeraig Ellian of Laxtal, and Airil of Nixa. Come. We will take you to our ddraig."

Hyantl spread his wings, though he waited for me to take to the air before he kicked off from the ground. He did not ask permission to take the lead position, but if he was to be our guide, then he had to fly in front of us. The remaining Axaatl warriors flew behind in close proximity.

Though my mind was full of questions, I never had the chance to ask them. The five dragons with their massive wingspan were able to fly much faster than we were. It was a struggle to keep pace. My wings burned with the exertion, but I didn't ask for the pace to slow. I would not shame myself by showing any weakness. Airil was able to stay on my wing the entire time, not once leaving my side.

I had never been to Axaatl before, so I didn't know how far away from the central lair we were, or even what it looked like. I imagined it would be fairly similar to Laxtal, given the similarity in terrain, and that it delved deep underground. There were no mountains anywhere nearby, so it couldn't rise towards the clouds like Xital's towering spire. There seemed no end to our flight though, not even as the sun started to sink down towards the western horizon. The amber light glinted off the surface of a wide river that flowed roughly from north to south.

Hyantl banked to the north and followed the river upstream. The water was murky brown as it slowly flowed on, making its long journey to the far-distant ocean. Here it lazily cut through the flat, lush terrain, which would surely have been verdant green in summer. Even so close to winter, the forested banks of the river extended for nearly a mile. Trees grew tall and thick, fed by the life-giving water that was so scarce in the northern plains. Here and there I could see the gentle splash of small mammals diving into the water. The air was alive with the sound of hundreds of little birds as they flew between the trees, calling out in alarm as we passed, warning us that the fish in this part of the river were theirs to hunt.

This far from the mountains there was no sign of the advancing human threat. I could only hope that Ddraig Aranat had been paying sufficient attention to the plight of his neighbours and acknowledge the danger to his clan if he did not act.

We followed the river for another hour, by which time the sun was almost touching the horizon. I was ready to fall from the sky. Every beat of my wings was torture, and I was no longer able to properly maintain my height. With every wing stroke I felt I was falling again. Keeping just by my side, I sensed Airil was in a similar condition, but Hyantl – flying about ten feet in front – could seemingly keep this pace up indefinitely. The rest of our guard flew alongside us, barely troubled by the pace. I could not help but admire the strength of the Axaatls. They would make formidable allies, or terrifying enemies. I hoped we were not the second envoys to visit this vast land.

I did not see the two nesses who approached until they were almost upon us. They ascended effortlessly to meet us, flying from somewhere around the gentle slopes of a small hill rising from the flat terrain. I noticed the river's meandering path almost completely encircled the hill, nearly creating an island within. The two newcomers ignored Airil and me and, having banked and assumed the same flight route as us, converged instead on Hyantl and the other Axaatls. One of the nesses, closest to Hyantl, was the deepest blue in colour I had ever seen on a dragon. The glistening from her scales in the failing light of the sleeping sun was disrupted by the many scars on her body, winding over her like jagged loops of string. She exchanged rasping whispers with Hyantl. Even though I couldn't hear what she was saying, I could detect enough venom in her tone to assume Hyantl was not receiving a friendly welcome back.

Hyantl nodded almost imperceptibly several times, before turning his head to address his Axaatl companions. "Mlara and Svetus, fly east and order Tehra to fly her army south. Fyrick and Iena, you will fly south immediately. You're needed on the borders." Hyantl barked his orders out stiffly. He then turned his head to address me directly. "Haeraig Ellian, please accompany Myvris," he said, nodding towards the blue-scaled ness. "She will escort you from here to our ddraig. I have other orders." Without waiting for an acknowledgement, he dropped and banked away to the west. At the same time, his companions all dipped their wings and circled away. Two flew east, with the others flying south. Airil and I were suddenly alone with Myvris and her companion.

"Come on, with me," Myvris said brusquely. She dipped towards the low hill. At last, it seemed our first flight in Axaatl lands was coming to an end. It was the only significant rise for many miles, and on the small strip of land that led to its base, two rows of stone pillars outlined a passage leading towards a large cavern. Those closest to the cave were topped by stone plinths forming a tunnelled entrance into the side of the hill.

My landing was not graceful, but I was simply pleased to rest my aching wings at last, not caring about the bemused looks I received from Myvris. However, we immediately set off across the lush green surface towards the strange structure, not having the chance to catch our breath. Airil let out a small groan and we both exchanged tired glances, both with weak smiles, knowing we would soon be able to rest. As we passed the first, I slowed and placed a paw on the pillar. I could immediately tell these pillars had been hewn by claw and the plinths they supported were separate slabs of stone. It was hard to image how many dragons it had taken to put these plinths into place.

"They were built by Clan Sxelt. You won't find this type of rock near Axaatl either. It was all brought here from the north." I turned to see the other ness, who had landed by my side. Although her blue scales sparkled in the dying light of the evening, hers did not have the same deep colouration as Myvris. "I do not believe Hyantl introduced me. Forgive him, Haeraig Ellian, he had pressing matters to attend to," she said with a formal bow, "I am Segrid. I shall have the honour of attending to you and Airil whilst you remain in Axaatl."

"They are truly remarkable," I said, too lost in the wonder of these pillars to pay attention to much else. From a distance they had looked like an ordinary dark grey rock, but now I was close enough to see the imperfections in the stone that gave it true beauty. Veins of silver shimmered on the surface, and specks of blue, gold, and green gleamed with a soft light. It took a great effort to tear my eyes away, and to not repeat my fascinated inspection of each pillar as we moved on toward the entrance of the hillside.

We followed Segrid and Myvris into the wide cavern mouth. Airil shivered the moment we stepped into the shadows. "This place was built by Nixan magic," he whispered, looking up to the dark ceiling.

Myvris bristled as she overheard the Nixan. "Our lair has been under Axaatl control for six hundred years. It has never been Nixan, and never will be, little dragon."

Airil shook his head. "I can feel an ancient magic in the stone. It's old. Older than anything I've felt before, but I know I'm not mistaken."

The Axaatl ness growled and turned away, refusing to respond to Airil's claims. I followed the Nixan's gaze up to the darkness above us, but I couldn't see what attracted his attention. Whatever feeling he had picked up, it was something I could not see or sense. Again, I felt a small pang of jealousy towards the Nixan and his amazing gift. I would give anything to be able to feel what he felt and experience the wonder of his magic. But I knew that would never happen. Laxtal dragons couldn't possess magic. Apart from Azlak, some corner of my mind reminded me. The seer was an anomaly that Clan Nixa had never been able to explain. No other Laxtal dragon had ever shown even the slightest sign of possessing magic. I sighed and resigned myself to the fact that I would never experience the thrill of wielding magic like Airil did.

While the Laxtal lair was a wholly natural formation, the caves having been bored out by hundreds of years of water erosion from an ancient underground river, the Axaatl lair was unmistakably draconic-made. I doubted Axaatl dragons alone had constructed this place – it seemed it would have been too massive a task for a single clan – but at the same time I did not believe magic had carved out the extensive and expansive tunnels that burrowed deep beneath the ground, as Airil had claimed. The deeper into the lair we delved, the more evidence I could see that this lair had been created by physical means. I paused to inspect a deep gouge in the rock, seemingly made by a claw. This was one of many I had seen already, but this was different. It was so large I could fit my whole paw into the cleft.

I looked around the wide passage as I continued down. It must have been wide enough for nearly a dozen Axaatl dragons to stand side by side with full wingspans. I began to wonder whether dragons had carved this lair after all. This was for something much bigger than even the largest Axaatl dragon.

"We are approaching Ddraig Aranat's chambers," Myvris said tersely.

The Axaatl ddraig had secreted himself deep within the lair, well away from the last remnant of sunlight that had likely dipped below the horizon. As it was in Laxtal, light came from a series of torches held in brackets along the walls of the passageway. A slowly meandering stream of smoke, caused by the multitude of flames, drifted slowly along the ceiling, heading towards the surface. Below the smoke, the air was clean, if not a little still. There was no sign of the human-made electric lights that Xital now boasted.

"Wait here for me," Myvris said, once we had gone as far as the passage could take us. A flat and smooth wall confronted us.

The ness seemingly disappeared before our eyes. I stole a quick glance at Airil, who seemed less surprised than I did. I moved nearer to him and understood why. From his position he had been able to see that Myvris hadn't vanished by magic, but instead had slipped into an angled fissure off to one side of the flat wall. Even with the size, this cunning design hid the entrance to the ddraig's chambers for all but those who knew the secret of the wall. This fissure was the only part of the lair I had seen so far that was to the scale of an Axaatl dragon.

"Haeraig Ellian, if I may ask, why are you here?" Segrid asked as we waited for Myvris to return.

"I'm sorry, I cannot say. I was sent here to speak to your ddraig alone. I hope you understand," I replied, sharing a quick glance with Airil to ensure that he wasn't about to reveal the reason for our visit. I had no need to worry. Airil's mouth remained firmly shut. His eyes were dark and cold, though they brightened considerably when he noticed me looking at him.

"Is it about Clan Xital?" Segrid asked anyway, ignoring my reluctance to discuss the matter with her.

"I really can't say," I replied again, firmer this time, clasping the blue stone at my throat. I met the eyes of the larger ness, and she immediately submitted to me. Her advantage in size meant nothing, as she gave way to my superior rank.

I was spared from having to deflect any further questions by the return of Myvris.

"You may both now enter," she said, stepping aside to allow Airil and me through.

Though Airil and I walked side-by-side through the fissure, the entry was tiny in comparison to the vastness of the chamber that lay beyond. It was far bigger than any single dragon would need. The ceiling formed an almost perfect dome. Its surface was highly polished, reflecting light back into the room. To one side of this huge cavern, was a pile of rugs that Ddraig Aranat seemed to use as bedding. From the opposite wall, a small stream flowed into the cavern through a natural fracture, pooling near the centre of the living space. The must have been a crack on the cavern floor to drain the water, as although the pool filled to just below the level of the floor, it did not overflow. Beside the pool stood the largest dragon I had ever seen. The blue-scaled behemoth stood at over four feet tall, and he flared his wings in a convincing display of intimidation.

Ddraig Aranat lowered his head by an inch. "Welcome to Clan Axaatl, Haeraig Ellian," he rumbled.

I bowed my head, while Airil almost flung himself to the floor as he paid his respect to the Axaatl ddraig.

"I thank you for seeing us at such short notice, Ddraig Aranat," I said. I focused on his shoulder, some six inches higher than my head even when I stood as tall as I could.

"We have been expecting you, Haeraig Ellian. Not necessarily today, but we knew Laxtal would come to us before long," the ddraig said. He bared his teeth as he smiled. "Your clan already has a formidable alliance with Nixa. Even if the clan of magic has had its wings clipped, you still boast an incredible force. Tell me, Haeraig, do you wish for Axaatl to join your cause also?"

"What I wish for is inconsequential, Ddraig Aranat. Laxtal does not approach Clan Axaatl on any personal or selfish mission. I am not here as a representative of my clan. I am here as a representative of dragonkind. Collectively we all face the greatest threat to our species since tales were first told. Only by uniting and fighting as one can we hope to survive," I said, my stare not wavering from Ddraig Aranat's shoulder. I needed to show him that his strength did not intimidate me, but at the same time, I had to show the respect his rank deserved.

"Well spoken, Haeraig. I was told you are young and inexperienced, but you speak with a maturity beyond your years. I am not blind to the events to the south and west. I too, know of what the humans are doing, and what Ddraig Tsona has done in Laxtal and Xital. But how do you know whether Clan Xital has already approached Clan Axaatl and sought my allegiance with them?" Ddraig Aranat asked, cocking his head to one side. "Who is to say whether I have already sided with Clan Xital, when Ddraig Tsona has an army of humans supporting him? Why should I side with Laxtal?"

I felt a cold clench in my chest. Surely we couldn't already be too late?

"Not all humans are our enemies," Airil said, holding his head down to the floor, as though he was talking with it, instead of addressing the ddraig. "Some humans rebelled, believing the slaughter of our species to be immoral and unjust. With their help and yours, mighty ddraig, we can defeat Xital. We only wish to defend ourselves against unprovoked invasion." Small swirls of dust danced to Airil's words, so close to the floor was his muzzle.

"Then you believe yourselves to be on the side of right and good?" Ddraig Aranat asked.

"Yes, Ddraig Aranat. Of that we are sure," I said immediately.

Ddraig Aranat snorted. "I care not for the virtues of right nor wrong. What can Laxtal offer Clan Axaatl that Xital can not?"

I had to think quickly. We needed Ddraig Aranat's support, no matter the cost to Laxtal. There had to be something our clan could offer Axaatl that Clan Xital could not. If it was not good or evil that motivated Aranat, then it had to be something tangible. We had no great artefacts, and little substance offering strategic advantage over our neighbours, other than the quality of the dragons who lived there. Then it occurred to me, the one thing that was unique to Laxtal, and what would make an attractive proposition to a warrior like Ddraig Aranat.

"I offer Clan Laxtal's stewardship in constructing a beacon network throughout Clan Axaatl," I said. I chanced a glance up to the ddraig's eyes to gauge his reaction. They had widened in either anger or desire; I hoped for the latter. For many, many years, the other ruling clans had been envious of the beacons that covered Laxtal. Though the beacons themselves were fairly simple, it was the chemicals used to manipulate the fire that had remained a closely guarded secret for generations.

"Haeraig Ellian, you offer a mighty gift indeed. If the offer is true, then I accept your terms," Ddraig Aranat said, as I lowered my eyes back down to his shoulder. "Never before has there been an alliance between three ruling clans, but I can bring you an offer in return. I have been approached by another clan, but it is not Xital. Ddraig Nunahra of Xigax has sent envoys to declare an alliance of northern clans, I believe in response to a message sent by Ddraig Krateos of Nixa. It is not three ruling clans who will fly together, but four. Humanity will tremble before the strategy of Laxtal, the magic of Nixa, the stealth of Xigax, and the brute force of Axaatl. Together, we will be unstoppable."

I breathed out in relief, just about managing to hold my shoulders and wings from sagging. I could barely believe what I had heard. This was not an alliance of three ruling clans, but four. That gave us a stronger army than any other. I did not know how many humans Tsona had at his command, but we surely outnumbered them now.

I barely knew what to say to such news. "I am grateful to you, Ddraig Aranat. We had feared we were too late in securing allies, for Xital is moving quickly. If we may ask for shelter here tonight, we will fly north tomorrow to strengthen our alliances."

Ddraig Aranat turned to the side, but always kept one eye on me. "You may shelter here tonight," he said, before pausing in thought for a moment. "Clan Reneza lies to the north. Our relations with them have been strained in recent years. Kyeuba, the ddraig before me, took refuge there following my defeat of him. I suspect Clan Reneza may plot to return him to power. I doubt they will provide you with any support, especially if they know you already have secured mine. I suggest flying south instead. Clan Lilisxi borders Xital. If Tsona has flown east, then you may be able to reach Lilisxi first."

"Lilisxi is small and weak. How could they help us?" Airil asked.

"Tchaa. They may not be strong, but it is better that they fight with us, rather than against," Ddraig Aranat said. The tone of his voice forced Airil to lower himself flat to the ground.

"I thank you Ddraig Aranat for your kind and wise words. We shall fly south in the morning," I said, lowering my head graciously towards the Axaatl ddraig. With little left to discuss, and after Ddraig Aranat promised he'd send an envoy to Laxtal to advise Anzig of our agreement, we were dismissed to go back to Myvris and Segrid. By the time we were shown to a small guest chamber on the other side of the lair, I was feeling proud with myself for my first meaningful action as haeraig of Laxtal. I had not faced the same danger Anzig had faced in his attempt to win Nixa's support, but my efforts had helped to secure the first alliance in history between four ruling clans.

Airil's wing draped over me as we lay together in front of the fire that had been lit for us. We had talked for a long time, discussing our plans for where to head after Lilisxi. We eventually agreed to visit all the minor clans that dotted the land to the south of Laxtal, before sweeping around to Clan Kern, the southernmost of the ruling clans. Xigax and Axaatl could take care of the north for us.

When we did eventually stop talking and settled down to sleep, our tails were entwined and my paw was clasped in his. My last waking sight was of his beautiful yellow eyes.

We flew all day to reach the Lilisxi lair. Airil, having never been to the clan before, was unable to transport us there in an instant, something that I was disappointed about. Ddraig Aranat had offered us a small contingent of Axaatl warriors to act as an escort for our flight south, which I had politely rejected. At the time, I could feel Airil's discomfort, as though he felt Ddraig Aranat did not believe he was capable of such a task, but felt it quickly turn to pride as I vouched for my present escort. The offer had humbled and honoured me, but I still trusted Airil to keep me safe; more so than four or five Axaatl dragons, no matter how formidable their fighting prowess was.

I relied on memory to guide us to the Lilisxi lair, which I remembered as being highly unusual for a draconic dwelling, as it did not bury down into the rock beneath our paws. Instead, it rose into the trees, with the dragons of Clan Lilisxi perching on the wooden boughs of the forest like any common bird. Without a defensible lair, the clan could never aspire to the prestige of becoming a ruling clan, but they were still arguably the most powerful clan near Laxtal's southern borders. Their ddraig, a feisty young dragon called Bakucic, had been a regular visitor to our clan when he had been haeraig. We had spoken occasionally, argued frequently, but I hoped he would now treat me with respect. I carried the Laxtal stone around my neck, so I represented my clan. I would not dishonour Anzig by bringing up fledgling disagreements, and I was confident Ddraig Bakucic would similarly act with dignity.

Day was beginning to surrender to the night, but we still had not arrived, or even laid eyes on the lair, though I knew we were flying in the right direction by following the great river south. We hadn't seen any dragons, but for a few specks in the distance that had vanished before we closed. As the darkness grew, so the cold intensified. Doubts were beginning to invade my thoughts, as to whether we would indeed find shelter for the night. I had seen no sign of caves, as the landscape in this part of the territories was almost perfectly flat. In the rapidly fading light, a sudden realisation hit me; there was no forest in sight either. Where was the forest-lair of Clan Lilisxi? Soon it would be too dangerous to fly, and we had nowhere to shelter.

Suddenly, Airil dipped his wings and reached out towards me. I instinctively reached out for him to take my paw. Were we under attack? I quickly scanned the charcoal skies, but could see nothing. I looked back at Airil, looking for a sign to where the danger was. I was not expecting to see a smile.

I had no time to react before an explosion of light obliterated my senses. An eternity forced into the smallest fraction of time as images flashed through my mind. Mountains, streams, grasslands, oceans, and forests came and went in moments that felt like years. Forests! The Lilisxi forest erupted from the ground. It looked like it was sprouting up beneath me. Twitching, bending, writhing, shaped by the forces of nature over eons; eons that passed by in less than a moment. Either I fell towards it, or the forest surged up past us, but we were plunging through the leaves, as bright colours started to swirl all around me.

Dragons shrieked from all sides, as we materialised right in front of them. Dazed and unable to form any words of apology, I staggered away, trying to furl my wings to a body that would not keep still. Momentarily, as my senses caught up with my trembling body, I was surprised to feel the ground under my paws. I slumped down onto my haunches.

"Sorry," Airil said as he sauntered up to my side, obviously not affected in the slightest by his magic. "I saw the forest on the horizon. I thought you might like to get here quickly."

All I could muster was a smile up at him. He smiled back, and that was all we had to say on the matter. Slowly, I lifted off my haunches and looked around us.

We had materialised near the edge of a small clearing amongst tall trees. A large fire was blazing in the centre of the clearing, around which was about a dozen startled dragons. One called out to send word to the ddraig, and several of their number flew skyward. I followed their flight up to the intertwined branches of the trees above. It was hard to see in the gloom beyond the firelight. I could just make out an angular structure amongst the branches. It was in stark contrast to the sinuous trees. A soft red glow was emanating from the corner of my eyes, but no matter where I looked, it was just out of sight.

One ness had recovered enough from our sudden intrusion to tentatively approach us. Airil had unfurled his wings slightly, but the Lilisxi ness displayed no threatening behaviour. In fact, she seemed terrified of our sudden arrival.

"You are from Laxtal?" she asked nervously. The firelight reflected off her cobalt scales as she lowered her head reverently.

"Yes. I am Haeraig Ellian of Laxtal," I gasped, still struggling to regain my true voice after Airil's magic had disrupted my senses. The ness's eyes widened in shock as she – and every dragon who had heard my words – flung themselves to the ground to pay their respect to a haeraig of a ruling clan. Dragons away from the clearing soon learned the presence and identity of their unexpected arrivals, as excited whispers spread through the clan, like the morning rays of the sun over the plains.

I approached the fire, a little startled at how the Lilisxi dragons recoiled from my way as I approached. The warmth of the fire was invigorating, and I was grateful for it. We hadn't been in the cold airs above the vast plains of Lilisxi for long, but with the setting of the sun, the chill cooling air still lingered in the thin membranes of my wings. I sat down next to the flickering amber glow, wrapping my tail around my legs for warmth. Airil sat alongside me, and cautiously placed a paw on mine.

"Sorry again if I scared you," he said quietly, as he stared into the fire. "I just couldn't stay in the cold any longer."

I rested my head against his shoulder. "That's alright. I was surprised, that's all. Maybe just warn me next time?" I replied, feeling his muscles relax as my reply reassured him. He sighed and put his wing around me as we fell into a comfortable silence, succumbing to the warmth and gentle dance of the flames. I knew Ddraig Bakucic would not keep us waiting for long. The Lilisxi ddraig would soon learn who his visitors were and would not dare ignore us. Our clans had remained informal allies ever since our mutual war against Clan Duma, according to Carlee's stories of that old campaign. I hoped he would honour the help we gave his clan then.

"Excuse me, Haeraig?" A small voice distracted me. An old ness had approached me, her head held so low that her chin brushed the short, trampled grass of the clearing as she approached. Her eyes never left my paws.

"Continue, please," I said when it seemed obvious the ness wasn't going to speak without permission.

"Forgive me for being presumptuous, but I feel that you must be warned. You are not the only one here seeking counsel from Ddraig Bakucic. Another ness arrived before sunset and demanded to speak with him. She's resting inside as we told her the ddraig was out hunting," she said, the faintest trace of pride evident in her voice.

"Who is this dragon?" I demanded, perhaps a little too harshly in my urgency.

"Haeraig Ilibela of Xital, Haeraig Ellian." The poor messenger flattened herself to the ground, but I had no time for her feelings now.

I hissed in dismay. I had hoped Xital would have continued their focus to the east, so this was bad news indeed if they had already turned their attentions to their western neighbours. The ness's words revealed something else; if Ilibela was still Xital's haeraig, then that meant I had not killed Tsona with the human's gun. Next time I vowed not to be so careless. I unleashed a growl that frightened the poor ness even further.

The arrival of Ddraig Bakucic emerging from near the top of one of the tallest trees surrounding the small clearing was all the poor messenger needed to turn and flee. The ddraig wasn't the largest of drakes, especially when compared to Ddraig Aranat of Axaatl, and was a couple of inches shorter than me. Even so, he held himself in a way that belied his status as a minor clan's ddraig. He was still a ddraig regardless of his clan's overall prestige. A space cleared for him to land directly in front of me, and he paused for me to lower my head to him before he spoke.

"Haeraig Ellian, it is good to see you again," he said. His voice was always light and pleasant, but from experience I knew that he was quick to anger and quicker to offend. To my cost I had learned not to treat him as a simple drake from a lowly clan.

"The pleasure is mine, Ddraig Bakucic," I said. Out of the corner of my eye I could see Airil bend his forelegs to give his respects to the Lilisxi ddraig.

If Ddraig Bakucic was surprised that a Nixan accompanied me, he didn't show it. He smiled in a testing manner that I recalled from our youth. "I know why you are here, Ellian. I'm sure you have already been informed another haeraig awaits an audience with me. What do you make of Haeraig Ilibela being here?"

"You came to see me first," I said quietly.

Ddraig Bakucic laughed. "That is true. What makes you think I didn't come here just to chase you away so the Xitals don't think I'm double-crossing them?" he asked.

"Because Laxtal has always protected Lilisxi and been a strong ally. What reason do you have to turn your back on us?" I replied. I felt a flutter of nerves. I had been sure Ddraig Bakucic would quickly declare his continued allegiance to Laxtal, but now I wasn't sure it would be that easy. Would Xital's arguments prove more persuasive?

Then he smiled and laughed again, wiping away all my doubts in a moment. "Come, Haeraig Ellian. Join me in the trees and we can discuss how Lilisxi can help you. Your companion may join us too," he said, before turning to the ness who had approached us earlier. "Keep Haeraig Ilibela away. If she asks for a reason, just inform her I don't want to see her."

"Of course, my ddraig," the ness said, smiling as she bowed her head.

I had never seen anything like the Lilisxi lair, with trees used by dragons as a place of shelter or refuge. Somehow the dragons of Lilisxi had manipulated these twisting boughs into a safe haven, just as other clans had carved through the stone. Thick, closely-knit tendrils grew down from the upper branches of many trees, creating an almost impenetrable wall of wood, which descended to the leafy forest floor. I couldn't tell whether these were natural or not, but these walls formed narrow, yet elongated chambers for the Lilisxi dragons to inhabit. Many of the trees had hollows carved into them, and as we flew up towards the canopy, dragons occasionally peered out from within. The whole clan lived in the trees. I had to marvel at the ingenuity of Lilisxi, to be able to fashion a home such as this without any cave system nearby.

Given they couldn't light fires within the trees, I was intrigued to see masses of small red crystals embedded into the wood. They gave off a soft red glow, and as I flew close to a large cluster of them, I also realised that they emanated a gentle heat. Airil was extremely interested in the crystals, and as soon as the three of us landed on a great bough just below the canopy of leaves, the Nixan pawed at a nearby crystal with intense curiosity.

"Ddraig, if I may? What are these?" Airil asked.

Ddraig Bakucic moved along the bough with poise and confidence, something I could not yet master. I still needed my wings slightly flared for balance as I struggled to stay perched on the bough. Some of my initial wonder for the clan was starting to diminish. This was how birds lived, not dragons.

"We do not know," Ddraig Bakucic said as he prised one of the crystals from its socket with a single claw. He held it up in his paw. It was smaller than one of his claws, but it gave off enough light to shine brightly, reflecting in his eyes. "It's some sort of natural magic. You'll find them scattered throughout the forest, but for some reason Nixa never showed interest in studying them."

The ddraig held out the crystal towards the Nixan, who excitedly extended his paw to accept the ddraig's offer to place it within his grasp. Airil brought the crystal up to his muzzle and stared into it as though entranced. Small sparks of amber and larger ones of red crackled from the stone as it moved in Airil's paw. "There is a lot of magic in these," the Nixan said, flicking the stone up before it vanished with a loud crack, only to reappear again on the branch, under his other paw.

Ddraig Bakucic seemed to show no interest and slipped past the Nixan, putting a paw on the massive trunk of the tree, next to a hollow lit from within by the same red glow. "Shall we?"

I nodded for Airil to follow the ddraig along the bough, not trusting myself to be able to get past him without suffering the ignominy of falling. Once inside, I was surprised. I had expected the chambers to be damp and cramped, with them being inside the trunk of a tree, but I was surprised by what I saw from the entrance. The floor was flat, on which I could count the many rings of the host tree, but the walls curved up and met in the middle in a perfect dome. I could see hardly any claw marks on the walls, but they were more pronounced on the ceilings; revealing how the chambers had originally been made. But, with time and numerous visitors no doubt, the walls had become polished almost smooth from repeated brushing from scales. With the crystals providing both light and warmth, there was no need for any fur rugs scattered around for bedding, which was just as well; it was small, but it was every bit as comfortable as any Laxtal cave.

"These are the guest chambers where you can rest tonight. But first, what are we to do with our little problem?" Ddraig Bakucic asked, shepherding the two of us inside the chamber. Airil quickly sat down and made himself small, his wings and tail wrapped tight to his body as the ddraig continued to speak. "How can we hope to defeat Xital and their human allies?"

"By overwhelming them with numbers. We need an army greater than anything dragonkind has mustered before. With the support of Xigax and Axaatl, we have that," I replied with confidence.

Ddraig Bakucic shook his head slowly, and for quite some time before he stopped and spoke. "I was at the council of Xital when your cousin proposed to steal the Axinstone. He seemed to believe that we could not hope to defeat the humans in battle. What has changed? Why do you think we can defeat them now?"

"At that time, we were broken and divided. And the humans still had the Axinstone. With it they were too powerful to fight. Now it's back in Nixan paws, and that power is Clan Nixa's to wield," I said, trying to explain as best I could what Anzig had told me. I knew there were doubts amongst my clan that Nixa could truly turn this war by themselves, but I wasn't going to let Ddraig Bakucic know that.

"So, Airil, it's down to your clan, is it?" the ddraig sniffed, turning my escort.

Airil immediately stiffened and uncurled his tail, which twitched nervously behind him, and dipped his head almost to the ringed floor. "Have you ever seen a Nixan with the power of the Axinstone coursing through their veins?" Airil asked the ddraig. When he didn't answer, the Nixan chanced raising his head slightly, looking between the both of us and revealing an excited glint in his eyes. With more confidence, he continued, "It is an incredible sight. You can see magic leaping from every scale like lightning from a cloud. Do you really think humans could stand up to that power and hope to win?"

A low growl rumbled from the back of the ddraig's throat. "You are confident, Airil, I give you that, but will confidence alone suffice? I do not think it will. Rumour has reached my trees that the humans have already defeated Nixa. Your strength is not as great as you believe. I think we are doomed to lose, but nor can I see an alliance with Xital. No matter what they offer, it will be rejected it, even if it results in the end of Clan Lilisxi."

"But you will still help us?" I asked falteringly. I shared his misgivings, but again I did not speak them. Airil had faith that his broken clan would be enough to turn this war around, but I too couldn't see how.

Ddraig Bakucic nodded. "Of course." He paused to think again, scraping a claw on the wooden floor in a strange pattern, small shavings spiralling up, revealing the sharpness of the ddraig's claws. "We have sufficient dragons to send a thousand to Laxtal. I cannot send more as I need to defend the clan's territories, but I hope you'll find the number sufficient."

It was more than I had hoped to receive from a minor clan, and expressed my gratitude to Ddraig Bakucic profusely, but he just bared his teeth in amusement. "I presume you will fly to Eivas next?" he asked.

Eivas was to the south-west of Lilisxi, but it didn't share a border with Laxtal as the small territory of Clan Duma lay between. Like Clan Lilisxi, they too were considered reasonably powerful for a minor clan and would make a good ally. They would certainly be more useful than the significantly weaker Clan Duma.

"I shall detain Haeraig Ilibela for as long as I can. The longer our negotiations last, the fewer clans she can influence," Ddraig Bakucic said, his grin widening. "Rest well tonight and fly at first dawn. Be reassured by the fact your Xital counterpart will not be quite so comfortable."

Abruptly, he bowed his head to the two of us as he moved to leave the chamber, which we scrabbled to immediately return; deeper and longer, in true recognition not only of his status, but in gratitude also for his promised alliance. As he unfurled his wings, he paused as he perched on the branches outside and glanced back, first at me, then to Airil. "Look after her, Airil, she's a good catch."

His raucous laugh was broken only by the sound of snapping twigs and falling leaves as he kicked off into the air. I spluttered in shock. Airil looked mortified.

# CHAPTER FOUR

**Anzig**

Ddraig Krateos was a strict and unrelenting teacher, never giving me a moment to rest or recover from the mental trauma he put me through. His justification for the harsh lessons was that I had already missed on many years of development for my magic. I had a long way to catch up. Failure meant risking myself, both through losing control of my magic and losing my mind amongst the thoughts of others, or by the simple act of discovery. If a Laxtal dragon realised I wielded magic, I would be stripped of my title.

Over and over again, the Nixan ddraig pushed me to control my magic, teaching me how to recognise where to find the power within me and how to unleash it. For three days I had done little else, ever since I had sent Ellian to Axaatl, with only a brief interruption to see the mysterious human Azlak had found in the caves beneath the lair. That had been two days ago, and still Ddraig Krateos, my father, refused to let me rest for long.

In those few short periods of time when he was not pressing me to develop my erratic magic, I struggled to keep control of the clan and to plan for the conflicts I knew were just beyond the horizon. Murmurs followed me whenever I left my chambers to eat. Whispers that I was spending too much time with the Nixan ddraig. Concerns about my loyalty to Laxtal. Even without the secret of my parentage known, they already doubted me.

I forced myself to ignore those whispers. Few dared to speak them aloud, and then never in my presence. If I was to keep my magic hidden, then I would need to pretend like nothing was amiss. That I had not heard the plots in the shadows.

I stalked through the lair and tried not to let my exhaustion show. Without Ellian, I had to take on the duties I would have delegated to her, tasks that only added to the weariness that pulled at my wings.

For the moment, I sought Azlak. I had not seen him since shortly after his human had left Laxtal, leaving behind simmering anger towards both me and the seer. Dragons like Marin had expressed their displeasure that a human had been in the lair, especially coming so soon after confirmation that Xital had broken that sacred law in their territory.

While I understood their concerns, the promises Azlak had made through the human were worth the transgression. I just wished I could make the other dragons see that, but they did not share the same belief Azlak held. Or the same desperation I felt.

Laxtal needed an army. We had lost so many dragons with the death of Ddraig Astar. Hundreds of our warriors had died in that ambush. Those who had survived were not enough if we wanted to stand any chance of defeating Tsona's army or his human allies. Without reinforcements from our neighbours, we had no hope of winning. Whatever aid this Esperance had promised might make the difference between victory or extinction.

The seer was in his usual chambers, almost as far down as the cave he had sheltered Esperance. Kaz was the first to meet me, bowing his head in greeting.

Azlak lay in the centre of the chamber, firelight flickering off his scales. At first, I thought he was asleep. Then he opened his eyes and inclined his head. Gold flooded into his eyes, chasing away the milky white of his magic. I was not the only one learning how to better control the power within.

"Have you heard from her?"

"Not yet, Ddraig." Azlak looked down to his forepaw as he answered. "It has only been a couple of days. She did not say how long it would take for her to get in contact with this army."

"Do you trust her?"

"With my life." Azlak stomped his paw to the ground and met me in the eye, an unexpected challenge that I struggled not to look away from. Seeming to recognise his aggression, the seer quickly turned away and started to pace, his tail thrashing in barely-contained energy that was unusual for a dragon who spent so much time beneath the surface.

I glanced to Kaz, but the Nixan kept his eyes low. "We're relying on her," I said slowly. I scuffed my paw as I took a hesitant step forward. "We aren't in a strong position right now. Without Nixa's full strength, we have no hope of winning this war. Even if Ellian succeeds in swaying Axaatl and some of our neighbours, we are going to struggle for numbers. Whatever Esperance has promised, human or dragon, we need them here soon."

"She promised aid," Azlak replied. He turned to face me again but kept his eyes at a respectful height this time. "She wants us to live. She thinks the world is starting to become aware of dragons again. For that to happen, we need to survive. We are doing everything we can to know how to do that."

I held my breath, then released it slowly. "Very well. But you come to me the moment you hear from Esperance, or if you See something that will help us."

"Always, Ddraig," the seer said, sweeping his head low.

A flicker of a thought reached my mind.

*Is he the one we need?*

I struggled to shut down the thought, closing off my mind as Ddraig Krateos had taught. My claws scratched against the stone as I tensed my jaw, drawing a confused look from both Kaz and Azlak. I wasn't sure which the thought had come from. I refused to look either of them in the eye, and before they could question me, I turned to flee their presence. They did not pursue me.

If even Azlak was starting to question me, then what chance did I have of controlling the clan? I needed a way to demonstrate my strength, but everything I tried always failed. Panic built up in my chest as I fled blindly through the deep tunnels, no longer sure where I was going. I didn't stop until I ran out of light, no more torches on the walls to illuminate the damp caverns.

There, so deep below ground that I could hear nothing but the echoed and muffled sound of water dripping, I unleashed the fears that had built in my chest. The scream that tore from my mouth reverberated against the rock, echoing down the tunnel towards whatever lurked in the shadows.

I screamed until my throat could take no more. Everything hurt. I just wanted to curl up and sleep. There were so many impossible things I needed. Knowledge I wished to be ignorant of. I wanted Astar to be the proud but distant father he had always been to me, for him to lead Laxtal. I wanted Carlee by my side. I wanted my magic to have never awoken within me.

I wanted…

I needed Keita.

There was no stopping the tears that flowed down my face. Not tears of weakness, as Astar had always told me. Tears that betrayed my heritage. Just one of the many things I needed to hide, or else the clan I had always called home would banish me.

*"They will banish you anyway if they believe you're derelict in your duties."*

I snarled at the unwanted voice in my head. There was no blocking that one out, no matter how much control I gained over my magic.

"Am I to get no peace from you, Mushussu?"

*"That is what it means to be a ddraig. Besides, your presence is required. The beacons have been lit."*

I groaned and held my head in my paws. There was always something demanding my attention. How had Astar made it all look so easy?

"I don't want to know the answer. Not now," I growled, sensing Mushussu about to give me another lecture on how Astar had acted as ddraig. I had no desire to listen to her as I walked back towards the surface. Though her dissatisfaction rolled across me, she remained mercifully silent.

It didn't take me long to reach the main chamber, my paws guided by Mushussu so I didn't lose my way after my wild run. I was thankful to the guardian for that, displaying some of her use in a way that didn't belittle, demean, and annoy me.

Almost the moment I arrived in the expansive chamber, several dragons quickly converged on me.

"Finally," Marin growled. He bared his teeth.

I ignored the green scaled dragon, instead turning to the albino by his side. "What do you know?" I asked, gesturing with a wing towards the beacon fire.

"A great number of dragons approaching from the north-east. Axaatl dragons," Yalle replied. He shoved past both Saya and Marin to stand in front of me. Vinzent lingered beside his mother.

"Ellian?" I asked, doing my best to ignore the pale blue eyes of the dragonet.

Yalle shook his head. "The beacons do not speak of any Laxtal dragons amongst their number."

My tail drooped. "To be expected," I said with a sigh. "She would have flown on to Reneza or Lilisxi to secure their alliances."

Marin growled again, louder this time, dragging my attention back towards him. "Are we really allowing other clans to send their dragons here?"

"We are if we want to survive," I said, growling back at the older dragon. Before he had chance to retort, I turned back to Yalle and spread my wings. "Fetch Ddraig Krateos and then meet me outside. I'd like you with me when we meet these dragons."

"Of course, Ddraig."

Marin and Saya did not follow as I flew for the surface. Vinzent did.

Though the dragonet followed me outside, he remained far from me as I waited for the arrival of the Axaatl dragons. Ddraig Krateos and Haeraig Zeena flew out with Yalle, arriving just before the first dragons appeared on the horizon. The two Nixans stayed a respectful distance from me. They were present to formalise the relations our clan had, and to display a show of strength to Axaatl. It was still my responsibility to be the strong leader expected in a union between three clans.

I scanned across the approaching dragons as they neared, searching for Ddraig Aranat. He was not amongst them. Worse, there was only about two hundred dragons.

A massive, green-scaled dragon led the Axaatl force. He landed a few feet in front of me, his wide wings kicking up a ferocious downdraft that buffeted into me. He offered no apology as he bowed his head. "Greetings, Ddraig Anzig. I come on behalf of Ddraig Aranat to confirm the alliance made by your haeraig. I am Hyantl, commander of the Axaatl army."

I chewed on my tongue as the gigantic dragon spoke. The words then escaped my mouth the moment Hyantl finished. "Is this an insult to Laxtal?" I realised the mistake almost immediately, but I could not stop the frustration from spilling out. "Where is Ddraig Aranat? And why has a clan as powerful as Axaatl only provided two hundred dragons?"

Hyantl dipped his head again, but such was his advantage in size that his eyes were still above mine. "My apologies, Ddraig Anzig. This war is being fought on more than one front. Ddraig Aranat has joined the bulk of our army in the east, where he is assisting Ddraig Nunahra to defeat Tsona. It is his intention to reinforce you once that mission has been achieved."

I suppressed a growl. I had hoped for a stronger contribution from Ddraig Aranat, but the implication that we had an alliance with Xigax as well as Axaatl was the bigger news. Of course they would need to deal with Tsona and his army, which had flown east from Xital. There were so many more of them than the humans encamped somewhere within Nixa.

"Very well," I said, lifting my head in a futile attempt to gain a little height on Hyantl. "We appreciate any assistance your clan is able to provide. We welcome you to Laxtal. Did you hear where Haeraig Ellian went after seeing your ddraig?"

"I understand she went south, to Lilisxi," Hyantl replied.

Lilisxi. If she had been successful, then dragons from that clan should start arriving soon. I could only hope that the minor clans were more generous with their numbers than Axaatl. It would do us no good if Aranat and Nunahra were able to defeat Tsona if we were destroyed by the humans. Only together could we succeed, and our alliance had already become divided even before we could fully join.

We would have to make do with what resources we had. I turned my head. "Yalle, can you arrange for space where the Axaatl dragons can rest. I'm sure they would like a place to sleep together."

"Of course, Ddraig Anzig," Yalle said, sweeping his wings low. There was something that looked like disapproval in his eyes. I deserved that. I had not been diplomatic in my exchange with Hyantl. I would need to repair that damage, both with the albino and the Axaatl.

I looked up to the massive dragon. "Hyantl, if you would oversee the training of our dragons. We lost a lot of our best warriors when my father died. We could use a stern claw to ensure our warriors are capable."

The Axaatl commander inclined his head. "I would be honoured to provide that service, Ddraig Anzig. Let me settle my dragons in and we can begin discussing what this alliance can bring for both our clans."

I could feel the eyes of Ddraig Krateos on me as Hyantl followed Yalle into the lair. Two hundred Axaatl dragons may not have felt like much, but their size meant they were an intimidating force as they squeezed through the narrow gap into the caverns.

Before I could receive any lecture from either Nixan dragon or Mushussu, I took to wing and fled in the opposite direction, towards the open plains. Perhaps if they believed I went to hunt, they would leave me alone. No one followed me.

*"We will need lessons in diplomacy."*

I sighed. It was too much to hope that I might be alone.

A cold wind blew as the sun sank towards the horizon. My wings sagged, the tips almost touching the ground. I longed for nothing more than to retreat into the lair and curl up by the fire, but the beacons were alight again.

In the two full days since Hyantl had arrived in Laxtal, he had taken command of training every adult dragon in the clan. No one was spared, not even me. He pushed us through a regime of exercise and drills, training our wings for stamina and strength, as well as building up an ability to fly in close formation. The Axaatl drake was relentless. The Laxtal dragons were too exhausted to complain.

The dragons who had alerted the beacon keepers flew from the southeast, but there was no indication that this was a threat coming from Xital. Tsona had not yet made his move. These were dragons coming to bolster our alliance, I was sure of it.

Sure enough, I recognised the brown-scaled drake that led the massive column of dragons that approached the lair. My eyes widened as I recognised the sheer number of them. This was a much greater force than Axaatl had provided.

Ddraig Bakucic of Lilisxi must have gathered almost every dragon in his clan for this. At least one thousand dragons followed him.

The ddraig dropped to the ground just in front of me, while the majority of those who followed him came to rest below the cliffs. I couldn't help but stare at them for a few moments. There was so many, and coming from a clan so small. Hope swelled in my chest. Whatever Ellian was saying, she was doing a good job at convincing our neighbours to join us.

"Ddraig Anzig, it is a pleasure to see you again," Bakucic said, bowing his head before me. "I would like to express my condolences for the loss of your father, but I am honoured to answer your call to ally against these threats Xital and the humans bring."

"I am pleased to welcome you to Laxtal," I replied, trying to keep the exhaustion from my voice. I partially turned and flicked out a wing, gesturing for the albino dragon just behind me to step forward. "Yalle will see to your needs and those of your clan. We have food and caverns for everyone, but we expect that your clan reports to Hyantl of Axaatl for training come the morning."

The Lilisxi ddraig bowed his head again. "I understand, Ddraig Anzig."

I felt the murmuring disapproval of Yalle's thoughts a moment before the albino opened his mouth. "We are fast running out of room, Ddraig Anzig. How many more must we accommodate?"

I didn't even give the albino the courtesy of looking at him. "As many as necessary, Yalle. We do not need to be comfortable these next few days and weeks. We simply need to be warm. Make it happen, please."

Yalle's continued grumblings stayed only in his head. "Very well," was all he said, and he quickly took Ddraig Bakucic and the Lilisxi dragons below the surface. The thunderous roar of a thousand pairs of dragon wings made me step back, staring with awe at the sudden growth in our power. We were still not yet at the strength we needed to be, but this was a great improvement.

*"Not the only thing that has improved."* Mushussu's thoughts were a frustrating intrusion into my mind. *"You handled yourself much better than you did with Hyantl. You are learning quickly, Anzig. We will craft a fine ddraig out of you yet."*

"At the expense of sleep," I muttered beneath my breath. But for the Lilisxi dragons as they flooded down into the gorge, I was all alone. "I'm tired, Mushussu. When does this start getting easier?"

The statue's sigh was so great I was sure I could hear the actual sound from my chamber. *"It doesn't, Anzig. To be a ddraig means you will always be flying in turbulent skies. What you are learning now will help you in navigating that turbulence. It will never be clear and still for you."*

I growled. "Then what good are you? If you're not even able to help me sleep and get some rest, then why do I bother listening to you at all?"

*"My magic is…"*

"Limited, I know," I snarled. I swiped at the dry grass between my paws, slashing through the stems with ease. "Leave me alone. I'm going to sleep by the fire so I don't have to look at you."

*"Don't do that,"* Mushussu said sharply. *"If you don't sleep in your chambers then my magic weakens further. I will not be able to protect you from harm."*

"Who is going to attack me here?" I scoffed. Lacking a target to glare at, I aimed my ire towards the half-full moon, chasing the sun across the sky towards setting. "I think I'll take those chances if it means a peaceful night."

There was no reply. I didn't even get a sensation of the guardian's displeasure. My mind was mercifully clear and filled with only my own thoughts. I breathed out slowly and closed my eyes. This was how it was meant to be. How long had it been since it had been this way for me? I hoped a good sleep would help me feel more normal and alert in the morning.

I woke suddenly from a dreamless sleep, momentarily confused about where I was. Then I recognised the firepit, still burning brightly, and the darkness beyond. I stretched out my legs and yawned, unsure whether it was daylight yet. No one else seemed awake, with a few dozen other dragons also choosing to sleep in the main chamber.

Then I realised what had woken me. Black scales. Menacing red eyes, and teeth that gleamed white. Maznar looked more like Nightwings.

I startled up to my paws, only just biting down on the yelp of shock before I woke anyone.

"Is that any way to greet your sister?"

"Keep quiet when you say that," I whispered, furtively looking around to make sure no one could have overheard her. It would only take one dragon to know that Maznar was my sister for the secret to spill out, and the spectre didn't seem overly concerned about keeping it hidden.

Maznar smirked. She sauntered away from the fire, towards the caves that led to the deeper parts of the clan. She glanced back at me a few times, waiting until I followed her. Reluctantly, I did so. If she had something she wanted to say to me, then I wanted her to speak it where there were no witnesses.

"Why? Are you scared of who you are? Do you not like being a Nixan?"

The angered snarl almost tore itself from my throat. I could hear no one else awake, but I didn't want to take the chance of someone overhearing our secrets. I hurried on, overtaking Maznar and leading her down to the dark. The crackle of the fire soon faded into silence, as did the gentle snore of sleeping dragons.

Maznar was finally a quiet shadow as I led her down towards the cold caves, where I knew we would be safe from eavesdroppers. It wasn't quite as private as my chambers, but I had no desire to return to Mushussu, whose thoughts had remained silent ever since I had fallen asleep.

I listened for any sounds of movement. There was nothing. We were all alone. There wasn't even much light to see by, with a few of the nearby torch sconces empty and cold.

"What was it you wanted to say?" I growled.

Maznar's insufferable smirk remained etched on her muzzle. "I simply wished to talk to you. I feel like you've been avoiding me all week. Perhaps you can invite our father and we can have a nice happy family reunion. Wouldn't that be nice?"

"Enough of that," I snarled. My claws tensed against the ground, tail thrashing.

"I'm not getting much brotherly love from you."

"I said enough!" I roared, surprising Maznar by slashing her across the muzzle. I stood still, panting as I tried to reign my anger in again.

The spectre slowly raised a paw to her muzzle. It came away bloodied and her eyes widened. "That's the second time you've drawn my blood, Anzig." She didn't sound affronted, if anything she sounded pleased, and not for one moment did the mad grin on her face fade. The spectre started to circle around me, but I resisted her games and stayed completely still, eyes only for the empty torch sconce directly in front of me. She was no threat to me, and I wanted her to know that.

I hissed in pain as twice she trod on my tail in her circuit around me. She prowled back into my line of sight and pushed her muzzle against mine, forcing me to look into her wild red eyes. If I took a step back, she took one forward, keeping us in constant contact.

"Do you know what happens to those who make me bleed?" she asked. Her hot breath was rank. She must have hunted recently.

"I am ddraig of this clan. There is nothing you can say to me that will make me fear you," I replied, keeping my voice even against her threats. I could not allow her to intimidate me.

Maznar snickered. "The imposter Nixan? Ddraig of this clan? I don't think so, my dear brother. It can't be long before you're thrown out on your heels."

I growled and tried to push Maznar away, but she stood firm. "We rescued you from the humans. Remember that," I snarled. I had trusted the spectre when no one else but Azlak had done so. I did not want to regret that decision.

"Yes, you did. Only after you tried to kill me."

"You tried to kill me first," I spluttered, unable to comprehend how the spectre could hold that against me. I had only wounded her as I had tried to stay alive, not out of any malice or ill will towards her. "I know you only did that because the humans were in your head, but I was fighting to survive. We freed you of that."

Finally, Maznar pulled away from me, giving me some room to move again. "That's where you're wrong, brother. You freed me of nothing."

I allowed my fear to show, taking a step back and fluttering my wings in distress. "The humans still control you?" I asked, my voice quavering in terror. The darkness that surrounded the ness seemed to grow steadily blacker, until the only thing I could see was Nightwings's demonic red eyes.

"They never controlled me to begin with."

I was powerless to resist as Maznar lunged for me. In one quick movement I was on my back, her claws at my throat. "I do not take kindly to those who injure me, brother. Last time you were healed. This time I will make sure that's not possible."

I screamed as her teeth seized my outstretched wing. Muscle and sinew stretched to breaking point. Frantically, I tried to push her away, but my claws could find no purchase against her scales.

Tendons snapped and the thin wing membranes shredded as her claws tore freely at whatever they found. I cried for help, but this far down in the lair there was no one to hear my screams. I could not even call for Mushussu. The guardian was silent.

With a loud pop, my wing dislocated, but the spectre was not finished.

Maznar pulled harder, her paw pressing into my throat and silencing my screams. My vision started to fade.

Flesh tore and bone splintered.

The spectre suddenly fell back, freeing my throat. I had not the breath to scream.

Her eyes gloated. My wing in her mouth.

Darkness took me, but even that couldn't spare me from her demonic gaze.

# ChAPTER FiVE

**Azlak**

Laxtal was busier than I could recall it ever being. With the influx of dragons from Axaatl and Lilisxi, we were already starting to run out of regular caves to house everyone. When I had not been training under the strict leadership of Hyantl, or using my magic to scour the future for assistance, I had been deep underground, helping to clear out some of the lesser used caverns of moss and grime. It was hard work, and I fell asleep quickly every night with sore muscles.

I had little time to myself, and few occasions to speak with Kaz about Esperance or her warnings about what was to come. I wished we had been able to spend more time with her, to learn more about what she was and to convince her to lend her magic to our cause. She had been silent ever since she had left the lair. Though I had been tempted to squeeze my paw and reach for her, I had resisted the urge. Such a thing was only to be for important pieces of news.

Despite the amount that I had to do, it never seemed to be enough for some dragons. Ddraig Anzig, especially. He came to me every day, sometimes multiple times, hoping for information on what to do next. I had not said it so bluntly, but I wasn't sure he had any plan. Haeraig Ellian was gathering the support of the surrounding clans, and Hyantl was training those who arrived, but Ddraig Anzig had done nothing with them.

Perhaps he was waiting for me. Waiting to hear what I had Seen of the future. I hoped that wasn't the case, as my visions were a mess of conflicting and contradicting possibilities. Nothing made sense, no matter how hard I tried to interpret them. All I had done was give myself a headache in addition to my sore legs and wings.

"It must have been another rough night. You've got that brooding look again."

I looked up to Kaz, who lay just across from me. With so many more dragons in the lair, it was getting harder to find somewhere to bask in the morning. We warmed our wings close to the base of the cliffs, near the ancient rockfall that sealed one end of the gorge.

"No more so than any other at the moment." I rose to weary paws and fluttered my wings, warm enough now after the long, cold night. The encroaching winter was really starting to bite now, the days shorter and nights colder. In so many ways, this was the worst time for humans to invade our lands. That was probably their intention.

"We'll find a way. Don't worry about it too much."

I knew Kaz believed what he said, but I could not bring myself to do so. There were still too many unknowns. Something obscured the future, something I had not yet Seen. If it was near, then there was little I could do to prevent it.

"We should…" I paused. I had been about to suggest going to the plains, where Hyantl would expect dragons to start showing up for training, but an unfamiliar dragon above us caught my attention, circling as though preparing to land.

"Is that…?" Kaz asked, following my gaze.

I nodded. My wings fluttered as I recognised the dragon, a newcomer to the lair. "Ddraig Bakucic. What could he want with us?"

It was clear the Lilisxi ddraig had no other target. He fluttered to the ground right in front of us, his wings quickly tucked to his side. Even though he came from one of the minor clans, he was still a ddraig. I bowed my head to him.

"You must be the seer, Azlak?" Ddraig Bakucic asked, though I could tell it was not really a question. He had heard of me before. My reputation usually didn't reach the clans beyond Nixa and Laxtal.

"What can I do for you, Ddraig?"

The Lilisxi ddraig glanced aside, judging how far away the nearest dragons were. He lowered his voice. "Ddraig Krateos said you are trusted by Ddraig Anzig. We have need of your assistance."

I blinked in surprise. A summons from three different ddraigs? It had not been long ago when such a thing would have terrified me. "Of course, anything at all."

Ddraig Bakucic flicked out his tongue. "We can't find your ddraig. No one has seen him since just after sundown."

"Not seen him?" I stepped back, horror pulling my wings out from my side. "How could he have gone missing?"

"I don't know. All we know is that he didn't return to his chambers last night. I… can't tell you why, but for a ddraig to sleep somewhere but his chambers is always a risk. I have chosen to do because I believe I am needed here, and Ddraig Krateos has no choice. But for Ddraig Anzig? It appears a foolish decision." The Lilisxi drake turned his head to the sky. The sun was already a few wing-breadths above the horizon.

If Anzig had been missing since sundown, then there were many hours where no one had seen him. I pawed at the ground. "Why do you need me? I See the future, not the past. I won't be able to find him any easier than other dragons."

Ddraig Bakucic shook his head. "It isn't your magic we need. You know him better than most, and no one else seems interested to know he's missing. Ddraig Krateos thought you were the best dragon to help us."

"Who else did you ask?"

The ddraig flicked his wings and partially turned away. "Two dragons who I believed were close to Ddraig Astar. I may have miscalculated their loyalty towards Ddraig Anzig. Marin and Saya are their names."

I only just managed to suppress the growl, reminding myself that this was a ddraig I spoke to. But the Lilisxi dragon could not have told two worse dragons that Ddraig Anzig was missing.

There was no undoing that now. It just meant that finding out where the ddraig had gone became more important. If Marin and Saya realised there was an opportunity to take control of the clan, then they would not waste such an opportunity.

"Where was he last seen?"

"By the fire, just after sundown. He wasn't there when dragons started to wake up this morning," Ddraig Bakucic explained. He flicked his wings and took a step back. "We have checked the obvious places, but he hasn't visited his chambers all night and no one has seen him fly out to hunt."

"Tracking his scent would be impossible," I said quietly. I wanted to stand and think, to work out a plan to find where the ddraig had gone, but staying still felt like inactivity and wasting time. There wasn't any of that to lose. "If you could show me where you've looked, Ddraig. I'll do my best to find him."

I waited for the ddraig to take to wing before following him, Kaz just behind me. A few curious eyes tracked our progress, but no other dragon took to wing. I doubted any had overheard the conversation. A missing ddraig would create some worry amongst the clan. For now, it was better to keep the news of Anzig's disappearance to as few dragons as possible.

Unfortunately, the two dragons I did not wish to see were waiting in the central chamber, as though they had known I was coming. Marin and Saya tracked us from the moment we arrived inside the lair, stood on the raised plinth by the fire. Where Anzig had been last seen. I struggled to put such thoughts out of my head. Surely they would not crawl so low as to attack the ddraig?

"Seems like it isn't just Nixans," Saya said as I landed nearby, her loud whisper clearly intended for me to hear. Marin sneered but said nothing.

I approached them, keeping my head held high, aware that as I did so I stepped in front of Ddraig Bakucic. The Lilisxi dragon didn't growl or try to push me back.

I stared at the dragon I had once called father. "Where is Ddraig Anzig?"

Saya flicked out her wings. Her eyes darted from me to Ddraig Bakucic. "Gone, if he has any sense. Fled the clan and left us to fix his mess."

A low growl escaped my throat, surprising Saya as she took a pace back. "Unless you heard him cede control of the clan, then he is still your ddraig and deserves your respect. Have you not put any effort into finding him?"

"Why would we want to?" Marin spat. "He is everything wrong with the dragonets now. No belief in the true strength of Laxtal and our ability to fly alone. He would do everything he can to weaken our clan, just as you would have done. I can't believe I ever managed to call you my son."

Marin's words did nothing to hurt me. They only built into my rage and frustration, boiling through my blood as though scorched by sunlight. I stomped my forepaw. "You should have no concerns other than finding Ddraig Anzig. Then we can start to fix the rot that has taken root in this clan."

Ddraig Bakucic stepped to my side. "Our alliance, our very survival, relies on the good nature of our clans. Laxtal has been gracious enough to provide shelter for my clan and many others while we prepare to strike back at the humans. We ask only that the dragons of Laxtal respect our presence."

"You have…" Saya growled, but Ddraig Bakucic snapped his teeth to silence her.

"Do not forget I am still a ddraig," the Lilisxi dragon snarled, matching the ness with his fury. "Watch your tongue or I will take matters into my own paws, as is my right and authority."

Both Saya and Marin held their tongues. Neither of them made any move to start a search for the missing ddraig. They simply glared at Ddraig Bakucic, but the drake made no step backwards. He was a ddraig, even if he was from a minor clan. His authority was the greatest here. The challenging dragons seemed to realise that eventually, and they both lowered their eyes.

Ddraig Bakucic kept the growl in his voice. "Start searching for him. This alliance needs a leader, and that is Ddraig Anzig. Without him we cannot win this war."

I pawed at the ground. Some of my visions had indicated that, but only when he was with Haeraig Ellian. Had I made a mistake in not informing the ddraig of this before he sent Ellian to the surrounding clans? I knew those alliances were critical to our success, but could another dragon have secured them? I feared my inaction might have changed the future. No visions had contradicted them, though. Perhaps we were not yet doomed.

"I'll start searching the lower caverns with Kaz," I said, my gaze lingering on Marin for a few moments. He returned my glare before looking away.

I did not wait around to see if Marin or Saya would assist in the search. Instead, I took to wing and soared above the chamber and flew towards the caverns that wound beneath the surface.

The expansive tunnels were no better a place to start than anywhere else, but something tugged my mind down there. It wasn't quite a vision or an understanding of the future. I Saw nothing about finding Anzig. Saya could have been telling the truth, that Anzig had fled his responsibilities and flown from Laxtal, but I could not bring myself to believe that.

I could think of no reason how Anzig could get lost in the tunnels though. He knew them well enough, like any Laxtal dragon, that he could always find his way back to the surface. A tension started to pull at my gut. Could there be some malice at work here? Surely, that was more likely than Anzig abandoning his duties.

Worry gave speed to my wings, and I hurried into the narrow caves before dropping to my paws. It was impossible to find Ddraig Anzig's scent amongst the myriad of smells, worse than usual given the sheer number of dragons residing in the central lair. I would never find him with my nose. Instead, I followed the gut feeling that pulled my paws forward, guiding me down the tunnels towards the cold caverns and the deep parts of the lair.

"Where are you going?"

I paused and looked back. Kaz struggled to keep up with my mad dash through the dark tunnels, lit only by the occasional torch. Even now that there were fewer dragons around, I still could not pick up Ddraig Anzig's scent.

"I haven't Seen anything," I said slowly, trying to put to words the confusion in my mind, "but I keep getting the feeling that I'll find him down here."

"You don't believe them, then? He's still down here?" Kaz stepped ahead of me, peering down the branching tunnel. Both directions sloped deeper underground, the walls rough and glistening with moisture.

"Definitely not," I growled. I lifted my nose and sniffed the air, hoping against hope that I could detect the ddraig. I thought I caught something, but it was so faint that I could not be sure how old it was. The scent was stronger down the left path though, towards the cold caves. "This way. We might not have much time."

I didn't know what I feared more. Ddraig Anzig wounded somewhere in the dark, or Saya and Marin plotting to overthrow him. I could only hope that Ddraig Bakucic was able to keep the rebellious dragons in check.

The darkness between the torches seemed blacker than normal, as though they hid the secrets of the ddraig's whereabouts. It took everything I could to stop myself from searching every tiny nook and cranny. If he was near, I would be able to smell him.

My nose wrinkled as I felt the frigid air from the cold caves wafting through the tunnel, bringing with it the scent of salted meat. That would overwhelm any lingering scent of the ddraig. I growled to myself. I couldn't be sure if this was the right way, but that strange sense of rightness pulled me on.

I closed my eyes for a moment and reached for the well of magic within me, trying, hoping to See something. The future stirred.

*"Here's here!"*

*The blue dragon leaped from the shadows, darting towards the bronze drake.*

*"We've found him."*

Kaz scampered ahead, beyond the entrance to the cold caves where the air might be fresher and less tainted with the scent of stored meat. Where was the ddraig? Where would we find him?

My paw slipped on something wet, immediately dismissing it as a trickle of water from the ceiling. I took a few more paces, eyes and ears alert for anything unusual. Only then did I realise that what wettened my paw was not water. There was a stickiness to it.

I lifted my paw to my nose. Not water. Blood. It dripped from a small crevasse, an unused path barely wide enough for a single dragon. Anyone much larger than me wouldn't have fit inside.

Already fearful for what I might find, I reached for the nearest torch and pulled it from its sconce on the wall. The firelight illuminated the narrow crack, and I squinted through the smoke and flame to see a dragon lying in the shadow. The shape of the body was wrong. It was completely still.

Blood splattered against the rock in copious amounts.

"Kaz! Quickly!"

I dropped the torch and groped into the darkness, my claws closing around an outstretched hind leg. With no thought to the safety of the dragon, I pulled hard, dragging him free of the crevasse. Blood stained against my paws, a steady trickle of it coming from the prone body. Kaz quickly ran close.

The dragon did not resist as I pulled them out. It was only once I had freed them fully from the crevasse so they lay on the tunnel floor, in the flickering light of the torch, that I could clearly see it was Ddraig Anzig I had found. It took me a few moments more to realise what was so wrong about the shape of his body. I stepped back, bile rising in my throat.

"Kaz," I choked. "Where are his wings?"

The Nixan's response was nothing more than a suppressed whimper, but even so he stepped forward and placed a trembling paw on Ddraig Anzig's blood-soaked back.

The ddraig was still alive. His chest fluttered with faint movement. His paw twitched in response to Kaz's touch, though he did not wake.

"Can you heal him?" I asked.

Kaz's voice cracked. "I can't heal what is not there. I can stop the blood, but I can't…"

He didn't need to finish to know what he meant. Anzig's wings were gone. There was no healing this. The ddraig would never fly again.

I bowed my head as magical light started to envelope the ddraig. A dragon without wings was useless and helpless. The sky was everything to a dragon, to stretch wings and soar on the thermals. Even just warming up in the morning relied on our wings. It would almost be a mercy to just let him die.

"It's… it's done," Kaz said shakily. I didn't want to look. I didn't know if I could bear seeing my ddraig in such a way. "He's weak, but he should come through. I've kept his heart beating. It had almost stopped. He'd lost a lot of blood. Well, we saw it all over the ground. I don't know how he survived so long as it is."

I didn't know if Kaz spoke simply to cope. It was certainly more than I was able to do, still staring down at the ground and refusing to lift my eyes. My mate hadn't finished either. "If only my brother was here. We'd be able to get him up to his chambers easily. We shouldn't leave him down here, but I don't know what else we can do."

Steeling my resolve, I slowly looked up. First, I saw Kaz's pleading eyes, desperate for direction on what to do. Then my eyes moved on to Anzig's shivering body. Blood still soaked his green scales, but Kaz had sealed off the wounds where his wings once had been. All that remained was small stumps of flesh, useless and pathetic. I reached out to him, my paw shaking as I gently brushed the side of his muzzle. He twitched slightly, but otherwise gave no indication he was aware of my touch.

"Who could have done this?" Kaz whispered, placing his paw on top of mine. I leaned against him, and he supported my weight.

My mind immediately turned to Marin and Saya. The dragon I had once called father would surely not be capable of this. I did not think him to be so cruel. Saya, however? Perhaps she was capable of anything, especially in pursuit of power for her son. Vinzent could be well placed to benefit from Anzig's death or injuries. Until the ddraig woke and was able to tell us who had done this to him, there were very few dragons we could trust. No one from Laxtal.

I turned to Kaz, wrenching my eyes away from the crippled form of Ddraig Anzig. "You should fetch Bakucic or Krateos. They're the only dragons I think we can trust at the moment. I'll keep guard here and make sure no one finds him."

"I'll be back soon," Kaz said, stepping away from Anzig, before turning to flee back towards the main part of the lair. He left behind a few bloody pawprints.

This close to the cold caves, I couldn't expect to be undisturbed for too long. I moved quickly to extinguish the closest torches to shroud us in darkness, hoping that would be enough to avoid detection. I then stood vigil over Ddraig Anzig, waiting desperately for someone to help us.

I couldn't help it. Long suppressed tears started to form in my eyes. It had been such a long time since I had cried that the wetness against my scales felt strange. Hope was surely fading. My eyes constantly moved down to the ruined shoulders of the ddraig and the absence of his wings. There was no help for him now, never enough to heal what he had lost.

So many futures died with those wings.

It was all I could do to hope that our survival as a species had not gone with them.

It was not long before Ddraig Krateos arrived, running through the narrow passages as though a human army was on his tail. I stood as soon as I heard him, spreading my wings to shield Anzig from view. Haeraig Zeena, Ddraig Bakucic, and Kaz followed not far behind the distressed ddraig.

"What happened to him? Please, let me through," Ddraig Krateos asked, trying to push past me, but I held firm and kept him away from Anzig.

"Please, wait. He's badly hurt, Ddraig," I replied, trying to stop the Nixan, but he kept trying to force his way through. Stubbornly I held my ground, placing my body between them. "Please, stop."

Though my heart pounded at standing up to a ddraig like this, the Nixan relented.

"What happened?" Ddraig Krateos repeated, his voice hollow and empty.

I explained to the ddraig everything I knew about what had occurred, but the gaps in my knowledge were immense. I couldn't tell the ddraig what he really wanted to know, and that was who had attacked Ddraig Anzig and left him a helpless cripple. When I finally lowered my wings Ddraig Krateos howled his grief, while Isikian and Haeraig Zeena both averted their eyes.

A low, savage snarl emanated from the back of Ddraig Krateos's throat. In alarm, I stepped out of his way before realising the reaction was not for me. "I swear I will destroy whoever did this to you," he said, holding Anzig's head in his paws and showing a tenderness I had not expected between the ddraigs. There was the slightest murmur of response from Anzig, but otherwise he remained still and quiet.

I placed my paw on Ddraig Krateos's tail. "We should take him up to his chambers, where he can rest properly," I said, hoping not to feel the wrath of the Nixan.

The ddraig's shoulders slumped as he nodded. "Of course, that will be best. Zeena, can you fetch Eule. I think her magic will be needed."

Zeena bowed her head and hurried off to do her father's bidding. I got no response to my questions about what Eule's magic was.

With a flash of amber light, the prone body of Anzig started to lift into the air. I looked into Ddraig Krateos's eyes, which shone with the same light that enveloped my ddraig's body. He appeared to be holding back tears, the strain of the constantly battling emotions taking their toll on the Nixan.

Slowly we made our way back up to the main part of the lair. Ddraig Krateos led the way with Ddraig Bakucic ensuring the path was clear. Anzig's motionless body drifted beside the Nixan as he carried him with his magic. I lingered behind with Kaz. He held me close with his wing as we walked, with me resting my head against his shoulder. No one spoke. There was nothing left to say.

As we approached the central chamber, I was sent ahead to keep away any wandering dragons while we waited for Haeraig Zeena to return with Eule. If Ddraig Krateos knew a way to keep Anzig hidden, then we didn't want anyone to catch a glimpse of him now. Though I was around a few corners from the main part of the lair, I could hear a lot of activity ahead of me. There didn't seem to be much concern for the missing ddraig, as the general mood appeared to be quite positive. I shook my head. Had Anzig's rule of the clan been poisoned to such a degree that no one even cared about his fate?

We didn't have to wait long for Haeraig Zeena to return, a copper-scaled Nixan ness hurrying by her side. I allowed Eule to pass, but the haeraig remained by my side.

"There isn't a Nixan here who won't be outraged at what happened, and we will help Laxtal find the attacker." She put her paw gently on mine.

"But what if the attacker is Laxtal? This wasn't just an attack on any dragon. This is the ddraig of the clan. It could only have been done by someone seeking to replace him," I whispered. I half-expected someone to overhear me and leap from the shadows, accusing me of spreading such lies against the senior dragons of the clan, but none came.

"No dragon would want to earn power that way. Such a vile act would not be treated with respect," Haeraig Zeena said.

I sighed. What she said was logical, but I still couldn't help but feel Marin or Saya was behind this. The haeraig looked like she had more to say, but she closed his mouth again as Ddraig Krateos and the others caught up with us. Anzig was still suspended in the magic of the ddraig, but even as I watched Eule put her paw on Anzig's body. There was a flash of white light and the two of them vanished.

"She's a teleporter too?" I asked in shock. I had thought Airil was the only survivor with that magic.

"Not exactly," an unfamiliar female's voice answered. I frantically looked around, trying to find the source, but Haeraig Zeena was the only ness present, and she hadn't spoken. "I haven't moved from where you last saw me."

My eyes focussed on the space between Ddraig Krateos and Ddraig Bakucic. I wasn't sure if I was imagining the slight shimmering I saw, like light reflecting off the surface of water. "You're invisible?"

"Yes. But we're not going to fool anybody if you keep talking to me," the empty patch of air retorted. I offered a quick apology before leading the group out into the central chambers. Apart from a few curious dragons nearby, no one even seemed to notice us. It was as though Eule had turned us all invisible.

Yalle and Marin were up on the raised dais in the middle of the chamber with Saya and Vinzent. The four dragons were quietly discussing something, but from this far away I had no hope of overhearing them. They had made no attempt to start the search for Ddraig Anzig. I knew soon I would have to let them know we had found him, but I didn't have the heart for that confrontation yet. I would have some heated words for the albino and the dragon I had once called father, but that could wait until Anzig was safely in his chambers. If they were oblivious enough to not see us crossing the central chamber then they didn't deserve to know what their ddraig's fate was. That was if they didn't already know. They could already be plotting how to convince Laxtal to follow their rule.

We soon took to wing to ascend to the small cluster of passageways behind the great fire. We rose through the air slowly, for the benefit of the three dragons helping to carry Ddraig Anzig. It would be taking a lot of concentration from Ddraig Krateos and Haeraig Zeena to keep Anzig in the air, not even accounting for Eule remaining in contact with him. I just hoped Anzig wouldn't return to consciousness as we flew.

Finally, we made it up to Ddraig Anzig's chambers. Eule removed her grip from Anzig's tail as Ddraig Krateos and Haeraig Zeena released him from their magic on his pile of rugs and blankets. I went forward and moved him into a more comfortable position, but that was about all I could do for him just now. He had never been a large dragon, less than an inch taller than me, but now he looked tiny without his wings; so thin and frail.

I had to blink a few times as I was sure something silver kept flashing past my eyes. No one else seemed to notice, so I dismissed it and moved it to the back of my mind. Ddraig Bakucic had immediately moved to light the fire and get some warmth into the chamber. Ddraig Krateos settled down beside Anzig and closed his eyes, though I could tell he was not about to fall asleep. His muzzle occasionally twitched in a silent snarl.

Eule had made a quiet exit, but no one else was willing to leave. We would all remain until Ddraig Anzig awoke. Partly we were curious. We wanted to know who had dared attack the ddraig, but we were also protective. No one wanted Anzig to come to any further harm, and we would fight tooth and claw to keep him from danger.

Ddraig Krateos was the first to break the silence. His voice was little more than a hoarse whisper as he turned his tear-streaked face around to look each of us in the eye. His gaze lingered on us all in turn, first his daughter, and then to Ddraig Bakucic, Kaz, and me. "I do not know if I should tell you this secret, but I feel you should all know the truth of the matter. But you must not share what I have to say with anyone outside this chamber."

"I understand," Ddraig Bakucic said, lowering his head in reverence to the older ddraig.

Ddraig Krateos took a deep breath. "Anzig is my son." He held up a paw to curtail Ddraig Bakucic's shocked cry of protest. "I only discovered that this morning. Three of my eggs were lost in the wild. One was Anzig. The second was the ness Maznar. And the third we don't know about, but..."

His eyes met mine as realisation reached us both in the same instant. "They would be a dragon with magic but not from Nixa," I said slowly. "Marin told me that my egg was found in the wilderness. I'm your son."

Ddraig Krateos choked back a sob as Haeraig Zeena hurried to her paws. "How is this possible?" the Nixan ddraig said. He rested his head against his daughter's. "I lose four sons, but I find two more and a daughter just days later."

I didn't know what to say. When Marin had rejected me, I had not expected to find my true father so soon. I was the son of the Nixan ddraig. Not only that, I was the brother of Ddraig Anzig. It was just too much for my mind to process, the sudden position of relative power I found myself in. I was older than Anzig by a couple of days, which placed me at a higher rank than him amongst Nixan hierarchy. In Laxtal, we were nothing. I had fallen nowhere, I already was nothing, but for Ddraig Anzig the loss of status would be immense. The loss of his wings would be nothing compared to the knowledge that he was not Astar's son. It was no wonder he had kept this knowledge hidden to all. I wondered how long he had known.

"Will our clan accept them?" Haeraig Zeena quietly asked her father.

"Our numbers are too few to pick and choose, Zeena. Any Nixan, no matter how or where they were raised, will be a welcome addition to our clan," the ddraig said. I couldn't help but smile, comparing the ddraig's words to those Saya and Marin had spouted out. They wanted just Laxtal dragon within their lair, and none other. They had opposed me when I had allowed the Xital outcast Selane to stay in our lair, and they had disagreed with me on everything regarding the Nixans. Ddraig Krateos seemed a much more accepting dragon.

"Once all of this is over, Ddraig Krateos, father, I think I should like to join you and your clan," I said firmly. I was in no doubt, there was nothing holding me to Laxtal but for Ddraig Anzig, and I doubted he would remain in Laxtal either, once his true parentage came to light. Even my mate was Nixan.

"Of course, my son, we would be glad to have you," Ddraig Krateos replied. He held open a welcoming wing, and I stepped into his embrace. He rumbled in a loud purr. "I could never have imagined my lost eggs would survive. I will always be in Laxtal's debt for the services they have done for me."

Haeraig Zeena stepped forward. "We will do whatever we can to repay that debt by helping your ddraig, however we can."

I moved away from Ddraig Krateos to look down at Anzig. My brother. Without his wings he looked so vulnerable. How could he ever hope to be a successful ddraig like this? Why had his wingless form never appeared in my visions?

Ddraig Bakucic flicked his tail as he addressed the Nixan ddraig. "I would wish to speak with you privately on this matter," he said, his eyes flicking towards the silver dragon statue perched in the alcove above the fire. "This is an unprecedented situation and will take wise words to resolve."

I got the impression there was a lot left unsaid between the two ddraigs. It was not my place to press them, but the questions burned in my throat.

"We can arrange that when my son is awake," Ddraig Krateos rumbled. He settled back close to Anzig's still and silent body.

My curiosity turned to a strange thrill. Anzig was the son of Krateos. My brother. The family I had always craved. Only the horror at Anzig's injury prevented any excitement beyond that. There would come a time when I could explore that new family I had barely dared hope for, but now was when we needed to ensure Anzig recovered from his sickening ordeal.

We fell into a silent vigil, rarely moving but for Kaz, who approached Anzig frequently and placed a paw on the comatose dragon's forehead. Pulses of magic occasionally emanated from my mate's paw, adding to the healing efforts he had already expended. No one disturbed us from outside the chamber, the business of the clan passing by without concern for their ddraig. Though I worried about what Saya and Marin might be doing in his absence, no one ever suggested leaving. We would stay as long as we needed to and deal with any problems when Anzig awoke.

Hours passed by. I could feel the cold chill of the night's air creeping into the chamber, not quite annulled by the fire. The lair had fallen quiet as most of the dragons had returned to their chambers to sleep away the cold night. I doubted any of them cared about what was happening in here.

Finally, Anzig stirred. He slowly opened his eyes and balefully stared around the chamber. Not once did he move his head to look at his back, though his eyes flicked in that direction a couple of times. When he spoke, his voice was hoarse.

"You should have let me die."

# CDAPTER SIX

**Ellian**

We had been flying hard for a full week since leaving Lilisxi and the treetop lair behind. Our wings were sore, but there was still one clan left to visit. Duma, Gyzlan, and Eivas had all pledged themselves to our cause, each ddraig promising at least five hundred dragons each. There had been no sign of Haeraig Ilibela, so either the Xital dragon had been detained longer in Lilisxi, or saw no need to bother with the other minor clans in the area. I hoped that continued, but if there was a clan she would visit to recruit to the Xital and human cause, then it would be our final destination. Clan Kern was another of the ruling clans, bordering Xital to the west and separated from Laxtal by a small band of minor clans.

If an alliance between four ruling clans was unprecedented, then five joining forces was something no dragon had ever considered. A full half of the ruling clans fighting as one force against a sixth. Anzig was responsible for one of those alliances, and Ddraig Aranat had secured the support of Xigax. But the thought that I could pull them all together and add Kern to the coalition gave energy to my struggling wings.

My hope was that, beyond the sheer numbers Kern could provide, they would be able to recruit the surrounding minor clans to their south and west, meaning I could return home and help Anzig. I was sure he would have a headache from trying to organise the thousands of dragons I had sent his way.

Like Laxtal, Kern was a flat land with little to break the monotony of the terrain. There were few trees, but the grass that grew here was thick and lush despite the changing season, with plenty of grazing animals to hunt.

I had been to the Kern lair a few times before, and though it was underground like Laxtal, the caves were quite different. Located just below the ground were long, winding tube-like caves, radiating out from a central point. When I had first come to the lair many years ago, they told me how the caves had formed from ancient lava flows that had literally melted the less hardy stone as it through natural fissures branching out from a long dead volcano.

As we reached the lair, it was obvious that the clan had already noticed our arrival. Several dragons watched us from the ground, though none of them rose to meet us. Descending from the sky, we landed near a gaping, jagged hole in bare rock that penetrated through to the caves below. My wings ached as I folded them to my sides, grateful that my paws were now supporting my weight. Dozens of dragons were lying in the evening sun, taking in the last of the heat before night fell. None of those dragons reacted to our presence, but the scouts quickly closed in on us before we could approach the cave entrance.

Two dragons approached, one drake and one ness. Their eyes fell to the gemstone around my neck. Both bowed their heads.

"I am Haeraig Ellian of Laxtal. I need to speak to your ddraig immediately," I said, before either of the scouts could speak.

The ness glanced through upturned eyes at Airil as he stood by my side. Her muzzle brushed through the lush grasses before her gaze turned to her companion. The drake nodded once.

"Of course, Haeraig, as you command. It will be my honour to escort you to my ddraig's chambers," the ness said quickly, spreading her wings ready to fly. As I unfurled my weary wings, I reminded myself that this would only be a short flight and soon would have the opportunity to rest them properly. With Airil on my tail, we took to the air, only to immediately swoop down into the lair. This initial descent, I had learned from my previous lessons, had been caused by lava fracturing to the surface; it was to be the only steep dive or climb in our journey within Kern's lair.

Our guide was unerring as she took us through the wide caves. They certainly didn't appear natural, as the blackened stone was an almost perfectly smooth-sided circle, but for a series of small grooves and ridges that ran horizontal along the sides. The floor, and partway up the sides, were coated in moss, fed by water that trickled down from large stalactites on the ceiling. Everything smelled damp. Unlike most underground lairs, these caves didn't dip deep underground, instead remaining almost level. There was no large central chamber, just a convergence of the winding tubes.

The ddraig's chamber was fairly close to the lair's entrance, and it was only a few minutes before the ness landed. She asked us to wait, and she slipped through a narrow crack in the wall. Firelight flickered out through the small gap, and I could hear the voices of at least three dragons abruptly stop. There was a brief pause, before the ness returned with an emerald-scaled dragon who I knew not to be the ddraig of Kern.

"Haeraig Ellian, we have been expecting your visit. I'm Haeraig Arath. Would you care to join me in my chambers close by?" he rumbled with a small bow of his head. Though Kern was one of the ruling clans, they were not on equal standing with Laxtal. We were still considered to be greatly superior, and as such the Kern haeraig was required to show respect towards me. I kept my head high.

"Please, lead the way."

The haeraig led us to his chambers. Like the ddraig's, they were situated through a small crack in the side of the curved cave. After about ten paces, the crack widened out, forming a small chamber. Unlike the smooth, moss-laden walls of the tube caves, the chamber walls were rough and uneven. I could see claw marks in the walls where draconic paws had carved it out. It was a humble dwelling for the haeraig of a ruling clan, but Arath didn't show any embarrassment for the state of his chamber. Instead, he set himself to lighting a fire in a small alcove, using a human-made gas device, ones that had become sparse in Laxtal.

Only once the fire had kindled on the stack of dry branches did Haeraig Arath turn and face us. "I am sorry you were unable to see Ddraig Lorkan, but she is already in an important discussion," he said.

I could not prevent the gasp of fear. "Clan Xital?" Were we already too late?

Haeraig Arath dismissed my concerns as he laughed loudly. "No, no, of course not! Xital has no business here. We have already chased away one of their emissaries. A group of nomads came to the lair a couple of weeks ago and told us everything that is happening to the north. One of the dragons, Mulner if I remember correctly, told us of Xital's treachery, and that we should have nothing to do with them."

It was almost impossible to hide the joy I felt at hearing news of my brother, and that he had become so active in helping the rebellion against Xital. I did wonder though, what had finally convinced him to take action.

"If I may, who is Ddraig Lorkan speaking with?" Airil asked, lowering his head respectfully towards the Kern haeraig.

"Ddraig Boruc of Vatrea," Arath said, much to my surprise. Vatrea was a fairly minor clan in the distant east, and that journey would have taken many weeks. Ddraig Boruc would have needed a good reason to fly such a distance. I had never met the Vatrean ddraig, but I had heard a lot of him from a few Laxtal dragons. It would be most beneficial if I was able to speak with him before we left. Judging from Airil's excited leap, he too would be keen to meet the ddraig.

Haeraig Arath smiled as he looked between the two of us. All of his teeth were showing and his eyes twinkled with excitement. "I know, I know. I can tell quite easily what you are seeking. We've known this discussion would happen for quite some time now."

"So will Clan Kern join us in the fight against Xital?" I asked him.

"Of course," Haeraig Arath said, bowing his head. "And what's more, we have already sent emissaries out to the nearby clans. All we lacked was your presence to confirm the terms of the alliance. If Ddraig Tsona didn't think we were serious before, he will now that three of the ruling clans have risen up against him."

"Five, now," I said quietly. If Kern were not aware of the fate that had befallen Nixa, then I did not want to share that information. "Clan Xigax has pledged support as well, joining with Clan Axaatl once they have dealt with the Nixan army. We will target the humans."

Haeraig Arath sucked in his breath, his tailtip quivering. "Five? Truly? These are days they will tell stories about for generations to come."

"First we must survive the days to come," I said. Stories were no use if there was no dragon left to tell them.

The Kern haeraig dipped his head. "Of course. My mother has already approved two thousand dragons to fly north to bolster your army. We have also sent emissaries to the surrounding clans to muster more dragons still. In total, we expect to send at least three thousand to Laxtal. Our warriors can leave tomorrow if ordered, and the remainder within the week."

My chest swelled in pride. "This will be an army unlike any other before."

"We can only hope it will be enough," Airil added. The Nixan scuffed his claws against the smooth stone floor. "These humans are dangerous. Even with the numbers we have, it will be no easy fight."

"Perhaps not," Haeraig Arath replied. "But it is better than flying alone against this threat."

We continued talking for a further half hour, determining some of the finer points of the alliance between the clans. Haeraig Arath didn't ask for much for his clan, just for some help in minor disputes that had broken out on their borders, as well as assistance in planning the carving out of a new lair towards their southern borders. I was happy to grant these requests as they seemed to be small payment for two thousand dragons and a more stable territory to our south.

Once we had finished our discussions, Haeraig Arath took his leave to check if his ddraig was ready to see us. I was fairly confident Haeraig Arath had discussed everything, and the ddraig would have nothing further to add.

"That went rather well," Airil said brightly. He placed a paw on mine. By mutual silent agreement, we hadn't discussed Ddraig Bakucic's comment back in Lilisxi, but this was the first time he had made deliberate contact with me since.

Again, there was that flutter of nerves I felt whenever I looked into his eyes. It didn't feel like a challenge when I met his gaze, and neither of us felt obligated to look away first. It was something I had never experienced with a drake before. Even with Vinzent, every time we spoke it was as though he was challenging me to accept his opinion, his position on a matter.

It was the Nixan who broke the silence once more. "You know, I've been thinking..."

What Airil had been thinking had to wait, as Haeraig Arath interrupted us with his return. He was accompanied by two other dragons. One was an old, red-scaled ness with scarred and tattered wings. I knew her as Ddraig Lorkan, and I bowed my head respectfully, but it was the drake who came in just behind her that caught my eye and piqued my interest.

If Ddraig Lorkan appeared old, then the dragon by her side was ancient. Ddraig Boruc's scales were grey, but the splotches of deeper black gave the impression that they had faded over time. He moved extremely slowly and with great care. It was his eyes though, that held the greatest indication to his venerable age. Even though they gleefully sparkled, in the brief moment I was able to hold his gaze, I could see the knowledge and memories from more years than I could even have imagined.

"Haeraig Ellian, it is a pleasure to meet you finally," Ddraig Lorkan said, bending a foreleg slightly as she bowed. "I trust my son has informed you of all you need to know?"

"He has, Ddraig Lorkan. We are most grateful for the terms we have been offered, and are honoured to accept them," I replied, dragging my gaze away from Ddraig Boruc.

"I am glad to hear it, Haeraig," Ddraig Lorkan said. "I apologise that I am unable to stay and talk further, as much as I would wish it. I have other duties to attend. I shall seek you out and formally confirm our alliance tomorrow. Until then, my son can show you the way to the guest chambers for tonight. Ddraig Boruc, can you remember the way to your chambers?"

Ddraig Boruc laughed. "I'm not that old, Ddraig Lorkan. I can remember the way just fine," he said. His voice was surprisingly musical, and not at all the crackling, dried up old voice I had expected him to have.

After Ddraig Lorkan had taken her leave, Ddraig Boruc offered to guide us towards the guest chambers instead, a task which Haeraig Arath was grateful to relinquish to him. The old dragon smiled as he led me out of the haeraig's chambers, with an excited Airil followed just behind.

"I hope you don't mind if we stay on paw," Ddraig Boruc said as we emerged back out into the wide caves. Neither of us offered objections, as my wings were sore from the flight, and I imagined Airil would be similarly tired. Then Ddraig Boruc paused and surprised me by turning in front of me and bowing so low he accidently bumped his chin on the mossy ground.

"I would like to formally introduce myself. I am Ddraig Boruc of Vatrea. I doubt you remember me, but I do recognise you Haeraig Ellian. I have seen you once before, many years ago. And you," the ddraig said, turning his head towards Airil. "Show me your paw. No, not that one. May I see the other one?" Airil quickly obliged by dropping his left paw back to the mossy floor and raised his right forepaw for the old dragon to inspect. "Of course, Airil. I thought it was you."

Airil blinked a few times in shock. "You remember me, Ddraig?"

Ddraig Boruc chuckled as he turned started to walk slowly along the passageway. "My dear young dragon," he spoke to the empty passage in front of him, "I may well be old, but I have quite the memory. I never forget a face, and though you share yours with your brother, I still remember that you lost a claw."

I paced up to Ddraig Boruc's side, marvelling at his memory. I wondered what else he knew, how many memories he had, that no other dragon could recall. Did he perhaps have some secret locked away that would help us win this war? Though I wanted to ask, I felt a little intimidated in his presence. He may be a ddraig from a minor clan, but I could not imagine this dragon submitting to anyone, for any reason. I didn't know what gave me that impression, but there was something about him that seemed greater than any dragon I had ever met.

The dragons of Kern certainly recognised who this ancient ddraig was, as any dragon that approached along the cavern floor, moved aside and paused their journey long before we reached them. All bowed their heads as Ddraig Boruc passed, whilst somewhat less attention and courtesy was afforded to Airil and me, even with the Laxtal gemstone hung around my neck.

"Why are you here, Ddraig Boruc?" Airil asked, finally speaking the question I had not dared to put to words.

The ddraig didn't answer immediately. His attention was momentarily captured by an orange patch of spiky moss growing on the rock as he ambled along. His head turned almost onto his back as he focused on the strange growth in the rock. Just before I felt he would tumble from his most awkward position, his eyes finally broke free, and he slowly turned his head away, back down the passage. "I am here because I need to be here," he said eventually. "That is kha'loi moss and comes from somewhere far to the south and west. It is quite, quite poisonous," he added, more to the empty tunnel ahead, than to his slightly bemused companions. We walked slowly beneath the lair's jagged opening to the surface; the sky overhead still held a little blue, but reds and oranges crept in, signalling nightfall. The sun's rays had long since left even the shallow depths of the entrance, and a chill lifted off the permanently damp rock. "But soon I need to fly north. If you are returning to Laxtal tomorrow, then I would like join you. Once before has dragonkind been in this much danger, and that six hundred years past."

"What happened then, Ddraig?" Airil's voice was a quiet whisper, as though we were speaking about forbidden secrets.

Ddraig Boruc stopped abruptly. He shivered, sending a ripple along his spine; his tail tip snapping aloud as it flicked violently. He lowered and half-turned his head to Airil, squeezing his eyes tightly shut. From the grimace on his face, it was obvious he was reliving a painful memory. "Fire. Pain. Death. The cataclysm was terrifying, and those few that survived were lucky to escape it. And yet, perhaps they were the unlucky ones, given what happened."

"And we face this same danger now?" I asked. The ddraig spoke as though he had witnessed those events, but that could not be possible.

"No. A different danger, but the threat is the same. Lose, and we face annihilation. But I do not wish to discuss such grim topics with you now," the ddraig said, his tone changing mid-sentence. Suddenly, it was as though he had broken free from a trance. Gone was the pain in his eyes, gone the wracking within his body. Moving away, he raised his head to look at the pink-tinged sky before we passed beneath the stalactite-encrusted rock again.

Airil cleared his throat and tried to speak to the old Vatrean a couple of times. Ddraig Boruc smiled politely as he waited for the Nixan, who eventually blurted out, "Ddraig, Kaz told me you taught him some of our old language."

Ddraig Boruc's chest swelled in pride. "That I did, yes. I'm the only dragon left who can still speak our noble tongue fluently. Ever since the cataclysm we have spoken human languages and have all but forgotten our own. Only sad reminders linger on. Perhaps someday I will teach you. It pays to know draconic history."

"I would like that," I replied. I knew that we had once spoken our own language, but I had never heard why we had stopped. It would be exciting to know more. A piece of draconic history for me to share. "Perhaps on the flight back to Laxtal?"

Ddraig Boruc's smile grew wider, until it revealed all his teeth. "An eager student? It has been a long while since I have had one of those from beyond my clan borders, apart from your brother, Airil." He unfurled his wings and held them over us. "If you are willing to learn, I am willing to teach. Anything you ever wanted to know about our history is here," he said, tapping the side of his head with his wing tip.

"Just how much do you know?" I asked in awe.

Ddraig Boruc's smile and eyes turned sad. "Sometimes I think I know too much. Some memories I wish could be purged. I have paid a heavy price for this knowledge. My biggest regret was my son, Tsoren." He sighed and smiled wryly again, the darkness from his eyes clearing. "But that is in the past. The past it is for old minds to worry over, not young ones. Look to the future with excitement."

He stopped outside a narrow gap in the side wall, formed with draconic claws. "These are my chambers. I believe the one opposite is intended for your use. Please forgive me, I would talk longer, but I am an old dragon who needs to rest. Tomorrow I will get to know both of you a lot better," he said. He placed a paw on Airil's shoulder. "I have lived long enough to know that fate and destiny have no bearing in this world. Gods and mortals speak of such thing, but none can wield it. I have, though, learned to recognise greatness amongst my fellow dragons. You both remind me of great people I have met and grown fond of."

I bowed my head in response to the ddraig's kind words, noticing Airil do the same to my side. I didn't know what great dragons he compared us to, but his praise flattered me. We bade the ancient clan leader a good night and let him retire to recover from his long journey in peace.

Though I the temptation of hunting tugged at my wings, I succumbed to Airil's request to head straight into the guest chambers. My hunger could wait, and my wings would be grateful for the respite. Besides, I didn't really want to be on my own without Airil.

The small cavern that had been set aside for visiting dragons was similar to the haeraig's chambers, in that it was small and roughly hewn by draconic claws. There was a small store of dry wood set aside near an alcove charred black from smoke. A few thin blankets covered part of the uneven floor.

Airil moved the blankets over in front of the alcove whilst I struggled to light the fire using one of the small human-made lighters. Warmth quickly permeated through the little chamber, though the smoke didn't disperse too well, due no doubt to the shallow angle of the outside passageway. Airil settled down on the blankets and held his wing out, ready for me to lie by his side. I quickly obliged, and he held me tight with both leg and wing. For a while we were content to just stare into the flickering fire, entranced by the beauty and the energy we saw in the red and amber light.

"Ellian, I've been thinking," Airil said, before pausing again. I could feel his head moving behind me, looking towards the chamber's exit, as though expecting an interruption. We heard nothing, but still he didn't continue straight away. His paw sought out mine and clenched it tightly. "I know I'm not of your clan, but... I've never been happier than when I fly with you. Would... Would you consider being my mate?"

"Do you mean that?" I demanded. The words were harsher than I intended. My heart had started to beat wildly, but I had to be sure. Especially after the last time a drake had asked me that question.

Airil's grip tightened on my paw. "Of course I do," he said, resting his muzzle against my cheek. "What sort of fool would say that and not mean it?"

I laughed in relief. "What sort of fool indeed," I said, not wanting to think about Vinzent anymore. That pain was behind me. Like Ddraig Boruc had cautioned, the past was not for young minds like mine to worry about.

I broke out of Airil's grip so I could face him, looking into his yellow eyes. "Yes, Airil. Of course I will."

He cried out in joy, pushing his muzzle against mine and holding me in his forelegs. He was trembling. "I was so afraid you'd say no," he whispered.

"And what sort of fool would say that?"

# CHAPTER SEVEN

**Anzig**

*Even in my dreams there was no escape.*

*I relived that moment over and over. I could feel her teeth tearing into my wings, again and again and again. I couldn't bear it. Shrieking in agony, I tried to escape, but I was stuck. Trapped beneath my sister, unable to do anything but endure my wings being torn away once more. Every time she spat them to the side, they were there on my back again, ready to be torn away in an agonising loop of torture.*

*"Why are you doing this to me?" I cried out, not expecting any answer. But one came. She moved, and standing over me were two copies of Maznar. One kept attacking my wings, but the other stared down at me sadly. I tried to lunge up to her, but I couldn't move, the jaws of her twin keeping me pinned.*

*"Oh my brother, just look at you." She shook her head slowly. "No one will ever treat you the same way again. Do you think they'll believe you worthy of being ddraig?"*

*"Is that why you did this?" I choked. Even in my dream, the pain was unbearable. But there was no escape from it. I struggled to endure every moment of it, each snap of a tendon, each shattering crack of the delicate bones of my wings. And then, that final agony and the brief moments of horrific absence before it began all over again.*

*The spectre before me sat back, even as her copy continued to savage my wings. She gestured with her paw. "It is not for me to speculate on the motivation of your attacker. But perhaps he might tell you himself."*

*"He? You did this to me," I snarled, putting as much venom into my voice as I could through the pain.*

*Again, she shook her head. "No, my brother. I want you to remember it this way."*

*Before I had chance to reply, she was gone. Fading into the darkness. The dragon pinning me down snapped at my wings again. I shrieked in pain. His silver scales gleamed in the dark. He leaned over my back, claws scraping into the agonising wounds where my wings had once been.*

*"Perhaps now you'll realise you were never meant to be ddraig," the dragonet hissed. His teeth snapped close to my eyes, as though threatening to take those next. "Laxtal is mine and no others."*

*I whimpered into the uncaring darkness as Vinzent tore my wings from my body again and again.*

I held my head in my paws, trying to erase from my memory the events of the last day. I simply wanted to undo everything that had happened, to forget all I had learned, and to heal the damage that I had suffered. It had not taken me long to grow weary of the constant sympathy I had received from Ddraig Krateos and Haeraig Zeena, or the silent pity from Azlak. Thankfully, they had left me alone at last, leaving me with just my thoughts and Mushussu for company. The guardian ness I could do little about, but at least she had kept silent for the time being.

I no longer knew what to do. If I ran the risk of my clan turning on me before, surely now my rule would be overthrown the moment my injuries became known, if my treacherous attacker had not already bragged about his victory. Against my better judgement, I glanced behind at my back, which looked bare and small without my wings shielding it. A shadow of the agonising pain knifed through me. My memories were vague and shadowy, but I knew who had done this. Vinzent had shown his ambition at last. His mother had long whispered in his ear. Now he had crippled me. I would never be whole again.

Though Ddraig Krateos had pressed me for answers, I had not yet told anyone who had taken my wings, knowing no one would believe me. I didn't dare sleep, fearing to plummet back down into my terrible dreams. I didn't want to relive it again. I couldn't endure that pain, but wakefulness was hardly any better.

"This is not the end," Mushussu said, finally breaking her silence. I heard her metallic paws crossing the stone floor, but I didn't raise my eyes to look at her, instead focussing down on my own paws. "Look at me Anzig."

I felt like I had no choice in the matter. Without even intending to, I obeyed the guardian and stared into her blank silver eyes. "What do you first notice about me, Anzig?" she asked, a sharp ring to her voice that I didn't like.

"That you're not flesh. You're something made of magic."

"No, not that. My body. What do you first see about my body," the guardian snapped.

I sighed and looked over the guardian's silvered form. There were several things that came to mind about her distinctive shape, but as my eyes roamed her back, I realised what she had been trying to point out. "You don't have wings," I said. Whereas I was sure that revelation was meant to uplift me, it just depressed me further. She was an artefact of magic, not of flesh and blood. She was not hampered by her lack of wings, which I most certainly was.

"Astar raised you to overcome every adversity. He would not want you to give up so easily," she said, obviously realising her previous attempt had not worked and changing her direction.

I scoffed. "I don't think he had this in mind." This was beyond anything a dragon could expect to happen to them. I had been crippled into something that was less than a dragon. There was nothing anyone could do to prepare for this. Once more I looked at my back and the scaled mounds that were all that remained of my wings. That was all that remained of a dragon's most prized possession, unable to give even a feeble twitch.

"You should accept your disadvantage and use it to turn into an advantage. Yes, you're bound to the ground, but that doesn't mean any dragon should assume you're toothless. If you are challenged, learn how to adapt your style to fight without wings," Mushussu said, poking a single claw into my sternum.

I growled and turned away. Her words meant nothing to the vitriol I knew I would receive from the clan. Vinzent had already made that clear when he tore the wings from my back. The guardian had no influence to sway their opinions of me, and even if I managed to defeat one, another would take their place.

Mushussu retreated to her alcove on the far wall. "If I can't convince you, maybe your brother will," she said, snapping her jaw together with a loud click.

I looked over to the veil that covered the entry to my chambers, before snapping back to Mushussu. "Brother?" I yelped. How many more dragons would come forward, claiming to be my family?

Mushussu had fallen silent with just a knowing smirk without any indication she had heard my question. I didn't have long to wait before I felt the presence of another dragon's mind close by. I was shocked to recognise the touch of the seer, Azlak. I glared at the guardian. What jest was she playing on me now?

"Ddraig Anzig? May I enter?" There was no mistaking the uncertain voice that drifted through the veil. It was most definitely the seer. Could he really be my brother, the third lost egg of Ddraig Krateos?

Though I had no real desire for any dragon to see me in such a weakened state, Azlak was one of the few I could tolerate, and I reluctantly gave him permission to enter. "If you came to offer pity, you can turn around now," I growled as the seer pushed aside the veil. I had no need for the pathetic sympathy thrown my way so far. No one could possibly understand what I was going through.

"I'm not here for that, Ddraig," Azlak said, keeping his eyes anywhere but towards me. He was scared to look at me. "I think there's something you needed to know, but I don't know where to begin." I could hear his thoughts racing as he tried to compose himself, trying to organise the words to reveal that he was also a son of Ddraig Krateos, to inform me that the Nixan had shared the secret of my egg.

"You're my brother," I said quickly, cutting across Azlak's annoying internal babbling.

The seer's eyes widened. *"How could he already know?"*

"Only my body is crippled. Not my mind. Nor my magic for that matter," I spat. I neglected to mention that it had been Mushussu who had told us of our relationship. I doubted the limitations of the guardian's magic would have allowed me to reveal her presence.

Azlak appeared rattled. I couldn't understand why. He already knew about my magic, so he shouldn't be so surprised that I was able to work out something such as this. Unless something else was bothering him. Once again, I tried to press my mind against his, but his thoughts were in such a mess I was unable to glean anything.

"Slow down, would you?" I growled, before realising I had made the request aloud. Azlak's mind registered his confusion at my demand, though he did well to hide it outwardly.

"I'm sorry, ddraig. I just came to tell you Ddraig Krateos… our father, he had to fight off Saya. She accused him of trying to take over the clan, like Ddraig Tsona did," the seer explained quickly, his words spilling out almost before he could think them. I pulled my mind out of his. It was clear what he thought. Without my leadership, the clan was starting to fracture. "No one has seen you for two days. Saya and Marin both think you've flown away and abandoned Laxtal. Vinzent has been asking for support for a wylax. Even Yalle doesn't think we should wait for Haeraig Ellian to return before declaring a new ddraig."

I snarled. At least four dragons were showing intentions of claiming the rank of ddraig. "We need you, Ddraig Anzig," the seer said, vocalising the conclusion to that thought.

"The clan doesn't want me," I replied, turning away from the seer.

"You don't know that," Azlak said, stomping his paw down hard. A sudden steel had come into his voice and he fearlessly approached me. "Rally the clan around you. Demand that justice be brought upon your attacker. Win them to your side."

"Since when have you been able to tell me what to do?" I asked bitterly, trying my hardest not to see the logic in the seer's words. If Laxtal knew that Vinzent had attacked me, his claim to be the next ddraig would fade like a forgotten wind. No one would support a dragon who had resorted to such tactics, except perhaps his mother. And yet, there would still be other challengers.

"Since I became your older brother," Azlak answered softly.

I growled and tried to look away from the seer, but he refused to leave me alone. I could feel his presence lurking uncomfortably close. He didn't move away, even as I lay down on the pile of furs in the corner of my chamber. Out of instinct, I tried to pull a wing over my head, only to feel a sharp stab of pain in my shoulder from the attempted movement.

A tear, partially from humiliation and part from pain, leaked from my eye and trickled down my scales. I furiously wiped it away, hoping the seer had not seen.

"You don't understand…" No matter how hard I tried, I couldn't keep my voice from descending into a whimpering sob.

Azlak's paw gently rested on my tail. I didn't have the heart to pull it away from his grasp.

"You are still the same dragon you always were," the seer said softly. "Nothing about you has changed where it matters."

I clenched my paw. How could he say such a thing? My claws ripped through one of the furred rugs, tearing several gashes through the fabric. My aching shoulders were testament to the changes I could not ignore.

"Anzig, please. Brother."

I whirled with sudden fury, striking Azlak across the muzzle and cutting deep through his scales. He yelped and jumped back, pain in his watering eyes.

"How can you look at me and say I'm the same?" I snarled. There was blood on my paw. I ignored it and stepped forward, advancing on the cowering seer. How could this have been the dragon I had trusted to lead the clan when I had flown to rescue Ellian? His mind was a flurry of frantic, desperate thoughts that struggled to form any coherent ideas.

"I… I know you are," the seer babbled, somehow forcing the words out.

I stomped my bloodied paw to the ground. "He took my wings, Azlak!"

The seer's eyes widened. "Who? Who did, Anzig? If you tell us who did this, then we can help you."

I snapped my mouth shut, anger still simmering through me. I wanted no help from the seer, or from anyone else who might throw their pity my way. More than that, I didn't want to see the treacherous Vinzent gain any satisfaction from seeing me grovel for help. No, I would deal with the dragonet myself, on my terms.

"Alright, I'll go," I snarled angrily, giving in to the seer's demand that I return to the clan. There was though, something else that bothered me, and I hated drawing attention to a significant weakness. "There's just one problem. There's a fifty-foot drop to the central chamber. I can't get down there."

Azlak paused, clearly having not thought of such a thing. Why would he? No dragon ever considered how the layout of their lair would appear to transform so dramatically should they lose the use of their wings. It was an unthinkable situation for a dragon, and never before had I thought so much about the sheer cliff walls, especially those around the central chambers and the gorge at the entrance to the lair. The structure of the caves trapped me in here, relying on other dragons to carry me in and out of Laxtal. For all my desire get my revenge on Vinzent my way, I was still reliant on others for such simple tasks.

"I'll get Ddraig Krateos. He carried you up here, he'll be able to get you back down," the seer said.

"You don't understand. I don't want to rely on anyone," I snapped. Anger faded to mere embers in my belly. I longed to curl up from the shame, but of course I was no longer even given the luxury of using my wings as a hiding place.

"For now, we'll compromise, but we'll find something to suit you, Ddraig," Azlak said, before bowing his head and disappearing behind the veil, in search of the Nixan ddraig. With my anger gone, I struggled to maintain the desire to stand before the clan. I feared what they might say. What they might do.

I only had a few minutes to compose myself before Azlak returned with Ddraig Krateos on his tail. The Nixan had a few words of sympathy for me, to which I responded by growling and trying to escape from his clutching paws. I had no need for his pity. I didn't want his help, but I found myself with no choice.

Gathering every scrap of courage I could muster, I led Azlak and my father out of my chambers, keeping a few paces ahead of them through the narrow, twisting passages that led towards the loud noises of the central chamber. Maybe Azlak had been right. I could hear many voices raised in anger at each other, and above them all roared Saya.

I hastened on, coming to a halt at the top of the sheer cliff, a fifty-foot plunge into thin air before me. Never had such a height terrified me so much. My head swam, and I took a couple of hesitant steps away from the ledge.

"Are you ready, my son?" Ddraig Krateos said, coming up by my side. I growled at him, unhappy that he had spoken aloud of our true relationship where other dragons could possibly hear us. I still needed to control the clan until Ellian returned. It seemed like no one had heard the Nixan speak.

I filled my lungs and roared at the clan. "Laxtal!"

My voice echoed through the massive chamber, and shocked silence greeted my words. All eyes were on me now. Then whispers started to spread. Some were shocked. Some were scornful. None pitying. Then a total hush fell upon the chamber.

I felt my paws lift off the ground and I tried my hardest not to flail and panic. I put my trust in Ddraig Krateos as his magic slowly carried me down to the far distant ground. My slow descent was nothing like flying, but it was as close as I would ever feel again.

Ddraig Krateos guided me towards the central dais, where Saya had gathered a group of her supporters. They didn't flee the dais, but they all retreated a few steps. I gently touched down and started to prowl towards them.

"Which of you would dare to call themselves ddraig?" I growled. I felt so small in comparison to the group of dragons attempting to stare me down. Without my wings I couldn't enhance my size, and I was already small enough. I would not allow them to intimidate me with their wingspans.

No one answered. The silence roared in my ears.

"Which of you dared to think I was gone?" My eyes narrowed as I gazed around the would-be challengers. Blood boiled through my veins as they fell on Vinzent, standing just behind his mother. "Which of you dared to take my wings and thought me defeated?"

With a nudge from his mother, Vinzent stepped forward. I grinned. The dragonet had identified himself without the need to bait him.

"I challenge you, Anzig," he declared, holding his head high.

I narrowed my eyes as I felt out for the power of the Axinstone, a harsh warmth always at the back of my mind. If I could not hope to win in a physical confrontation, then I would use whatever tricks necessary to defeat any challenger. If that meant using my hated magic, then so be it. It was about time it benefitted me.

Vinzent started to circle me, and I was not blind to the fact he slowly unfurled his wings, taunting me with their very presence. "I'm sorry for this, Anzig," he said, no evidence of his contrition visible in his posture. A trick to lure me into submission. I was offended he even thought that would work.

"What are you waiting for," I hissed, trying to goad the young dragon into attack, turning on the spot to keep facing my foe. I could already feel his mind. He had mixed feelings. He respected me too much to attack, but he didn't want to disappoint his mother by backing away. This had been her idea, she had forced him into a confrontation he did not want. A puppet dancing to the strings Saya held. Now I would hold the strings.

Curiously, I could find no remorse or regret in the dragonet's mind. It was as though he didn't care about the injuries he had caused me. Like that had been nothing for him.

My anger smouldered as I kept a firm grip on Vinzent's mind, waiting for the right moment for my mental strike. The young dragon wasn't yet aware of my presence in his mind, and nor did I expect him to be. He would be completely unprepared for what was about to happen. The training from Ddraig Krateos had opened new possibilities with my magic, and I was confident in my plan.

With my magic in Vinzent's mind, I predicted exactly when he was about to attack, and I deftly stepped aside from his lightning lunge. I gave him a firm kick in the ribs for good measure. My claws raked his side, drawing blood.

I could feel Vinzent's seething realisation at the ignominy of suffering the first injury. Twice more he tried to lay claws on my scales, but both times I avoided his attack, and parried with a lunge of my own. Much to his disbelief, Vinzent was soon bleeding from the initial wound to his side, as well as a slash on his right hindleg and another on his muzzle. He had yet to lay a single claw on me.

Then Vinzent looked into my eyes and recoiled. My magic snapped and I grew disorientated.

*I blinked and looked into my own face. My eyes were as white as Azlak's when he Saw the future. Pushing Vinzent's mind aside, I forced the silver dragon's forelegs to drop. "I surrender," I said with his mouth, before retreating from his mind.*

I looked down on Vinzent, whose eyes spoke his confusion of what had just happened. He had surrendered to his wingless ddraig in front of the whole clan, and he wasn't sure how it had happened. For the time being he was submissive. He didn't understand his decision, but he had no choice but to obey it. He had lost his challenge. He had uttered the words of concession.

Others were not so easily cowed. Saya shoved her son to the side to take his place. Her eyes were narrowed in unshielded hatred. "You will not rule this clan, lizard," she hissed. She spread her bronze wings to their full extent. The gentle scaling on her wingarms glittered in the firelight, and I was sure her delicate movements were meant to accentuate every gleaming flash.

"Is that so?" This time I wasted no time in seizing Saya's mind, finding it easier to slip my magic into her head and take control.

*I furled her wings against her back and kept up a pretence that she was in control of her actions by pacing around me. It wasn't easy, directing two bodies at once, but it only took a few seconds to achieve it, getting Saya to circle around me, whilst I slowly pivoted on the spot to keep us staring at each other.*

*"I should have done this the moment you chased Tsona away," the ness snarled. I had allowed her continued use of her voice, but now I blocked her access even to that. I had full control over her every action, her every thought. Through her eyes I could see Vinzent retreat to Yalle and Marin as they watched our struggle for power. They looked scared. They had seen how easily I had subdued Vinzent.*

*I pondered what I could do to Saya. I had access to everything there was about her, I could sort through her memories and learn anything I liked should I choose to do so. This must be how Maznar felt when she sifted through a dragon's dreams. Through the ness's eyes I watched as a mad grin spread across my face. It was time to humiliate the ness completely.*

*Searching through Saya's mind, I found the area I needed. I released my grip on her and focussed all magic on her subconscious impulses and prevented the inflation of her lungs.*

Saya's face twisted in a silent snarl as she continued to circle around me. I calmly stared back, waiting for her to realise something was wrong. It happened as she tried to speak, the deep breath never coming, her mouth making all the movements but no air passing through her throat to provide the sounds. Her paw went to her neck as she retched, trying to get some air to her lungs. Her eyes dilated as she started to panic, her wings thrashing. No one dared approach the ness. Not even Vinzent, wild horror in his eyes, stepped forward to help his mother.

I grabbed hold of Saya's chin and pressed my head against hers. Her eyes were already starting to darken as her mind began to slip.

"Do you surrender?" I demanded.

The ness struggled to nod against the strength of my hold on her. I glared into her eyes, leaving her in no doubt that she was mine.

I released her, physically and mentally, and she collapsed to the ground. She took in frenzied gulps of air as Vinzent finally rushed forward to help her, dropping to the ground at her side. He gently cradled his mother's head in his paws as she choked and wheezed on every breath.

"Do I have another challenger?" I snarled, searching for any new rivals, seeking out any who dared threaten my rule. There were none. In every face I saw one emotion. Terror. No one dared to even look at me, averting their eyes completely and taking a few steps back in deference. I was wingless, but the clan wouldn't dare to oppose me now. Perhaps I wouldn't need Ellian to take over after all. I had faced the dragon who had torn away my wings and defeated him. No one else dared to face me, wings or no.

Only one dragon met my eyes as I stared around the chamber. Only one was not terrified.

I snarled as I considered the disappointed eyes of my father. His opinion didn't matter to me. How I controlled my clan was not his concern.

Laxtal was mine.

# CHAPTER EIGHT

**Mulner**

It had been over a month and a half since Ellian had allowed humans to take up residence in my territory. In those seven long, agonising weeks, they had been busy constructing enough wooden shelters for them all to live in. As I soared over the small village they had created, I begrudgingly allowed a moment of awe towards the progress they had made. The humans had come to us with nothing after they had voluntarily banished themselves from their own species, opposing the war that had broken out between humanity and dragonkind. Now, where once was open grassland, stood wooden shelters neatly arranged in small groups. They used these for shelter, ignoring my generous offer of the caves.

Most of the humans gathered near a cluster of smooth black panels assembled not far from the small houses. I had never seen anything like them before, and nor had I been able to understand James McArthur's explanation for them: something about stealing the energy from the sun. It had not made sense to me.

I scanned the ground, trying to find the leader of the human exiles. We had sent some of his number out to spy on George Symons's army and were expecting them to return any time now. I wanted to hear everything they had to say. News had reached us of the devastation of Nixa, and it filled me with dread that their next target could be Laxtal. We were sure that the three minor clans that lay between the clan of magic and my homeland would not interest the marching humans.

There had to be some weakness to exploit without having to risk everything by attempting to kill their leaders. If there was one, we were yet to find it, and James was out of ideas. Every possible vulnerability the human forces presented looked secure again. He seemed as lost as I was, though I would never admit such a weakness to the human. They must never know that I already felt resigned to defeat.

Two other humans were with James when I at last found him, as was Cinson, the Xigax dragon who had been a part of my small clan of exiles for almost two years. The other humans I recognised as Sophie Carter and Amanda Jones, who had also been officers of a similar rank to James before their desertion. As the three most senior humans in their army, they had taken on the responsibility of ruling the small breakaway force, of organising them into something self-sufficient.

The shorter of the two women, Sophie, signalled me to land as I flew overhead. I did not trim my wings to descend straight away, not wanting to give the humans the impression that they could control or summon me at their will. I would land in my own time. Circling around as though scouting the surrounding area, I squinted into the bright sunlight. The rise of the moon during the night past had brought with it the arrival of winter, but the air still had a lingering autumnal feel.

I could see nothing of interest. No unexpected movement of human or dragon. The war had not come to these parts, and I hoped it would stay that way. Recognising that I had no further reason to stay away from the humans, I sighed to myself and trimmed my wings to descend.

I announced my presence with a growl, staring down Cinson before turning the ire of my gaze towards the humans. Like all their kind, none of the three humans met my eye for even a moment, yet they did not seem concerned with constantly submitting to my authority. I got the impression they were not even aware they did.

"We were about to send someone out to look for you. We've been trying to find you all morning," James said as I landed. The human was looking to the trees a few dozen feet behind me.

"You have news?" I asked, glaring at him for having the temerity to think I could be summoned at his call. If he noticed my stare, he made no attempt to respond to the challenge and meet my eye. Whereas before I would have revelled in the small victory, now it just felt hollow. Forcing the human to look away meant nothing when he never looked me in the eye to begin with.

"The army has started to move again, but they aren't following the path you feared. They aren't going south. Instead, they're moving further north, beyond the ruins of Nixa," James said, as though no mental battle had just taken place.

I growled, surprised by the news, but at the same time elated. Perhaps Laxtal was not their next target, though of course I allowed myself a moment of fear and sympathy towards the clans north of Nixa. They would need to be warned of the potential threat, if we could spare the wings.

"I want to speak to David," I asked, referring to the man who had taken control of the small group of human spies. I needed to know everything that the humans had learned. "Take me to him."

James blinked a couple of times. "He's not back yet."

"Well take me to whoever brought you the message," I growled, annoyed at the human's lack of initiative. Anyone who had helped pass on this information would be worth my time, unlike this ignorant and idiotic human.

"None of them are back yet," James said, spreading out his hands.

I snapped my jaw shut and glared at the human again. This time he did meet my eyes – just for a moment – before looking away. His skin had reddened. I growled again before turning my attention on his companion, Sophie. "Are you going to talk sense? How do you know the humans are going north if none of the spies have returned?"

Sophie smiled as she pulled a small, black device out of her pocket and held it out for me to see. Around the edge of the dull, smooth surface was a border of shimmering light. It appeared to contain every colour imaginable, all intermingled with each other yet, at the same time, distinctly separate. It made my eyes sore just to look at it.

"These allow us to communicate with anyone else who carries one, no matter where else on Farenar they are," the human woman explained, brushing her hand against the edge of the thin, stone-like block. She leaned down towards me and lowered her voice to a conspiratorial whisper. "They say that these were first made by Jalen."

"They?"

"They do, yes."

I scoffed and turned away from the human. She was no better than James, but at least she had given me some sort of answer that the so-called leader of the humans had been unable to provide. Not that her explanation made any sort of sense anyway. How could those little black stones communicate with someone who wasn't there? I sneered again and put it down to some sort of Human-Nixan magic.

"So, when are they coming back?" I asked, not expecting a satisfactory answer from the humans. Two had been most unhelpful, and the third hadn't even spoken to me yet. This other woman, Amanda, had steadfastly refused to even glance in my direction; she maintained a look of nervous fear frozen on to her face. To my surprise, I did get an answer to my question, and it was the Xigax dragon who responded.

"Tomorrow morning," Cinson said with a respectful bow of his head. Finally, a simple answer that made sense without any need to answer an additional question I had not asked. Of course it had come from a dragon. "I spoke to Tsulus through the... thing. It was so strange, hearing his voice but not picking up his scent. It is an unusual magic, Mulner."

Cinson had turned his back on the humans, ignoring them as though they weren't there, or were of no importance to him. Following his example, I turned away from the humans and started to walk towards the small forest, gesturing with a wing for Cinson to follow.

"We'll just wait here then, shall we?" I heard James say to our retreating backs. I responded with a snarl, not bothering to dignify his irritated tone with a spoken answer. I wished for an intelligent conversation, and that ruled out the three moronic examples of humankind. If they truly did have information for me, then it could wait until I'd learned what I could from Cinson.

"Any word on Ellian?" the Xigax dragon asked softly as we entered the shade beneath the trees.

"Not since she left Kern. She should be back in Laxtal by now, but surely she would have sent word," I replied. I couldn't help but fear for my sister. Ever since I heard she had been taken prisoner by the vile traitor Tsona, I had been worried for her safety. She was a strong ness, and I knew she could fend for herself, but no dragons flared their wings against Clan Xital without consequence. Something had delayed her flight home, and once already Cinson had persuaded me not to fly out and look for her. I didn't know if I could resist a second time.

"She'll be alright," Cinson said.

"I wish I shared your faith." I looked up through the canopy of leaves above our heads. The sky above was clear with a strong southerly wind creating quite some noise amongst the trees. Perfect weather for flying from the southern clans. If Ellian was on these winds, then she would travel easy and fast.

"She's strong, Mulner. Stronger than perhaps you realise."

"I know what she's capable of," I snapped, coming quick to anger at Cinson's insinuations. She had been out of my life for so long, but that did not mean I was unaware of her feats. Astar's death had shaken the clan, and if rumours of Carlee's demise were true, then that elevated Ellian to being one of the most important dragons in Laxtal. She made a better leader than our ddraig, though I would never vocalise such thoughts to anyone, even my sister. A ddraig's rule should be absolute and without question. Especially from a nomad such as myself.

"I didn't mean – ugh. I think the human is calling you again. Shall I go see to him?" Cinson said, swinging his head around as the sounds of human shouts drifted through the forest.

I wondered what the confounded creatures wanted this time. If it was another painfully trivial matter then I would have to find some better way to avoid them. I would give them this one last chance to be either interesting or useful, and I led Cinson back out of the small forest. The humans sounded excited, but as they spoke over each other I couldn't make out what they were saying.

James was holding a strange device to his face. He had called them binoculars last time I'd seen them, and he said they allowed him to see things from much further away. I followed his gaze up into the clear azure expanse. My heart almost leaped out through my throat at what I saw. Dragons. Three of them, so far away I couldn't identify them, but I didn't need to. I knew. It was Ellian.

Ignoring the humans and Cinson, I spread my wings and powered up to meet them. I had no idea why my sister had come back here, rather than going straight for Laxtal, but I didn't care. I just needed to know she was safe and well.

As I approached, they deviated from their heading to converge on mine. They had seen me.

Ellian was flying in the middle of her two companions. On her left flew a dragon I recognised – the Nixan Airil had been a near constant companion to my sister when they had last been here. The other dragon I did not recognise. He was an old grey-scaled dragon whose wings looked like they were starting to suffer.

I called out Ellian's name, and the wind carried her response back instantly. It felt like only a moment before we embraced mid-flight. I took her weight in my wings as I held her tight.

"You shouldn't have come back," I told her, but that didn't matter now. She had returned, just after a circuitous route. I silenced her attempted apologies as I released her, allowing her to glide down to the ground with her own wings.

We ignored the humans' calls to land by them, instead returning to the small cave overlooking the river and taking to the ground there. The stranger went straight for the water and took a long drink, before spreading his wings and lying in the grass. He seemed exhausted, but in the brief moment I caught his eyes I saw the curiosity and exuberance of a drake in his youth. But most of all I saw incredible power. I had no idea who this dragon was. There were very few dragons I would submit to, but I couldn't help but avert my eyes from this stranger.

"Greetings, Mulner of the nomadic clans," the stranger said, nodding his head just slightly. "I have heard a lot about you from your sister. She tells me some remarkable things about what you are doing here. I have not seen humans and dragons living together in equality for such a long time."

"I will admit they're proving difficult to get along with, but Ellian asked me to try," I replied, glaring at my sister. She only laughed. "You'll have to forgive me though. I do not believe I know who you are."

"My apologies Mulner. Of course, I am yet to introduce myself. I'm becoming quite forgetful in my old age. I am Ddraig Boruc of Vatrea," he said.

"Forgetful?" Airil asked in shock. "Ddraig Boruc, you know more than us all combined." The Nixan had wasted no time in placing his wing around my sister. I frowned. I would need to keep a watchful eye on those two. After the way Vinzent had treated my sister, I was not prepared to let another drake get close to her if he was unworthy of my sister's affection.

Ddraig Boruc chuckled. "But I have also lived considerably longer, young Airil." The old dragon looked up to the sky as though something had caught his attention. I followed his eyes but could see nothing. The only clouds that broke the perfect sky were a long way to the south. The ddraig had noticed my gaze. "You won't see what I'm looking at, Mulner. I look at currents of magic as they flow, much like a river through the air."

"And you still won't tell me how you can see that," Airil grumbled. This sounded like something the Nixan had been going on about for a while. The Vatrean ddraig remained silent as Airil continued. "Only Nixans can sense magic, but I've never heard of anyone being able to actually see it. It's completely unheard of."

"Unheard of doesn't make it impossible. I have told you already. I'm not Nixan. I'm something much older and more powerful than that. I am also the last," Ddraig Boruc said with sorrow, still looking up to the sky. His voice dropped down to a whisper, so quiet that I wasn't sure if it was for our ears. "It's definitely changed. Something has taken place to the east, like the remnants of a great explosion of magic, still drifting on the wind."

"Could that not be the destruction of Nixa you see?" I asked. Despite the old dragon's assurances I would not be able to see what he could, I still gazed up to the clear sky.

Ddraig Boruc did not lower his head. "No. I see that also, but this is something different. Something else has taken place, more recently than Nixa. Perhaps two weeks past, and to the east. Something was found. Or, could it have been someone?"

His eyes shone with the magic he saw, glowing beacons of golden light. Then he blinked and the light was gone, as though it had never been. Slowly he moved his head down to look at the perplexed Nixan. I could tell already that this was a dragon of many secrets.

"Soon we will have to fly to Laxtal, but you needed to see your brother, Ellian. And I wanted to meet these humans you live with, Mulner. I feel they would be most fascinating company," the ddraig said.

"I think you'll find you're wrong, Ddraig Boruc. They're obtuse and irritating and know nothing of our ways," I muttered darkly. No dragons should look forward to meeting humans.

The ddraig just laughed, a dry chuckle that shook his body from muzzle to tail tip. "They haven't always been that way," he said after a few moments. "And maybe one day they'll understand us better once again. But they won't do that if we don't give them a chance. That's what I'm here to do."

I bowed my head, seeing some sense in the ddraig's words, even if I still believed they didn't apply to these particular humans. Having had a few weeks to get to know them, I had come to the conclusion they were all as idiotic as each other. Even so, we had to start somewhere, and if these humans could help us defeat the ones who threatened our territories, then we would still be grateful towards them. I just hoped they wouldn't act like they were our betters. I would hate having to submit towards a human.

"I'm sure you'll find plenty of opportunity to meet them then. In fact, here they come now," I said. The humans had just come into view, on the far side of the river. For creatures without wings, there weren't many places to cross the river without getting wet, but human ingenuity had temporarily startled me a few days back when they had constructed a bridge from fallen trees. It was simple and rudimentary, but they had told me they'd already started work on constructing a more permanent one. That had shocked me out of my state of awe. I had thought the shelters had just been to house themselves before they moved on again. Now they were making permanent marks on the land. Land I claimed as my own.

I glared at the three humans as they carefully crossed their narrow bridge, hoping that one of them might slip and tumble into the water. They were surer-footed than they looked, as once again they denied me the amusement of them getting wet.

Ddraig Boruc slowly rose to his paws to meet the three humans, while I took Ellian and Airil away, eager to put some distance between myself and the humans again. We took refuge in the small cave, where we were joined by a couple of other dragons. Our numbers had swollen in the past few weeks, mainly from dragons who were fleeing the clans controlled by Ddraig Tsona, or those that were under threat from the advancing human army. With them came small snippets of information that had allowed us to build a better understanding of what was going on throughout the clans. Two survivors from the devastation of Nixa. Both Nixans were out hunting, but Airil was glad to know at least two more of his clan had survived.

With a little prompt, Ellian began to recount the tale of her adventures since leaving me behind, what felt like so long ago now. With some digressions from Airil, who had been by her side almost constantly since her rescue from Xital, I was able to add to my knowledge of what was happening in the draconic territories. It did not make for pleasant listening. Though most western clans were united against the human invasion, Xital had sided with the humans, and were forming their own army to fight those who opposed them.

Soon every dragon would flock to Laxtal.

"Why did you come back?" I asked my sister, once she had fallen quiet. Surely she would be most needed with Ddraig Anzig.

"I made a promise that I would come back here, but I never did. There was always something else I needed to do, but flying back from Kern would take us near here anyway. What haeraig would I be if I couldn't even keep my word to my brother?" she said, leaving the side of the Nixan dragon for the first time to place her head on my shoulder. Her paw rested on the jewel around her neck that marked her as haeraig of Laxtal. "Besides, Ddraig Boruc has been really eager to meet James and the other humans ever since he knew they were here. He seems to feel they're vital. We'll only stay for a day or two, to give the ddraig a chance to recover, but we will be needed in Laxtal again."

I pulled away from Ellian, looking out into the light that streamed into the small cave. I could just about hear the loud voices of James and his two companions as they talked with Ddraig Boruc.

"Will you come back with me?"

I couldn't meet Ellian's hopeful gaze. I paced back to the cave mouth. "My place is here, Ellian. I made a choice never to return to

Laxtal. Too many dragons depend on me here for me to abandon them. I'm sorry."

"I understand," Ellian said, following me and sitting by my side, though I could tell she disagreed with my opinion. Airil hung back awkwardly.

My demesne was starting to change as human influence spread. The forest was a little smaller now, a cluster of dying stumps marking where the humans had cut trees to make their homes and bridge. Only the river remained untouched by the humans, flowing as it always had done from the mountains in the west. This was my place in the world. Laxtal would not need my help in their struggle.

Though I had my doubts, in Ddraig Anzig they had a capable leader, even if he was no match for the legendary figure his father had been. At least my sister would fly by his side to correct his mistakes.

That would not be my place. I would stay where I always did, watching on from my home, content to stay obscure and unknown, forgotten by everyone in the clans. I was not needed in this war.

# CHAPTER NINE

**Ellian**

For three days we had rested, and to me it felt like three days too long. I respected Mulner for wanting to stay here, but it was not my place. I needed to get back to Laxtal, where I could make a more telling contribution to the war. Our wings were fresh and Ddraig Boruc had learned what he desired from the humans, though he had not shared the details of those conversations with James McArthur. The old ddraig would be joining us upon our return to Laxtal. We needed only to fly for half the distance, as Airil was confident he could carry us the remainder with his magic. I was thrilled; it had been too long since I had last experienced those few moments of incredible wonder.

I had wanted to promise Mulner that I would return to see him again as soon as possible, but I knew I could not make any such assurance. As haeraig of Laxtal I knew I would take on greater duties for the clan and would be unlikely to have the chance to escape until we were victorious. Or defeated. If he wanted to see me, he would have to come to Laxtal.

I had taken advantage of his company while I could, spending almost every waking moment with him, Airil usually accompanying us when he wasn't shadowing Ddraig Boruc amongst the humans. I had been fascinated by what the humans had accomplished in such a small amount of time, much to my brother's chagrin. He had attempted to convince me how much they were ruining his territory, but I had just marvelled at how they could create so much from the landscape.

James McArthur had been pleased to see me again. The human leader had given me a short tour of everything his group of fifty had achieved in my absence. Though I understood little of their technology, it had done nothing to diminish the awe their endeavours inspired. He also promised their support should Laxtal come under direct threat. Whether our clan could accept such aid was yet to be determined.

Once we finally took to wing, Ddraig Boruc took the lead position, as was his right as a ddraig. He dictated the pace, faster than I had expected. An urgency fuelled his wings as he led us eastwards away from Mulner's little clan, towards the border of Laxtal. The seasons had turned during our rest, a chill winter wind blowing at our backs.

It was only a few hours of flying before Airil called us down to land. We had just entered Laxtal territory, and I could see a couple of unlit beacons below. Either the keepers hadn't seen us yet, or my command to garrison all the beacons had gone unheeded. I couldn't imagine Anzig would knowingly neglect such a crucial part of our defences. Even if we were expecting the human army to attack from the west or north, it would be foolish to neglect the southern boundaries.

I led my two companions down to the closest beacon, wanting answers as to why their vigilance had lapsed, before returning to the central lair. Perched atop a large structure carved from the bedrock of a low hill was a bundle of firewood on a blackened patch of stone. I landed by the firewood and furled my wings. I listened, but there was no sound from inside the chamber beneath the beacon. No dragon came forth to apologise for their inattention.

"Do you smell that?" Ddraig Boruc asked as he landed by my side, the backdraft from his wings kicking up a vortex of small twigs and dead leaves from the firewood.

I nodded. Death hung heavy on the air. I feared what we would find here.

Airil descended into the small hollow that served as shelter for the beacon's keeper. His blue tail had barely disappeared into the shadow before he called out. "She's in here. It looks like she put up a fight."

The Nixan came straight back out, spreading his wings to prevent me from going past him.

"Human?" Ddraig Boruc asked. The Vatrean hung back, inspecting the stone in several places around the beacon, occasionally pausing to claw out a patch of weed or moss and holding it close to his eyes to identify it.

"No. Dragon. She was savaged by claws," Airil said, holding his head low.

Ddraig Boruc paused his search for a moment, before sighing and shaking his head. "Dark times will fall when dragon kills dragon in cold blood. When the lost rune of the gods is found once more, when the wingless amongst us flies the highest and the eagles of war descend in peace. When dragonkind seems doomed to fall, that is when the night is darkest and the glorious dawn returns once more," the ancient ddraig chanted.

"What was that?" I asked Ddraig Boruc.

He shook his head with a wry smile. "Just something someone very wise told me long ago. This just reminded me of that, and maybe, just maybe, it might give us some hope."

"A Nixan seer told you that?" Airil asked, finally stepping away from the entrance to the small cave.

"No, it was no dragon. He was a werewolf who lived very long ago. There is more magic in the world than just your clan, young Airil. Much greater magic, too," Ddraig Boruc said, shaking an admonishing paw at the Nixan. It was something the Vatrean had mentioned several times before, but Airil was finding it hard to believe that magic existed beyond Nixa. Even after stories of humans being able to use magic, they were considered flukes and freaks, and only the clan of magic had rightful access to the mystical art.

I had other concerns on my mind. If the beacon keeper had been killed by another dragon, it could be an attempt by another clan to learn the secrets of the beacon flames. Only Laxtal knew how to create the intricate colours in the fire that could differentiate between threat and friend, dragon or human. The beacon fires were a coded network across the clan, and only Laxtal knew their secrets. That was also the terms of the alliance I had promised to Ddraig Aranat of Axaatl. His clan would learn the secret too. I had to know if the beacons were under threat.

Before Airil could stop me, I barged my way past him and into the shadows of the little burrow. Momentarily, my eyes struggled to adjust to the darkness, before a grisly scene unfolded before me. Blood splattered the walls, the crimson stains still slightly damp. In the middle of the floor lay the ness who had been keeping the beacon. Airil had chosen his word well: savaged. Her killer had not been content with a simple bite to the throat. Her mangled body was testament to both the fight she had put up, and the ferocity of her foe. Her scaled hide had been rent in dozens of places, her wings beaten and torn. I didn't want to keep staring, but I could only look away when Airil placed his paw on my tail.

Averting my eyes from the savaged corpse, I scanned the rest of the room. There, in the far corner, was the cache of chemicals and powders the keepers used to manipulate the flames. Taking care not to stand in the blood stains that soaked into the dirt floor, I jumped across the chamber. It was completely untouched. Everything was all still here. Possession of the beacon's secrets was not the cause of this attack.

With precision, I eased out a particular black stone which threatened to crumble apart in my claws. Ignoring Airil's questions, I walked back outside with an awkward three-legged gait. I knew we had to spread the knowledge of this attack. The other keepers needed to know of the danger they could be in. An unknown attacker had brutally slain one keeper. I could only assume that others would be a target too.

At my request, Ddraig Boruc used the human-made firelighter that was always kept just beside the firewood to create a roaring blaze. If the other keepers were still alive, they would soon react and light their own fires, and the message would spread across the clan. I crumbled the small black stone in my paw and threw the powder into the fire. Black flames erupted with a tinge of purple, sending a warning of murder and treachery within our territory.

I looked towards the horizon in anticipation. The warning would be useless if the other keepers were dead.

"Look, there," Airil said, pointing with a wingtip to the north. Another beacon burst into life, and a moment later it also burned with the black and purple flames. Then a second lit, and a third, further away, faint on the horizon. The keepers were alive. My warning would reach the central lair.

"We shouldn't linger," Airil said, his eyes spellbound by the mystical flickering of the fire. "Whoever attacked the ness here may not be far away. They could easily come back for us."

"We can't just leave her though. She deserves a dignified rest at least," I said. It would not be right to leave the ness's body for the wild animals to further destroy. It would disrespect her memory. She was not carrion for the wildcats. Somewhere, not too far away, would be a small outlying lair where this ness had lived. She would have friends and family there. Soon they would mourn their fallen companion.

I touched the azure gem at my neck, the symbol of Laxtal's leadership. It represented the power, responsibility, and duty I owed all members of the clan. The least I could do for this ness and her family was to provide her with a noble and fitting eternal rest.

"Do your clan burn their dead?" Ddraig Boruc asked, looking towards the southern horizon.

"Only if there is no other option," I replied. We preferred to bury those who had passed on. There was an expansive burial ground to the south of the central lair, where the ground was soft. Thousands of Laxtal dragons lay there amongst the forests and rivers there, at peace in the tranquil surrounds of nature.

"There is no other option," Ddraig Boruc said, pointing with a quivering wing to a dark patch in the sky. I almost dismissed it as a cloud, but then I realised it moved against the wind. It turned slightly, and I saw it for what it really was. Anzig's stories of the monster he had encountered over the mountains came to mind.

"Nightwings," I whispered in horror. How could she be here? Anzig had said she had fallen into the ocean.

"It can't be," Airil said, also looking up to the great spectre. "Nightwings had black scales. This one is green. It can't be her." The Nixan had seen what I had not. This was not Nightwings.

"Then the humans have created another demon," I said tersely. The monster was circling around one of the other lit beacons like a carrion bird. Swiftly it descended and disappeared again. I closed my eyes, fearing the life of one of the other beacon keepers. Had we given them enough warning to escape?

"If you wish to cremate your clanmate, now is the time. That dragon doesn't seem like it's here to negotiate," Ddraig Boruc warned. He spoke wisely, galvanising Airil and me into action. There would be no time for ceremony, but we would do what we could for the ness.

With the ddraig keeping watch in case the demon should approach, I hurried down into the little burrow with Airil following just behind. The brutal scene no longer shocked us. There were more important things to concern ourselves with.

"Do you think that creature did this?" I asked Airil as we struggled to lift the ness's body onto my back, trying to ignore the oozing blood seeping onto my scales, staining them red.

"Too big, isn't it?" Airil replied with a shrug, before taking the ness's forelegs over his shoulder. It was awkward, but together we were able to half-carry, half-drag the lifeless body up to beneath the open skies once more.

We gently placed the body next to the fire, which had started to spit orange and yellow once more. A deep concussive thrum filled the air, followed by an urgent warning from Ddraig Boruc.

I didn't even need to look up. The creature was coming.

Frantically I pulled down on the pile of firewood, trying to pull some down to cover the ness's body. If I could just get the flesh to light...

"Leave her, Ellian," Ddraig Boruc whispered frantically, edging closer to Airil.

"I can't. This needs to be done," I cried, trying to block out the steadily growing volume of the monstrous dragon's wingbeats. All I needed to do was pull the flames down to cover the ness's body, and it was my duty to her that she was not left alone until it was done. I tore at the burning foliage at the bottom of the pile, ignoring the heat searing my scales as I tried to unbalance the towering inferno of flame.

Twigs and logs snapped and crackled as I dislodged enough to send the whole bonfire crashing down. I leaped away with a squawk, taking to wing briefly to avoid the flaming debris. Grounded, I hurried over to Airil and Ddraig Boruc, but as I did so I caught sight of the monster, close enough now that I could see its ferocious yellow eyes. The beast roared, a deafening sound that assaulted my ears and blurred my vision.

Airil held out his paw for me to take, holding a firm grip on the ddraig's paw on his other side, ready to take us away from here. The ness's body was alight. She had her pyre. My duty here was done, and I reached forward for my mate and for a brief moment we touched.

The ground shook as the creature landed, and in the shockwave I fell back and away from Airil.

Airil's pupils dilated, but it was already too late. A loud crack and my mate was gone.

I was alone in the company of a monster. My eyes darted from side to side, looking for some sanctuary. The small keeper's burrow had offered little shelter to the ness, but it was all I had for safety. I dived towards it just as the monstrous dragon lifted its head up over the edge of the stone slab. His head alone was larger than my body, and a crown of horns adorned the top of its skull. He was a Xital drake, many times larger than even the biggest Axaatl dragons.

I fled into the small chamber, cowering in the far corner as the monster hauled itself up on to the beacon. Giant claws crumbled the rock as it moved around with purpose. A deep rumbling reached my ears, and it took me a moment to realise it was laughter. The creature was laughing at me.

"Another little dragon to chase?" the creature said. The oversized dragon crouched in front of the entryway, cutting off the small amount of light that had illuminated the chamber. In the complete darkness I could see nothing, and I tried not to move and make a sound, but I knew it was pointless. The creature couldn't reach me here, but nor did I have any chance of escape while it sat and blocked off the only exit.

"I'll give you the same choice I gave the others, little dragon. Either I kill you, or I take you back to Xital and subject you to their magic," the creature said.

I couldn't help myself. "Xital has no magic," I squeaked, before remembering that I was trying to remain silent. This wasn't like what Airil believed. Nixans weren't the only users of magic in Farenar, but they certainly were the only dragons who possessed the ability. No Xital had ever used magic.

The monster snickered. "With human help we can. I am the result of such magic, and the future of dragonkind. You would be wise to accompany me, little ness. It is humans who will lead us to the future, not your pitiful Laxtal leaders," he sneered. I thought I could see a little bit of movement in the darkness, and the slightest flash of his yellow eyes. "Come, little one. Let us speak in a civil manner. I am Garus of Xital. I wish to know your name."

I was not going to give this creature my name, fearing that somehow it would provide some power over me. I was haeraig of my clan. If I were to fall into the claws of Xital once again then I would be powerful leverage for them. I must not let this dragon know who he had trapped beneath him.

"Nothing?" the dragon purred, pulling his head back to allow a little light into the chamber. All I could see was Garus's terrifying visage as he leered down at me. I concealed the gem at my neck with a paw, hoping he didn't see the symbol of Laxtal's power. "Then you shall meet the same fate as the others."

The dragon took in a deep breath, just as a deafening crack resounded from just by my right ear. A flash of blue and I felt a touch at my side.

The monstrous dragon exhaled, and a stream of flame roared from his gaping mouth.

I shrieked as darkness took me. Red flames licked the corners of my eyes, as shafts of coloured light danced in front of me. Shapeless, formless they spun and swirled, dazzling me as the echoes of an enraged roar vibrated through my body. All the while a pressure on my paw kept me safe.

The light almost blinded me, and I gulped in air to my seared lungs. Fresh air. Grass was beneath my paws. Before I even had time to react, Airil was holding me tight, his wings wrapped almost completely around me. I returned his embrace, still trying to slow my racing heart. My brain and senses finally caught up with reality. I was safe.

"He breathed fire?" I asked in shock, more to myself than Airil, barely believing the evidence of my own eyes and the singes to my body. Legends told of dragons being able to spit fire long ago, but it was no more than that. A vague story almost lost to the depths of time.

"I'm so sorry," Airil was saying in a shaky voice. I wasn't sure he had even been aware of the attack. He was exhausted, and his tight grip on me started to slacken. I pulled back a little from my mate and looked into his eyes, holding his head with my wings, preventing him from looking away.

"You came back for me, that's all that matters," I said. He had not meant to leave me behind, and I had come out of it alive. We had also learned something new. Humans and Xital dragons had created at least one of these Nightwings-like monsters. After fending off a few more apologies from my mate, I attempted to take stock of where we were. We hadn't quite made it all the way back to the main lair of Laxtal, that was still an hour's flight to the north. Ddraig Boruc was a few feet away, his wings spread out as he lay in the sun, gaining some warmth whilst he could.

With a sheepish Airil on my tail, I approached the ancient ddraig and recounted everything Garus had said. Every dragon allied to our clan needed to know about this, and the Vatrean ddraig may be able to delve deep into his incredible memory to find a similar occurrence. I did not expect him to leap up to his paws, wings still trailing on the ground as his eyes widened in shock. It was by far the most active I had ever seen him.

"Repeat everything you just told me," the ddraig said quickly, urgently.

Once more I repeated Garus's words, paying close attention to the ddraig's reaction. I hadn't realised his eyes could widen further, but they did.

"Why him? Why now?" he hissed, his eyes going dark as he pondered this new information. He offered no elaboration. He whispered to a person not present, eyes drawn towards the cloudy sky. "Dirus, help me understand."

"Has this happened before?" Airil asked. My mate's wing still held protectively over my body. I doubted he would let me out of his sight for some time to come. I gently leaned into him, welcoming the touch of his scales against mine.

"It has not," the ddraig replied, his words slow and thoughtful. "We should hurry to Laxtal. The portents that this event holds could have wide-ranging effects beyond even I could realise. Everything I thought I knew about this human George has just changed. I don't know how he has done this, but… I'm sorry, I just don't have the words for this right now.

"I am glad that Ddraig Krateos survived the attack on Nixa. I feel he is the only one I can discuss such matters with. Of all dragons alive today, he knows the most about the Axinstone. Maybe together we can work this out, but we must hurry."

I tried not to be too fearful by Ddraig Boruc's words, but if this was something he had no knowledge over then I couldn't help but feel a little intimidated by the magic that had created Garus. I had experienced a little of what the humans and Xital dragons had planned during my time in captivity there, but this monster had been kept completely hidden from me.

Ddraig Boruc was silent as we took to wing once more, for what was hopefully the last time before returning to Laxtal. Nothing I could say to the Vatrean was able to coax him from his silence; he was clearly in deep thought about what had happened at the beacon, and what it meant for the future of dragonkind.

I hoped we could start uncovering answers once we returned home, and not further questions. The time had surely come to turn this war around. If the enemy were to find any more weapons, then the alliances I had secured would all be for nothing.

We needed to act, and soon.

# CHAPTER TEN

**Azlak**

I was glad to see the back of the ddraig. In the week since his demonstration over Saya and Vinzent, he had been quick to anger, sharing violent rows with anyone who disagreed with him. As far as I could tell, he hadn't been using his magic to influence any of his fights, but it was almost impossible to tell. I didn't know what he had done to Saya, but I didn't have the courage to ask him for fear of retaliation.

Ddraig Anzig had dismissed me from his chambers after harshly condemning my attempts of discovering a way to defeat the human army. Apparently, my efforts in gaining Esperance as a powerful ally had fallen short. A toxic feeling had consumed the lair, and I longed to escape, if only for a short time. Taking Kaz with me, I sought a little peace with just my mate for company.

We flew to the south, away from the flocks of dragons enduring the rigorous training from the Axaatl commander, Hyantl. Everywhere I looked were unfamiliar dragons from so many different clans. Laxtal had never been busier, but it was no longer a welcoming place. Discontent was simmering beneath the surface. Some senior dragons protested at the lack of space and the favour seemingly bestowed upon dragons not from the clan. Few Laxtal dragons were happy with the situation, of having to share the lair and hunting grounds with so many of our neighbouring clans. The sooner we could strike out at the humans who patrolled through the Nixan territory and chase them away from our land the better.

I dreaded to think what it would be like when Esperance's army arrived.

I glanced down at my paw, tempted to squeeze it just for the chance to talk to Esperance once more, but I resisted. I doubted she would appreciate the disturbance just because I had some doubts over the ddraig's leadership. Esperance had already confessed she didn't like Anzig. I didn't want to hear those words again, though right now I had to admit she had a point. He was not the brother I had longed for.

Kaz flew a little closer, brushing his wingtip against mine. At least with him around I knew happiness wasn't far away. The grief I felt towards Anzig's descent was nothing compared to the uplift I got whenever I looked into Kaz's eyes. In his paw he carried Esperance's rune, keeping true to his promise never to let it out of his sight.

We landed about twenty minutes away from the lair, not far from one of the inner beacons that helped protect our territory. On several occasions, Kaz had asked me if we were able to go to one of the beacons, but each time I had refused. He may be my mate, but that was still a secret known only to Laxtal dragons. I ignored the little voice in my head that told me I wasn't Laxtal, and nor had I ever been. I was a son of Ddraig Krateos and a Nixan. As the clan of magic had always tried to claim.

I was no longer sure I would stay in Laxtal after this was all over. What was keeping me here? Only my duty to help Laxtal defeat the humans, and nothing more. One day I would fly far away from here and explore the world. With Kaz by my side there was nothing I couldn't do.

*A mountain loomed high, towering above the surrounding peaks. Far below were meadows of green and red, dotted with small human villages. Near the summit of the great mountain was a small flat shelf, backing on to a sheer cliff that climbed all the way to the distant peak. The little shelf offered a perfect view of the country below, and a human-like woman with glowing silver tattoos sat there, eyes grey as slate that took in everything. By her side lay a small dragon, scales of gold shining bright.*

*The dragon stretched up to whisper something to the four-armed woman as he pointed with a wingtip towards a line of blue; the distant ocean. A wisp of smoke was starting to rise from a city on the water's edge.*

I had never Seen that place in any of my visions before, nor had I been there physically. It wasn't part of the Sxinix Mountains, but instinctively I knew where it was. Mount Ehran. Esperance's home in the far distant south. I longed to fly there now.

The smell of burning brought my mind back to reality. I blinked a few times and followed the trail of smoke that had started to drift across the sky. It came from the beacon, just visible through the trees.

"Purple and black flames?" I queried aloud, trying to work out what that indicated. I had never seen such colours before, but I knew Kaz would be no help in trying to decipher it, even if he had been paying attention to the flames. He had eyes for something else, and he peered through the smoke haze towards three specks against the clear sky.

My mate cried out in joy. "Airil!"

It took me a moment longer, but he was right. Airil had returned with Haeraig Ellian, though I didn't recognise the third dragon that flew with them. We quickly flew up to meet them, and Airil and Kaz danced through the air together as I took to wing between Haeraig Ellian and the stranger. I could tell he was an old dragon, his grey scales starting to fade in places, but in his eyes, he still seemed to be a young, inquisitive dragonet.

"We need to see Ddraig Anzig right away," the haeraig said, treating me with considerably more respect than I had ever heard in her voice towards me before.

"I wouldn't advise that right now, Haeraig. There are things you should know first. May we land, and I can tell you everything that has happened since you've been away," I said, holding my head low as I spoke to my haeraig.

"Of course," Haeraig Ellian said, her voice quivering with apprehension. She turned to her companion, the stranger I didn't know. "Are you alright waiting a little longer, Ddraig Boruc?"

The old dragon nodded his head slowly. "The magic I sensed has passed, almost as quick as it arrived. Whatever it was is no longer here," he said sadly.

"Magic?" Kaz called out, slowing down and returning to us as we started to descend. It was almost impossible to tell him apart from Airil. "That would have been Esperance, but how could you know she was here? You're not Nixan."

Ddraig Boruc almost fell from the sky. "Esperance? Here?" he squawked. He flapped his wings, barely able to stay aloft in his distress. "When?"

"She was here about two weeks ago. Do you know her?" Kaz asked the older dragon, who looked towards my mate with sorrow in his eyes.

"Two weeks? Yes, that would seem about right. Yes, I know her, from a long time ago. I would very much like to hear this story when you get the chance," Ddraig Boruc said, before falling into a contemplative silence.

Ddraig Boruc said nothing further as we landed, and I started to explain what had happened in Laxtal since the haeraig had left, what felt like so long ago now. Though I said nothing of the ddraig's true parentage, there was still more than enough to shock the haeraig into hiding her face behind her paw. I didn't explain the manner in which the ddraig had defeated his challengers, but I didn't need to. It was clear Anzig was bitter about the loss of his wings, and rightfully so, but he was in danger of taking his anger and frustration out on those who didn't deserve it. I could only hope that having Haeraig Ellian around would help calm him down again.

All the while I was speaking, Airil and Kaz were talking to Ddraig Boruc. My mate was explaining how we had come to find Esperance in the caves below the lair, and what she had promised us in return for helping her. The ddraig listened without speaking, a wistful look on his face. Kaz had relinquished the rune for the moment, allowing the older dragon to run it through his paws.

Despite my warnings about Ddraig Anzig, the haeraig was still eager to report to him as soon as possible. She left with Airil, but Ddraig Boruc stayed behind, eager to hear more about Esperance. When we told him about the slates Esperance had given us, he gasped in shock. "She chose you as her envoys? I hope you both realise how great an honour that is."

I had a feeling there was a lot Ddraig Boruc wasn't telling us about Esperance, but I didn't feel comfortable questioning him on the matter. His presence felt far greater than the span of his wings. Instead, it was the ddraig who asked how many survivors there had been in Nixa. Neither of us had been there during the devastation of the clan of magic, but both of us had felt a personal loss. Kaz of course had lost so many of his friends and family when the humans had broken through the clan's magical defences. I had lost Nataik, the Xigax ness who had become as close to a friend as I had known on our journey across the mountains and into Kernow.

The old dragon was pleased to learn that Ddraig Krateos was in Laxtal, and he asked if we could arrange a meeting with the Nixan. I stuttered in my response, unsure that I would be able to promise such a thing. Ddraig Boruc was insistent though, and it did not take long to persuade me to seek out the Nixan ddraig.

I left my mate and the old ddraig behind as I flew off in search of the Nixans. Truth be told, I had no idea where to even begin looking, as I hadn't even seen Ddraig Krateos or his daughter since the previous morning, when the two had gone out hunting with a couple of other survivors from their clan. I wanted to avoid going into the lair if I could, not wishing to get involved with the toxic atmosphere that was pervading the clan.

A large group of Axaatl dragons were resting near the gorge at the top of the lair. As always, I couldn't help but feel a little intimidated by their sheer size. Scattered amongst their number were dragons from Lilisxi and Kern, the latter having arrived the previous day. Other clans it seemed were fine with mingling with others. It was only the senior dragons in our clan that were taking an aggressive approach to any outsiders.

There was little activity below as the military drills had ended for the day. Most of the dragons spread out on the grass with their wings outstretched, catching as much of the afternoon sun as they could. I doubted there would be any real movement from them until the air started to chill in the evening. I couldn't see a single Nixan amongst them, so I flew on to the hunting grounds to the north.

Compared to the famed Nixan hunting grounds, the Laxtal ones were sparse, but we always had sufficient prey to feed the clan. Large herds of deer prowled the plains that separated Laxtal from the small clans on our northern borders, as did packs of wildcats and other predatory creatures. Here and there I could see dragons circling the sky with a few hunting eagles stalking the distant deer. The herbivores seemed oblivious to the fact that we stalked them, but then they seemed oblivious to everything but where the grass was greenest. They lived simple lives.

I was about to give up and turn around when I caught the briefest flash of bronze scales. Ddraig Krateos appeared to be alone, flying back towards the lair. I hurried up to meet him, not wanting to lose him again amongst the chaotic movements of the hunting dragons.

A few eagles squawked as I flew close to them, and for a moment I thought one of them was about to strike out at me, before it wisely reconsidered. Even as one of the smallest dragons, an eagle would not pose much of a threat towards me. Its talons and sharp beak, so effective on deer and cats, were not strong enough to puncture our scales.

I called out to my father once I was close enough for him to hear me. He lifted his head and quickly turned his wings to angle away from the hunt.

"Azlak? How can I help you?" He made no reference to his relationship with me, but there were enough dragons around who could overhear us. For now, that needed to remain a secret.

I dipped my head in respect as I approached, my legs tucked up against my chest to keep my flight stable. "Ddraig Boruc has requested your presence. He has something he would like to discuss with you. He claims it is important."

Ddraig Krateos yelped and almost fell from the sky. His wings fluttered as he struggled to regain his flight, almost matching the old ddraig's reaction so perfectly that it drew a smile to my muzzle. "Ddraig Boruc? He's still alive? I haven't heard from him in years, since I was a young haeraig. To receive a summons from him can mean many things, all of them fascinating."

"It seems curious that he's the ddraig of such a small clan if he's so well respected," I said, flicking the tip of my tail as I angled around to fly alongside my father. I still led the way, flying half a body length ahead of the Nixan ddraig.

"He has never shown much interest in power like most clans," Ddraig Krateos replied. "He prefers to consider our history, putting together what fragments remain from before the cataclysm. I personally don't care much for it. That happened centuries ago and has no relevance to today, but if Boruc is here, then perhaps there is something to be learned from the past."

I wondered what Ddraig Boruc had to share with us, and I hoped that I would be able to listen in to the conversation. There would be a lot to learn. I already had so many questions I wanted to ask the older ddraig.

As we flew back to the lair, I used the slate in my paw for the first time. I squeezed hard on the small lump in my paw, thinking hard of Kaz as I did so. I felt the little pebble beneath my scales start to vibrate, a curious sensation that made my foreleg twitch uncomfortably. Ddraig Krateos watched on with interest from beside my wing.

A phantom image projected into the air in front of me. To begin with it was just a mess of colours with no discernible pattern, but slowly it resolved into the shape of Kaz's head, bobbing up and down slightly as he flew. Ddraig Krateos's sharp intake of breath spoke of his shock.

"I have Ddraig Krateos. I can meet you and Ddraig Boruc outside the lair," I said uncertainly, unsure if Kaz would even be able to hear me, or if I was speaking to nothing more than a ghostly projection. I was delighted to see my mate nod in response.

"We'll be there soon," he replied, his voice slightly distorted but still understandable. I squeezed my paw again and the image faded to nothing.

"What was that?" Ddraig Krateos asked, his eyes wide with wonder. This was something even he had never seen before. Slightly embarrassed by his attention, I recounted everything Esperance had told us about the slates. By the time I had finished, we were landing by the gorge, a little distance away from where the Axaatl dragons sprawled out. My father took hold of my paw, pressing down on the slate. There was no response at all to his touch.

"There is magic greater than ours in this world," he whispered in awe. Few Nixans were willing to admit that, and before meeting Esperance I had thought the same. The world as dragons saw it was changing, becoming bigger and far more powerful than we could ever have realised.

My father asked me a few questions about Esperance while we waited. I could answer only a few, as Esperance was still a great mystery even to me. I knew next to nothing about her, but she had given me a great honour in choosing Kaz and me to be her envoys amongst dragonkind. Then Ddraig Krateos uttered words I never thought I'd hear.

"If only I'd have known you were my son earlier. You are a fine dragon, Azlak, and I am proud you are part of my family," he said, stunning me into silence. Marin had never shown such sincere praise before, only a reluctant acceptance that I was not totally useless after guiding Ddraig Anzig back with the Axinstone. I didn't know how to respond to my father's words, and I mumbled an awkward thanks. It was enough for Ddraig Krateos, and he held his wing around me.

We only needed to wait a few minutes for Kaz to arrive with Ddraig Boruc. The two ddraigs greeted each other warmly, before the Vatrean went straight to the point he wished to make. He told us about what he had seen on the borders of Laxtal, of the monster they had encountered there. I was the only one present who had witnessed Nightwings, and the prospect of another such creature was utterly terrifying.

"You said you met such a creature in Kernow?" Ddraig Krateos asked, turning to me.

"We did," I said, shivering slightly in fear, both at the thought of speaking to two ddraigs, but also of the monster that was out there, on the edge of Laxtal's territory. "She was Nightwings, created by George as a weapon to defend his island from dragons. She is... or was, at least, Maznar."

Ddraig Krateos growled, curling his forepaw into a tight fist. "The humans will pay for what they did to her. She knew nothing but captivity before you brought her home."

Ddraig Boruc frowned. "Can we be sure she's free of their magic?"

"I believe so. She certainly tells us she is free, and I believe she can be trusted," I said, tucking my wings in tight against my body as I sat down.

Ddraig Krateos started to prowl back and forth, his wings unfurled slightly, dragging across the ground as he walked. "We should get someone to go through her mind, so we can be certain. Once your brother is more approachable, we should ask him," he said, meeting my eyes for a moment. I shivered at the prospect of asking Anzig anything, especially to do with his magic.

"That shouldn't be our main concern right now," Ddraig Boruc interrupted. The old dragon looked at the three of us in turn. Only my father could hold his eyes. "I do not believe the humans could have created Nightwings without the Axinstone, but if Azlak is right, and there was only one when he stole back the rune, then how have they created this new one, Garus?

"It doesn't make sense. Only the Axinstone has the power to do that to a dragon, and nothing else. No mage or wizard has that strength on Farenar. Not even Esperance." Ddraig Boruc tapped his claws on the ground. "They have been trying for so long."

"What exactly are you suggesting, Boruc?" Ddraig Krateos asked, pausing in his pacing to sink his claws into the soft earth.

Ddraig Boruc didn't answer for a moment, flicking his teeth with his tongue as he thought. "Either the humans can tap in to the Axinstone's power without having direct access to it, or what was stolen back is not the real stone. Or there is a traitor who has handed the Axinstone back to the humans, substituting a fake to avoid suspicion."

"Impossible, all of them. I know it's the Axinstone. I can feel its power from here," Ddraig Krateos countered with a vigorous shake of his head.

"Can you know for certain? I don't mean to question you, Ddraig Krateos, but even the greatest of us can be fooled by a skilled deception. This would not be the first time I have seen such a trick," the Vatrean ddraig said. "If you would consent, I would like to check for myself."

Ddraig Krateos snapped his teeth. "Very well, if only to prove you wrong. Zeena is looking after the Axinstone. Wait here for me, and I shall return soon with her." Without waiting for a response, the Nixan flared his wings and launched into the air, soon diving out of sight as he passed into the deep gorge.

We waited in silence for a short while, Ddraig Boruc sat with his head bowed and eyes dark in thought. Though a dozen questions burned at my throat, I did not dare open my mouth to break the silence.

Close by, Kaz kneaded the soft ground with his forepaw, the other paw clasped tight around the shard of stone found with Esperance.

It did not take long for Ddraig Boruc's gaze to also turn to my mate and the rune he held. "May I see that, please? I wish to study it a little more."

Though the ddraig had already held the rune once, Kaz still shared a quick sharp glance with me, as though asking my permission to hand over the precious shard of stone. I nodded once, and my mate relaxed a little before approaching the old ddraig.

"Absolutely remarkable," the old ddraig whispered, delicately taking the rune into his claws. He leaned back on his hind legs to free up both paws, turning the stone over gently between his claws to peer at both sides, lingering on the fiery leopard's head. "I never thought to see another one of these again."

Kaz tilted his head. "There are more?"

Ddraig Boruc didn't look up. "There are eight in all. Individually, they don't do much. But together…"

*A gold dragon, bleeding from a wound in his chest, limped out of the mouth of a dark cave. In his forepaw he held a shard of stone, the golden outline of an otter on its surface.*

I got the impression the ddraig was about to start explaining something else before the sound of approaching wings alerted us to the return of my father. Ddraig Boruc quickly returned the rune to Kaz.

"I am sure Esperance impressed upon you the importance of keeping that safe," the old dragon said, glancing up to the sky and watching as the two Nixans began to descend. "As envoys, it is your duty to protect it. Soon, I hope, you will know more. But for now, just know that empires have fallen for just a single one of these runes. If knowledge of its whereabouts became known, it will be more than just the armies of Trevena descending upon Laxtal. If they knew about two…"

Anything further Ddraig Boruc had to say faded to quiet mumblings as Ddraig Krateos and Haeraig Zeena landed either side of him. In the haeraig's forepaw was the Axinstone, the ness clutching it with the same protective strength as Kaz with his rune. For the first time, I got the chance to see them both together.

The runes were remarkably similar; almost the same shape and size, as though a replica of each other. The only significant difference was the head emblazoned on the flat surface; one a dragon and the other a leopard. Then there was the power that came from the Axinstone, the magical energy radiating out from within. Surely it couldn't be a fake. I could feel the heat invigorating me like the morning sun on cold scales.

Haeraig Zeena placed the Axinstone on the ground between us all, keeping a protective paw to shield it from anyone who wished to touch it.

Ddraig Boruc approached the Nixan haeraig. "May I?" he asked, reaching out with a paw towards the Axinstone.

"You are not Nixan. I don't advise touching it," Haeraig Zeena said, pulling the stone away from Boruc's reach.

The Vatrean laughed, a slow dry chuckle. "I have held things of much greater power in my paws, young haeraig. I do not fear the Axinstone. I am something far greater than any Nixan."

Haeraig Zeena growled, but pulled her paw away from the Axinstone, giving the older dragon access to it. Everyone tensed as Boruc placed his paw on the stone, but nothing happened but for a small crackle of magic energy.

Like he had done moments before with Kaz's rune, Ddraig Boruc turned the Axinstone over and over again in his paws, holding it close to his eye as he inspected it. A shower of golden sparks ignited from the surface in response to each touch of his claws. The magical discharges alone should have been evidence enough that it was genuine, but the Vatrean was not yet convinced.

"Most runes hold no magic of their own, but even so, it takes a remarkable amount of magic to imitate them," the old ddraig explained. His claws scraped across the glowing shape of the dragon head. He left behind a small scratch to mar the fiery outline.

Ddraig Krateos edged forward. "Careful, Boruc. We need this intact."

The Vatrean drake slowly lifted his head to meet the Nixan's gaze. "I agree that we need the Axinstone, both to fuel your magic and to keep it away from the humans. This, however…" Boruc held either end of the stone in each paw.

The Axinstone snapped in two. A shockwave of magical heat pulsed out from the shattered remains of the stone.

"What have you done?" Ddraig Krateos howled, leaping back, his paw partially raised as though to strike.

Haeraig Zeena hissed her aggression, lowering her head as she stalked forward a step.

"If that were the real thing, I could not have done damage to it," Ddraig Boruc said coolly, staring the Nixans down and freezing his would-be attacker with nothing more than a glance. The Vatrean threw one half of the broken stone to me, and I struggled to catch it in time. "What do you see in there, Azlak?"

I looked down at the broken Axinstone. It was not what I expected, a solid stone, but was instead a blood red ruby with a stony exterior. I tilted my head in confusion. I had seen something like this before. Magic sparked as I ran my claw over the ruby core. "This still feels powerful."

Kaz reached for the second piece of the stone, running his claw over the ruby within. "There is magic here," he said, turning accusatory eyes towards Ddraig Boruc.

"Of that there is no doubt. But this is not draconic magic. It is natural in origin, but almost certainly altered by human means. I do not know for what purpose this has been planted with us, but I do not think it was for the good of dragonkind. The real Axinstone is still out there, probably in the hands of George Symons.

"I don't know how long you have had this fake. It could well be that you never possessed the real stone, but you must prepare yourself with the knowledge that a traitor may be amongst our midst. It would be wise to keep this revelation a secret, but you would do well to dispose of this false Axinstone as soon as possible. I don't trust it, and I fear the human magic within could be used to harm us."

Slowly Ddraig Krateos lowered his paw. "And how do you propose we do that? What's left of my clan looks to this as a symbol of unity and of hope. They're going to notice if it just disappears," he snapped.

"We use this instead," Ddraig Boruc said, picking up Kaz's rune from where it lay on the grass. He ran his paw over the surface, and the outline of the leopard's head blurred and reformed into that of a dragon. "It is only an illusion, but it should convince pretty much everyone."

Ddraig Krateos shook his head. "It may look the same, but we'll notice the difference. It won't feel like the Axinstone, it doesn't have the same magic."

"You didn't notice you possessed the fake, even when you held it in your paws," Ddraig Boruc pointed out, eliciting an angry snarl from my father, but nothing more. "It is the only option. We just don't know what this magic is capable of."

"If you're wrong…" Ddraig Krateos warned, giving Ddraig Boruc a withering gaze, but the Vatrean was more than his equal.

"I'm not wrong. I know more about these runes than you," was the calm reply. I couldn't help but marvel at this old dragon, ddraig of a small clan from the distant east. He treated every dragon as his equal, no matter their rank or clan and always seemed to be without fear.

"Then destroy it if you must," Ddraig Krateos said with a growl. "Our efforts should turn to finding the Axinstone once more. If what you say about these enhanced dragons is true, then we can't allow humans to continue using our magic against us. It must be under our control."

"But how will we find it? We have no idea where it is," I said, drawing the attention of the two ddraigs. While Ddraig Krateos seemed a little disheartened by this point, Ddraig Boruc just chuckled.

"Where George Symons is, the Axinstone will not be far away. If we find him, we'll find the Axinstone. It may take another act of theft, but I can take a small group of trusted dragons out to reclaim it," Ddraig Boruc said, before turning to face me and Kaz. "I will need one of you to accompany me, so we can keep in contact with the clan through those slates."

I looked over at my mate and saw a brief flash of fear in his eyes. "I'll go," I volunteered, despite the same fear in my gut, and knowing that I could well miss the arrival of Esperance's army. "I already know of George and the humans. I'll fly out with you, Ddraig Boruc."

"We may have need of a healer," Ddraig Boruc suggested, looking towards Kaz, his eyes narrowed in thought.

"Then with your permission, Ddraig Krateos, we would take Isikian too, if he is willing," I suggested. I hadn't seen much of the healer who had accompanied me over the mountains. Of course, he could view this as even more a suicide mission than the last and refuse to come, but as our ddraig gave me permission to ask him, I was hopeful I would be able to persuade the healer. I didn't want to leave Kaz behind, but I understood the logic in Ddraig Boruc bringing only one of us. These slates had been a great gift from Esperance, and we needed to use them for the good of all dragonkind.

"Very well," Ddraig Boruc said, dipping his head. "Please ensure you are ready to depart with the sunrise tomorrow. We will have a long flight ahead of us."

Haeraig Zeena tentatively reached out to take the altered rune in her paw. Her claws closed around the stone. "If we are to keep up the ruse, then I should hold onto this," she said, keeping her eye on a bristling Kaz.

"Look after it as though it was the Axinstone," my mate growled, showing no fear before his haeraig.

As though startled by the aggression and lack of decorum, Haeraig Zeena bowed her head. "You have my word, I promise you this."

Ddraig Boruc spread his wings. "I shall find Isikian and prepare him for tomorrow. Ddraig Krateos, if I may borrow your time for a little longer."

Though Kaz spread his wings, he remained on the ground as the two ddraigs and haeraig all took to the air, taking with them the rune and the shattered remains of what we had believed to be the Axinstone.

We would have to put our trust into Haeraig Zeena that she would keep the rune safe.

I sighed and turned to my mate. We would have a few more hours to share each other's company before nightfall, and then a journey apart again. Though I would not be leaving until morning, I still needed to hunt and rest so I could be ready to fly without the need to bask in the sun for too long. We wandered away from the lair on paw, content in our silence for now.

We settled close to the shadows of one of the small forests that grew near the lair, a bed of golden leaves littering the floor. I couldn't help but wonder whether I had made the right decision to leave Laxtal again. Ddraig Boruc had seemed so sure that we needed to find George and steal the real Axinstone, but how could we hope to do that and survive? It didn't sound like Ddraig Boruc wanted to take many dragons at all, just three of us in fact. It had been enough of a challenge with eight. At least this time though, we wouldn't be crossing the mountains. We already knew George was in draconic lands.

After an hour to ourselves, we both hunted, working together to take down a large hare with relative ease. The mammal had fattened up for winter, providing us with more than enough meat to satisfy our bellies.

Once we had fed our fill, we left the rest of the carcass for the wildcats and scavenging birds to consume. With the onset of winter, much of the prey had already flocked further south to escape the cold. With so many more numbers flooding into Laxtal, we would soon need to make plans to move or else we would run low on food. The nights were getting colder as well, meaning proper shelter was more important. I was not looking forward to sleeping away from the lair. I could only hope we would find caves to sleep in.

Anger and tension continued to simmer inside the lair when we eventually returned, close to sunset. Scuffles broke out, and the angered shouts of dragons echoed through the caves. We ignored it all, hurrying through the main chamber and into the narrow tunnels below.

My chambers were quite far down in the lair, not too far away from the crack that led to the underground river. I had planned to try and claim somewhere better and warmer as I acted as ddraig in Anzig's absence, but I had never seen the opportunity. Now it seemed pointless. I doubted I would be calling Laxtal home for much longer anyway.

Though the air was cold, I had been able to scavenge a single human-woven rug for my own. But for a few other small trinkets scattered around the tiny chamber, it was all I owned. Though the night air was cold, as I curled up in the rug with Kaz's wing unfurled over my body I knew I had all the warmth I could ever want. We muttered a few words to each other, but it wasn't long before we both fell into slumber.

Late into the night a small vibration in my paw disturbed my sleep. Lazily I pressed the slate, and with tired eyes I watched as the visage of Esperance appeared in front of me. I was too exhausted to do anything but smile and murmur a greeting. Kaz's head lifted beside me, also blinking sleepily into the light.

"Your army is on their way. Two days at the most. Alaron and Kyrus know to ask for you both," she said, appearing to be fending something or someone away. "And once again, thank you. I believe I have chosen you well in aiding me."

Before I even had chance to respond, Esperance had gone – her image and voice lost to the darkness once more. I closed my eyes and dreamed of strange, four-legged birds.

# CHAPTER ELEVEN

**Anzig**

I could not stop pacing. Back and forth, back and forth. A constant movement of paws as I wore out a path doing endless laps of my private chambers. Nothing could get rid of my restless energy, no matter how long I prowled for. I knew exactly what I needed, but it was the one thing denied to me. I longed to soar through the sky, to feel the wind beneath my wings.

I did not look back at the scarred ruination of my shoulders. I could not, lest I sink back into hopelessness. If I paced, I kept up my energy and my anger. That was all that was keeping me in control now. The clan was splintering beneath my claws, with too many numbers flying in each day to keep control, especially when dragons like Marin continued to plot against me. I had shamed both Saya and Vinzent, but not silenced them.

And now one of the few dragons who still supported me was gone. Azlak had flown at first light, taking with him Isikian and a newcomer to the lair. I had not even had chance to speak to Ddraig Boruc before he had flown off again, taking the healer and my apparent brother on an unknown mission. No one had bothered to tell me what urgency fuelled their wings. I had only learned of their departure through Ddraig Krateos, and it hadn't occurred to me to use my magic to learn from my father's mind until he was already gone. I had no desire to reach out to find him now, lest I lose myself amongst the thousands of dragons in the lair.

One source of minor relief had been the return of Ellian. Her presence allowed me to retreat to my chambers more frequently, taking me away from the pitying scorn the dragons of Laxtal gave me. She could rule when the shame of my wingless form grew too much.

My haeraig had asked who had attacked me, but even to her I had said nothing. She had been close to Vinzent once, and though that romance had cooled, I still couldn't be sure if I could trust her fully. If she knew that it was her once-mate who had attacked me, she might decide Vinzent was the better choice to lead Laxtal.

"That way lies foolishness," Mushussu said, breaking into my thoughts as she always did when my mind turned to introspective melancholy.

I snapped my teeth at the guardian to silence her. She simply watched me from her perch above the fire, her silvered body shining in the light but reflecting nothing.

This was not how any of this should have gone. Ever since Azlak had convinced me to fly into human lands, everything had gone wrong. Everything had been stolen from me. My father, my identity, and now even my wings. Becoming ddraig of Laxtal was meant to have been my destiny, but it wasn't even that. I was not a Laxtal dragon, but Nixan. I was a fraud who deserved nothing, and yet I couldn't bring myself to loosen my claws on power. Despite everything, I still wanted to be the ddraig. I refused to let that go, no matter what fate put before me. Now that I couldn't fly, I would simply have to clamber over any obstacle in my way.

"You may not be Astar's flesh and blood, but you still have his tenacity."

I growled at Mushussu again for her unwanted intervention. "Didn't I say to be quiet?"

"No, you didn't actually," the guardian replied. She inspected her claws as she sat back, her sinuous body curled around itself. "I am here to advise and to guide you. It would be worthless if I were to remain silent whenever you asked it of me. You would have me rendered mute if you had your way."

"If only I were so lucky," I muttered, shaking my head. I then sighed and looked up to her. "But go on, I can tell you have something to say. You might as well get it over with."

Mushussu jumped down from her alcove and encircled me with her long body. Her whiskered muzzle bumped up against mine as she forced me to stop pacing. "Your haeraig has gathered a great army for you, consistent of many clans. You have haeraigs and ddraigs from nearly a dozen clans in Laxtal, but not once have you summoned them to a council to determine your strategy for the upcoming battle.
128

Numbers will mean nothing if you do not have a plan for what is to come."

I growled. "Why would they listen to me? None of them would respect what I have to say."

"Anzig, the only one limiting what you can do at the moment is yourself," the guardian said, her metallic voice ringing in my ears. She did not move, keeping me trapped within her sinuous coils. "The clans are here because they trust your leadership and believe that the best way to win this war is together. The best way to lose that respect is to ignore them, as you are currently doing."

I snapped down on a snarl as I tried to turn away from the guardian, contorting my body within the tight circle of her coils. While I knew she was right, to an extent, I resented that she had to point it out to me. Of course I needed to maintain the alliances Ellian had been able to secure, but I didn't want to see anyone if I could help it. I dreaded to think of what pity I would get from the other ddraigs.

"Fine. If it will get you to be quiet, I'll try to meet them soon."

The guardian relaxed her body and stepped away. "I know you don't appreciate my advice, but I am here to guide you as best I can."

Again, I managed to bite down on the growl that immediately tried to loose itself. No, I didn't want Mushussu. The dragon I needed was Carlee, but I would never get any of her advice again, thanks to my own stupidity. My claws scraped at the stone, the floor still flat despite my endless pacing.

"You also need some sunlight," Mushussu said, her blank eyes turning back to catch my gaze. "When was the last time you went outside?"

"What's the point? I can't bask properly anymore." I hung my head and squeezed my eyes closed, frustrated at the tears that threatened to build. "And there's too many dragons out there. Even with Krateos's training, I can't hold them all back. I like the quiet in here."

I could feel Mushussu's amusement, though she said nothing to contradict me. I shook my head. Of course, my chamber wasn't as quiet as I desired. Her voice still irritated me, but at least the guardian was the only other dragon in my head. It was better than out in the lair, but I knew that was where I needed to go. Laxtal needed to see me and remember that I was their ddraig.

"Do you wish to wait for Ddraig Krateos first?" Mushussu asked.

Did I really want that? If I called for my father, then he would be able to help me down into the main chamber, giving me the poor replacement for my wings. Was I really going to be reliant on him for my entire life? There was only one answer to that question.

"I don't need him," I growled at the guardian. Before she had chance to reply, I pushed through the veil and into the narrow corridor beyond. Leaving the guardian behind was not so easy, and her disapproval simmered in my mind, but at least I could no longer hear her directly.

*"What are you planning on doing?"* Her voice sounded loudly in my head nonetheless.

I had thought it was obvious what my intentions were. I resisted the urge to look back towards my chambers. "I'm going to climb."

The guardian was silent for a moment. When she spoke, it was with barely restrained frustration and a ring of metallic anger. "My magic will protect you from harm, but it does not make you immune. If you continue with this stupidity, then you will get yourself hurt again."

I reached the end of the passage to stand on the ledge overlooking the great chamber. No one looked up at me, ignored by the clan. Hundreds of dragons gathered inside the chamber, all engaged in preparing the clan for war. Warpaints were mixed, food preserved, with small scuffles breaking out and quickly quelled by the massive Axaatl dragons patrolling through the cave. Hissed protests followed, but none of the small scraps led to further violence.

I tensed my claws against the edge of the sheer rock wall. I swallowed nervously as my vision spun, trying to wet my dry throat. Funny how I had never noticed just how high my chambers were before losing my wings.

*"No one will think any less of you if you called for Ddraig Krateos to help you."*

I slammed my tail against the ground as I searched for the first clawhold beneath me. I needed no one.

Reaching out with my forepaw, I snagged a claw into the first crack, then swung my body around before I had the opportunity to stop myself. My heart thundered away inside my chest as I tried to ignore the drop, once something I had never considered.

Using tail and hindpaws to find clawholds, I slowly began to descend. My weight pulled down on my forepaws, shoulders burning from the exertion of the slow and careful movements.

While I could feel Mushussu's discontent simmering, the guardian wisely didn't speak. I doubted she wanted me to get distracted. It took all my focus to tap the stone beneath me with my tail, then extending a hindleg down to dig into the cracks I found. My forepaws were easier, able to see those clawholds.

Whenever I looked down, the ground seemed no closer, and yet the ledge above looked an eternity away. My forelegs trembled and for a moment I was sure I was about to fall. I pressed my belly to the wall and squeezed my eyes closed, taking in a deep breath. Whispers filled my mind. Whether they were spoken aloud or mere thoughts I did not have the concentration to determine.

A flutter of Mushussu's thoughts touched against mine, wordless yet comforting. The tension in my muscles eased slightly, just enough to reach out for the next clawhold.

The climb down seemed to take an eternity, before I was finally surprised when my tail batted against flat ground. I looked down to see the bottom of the sheer wall, confirming with my eyes that I had completed the painful clamber down the rockface. I leaped the last short distance, my shoulders aching as they took my weight in a more conventional position.

A couple of dragons edged away from me, wings flared before they recognised who I was. Though they offered a hasty apology, I ignored them and continued on my way. Climbing down was the hard part. The climb up towards the surface should be easier.

Just as the way down from my chambers had looked so much further, so too did the climb up look daunting. I craned my neck, squinting to find the second tunnel leading towards the surface amongst the shadows. I could barely see it in the gloom in the upper reaches of the chamber, partially obscured by the thin layer of smoke that lingered near the ceiling.

Once again, I began to climb before my courage could fail me. If Esperance had been able to scale the walls out of Laxtal, then so could I. No human was going to be able to do better than me, not in my home.

Hauling my body up the rockface was still a challenge. My forelegs burned from the exertion, my breath coming in short, sharp pants as I struggled to keep moving. I knew that if I stopped, I would lose grip and fall.

Wings fluttered close by. I did not dare turn my head to see who flew near me, for if I did then I would surely miss the next clawhold and slip. I grunted and flicked my tail out, hoping to show the dragon I did not wish to speak.

The dragon did not respect my wishes. A familiar voice spoke, once a voice I cherished more than any other, but right now I had no desire to speak with Keita. "Ddraig Anzig? You don't need to do this. I can help you up."

I growled as Keita thudded against the rock, finding clawholds of her own and settling her wings against her back. I ignored her, reaching out for another place to grip.

Keita didn't go anywhere. "Anzig, please. Let me help you, or else you'll just end up hurting yourself again."

"Do you think so little of me?" I spat, the words coming from my mouth before I could hold them back.

"No, it's not that," Keita whimpered. A couple of stones fell as she moved her claws, pushing back into the air so she could laud her wings over me. "I just wanted to help you."

Grunts of exertion punctuated my deep growls as I tried to pick up the pace, eager to reach the top before Keita got any ideas of grabbing hold of me. I could already sense the thought in her mind. "I don't need your help. Or anyone else's, for that matter."

A small sigh. Then retreating wingbeats. I was alone once more, but I doubted it would be for long. Keita would not keep my words to herself. My climb continued, my focus returning onto the wall as I did my best to ignore the ever-growing drop beneath me. A small thought entered the back of my mind, wondering if perhaps I should have asked Keita to stay with me. Not to help me, I didn't need that, but just to catch me if I did fall.

No. It was better that I didn't have anyone at all. I could prove that I was still capable. No one needed to help me or watch me.

Sure enough, I was able to reach the top of the cliff and haul myself up onto flat ground once more. I took a moment to rest, belly on the floor as I sucked in several deep breaths. I groaned as I dragged myself back to my paws, not wanting to show weakness to any dragons who may have been watching on. My mind couldn't sense anyone watching, but I wanted to take no risks.

Despite my resolve to hide my weakness, my legs shook with each step. I could barely breathe as I limped towards the surface, the gentle incline of the winding tunnel feeling almost as steep as the wall. Each lungful of air stabbed at my lungs like sharp claws throttling my neck from the inside out.

How long could I really expect to do this?

Pawsteps thundered close behind. I suppressed a groan as I turned my head, just as the Axaatl commander addressed me.

"Ddraig Anzig? If I may?"

Hyantl towered over me. I struggled not to feel intimidated by his size and obvious strength. But as his eyes drifted towards my back, anger swelled up within me again. "I don't need or want your help."

Hyantl stepped back. His eyes dropped to gaze at my paws. "Of course. I simply thought I would offer my assistance in training you," he said, flicking out a wing to stop my immediate growled protest. I glared at that wing in jealous fury, but I did hold my tongue for a moment longer. "You are going to need to strengthen different

132

muscles. I can show you exercises to do that, so you won't miss your wings so much."

A different kind of heat flared beneath my scales. I dipped my head, partly in respect, but also to hide some of the shame that warmed my face. My claws scratched at the unyielding ground. "Then I apologise for my harsh words, Hyantl. I would be grateful to receive your training."

The Axaatl drake lifted his forepaw and bowed low. "Tomorrow, then. It was a terrible injury you suffered, Ddraig. You have my respect that you refuse to let it best you."

I flicked my tail as Hyantl retreated towards the main chamber again. I stared into the shadows until I could no longer see him. Only then did I turn and continue my walk to the surface.

The Axaatl dragon had given me something to think about. Perhaps not everything was lost. He could help me improve my strength and stamina, learning to put more focus onto my legs, now that I couldn't use my wings. The lair would never feel as easy to traverse again, but if I could move around without exhausting myself then that would be a great advantage.

My vulnerable sense of optimism threatened to collapse when I emerged into sunlight at last. There, I faced the sight of the steep edges of the gorge, rising far higher than any wall inside the lair. Only a thin slice of the sky was visible, mostly grey clouds with occasional patches of blue between them. I scanned the cliffs, searching for an easy way up, though I already knew it did not exist.

A couple of hardy trees clung to the side of the cliffs, but there were no paths. If I wanted to get up to the plains, then I would have to climb.

Partly in hope, but also to give my shoulders a rest, I slowly ambled down the gentle slope of the gorge, following the valley floor as it wound back and forth. Bones littered the ground, scattered amongst the dry grass and occasional shrub, largely reduced to a collection of spindly sticks with the onset of winter.

I looked up as I walked. The steep slopes either side of me felt like a cage, trapping me within Laxtal. Everything about my home was suitable to dragons with wings, with no thought given to those who could not fly. Humans would have difficulty trying to get around, and now I suffered the same indignity. Even as the ddraig, did I have the authority to demand changes made to the lair so I wouldn't have to climb everywhere? If there was already resistance to my rule, I was sure protests would arise.

I batted away a loose stone. It was quiet in the gorge, even with a few dragons flying overhead. None of them stopped or even gave any indication they saw me. No one walked through the gorge. There was never any need. But for the single cave entrance, there was nothing else down here but stones, sticks, and bones. Only an occasional animal fell from the cliff tops and was quickly dispatched and taken to the cold caves for preparation, but that attracted our hunters through scent or sound.

I was invisible to them. Useless and pointless. Everything I had longed for had turned out to be a false promise of a good future. How much of this had Azlak Seen? Had the seer been mocking me behind my back before the rest of the clan had joined in?

My walk soon ended at the end of the gorge. Though it had once been open to the plains beyond, a great landslide had torn down the cliffs on both sides to completely obstruct the gorge, blocking off the last hundred feet of the valley. None of our history recalled when such an event had happened, but it added to the security of our lair and kept humans out. Now, it kept me in.

I put my paw on the nearest mossy rock and looked up, the top of the ancient rockfall almost as high as the sides of the gorge. There was no easy way up.

Magic brushed against the corner of my mind. I had no chance to prepare as I rose from the ground, paws scrambling for grip on the rocks but finding nothing. I snarled as I floated away, the bottom of the gorge receding into the distance as the Nixan magic gripped my body tightly. I twisted my neck to see the familiar bronze scales of Ddraig Krateos swoop by, his wings almost silent on the wind.

Under the guidance of my father's magic, I soared over the rubble of the landslide in a poor imitation of flight, before gently landing on the far side, on the edge of the sloping descent to the hunting plains. The moment his magic's touch slackened, I bounced away and spun, teeth bared in a snarl as the Nixan landed.

"I didn't need that," I spat, making sure to get in the first word.

Ddraig Krateos blinked and stepped back. His head tilted slightly to one side as he met my gaze. "I saw you struggling and thought you needed help."

I swiped at the grass, ripping up several strands which snagged on my claws. "I was perfectly capable of getting here by myself. I am ddraig of this clan and not some helpless hatchling. Or are you so besotted with learning I'm your son that you forget I'm not fresh out of the egg?"

"I… no. That's not true," the Nixan said, his eyes flicking up towards the sky. Making sure there were no dragons to overhear us. He took a hesitant step forward. "I know who you are, Anzig, but it is no weakness or shame to need help."

I glared at Ddraig Krateos until he looked away. My tail quivered as fury overwhelmed me. "I am ddraig. I cannot show weakness like that."

The Nixan turned away, his wings drooping so much that the tips dragged across the grass. "I am sorry that you think that way, my son. I don't know what Astar taught you, but being a ddraig is not showing no weakness. It is recognising when you need help and asking for it. It is knowing your limitations and trusting those around you to do what needs to be done."

I scoffed and turned my back on him. "Asking for help. Is that what you did?" I snarled and wrapped my paw around a small stone, feeling the sharp edges dig against my scales. "Perhaps if you'd asked for help your clan wouldn't have been destroyed."

Krateos whimpered. I refused to look at him, instead staring intently at the base of the cliffs and trying not to tremble with rage.

"You are right," the Nixan whispered, so quietly I could barely hear him. "If I'd have asked for help in defending my clan, then I could have saved them. If I had listened to what I was being told. If I had listened to Nataik and trusted her opinion."

Regret billowed through the Nixan with such strength that I could not block out his emotions. I grimaced and squeezed my eyes shut, claws tensing against the dry earth as I struggled to control my magic. Deep breaths. In and out. Slowly, my own thoughts returned to the surface as I fought against the ddraig's conflicted regrets. Understanding rose from the murky depths of his thoughts as I realised just what he regretted.

I faced my father again. "She warned you, didn't she? Nataik told you about the threat to Nixa and you ignored her." A low growl came to my voice as I took a prowling step forward. My shoulders twitched as instinct tried to flare my wings. "You dare to lecture me about accepting help when you refuse to show that same weakness? When you would rather see your clan burn than accept help?"

Ddraig Krateos covered his face with a paw. "Yes, I let my pride get the better of me. I refused help when it would have saved my clan. Please, Anzig. Don't make the same mistakes as me. Don't think you have to do everything alone, just because you're ddraig."

I shook my head. "I used to be scared of you. I used to think you were like Astar, powerful and strong. Now I can see what you truly are. Weak and vulnerable. As if I could ever be proud of a father like you."

"I don't ask you to be proud of me. I just ask that you learn from my mistakes," Ddraig Krateos whispered. He lowered his paw to rest against his muzzle, though he didn't seem able to meet my gaze anymore.

I growled. "I don't want or need your help. I will rule Laxtal in the way I think best."

Without giving the Nixan chance to respond, I shoved past him and ran down the hill. No pawsteps followed me, so he was wise enough not to give chase.

I didn't know where I intended to go, just knowing that I needed to escape the lair for a few hours. Hunting, perhaps. I had eaten little since losing my wings, though hunger did not yet gnaw at my stomach. Testing my claws and skills on the ground against prey would be a good way to learn what I could still accomplish.

I even managed to shake off the disapproval that emanated from Mushussu. The guardian would have words for me later. I vowed to ignore them all.

Evening was swift, the sky darkening rapidly as the sun sunk towards the horizon, flitting occasionally between thin wisps of cloud that blew across the sky on a strong wind. My only kill was a small rabbit, barely out of adolescence, that had not been quick enough to escape my claws. I had not eaten much before disposing of the carcase and washing my muzzle and paws in a stream.

I knew I wasn't alone for a full ten minutes before the dragon watching me decided to step out of the lengthening shadows. Even still, Maznar said nothing as she settled down on the bank of the stream, dangling the tip of her tail in the water. She seemed to ignore me, and I was happy to ignore her as well.

It couldn't last.

"You know they're all mocking you," the spectre said at last, breaking the silence between us.

I grunted. There was nothing to say to that. Of course I already knew. Even the birds tormented me, one of them chirping to the sunset in the bare branches just above my head. If I had wings, I would have been able to reach the noisy avian. Instead, I had to listen to its irritating song.

Maznar refused to let the silence return. "I've been listening to them. Behind your back or to your face, it doesn't matter. They think you're weak and can't do anything for yourself anymore." She put on a mocking tone. "Oh, let me help you with that. I can do that for you. You can't do that by yourself, let me help."

I growled, but still said nothing. I turned my gaze towards the ness. Her piercing red eyes flashed in the sunlight.

"It must be infuriating for you." She dipped her head and turned away, looking towards the lair. "All they want to do is help you, but they don't understand what that means to someone like you. A ddraig shouldn't be weak, and all you want to do is show your strength. And so they mock your weakness."

"No matter how many times I tell them, they keep trying to do everything for me. It's demeaning," I admitted, finding my voice at last. I sighed and curled my tail around my hindlegs.

Maznar inspected her claws. "You know they'll never stop. They'll keep trying to help you until you have no power or respect left. You'll lose the clan to your haeraig if you don't stop it."

I hurled a loose stone into the stream and watched it sink. "If only I knew how to do that."

Out of the corner of my eye, I saw Maznar grin. She exposed her fangs as she rose to her paws. "You know what you need, brother. You need wings."

I scoffed and looked away. "Kaz said it was impossible. Nothing is going to let me fly again, even if I wanted that help."

"I'm not talking about asking for help, Anzig. I'm talking about taking what you need. Demanding it, not meekly hoping someone will help you," the spectre growled. She grabbed hold of my muzzle and forcibly turned my head so I looked into her crimson eyes. "No dragon is going to give you what you need, but there is someone else who can."

The spectre was going to make me say it. I growled as I spat the word out. "Who?"

Maznar smirked. "George."

I tore myself free from her grip and stepped back, ignoring the pain on my muzzle where her claws had ripped through the scales. "You would have me go to that human and beg for help?"

"No, I would not," Maznar snarled. She flicked her wings out wide, taunting me with them. "I would have you go to George and demand that he restore your wings. I would have you take from him what you deserve, and you use that to rebuild your control over

Laxtal." She stomped her paw to the ground. "You are the ddraig of this clan. You deserve the respect of your dragons and you deserve your wings. Don't beg for them. Take them."

"He'd never listen to me."

Maznar tilted her head. "That doesn't sound like the strength of a ddraig to me." Her eyes twinkled. "George is not the monster you believe him to be."

"He's killing dragons at will," I hissed.

"That is not George's will. That is... another." The spectre hesitated. I got the sense she was about to say one thing, then changed her mind., but she hid her thoughts well "But I don't think you'll have much of a choice soon, Anzig. I see how things are moving here. It won't take long before your respect has eroded so much that Ellian will be ddraig in all but title. And how soon after that until she takes even that from you?"

I trembled. "She wouldn't do that, would she?"

Maznar kept her wings unfurled, even as she placed her paw on my shoulder. "She would, if she thinks she's stronger than you. Take what you need, Anzig. It is the only way."

I didn't have chance to reply before the ness kicked off with her hindpaws, beating her wings and buffeting me with her downdraft. I was forced to look away and close my eyes so they weren't filled with dust and dirt. When I was able to open them again, Maznar was gone, already halfway back to the lair and almost invisible in the growing darkness.

Was she right? Was I really going to lose the clan I had sacrificed so much to lead? I had lost my mate, my father, my mentor, and even the dragon I believed myself to be. Would I lose Laxtal on top of all of that?

I turned to face north, to where I knew the humans to be, far beyond the horizon. Could I really go to George and demand my wings? Would he even listen to me? And who was this other Maznar had hinted at? I doubted I could trust George, but if he was the only way I could keep control of Laxtal...

I shook my head. Foolishness, that's what it was. Ellian was my haeraig. She wouldn't plot to take control of the clan. I knew I could trust her.

And if I couldn't? Then I would take what I needed.

# CHAPTER TWELVE

**Ellian**

I sat perched on top of the cliffs, my wings tucked tight against my body to protect me from the strong southerly wind. Dark grey clouds tore across the sky, casting a patchwork of shadows against the plains. There was no smell of rain on the air, but as winter's claws dug in deeper, there was always a chance for the weather to change dramatically and with no warning.

Despite the cool morning air, I had given up trying to bask in the limited sunlight. I had no desire to chase after the limited patches as the clouds raced overhead. If I needed to warm up, then I could return to my chamber and curl up in front of the fire.

Instead, my focus was on the two dragons far below me, close to the blocked entrance of the gorge. I could hear Hyantl's barked commands from here, carried on the wind, as he gave Ddraig Anzig a private session. Starting the previous morning, my cousin had started the long work to strengthen his body in ways a dragon didn't normally need, trying anything he could to account for the mortifying absence of his wings. I hoped the activity would also help burn off some of the aggression in his system, as he had spent much of the last few days growling and snapping at anyone who got too close to him.

The focus of my attention had not gone unnoticed by my companions at the top of the cliff. While Ddraig Anzig was busy, a few ddraigs and haeraigs from the other clans had taken the opportunity to borrow my time. We were still awaiting the arrival of

Haeraig Arath of Kern, but even without him there was still an impressive gathering.

Bakucic was the only ddraig present, the brown-scaled drake standing just behind my shoulder, also gazing down towards the plains. Haeraig Zeena was the representative for Nixa, the Axinstone as always clutched tightly in her paw. With her were the haeraigs of Eivas, Gyzlan, and Cuine. Haeraigs Attevur, Bazru, and Efferis had all come to Laxtal on behalf of their ddraigs, all arriving a few days earlier with the massive force sent by Kern.

"Do you really think he's capable?" Ddraig Bakucic whispered.

My gaze snapped from watching Anzig and Hyantl towards the Lilisxi ddraig. My claws tensed as I battled the urge to defend my ddraig and the requirement to give the Lilisxi drake the respect his rank deserved. I matched his gaze for a few seconds before looking down to his throat. I could do nothing about the growl in my voice. "He will be capable, yes."

Ddraig Bakucic nodded once. "A lot depends on it."

Haeraig Zeena approached, walking awkwardly with the Axinstone clutched in her forepaw. She had refused to let the precious artefact out of her sight, not even letting her father carry it. "He will not have much time to train. Once this promised army from Esperance arrives, then we will be at our full strength. We will need to know what to do with that strength."

I glanced between the ddraig and haeraig, with the three other dragons just behind them. Above us, I caught a flash of emerald green scales as Haeraig Arath finally joined us, soaring down on wide wings. We cleared some space for him to land, quick greetings shared around the powerful gathering. A little apprehension fluttered in my chest, both at the thought of being amongst such strong company, but also the purpose behind the meeting. I was sure there was a reason why these dragons had not wanted to speak to Ddraig Anzig. Bakucic's question had given that away.

It was Haeraig Arath who spoke first. "The humans appear to have stopped moving, according to our scouts. They have settled in a place north and west of the Nixan lair, close to the mountains. It does not appear to be a strongly defensible location, so there must be some other purpose to why they have chosen that spot."

"There are plenty of caves in the foothills and mountains there," Haeraig Zeena said. She looked to the north, as though peering beyond the horizon to find those caves. "Some of those are places of natural magic. It could be possible the humans are intending to use this, though I can't be sure why at this stage."

"Surely there's nothing out there with as much power as the Axinstone," Ddraig Bakucic declared, his head held high.

Haeraig Zeena's eyes flicked down. Her paw tightened around the precious artefact. "No. Nothing."

"Then we need to get closer to them," Arath said. He remained standing, starting to pace around those of us who had sat down. "But for this promised army from Esperance, our numbers should not swell appreciatively, but we are already straining the hunting capacity for Laxtal. If the humans have settled, then we should fly north and encamp ourselves in Nixan territory, where the hunting will be better."

The Nixan haeraig shook her head. "Our lair was shattered in the human attack. It is not habitable at the moment, and there is nowhere else that can hold our numbers. With winter setting in and the temperature getting colder, we would have nowhere to shelter."

"And if we stay here, then we risk starvation, or missing any sudden movement from the humans," Arath replied. He turned to look at me. "How much food would you say we have, based on how much prey we can hunt at this time of year?"

I flicked out a wing as I thought. I had been down to the cold caves the previous day, inspecting how much salted meat we had in reserve, diminished thanks to the brief but brutal rule of Xital. "A couple of weeks, at least. Maybe up to a month, but I don't know how big Esperance's army will be. That will change things."

"Then we can't risk staying here too long," Ddraig Bakucic said. A murmur of agreement rippled around the gathered dragons. "We will need to fly soon."

A quiet voice spoke up as Haeraig Efferis of Clan Cuine stepped forward. "It would be no dishonour if Ddraig Anzig recognised that he must remain in Laxtal. Many ddraigs have remained behind, either because of age or a desire to protect our territory. He must understand that he can't fly with us, nor can we risk slowing down so much that he can keep up on paw."

The haeraig of the small, southern clan bowed her head as all attention turned to her, but she did not back away. Even though her clan possessed little power, she was still a haeraig. But for Ddraig Bakucic, she was on equal ground to everyone else.

I understood the logic in her words. Anzig would not see it the same way. He would want to be there with us. Being left behind would absolutely be an insult for him.

"We will find a way to accommodate him," I said slowly. "Laxtal will want our ddraig with us. We will do whatever we can to allow him to join us when we fly to Nixa."

"That may not be possible," Haeraig Zeena said. She sucked in her breath and looked over my shoulder, out across the plains. Her eyes widened. "Is that one of your beacons?"

I whirled around to follow her gaze. Sure enough, close to the horizon, the nearest of the southern beacons was ablaze, billowing smoke into the sky. It took me just a moment to recognise the colour and nature of the flame to understand the message. A large number approached. They were in the air, but they were not dragons. This had to be the army Esperance had promised us.

I bellowed out to Anzig, hoping to catch his attention. Hyantl looked up. A moment later, my cousin followed the Axaatl drake's lead. I flicked out a wing to point to the beacon, realising a moment later that my cousin might think I taunted him.

"Beacons!" I shouted, hoping Anzig would realise what I was trying to draw his attention to. "Get up here!"

I was relieved to see Anzig turned to follow the direction of my wing, though I wasn't sure if he could see the beacon from so low. He then turned to run perpendicular to the cliffs. The nearest way up on paw that didn't mean he had to scramble up a vertical rockface was almost a mile away. It would be a long run.

Haeraig Zeena stepped up beside me. Her neck craned into the sky, searching for some glimpse of what approached.

"What do you think she sent?" the haeraig asked.

I shrugged. I had not met this human who had promised the army, though I wished I had. It didn't sound like she was from across the mountains, and it was not a human army that came, unless they had learned to fly.

"How far away are they?" Ddraig Bakucic asked, coming up on my other side. He squinted as he looked towards the horizon.

"If they fly as fast as a dragon, and if the beacon keepers were all alert, then about an hour away," I replied. I could see nothing yet, but the beacons stretched for many miles away from the central lair. The approaching army could be anywhere in our territory, though one thing was for certain. They were coming this way. Our grand alliance of clans was receiving our final numbers. After this, there would be no more strengthening. The pressure would be on to act.

The gathered haeraigs dispersed for a time. Haeraig Zeena left to fetch her father, while the others vowed to return before the army arrived. I remained where I was with Ddraig Bakucic for company, largely unmoving as I kept up my vigil on the horizon. Hyantl joined us, the large Axaatl dragon flying up instead of following Anzig on paw.

My cousin arrived just before Ddraig Krateos, his chest heaving as he struggled to keep moving after his long run. Though I could see the suffering he put himself through, he managed to keep his head high once the Nixan ddraig landed. He even managed to hide the tremble of his paws, though I spotted it before he stood amongst the longer grass near the edge of the cliff.

Curious dragons emerged from the lair, drawn outside by the beacon fires. In all, nearly one thousand dragons gathered on the slopes surrounding the gorge, with around one hundred more spread out across the lower ground below me. I noticed that few of them were Laxtal dragons, with most being the reinforcements provided to Laxtal from our neighbours.

Yalle was one of the few Laxtal dragons to emerge. The albino drake quickly made his way up to us, landing close to Anzig and exchanging a few quiet words with the ddraig.

Excitement gradually built as whispers and questions rippled through the growing crowd. No one knew what to expect, even as the first dark smudge on the horizon grew. Something moved through the sky, less than an hour after the beacons were lit. They moved quickly, directly towards the lair. From such a distance, it was impossible to know what they were. They flew like dragons, but already I could tell they were nothing like us. My claws gripped the ground tightly as excitement slowly shifted towards unease and confusion.

More of the strange creatures dipped down from above the thickening layer of grey clouds. They were bigger than I first thought, growing larger with almost every wingbeat as they began to descend. I got the impression of wickedly sharp beaks and feathers. Were they some kind of great bird?

"Clear room!" I bellowed, addressing both the dragons on the lowlands and on the hill.

Dragons of all clans obeyed my command, quickly clearing space for the approaching army to land. Many dragons fled entirely, retreating into the lair to escape the strange creatures as they finally came close enough to see clearly.

They looked like birds, but their body structure was closer to that of a dragon, only around four times the size. They had wings and feathers, like an eagle or a similar bird of prey, but that was where the resemblance ended. Their feathered forelegs ended in wicked talons, with hindquarters furred like a wildcat. I had never seen anything like them before.

The first of these strange creatures landed in the middle of the rapidly expanding clearing vacated by the gathered dragons. With a quick count I estimated over one thousand of these creatures. Those who found no space to land circled a little longer before coming to ground beyond the steep slopes that led down to the wide-open flatlands.

One creature stepped forward from the rest. He had a purple sash around his neck, hanging beneath one of his forelegs. Deep brown and burnished gold feathers and fur adorned his body. His cold blue avian eyes met mine, and his sharp beak clacked as he trotted forward, clearing the gorge without even having to open his wings.

I craned my neck and resisted the urge to step away. This bizarre creature was taller than any human I had seen, at least three times my height. Each one of his taloned forepaws looked large enough to grip entirely around my body.

"I come seeking the dragons Azlak and Kaz," the creature said, his voice surprisingly smooth for having to get the words through a beak.

Even as I wrestled with the urge to retreat, Anzig fearlessly stepped forward. "I am Ddraig Anzig of Laxtal."

"Then you are not the dragon I seek. Bring Azlak or Kaz. I speak to no other," the creature said, interrupting an indignant Anzig before he was even able to complete his introduction.

For a moment, I thought Anzig was about to protest further, and I eyed the creature's ferocious talons with a wary eye. I had no doubt they could slice through a dragon's scales with ease.

Thankfully Anzig backed down. "Find Kaz and bring him here," he barked out to Yalle. He need not have worried, for the albino had not even had the chance to spread his wings before the Nixan he sought flew up from within the gorge, landing just in front of me to face the creature.

"Oh, you're gryphons," he said, eyes wide as he lowered his head and spread his wings. He didn't seem at all shocked by the creatures. "I am Kaz, envoy of Esperance. I welcome you to Laxtal."

The gryphon lowered his head in response. "I honour you with my name, Prince Kyrus, heir to the Crown of Golden Feathers and envoy of Esperance. I am at your service."

As the gryphon moved, I caught sight of something on his back. A grey-scaled dragon lay there, curled up in a tight ball amongst the gryphon's feathers. The movement of his mount caused the dragon to start awake, raising his head and trying to scramble up to his paws on the uneven surface. There was something odd about the way he moved, but I couldn't quite place what it was.

"We there already?" the dragon muttered sleepily. "Damn it, Kyrus. You said you'd wake me."

The gryphon snorted in what I could only assume to be amusement. His eyes had lightened momentarily. "This is Alaron.

144

Envoy of Esperance and commander of her armies. Poor thing needs his beauty sleep, not that it helps much, if you ask me."

"Oh shut it, you overgrown bird," the dragon said sleepily. "Pleasure to meet you, I'm sure." He shook his head as he half jumped, half fell off the gryphon's back, who almost immediately turned to start preening the feathers that had been pressed down by the dragon's weight.

My shocked intake of breath was shared by the haeraigs and ddraigs who stood with me, but only Anzig had the confidence to hesitantly step forward.

"Your legs? What happened to them?" he whispered.

The strange dragon had no forelegs, with not even a scar where his forelimbs should be. Instead, he used his wings to walk. I looked into Anzig's eyes, and I saw the same horror he had reviled when we had looked upon him.

Alaron did not walk like a cripple, but with confidence and poise that suggested the injury was an old one. "I'm a wyvern, you fool. This is what I'm meant to look like. Don't know how you're meant to fly with those extra legs weighing you down," he said, before yawning widely. He rubbed his eyes with a wingtip and blinked a few times, then looked at Anzig for the first time. "Of course, you aren't flying anywhere," he added in a quiet voice.

Anzig growled, but surprisingly didn't say anything to retort the wyvern's words. "I am Ddraig Anzig of Laxtal," he said instead, repeating his interrupted introduction from before. "We are glad to have you here." His words lacked sincerity.

The wyvern was slightly taller than Anzig, even without his forelegs to prop himself up. Now that he was a little closer, I could see that his wings were different to ours, located further around on his shoulders, more on his side than his back. The bones that supported them seemed stronger, though I supposed they had to be, given he used them to walk. He also had a small set of claws about halfway down the leading edge of the wings, which I imagined functioned as his paws. The end of his tail was tipped by a claw-like barb. He was such a curious creature, even more so than the gryphon behind him, simply because he was so close to a dragon, yet so wildly different at the same time.

If Alaron took offense to Anzig's pointed words, then he did not show it. His strong wings rustled, before he yawned again. "Kaz and Ddraig Anzig, if you could join me and our great prince here, we can discuss how we can best fulfil Esperance's promise to you. Though first I must ask if you have any coffee here."

Anzig tilted his head. He wasn't the only one. "No. What's that?"

Alaron clicked his tongue. "What's that?" he mimicked. He sighed. "I really hope you remembered to bring coffee this time, Kyrus, or else I'm going to have a monstrous headache later."

"And you're going to give me one with your complaints," Kyrus chirped. His bright blue eyes sparkled with amusement, even as he guided the grumbling wyvern away with one massive, taloned forepaw. Kaz hurried after them both, but I could see Anzig hesitate. Then the ddraig seemed to remember a thousand expectant dragons watched his every move. He followed Kyrus and Alaron without a backwards glance.

As they moved far enough away to be out of earshot, I turned to look at the army Prince Kyrus and Alaron had brought with them. One thousand gryphons, most of them settling down near the trees on the plains. With their size, there was no chance they would be able to fit inside the caves of the lair. I could only hope they didn't mind sleeping beneath the stars. Of course, that still left the issues of food. Already we were straining the resources of the clan to feed everyone. Gryphons I was sure would need a lot to eat; Laxtal would not be able to provide for them for long.

One month I had estimated, before we ran out of food. Surely that would be much less now.

Ddraig Krateos had clearly thought of the same thing. We had strength in numbers now. It was time to act. "Haeraig Ellian, we will not be able to hold these numbers for long, but there is one last ally we have not considered. Did you say there were humans allied to our cause? If they're serious about living this side of the mountains, then they should answer our call if we need them. Would you be willing to send a messenger out to them?"

"I'll find someone, Ddraig," I said, bowing my head and taking a few steps away towards the gorge. Many dragons had already retreated underground, fleeing the great size of the gryphons. I didn't blame most of them, almost wishing I could do the same. But, at the same time, I was thrilled by their arrival.

I reluctantly left to find someone to carry the ddraig's message. Those creatures who had descended upon our lair were fascinating, and I wanted to learn as much about them as I could. I knew I would seek out their company again at the first opportunity. For now, I worried only about what Ddraig Krateos wanted James and his group of humans to know. I couldn't help but wonder if Mulner would join the humans if they came. This could be one of the greatest moments in draconic history. Would my brother really want to miss that? If I were to be honest with myself, he probably would. He cared not for the comings and goings of greatness, instead preferring to live a simple existence as a nomad. I couldn't help but feel some envy towards that.

It didn't take me long to find someone to fly to Mulner's lair in the west, as there were several dragons in the upper chambers generally reserved for messenger duties. The ness who was to carry my message fluttered her wings in fear at the prospect of flying to seek out a human but offered no vocal protests. She had little choice in the matter. I was her haeraig after all.

I watched the messenger leave, then followed to return to the surface. When I did, I saw the gryphon prince had also returned, leaving Anzig and Kaz to continue their discussion with Alaron. Kyrus bent his feathered forelegs and bowed. "You are haeraig?" he asked, the word forming strangely from his beak.

"I am, yes. Haeraig Ellian of Laxtal," I replied, bowing my head towards the gryphon. I tried not to feel intimidated by him, but the top of my head barely even came to his knees. Even the Axaatl dragons looked small in comparison to the gryphons.

Kyrus chirruped in delight, his earlier coldness seeming to vanish into the afternoon sun. Perhaps it had never been there to begin with, and it was only the shock of seeing such a bizarre creature that had placed the emotions in my mind. "If I may ask for you to join me on a short walk?"

I glanced briefly at Anzig, still in discussion with Alaron, and then to Ddraig Krateos and his daughter. They were also talking to each other, Ddraig Bakucic an attentive ear. I doubted they would even miss me if I left, so I assented to the gryphon's request.

After a short glide down to the plains, we passed through the field of gryphons towards the small forest to the north. Though a path quickly cleared for Kyrus, I had to be careful to avoid their talons and claws. There was not as many colours amongst the gryphons as there was in dragons. Most were golden or brown in some variety. Feathers came in all patterns, and every last one of them seemed perfectly groomed. Those few that were a little dishevelled were busy preening and maintaining their feathers with barely an eye for anything else.

As we walked, Kyrus told me a little about where he came from, a land to the south and east of the draconic territories. He spoke of roaring oceans and towering cliffs, of stony beaches and an abundance of fish to hunt. His mother currently wore the Crown of Golden Feathers and had ruled over the gryphons for almost forty years. It would be another forty at least before Kyrus expected to wear the crown upon his feathered head. Any dragon would be proud of a forty-year rule. Eighty years was completely unheard of – few dragons even managed to live to see their eightieth year.

Though Kyrus talked at length of his homeland, I figured that was not the reason for our sojourn from the others. We had started to skirt the edge of the hunting grounds, where the herds of deer sniffed in alarm at the scent of this new, unknown predator.

"Esperance warned me not to trust your ddraig," Kyrus said, finally getting to his motive. "She thought he carried too many secrets, and tried too hard to be the leader he wasn't. False, I believe she called him." The gryphon's beak clacked his disapproval.

I had not seen this mysterious human, but I wondered why she could think she knew so much about my cousin. Words drifted back to me from the depths of my memory. Hadn't Astar once doubted Anzig as a leader? I shuffled my wings as I thought, my loyalty towards my ddraig and cousin tested by Astar's doubts, and now those of the gryphon.

"I don't know that I agree with you, or with Esperance," I said, trying to avoid sounding timid before the gryphon.

"It would be unwise to allow the wingless one to lead your armies in to battle. This is not the time to risk any weakness," Kyrus advised. His talons and paws crunched heavily on the sticks and leaves that littered the forest floor. In contrast I made almost no noise at all, my much lighter pawsteps able to avoid the bracken and debris. Only a few of the hardiest leaves still clung to the trees, mostly golden and brown much like the gryphon newcomers. Soon nothing would remain, save bare branches creaking in the wind.

"I'm not the one to take that away from him," I answered after a while. I had to crane my neck to even attempt to meet the gryphon's eye, but not once did he glance down to me. His focus was solely above us, at the lifeless and dull foliage still clinging to the trees.

"Are you not his haeraig? Surely leadership should fall to you if your ddraig is incapacitated in any way?"

He was correct. Should Anzig prove a poor leader, then it was my responsibility to remove him from power, lest another dragon from within the clan step up and challenge him. I knew it was my responsibility, but I didn't know if I could have the heart for it. He had suffered so much recently, and I didn't want to be the cause of more pain. He had lost father, mentor, and now his wings. Could I take his clan from him too?

"I understand I may have given you some difficult things to think about, Haeraig Ellian, but you mustn't let family loyalty blind you now," Kyrus said, coming to a stop as he looked down at me. A crest of small feathers rose against his neck. "We are here to help you, but not to fight your wars for you. I have followed Alaron here because he is a strong leader, though he is no gryphon. If your ddraig proves to be weak, he will soon lose our respect, and we will return home, regardless of your bargain with Esperance.

"I say this not as a threat to you Ellian, nor as an attempt to spur you to act on what you do not wish to do, but you must know the potential consequences if you fail to act. I have seen many battles. I know the difference between a competent leader and one who is not.

"I will not remain if doing so will mean throwing gryphon lives away pointlessly."

While I understood the reasoning behind Kyrus's advice, I knew I would have to think long and hard before I made any decisions. Did I really think I could be a better ddraig than Anzig? I would have to be certain if I decided to challenge him. The clan, and even all dragonkind, could not afford a period of instability. That would be much worse than a weak ddraig.

"I apologise, Haeraig Ellian, if it seems like I am meddling in affairs which are not mine, but I only seek to strengthen your cause in ways I see fit. You do not need to heed my advice, but only recommend you learn from my experience," Kyrus said, starting to move once more. I bounded to keep up with the large strides of the gryphon.

Once more, Kyrus talked of his homeland as we began to return to the lair. His roost was located at one of the most western points on the continent across the ocean – a tall spire of glittering rock that shone in the morning sunlight, rising high above the roaring ocean. Fifty thousand gryphons lived there, and at the summit stood the Aerie, home of Queen Hera. The gryphon's silky words conjured an image of a place of pure beauty, and I longed one day to witness it. Perhaps Airil could take me there, before realising should I become ddraig, I wouldn't have so many opportunities to leave the clan.

I spent a little time describing our lair to Kyrus, but no matter how I tried, I couldn't match his beautiful painting of words. There was no doubt in my mind that Laxtal was one of the most beautiful places I had seen, even now winter had its grip on the trees, but there was nothing striking about it. We had nothing as awe-inspiring as a gleaming tower of rock that could mark our territory, leaving strangers in no doubt where they were. I almost felt embarrassed, but the gryphon was polite enough as he listened.

Most of the gryphons had gathered in small groups. There was much conversation between them in a musical, chirruping language I couldn't decipher. It was like a dawn chorus, with birdsong filling the air.

Up on the hill, on the other side of the gorge, Ddraig Krateos was still with Anzig, Kaz, and Alaron, though Haeraig Zeena and Ddraig Bakucic were no longer present. Few dragons remained, most having vacated in fear the moment the gryphons had landed. Those few that lingered were the brave and fearless. I recognised just three Laxtals amongst them – Saya and Vinzent, as well as Keita, the daughter of the albino Yalle. None of them interfered in the conversations on the far side of the gorge, but they were listening with interest.

Alaron was learning all he could about the human army, asking Anzig and Ddraig Krateos questions about their strengths and movements. Thanks to the information my brother had gathered, we were able to provide a decent representation of the human army, and what we believed their intentions to be. The wyvern didn't seem too impressed though.

"Why have they been given free access to your territory? Why haven't they been harassed at all? You have many thousands of dragons here, just sitting idle," Alaron asked, as I took my place by Anzig's side. Kyrus returned to standing just behind the wyvern.

Ddraig Krateos rumbled an apology. "That had been our task, before the humans destroyed our lair," he said, quickly ducking his head.

"There should have been someone replacing your duties then, once your clan was no longer able. Ddraig Anzig, why had none been arranged? You have the numbers," the wyvern said, pointing an accusing wing at my cousin, who had nothing to say for himself. I said nothing of Ddraig Boruc and his mysterious quest he had taken with Azlak and Isikian. That would only have raised some questions I would be unable to answer.

"And Haeraig Ellian, why don't you come and tell me all about dragon you ran into the other day?" Alaron asked, turning to me. For the first time I looked into his eyes. They were yellow like a wildcat's, fierce and intense. I met them without looking away.

"Of course," I replied, before delving into the tale once more. By my side, Anzig seemed to diminish as I told of the enhanced dragon. Had he been so deeply scarred by his encounter with Nightwings that he was unable to even hear of another such terror? I suddenly feared how he would react if another such monster were to face him. I kept such emotions from my expression as I spoke. It would not do Anzig's confidence any good if I started openly doubting him, even if I did start to believe Kyrus's warnings were correct.

The gryphon caught my eye and nodded slightly. Either something was visible on my face or in my wings, or Kyrus had also seen the same signs in Anzig and reached the same conclusion. My cousin was weak.

Soon I would have to challenge him for control of the clan.

For the sake of dragonkind, I had no choice but to win.

# CHAPCER CHIRCEEN

**Mulner**

I almost refused to believe the messenger when she relayed what had happened in Laxtal; massive, feathered creatures had landed and declared allegiance to our cause, and now Laxtal required the presence of their allied humans. Though the messenger had only arrived an hour ago, James McArthur was already preparing to depart. I thought I would have been glad to see them go. Now that they were leaving, I wasn't sure I was going to enjoy the silence they would leave behind.

Cinson stood by my side as I looked down on the small village they had created. In the shadow of the rocky outcrop in which we lived, the humans had created an impressive sight. The Xigax dragon's tail was restless, twitching back and forth. Something was on his mind, but as of yet he had not breached our silence.

Night was starting to fall though, and the humans would not be leaving today. They planned to march on at first light, likely before the earliest rising dragons emerged from the cave to bask in the morning sun.

"You should join them," Cinson said at last, freeing the words that had held fast on his tongue for some time now. "We should all join them. They'll need all the help they can get."

I stared at the Xigax dragon. "I vowed never to return. I will not go back," I said adamantly. It had been quite some time since Cinson had asked me that question, and I had thought that argument had long ago ended in my favour.

"Even at the expense of dragonkind?" Cinson said quietly, keeping his eyes firmly on the activity below.

I growled and spread my wings, contemplating flying off before changing my mind at the last moment. This was not something I could choose to do. Laxtal was not a place of good memories for me. I had watched both my parents die there. To me it was a place of sickness and death. It was not a home for me, and but for my sister there was no one in Laxtal I cared for. But Cinson was right. They needed all the help they could get, for they were one of our last hopes in defeating the humans that threatened our existence. If Ddraig Tsona and George Symons had their way, dragons would be little more than pets at the beck and call of humanity, forced to move from our traditional homes as the human country of Kernow expanded beyond the mountains that had long been the border between us.

"I will not do it," I snarled. I had been doing enough to help from here. Why would Laxtal need me to return?

Still not looking towards me, Cinson shook his head. "Then expect to be left alone. I will be flying out tomorrow, and I expect almost everyone will be joining me. Don't let your pride rule you, Mulner," the Xigax dragon said. He didn't give me a chance to answer, spreading his wings and leaping off the bluff, soaring down to the river below. He met a few dragons down there, dragons I had thought were loyal to me no matter what. A few of them looked up at me and shook their heads. They were leaving me.

That night, I lay alone. No one tried to convince me to leave with them. They all must already have known I wouldn't change my mind.

I used the silence of the night to think about what I really wanted. Did I want to simply be a dragon on the edge of the action, never really involved in the most important events of our time? I snorted to myself, drawing the sleepy gaze of a few of the nearby dragons. Of course I did. I had never had any intention of living a life filled with adventure. If Cinson was wanting to take my dragons away from me and lead them to their likely deaths, then he was welcome to it.

It was a cold night, and though the fire burned brightly, I could still feel the chill night air blowing in through the cave mouth. I wasn't sure if it was entirely my imagination or not, but I thought I could hear wings beating on the wind, wings of a creature much bigger than any dragon. My last waking thought before dropping into restless sleep was that it was probably my mind playing with the idea of the feathered creatures who had landed in Laxtal. There simply wasn't anything big enough to make such a noise.

True to their word, the humans had already gone by the time I emerged into the morning sunlight. A few dragons were already awake, Cinson included, their wings spread out over the grass as they tried to warm up. A few acknowledged my presence, but to most I was a ghost drifting by. The petty fools. I had done nothing wrong, and yet they treated me like a pariah, like I had committed some great evil.

I said nothing to them, and them to me, as the hours passed by, and they prepared to leave. Not a single other dragon was going to remain behind – my little clan was abandoning me here. I was a ddraig without dragons.

By the time midday had passed, I was alone. Just before he had taken to wing, Cinson looked like he was about to approach me, but I glared him away. I knew he was going to try one last time to make me join them, but they would not dissuade me. I would remain here, alone if I had to. There could be no shame in that.

I took some time to hunt, stalking and killing a rabbit with ease. The docile little things never even knew I was coming before I killed them with a quick bite to the neck. One moment they had been happily chewing at the grass, the next they were my meal. The rabbit was me, I decided. In an instant, I had lost my clan and everything I had lived for over these last few years. This was meant to be a refuge for the lost and the clanless, and yet they had spread their wings at the first chance to fly to Laxtal. Did this war really mean that much for them?

Losing my appetite for the remainder of my meal, I left it for the scavengers. I could already see a few wildcats lurking nearby, hoping for any scraps. As I spread my wings, they fought amongst each other to get the best of the rabbit. I left them to it. I had no cares for the comings and goings of the cats.

My little domain felt empty now, and I soared over it a few times, hoping to find some sign that just one dragon had remained. I'd even take a human. Any sign that at least someone was still loyal to me, but after the fourth pass over the hill I gave up, dejectedly sinking down to lie by the river.

The leaves were really starting to fall from the trees now. Copper leaves almost choked the river as they slowly drifted on the current to the far distant sea. How many would eventually reach that far-distant destination? What sights would they see? They would surely travel further than I could ever hope, stuck here through my own stubbornness.

I gripped the soft earth in my claws and howled to the empty sky. I was not expecting it to answer back.

A deep, earth-shaking roar returned my cry, a terrifying noise that sent me fleeing straight to my cave. Nothing I had ever heard of could make that sound, and I did not wish to linger and meet whatever had created it.

I reached the cave just in time. A deep, percussive thrum heralded the wingbeats of a vast creature, and from the safety of underground I was able to see a shadow pass overhead. Rock cracked as the creature landed on top of the hill, right where I had been standing with Cinson the previous day. Just a few feet of stone separated me from the creature now, but I didn't believe it knew I was here.

"I was sure I heard… There are scents here, but they're a few hours old at least," a loud draconic voice said. It was unmistakeably a dragon, but as he moved above me his weight on the rock was far greater than any should possess. It reminded me of the strange creatures that had descended on Laxtal, but the messenger had been clear. Those creatures were more like birds than dragons.

"You're better than that," a second voice said, this one human. The dragon growled in response, a deep, gravelly noise that reverberated through rock and bone. "Come on, they're waiting for us. We fly north!"

The human yelled out to unseen companions, but they answered. Three other monstrous dragons roared out, and their wingbeats shook the trees so hard they shed even the hardiest of amber leaves. I crept as close to the cave mouth as I dared so I could watch the dragons fly away. Each carried at least one human on their back, and all were impossibly large. I simply couldn't believe what I was seeing. Their wingspans must have been well over fifty feet, an utterly impossible size for any dragon. These were not the creatures who had come to Laxtal.

I couldn't see if the dragons were Xital, but it was clear they were working with the humans. Was it human magic that made them so large? Ellian had to know. I had to warn her.

I didn't even hesitate.

I flew east.

There were no sounds of pursuit, so it seemed the monstrous dragons hadn't known of my presence. I had been fortunate, but I could not count on such luck again. I pushed myself hard, wanting to create as much distance as I could between myself and my old lair.

I saw no sign of Cinson and his group of dragons as I flew, but as night started to fall, I didn't even think about pausing. They would have stopped to rest for the night, but what I had seen didn't allow me to sleep. If Xital was creating an army of monstrous dragons, then Laxtal needed to know about it.

As the stars came out, I wondered why I didn't fly at night more often. The skies were almost completely empty, though I could hear a lot of movement below me in the shadows. I could hardly see beyond the end of my own muzzle, but I fixed on to a single star in front of me to keep flying straight. Without being able to see any of the landmarks along the route, they sky was all I had to navigate. The light of the moon and stars glinted off the occasional river and lake, but nothing else reached my eyes of the land below. I could have been flying over nothing but shadow. At least I wouldn't be able to see any of the familiar but long-avoided landscape below to remind me of where I was going.

I started to tire quickly as the cold sapped away my strength. My wings became stiff, and I laboured with each beat. There were still many of hours of flight left, and it was only through force of will that I was able to keep going.

The shadows seemed to reach out towards me. I had never felt so cold before, and it was hard to tell if I was even still moving. Other sounds started to reach my ears, more unsettling ones. Somewhere in the distance a dragon roared, followed by high pitched shrieking and chittering. It sounded like bats, and they were coming closer.

Though I should have no fear of bats, the chill pervaded my heart, giving me fresh impetus to keep flying, and to hurry. My efforts were useless though. My wings were too cold to do little more than glide, and I was slowly sinking down towards the shadows. They would be no protection from the hunting bats. The shadows were their domain. If they were seeking me, then they would find me with ease.

The sound of dry leaves rustling in the leaves warned me of how low I had sunk, and a few weary beats of my wings stopped me from falling beneath the canopy. The light of the moon dimmed in a thousand shadows, and I cast a tired glance up. Bats covered the sky, each as large as a dragon. An ordinary dragon, but monstrous for a bat. Whatever their destination may be, I had no more strength to continue.

Leaves and slender branches whipped at my underside as I brushed against the canopy of trees. Another beat of my wings lifted me clear before the forest abruptly ended. I fell into the darkness below, coming to a sudden halt against the ground.

Not too far away a fire flickered. A tall, pale man looked in my direction but didn't move. He melted into the shadows as the cold finally defeated me.

I woke to the sun on my back and a bird chirping nearby. It took me a few minutes to even realise where I was, and why I was lying in the middle of an unfamiliar field. The remains of a small campfire still smouldered not too far away. Slowly the events of the previous day started to filter back through my mind. The sky was clear now, with no dragons or bats of any size in sight. I hoped those creatures hadn't been going towards Laxtal. From what little I had seen of them; it had looked like a formidable army.

Though I tried to stand up and keep moving, my legs and wings simply wouldn't respond. The cold had sapped all my energy, and all I could do was crawl forward a few pathetic steps before collapsing to the ground again. I managed to reach the abandoned campfire, where I had seen that pale figure in the night. I didn't know how it had failed to see me, but I was glad of it. The charred firewood still gave off some heat, so I lay down with my wings spread out beside it. Anything that would help put some warmth into my aching body.

As I started to wake up, I became aware of a stinging in my neck. I pressed my paw against the pain, and it came away with a couple of spots of blood. I dismissed it as nothing to worry about. A branch must have struck me as I descended through the trees. With my paw, I felt two small holes that had pushed in between my scales, with a couple of sharp ridges where the scales had broken. It would heal.

I tried to get my bearings, working out where I had blindly flown to in the darkness. From the ground, I could see no defining feature – no hill to break the flat plains that spread out for miles in all directions.

Behind me was the forest I had just avoided flying in to, but those dotted the western territories of my home clan, so it didn't help me work out where I was. I would need to get into the air and hope I could see something then.

Some dark thought kept eluding my mind. I was sure I was forgetting something important, but as I ran everything through my mind, I could find nothing. Cinson left. The monstrous dragons. The bats. Everything was there, but I was sure something still eluded my mind's grasp.

It took an hour before I felt strong enough to fly again. I still felt an icy chill in my blood, but it didn't restrict my wings anymore. Spiralling straight up so I could hunt for landmarks, I tried to shake the fear in my heart that I was already too late. If the bats had been heading for Laxtal then the clan would not have had chance to react. Slaughter would have been the only outcome.

Finally, I caught sight of a rock formation I recognised to the north of me, an outcrop I knew to be not far to the south of the lair. I felt relieved. Not only had I flown most of the way to the lair in the night, but the bats would surely have safely passed the lair.

I pushed on, flying north as fast as I could manage. Below I could see many of the beacons that scattered across Laxtal's territory. They all remained unlit, though there were signs many had recently been alight. The bats may not have taken the central lair, but I feared something had happened to the beacon keepers. It would have to be something to worry about later. Now I needed to steel myself for my first glimpse of the central lair in many years. Just once had I been back since I had banished myself, and then I had only reached the gorge. This time I would have to go further.

My wings shook as a steep hill rose out from the flatlands. The hill was dissected almost in two by a steep-walled gorge that had been blocked off at one end by an ancient rock fall that had probably redirected the river that used to flow there. North of the gorge, the land remained at a higher elevation, keeping the old riverbed out of reach for anything without wings. I had returned.

There were a few dragons on the upper slopes of the hills, above the deep gorge. There was no sign of the strange creatures that had come to Laxtal, nor of Cinson and the other dragons who had left me. None of the present dragons paid any attention to me as I flew past, trying to remember where the entrance to the lair was. After a few minutes I found it, landing just outside on the springy bracken. I could see the flickering flames of the torches inside.

The first step was the hardest, but after that the others came easier. Long forgotten memories rose to the surface, the agony of losing my parents to illness and injury, but also the joy of so many years spent playing with my friends when I had been a young dragonet. I slowly padded down through the narrow passages, ignoring all the ones I knew to lead to nowhere. It wasn't long before I found myself looking down on the central chamber. Kept alight by uncountable numbers of torches, as well as the few small cracks near the ceiling, the chamber shrouded with many shadows in the corners. To my eyes it looked like dragon filled every nook and cranny.

In the very centre of the chamber was a raised dais, surrounded by a ring of small stalagmites. Ellian was there, with a few other dragons. Two of them I recognised as Nixan, but the other two were strangers. As I flew down to meet them, I realised they were both crippled. One was without wings, and the other without forelegs. What had happened here to create such injuries?

It was only once I got close enough to land that I realised the wingless dragon was Ddraig Anzig. I couldn't help but stare at the useless scars that adorned his back where his wings should have been.

My claws clicked on the stone as I landed, and only then did the ddraig turn and notice my stare. He narrowed his eyes in anger. "What?" he snapped. I didn't have the courage to ask how he had gained such injuries, but nor did I have the force of will to look away.

At the sound of his voice, Ellian turned around, and her eyes widened in shock. She shrieked my name and bounded over to me, embracing me in her wings. "You're back. I can't believe it, you actually came back," she said, holding me tight. She held her paw over the wound on my neck, her eyes growing wide in concern. "Did something bite you?"

"It was nothing. I flew into a tree, that's all," I said, fighting to free myself of her grip. Eventually I was able to fight free from my sister. Ddraig Anzig glared at the ground by my paws, a fury in his eyes the like of which I had never seen before. I recognised the two Nixans now. They were Ddraig Krateos and Haeraig Zeena, and I bowed my head to acknowledge them.

I turned to the grey-scaled stranger, noting how he used his wings to stand. "Don't even say it," he said, before I even had the chance to ask the obvious question. "I'm a wyvern, not a dragon. And I hope I don't have to explain that to every new dragon I meet. This is how I'm meant to be."

I nodded without saying a word. I didn't know who this creature was or why he was here, but already I knew I didn't want to start an argument with him. Even lacking two of his legs he looked like a fight I couldn't win. His chest and leg muscles were immense, and the small claws on the leading edge of his wing were sharper than any I had seen before. And that was even before considering the wicked barb on his tail.

The wyvern huffed and turned again to face the ddraig. "As I was saying, we need to find some strategy to counter this enlarged dragon. It alone can kill hundreds."

"You know about them?" I asked, unable to help myself from interrupting. If they already knew about these dragons, then there was little point in me coming here after all. The only news I had now was of the bats.

"Them?" the wyvern asked, tilting his head back towards me. "We only know of one."

"I saw five yesterday morning. That's why I came here," I whispered to the wyvern's clawed wings. I heard a sharp intake of breath from Ddraig Anzig and a shocked murmur from Ddraig Krateos aimed at his daughter.

Suddenly I was the focus of all the attention from four dragons and the wyvern. "Tell us everything," Ddraig Krateos asked.

I took a deep breath and recounted everything that had happened to me over the last day.

# CHAPTER FOURTEEN

**Azlak**

I had never known what it was like to look down on so many humans all together, and now I had the opportunity, I wished that I had never done so. It was the first time I had been able to truly appreciate the magnitude of the task dragonkind faced if we were to earn our survival.

We had come beyond the northern borders of Nixa, west of the territory of Clan Turaxa and north of the refuge mountain of Kxisila. We weren't far from the pass where I had crossed the mountains with Ddraig Anzig, returning from human lands with the Axinstone. The terrain was rugged and harsh, with a multitude of small hills and valleys punctuating the horizon. There was very little out here that could be of interest to the humans, nothing but a few minor lairs that were home to a hundred dragons at most. Some of the local dragons, who had lingered despite the human threat, told us the army had not moved at all for several days now. It seemed they were waiting for something, but the dragons weren't sure what.

The human camps spread out over a great distance, stretching almost as far as I could see in either direction from my vantage point on a small bluff. A couple of thin trees obscured me from any potential prying eyes, but it wasn't long before my confidence failed and I returned to Isikian and Ddraig Boruc. We had found shelter in a small cave frequented by nomads and other travellers. It was little more than a tiny, three chambered cave, but it suited our needs perfectly. My two companions looked up expectantly as I returned.

"Still no sign of him," I said, shaking my head. We had been here for almost a full day, now a week since leaving Laxtal, but we had yet to sight our target. George had been absent, but the camp was large enough that he could be anywhere within. Occasionally I felt the power of the Axinstone pulse out from the camp, so we knew we had come to the right place at least. We certainly weren't going to give up so easily. We would try again in an hour.

With great effort, I resisted lying near Isikian, instead curling up on my own a short distance away. The Nixan had been one of my closest friends since flying across the mountains together, but I sorely missed the company of Kaz. Absently I toyed with the slate embedded within my paw, but I did not succumb to the temptation. We had both promised each other we would only use them when the need was great. Though we were sure Esperance would not give us anything harmful, we had no way of knowing if their magic could have any adverse effects.

Once more we discussed a strategy on what to do once we found George. With just the three of us we knew we would be unable to take it by force. It would be another act of thievery, likely during the night. I shivered at the prospect of having to go out and fly in the darkness. I had done it just twice before; once with Inilta's magic to help warm me. This time we would be without that luxury.

After a while, Isikian went out to try his luck spotting George, leaving me alone with the ddraig, who had been quiet and lost in pensive thought for most of the day. When he did speak, he was vague and unclear, always referring to events and places I had never heard of. Sometimes I got the impression the old dragon did not even realise I was there, and he was simply vocalising his thoughts to better sort through them. The name 'Tsoren' repeated frequently.

*A dark cave loomed all around. "The power of one or all," the old, grey-scaled dragon said. Two other dragons listened to his words, one was gold, and the other blue. There were seven runes of stone laid out in a circle between them. The older dragon held an eighth in his tail. "You have the power to join or destroy. The choice can be yours alone."*

*"I never asked for this," the gold dragon whispered, holding his head low.*

*"Every one of the Eight had this same choice to make," the old dragon replied.*

*"But they chose this path," the gold replied, nudging one of the runes with his paw.*

*"Not all of them."*

*"And what did they choose?"*

*"That much should be obvious, at least."*

*The gold dragon sighed and turned to the blue by his side. "I don't want to lose you though. If I do this... If I do this I won't be the same."*

*The blue gently rubbed heads with his companion, a pained smile on his face. "Didn't Esperance tell us she had to give up her love to finish her quest? If she could make that decision, then so can you. Besides, I can find them all again after."*

*"Are... are you sure?" the gold dragon said.*

*"Do it," the blue said, taking a step back. He made sure he didn't once lose eye contact with his companion.*

*"Very well. Pass me the Axinstone." The gold held out his paw to receive the eighth and final rune. Magic seemed to take physical form as drops of blue light dripped from the radiating stones. The three dragons disappeared as the liquid light grew ever more intense.*

"The power of all or one?" I whispered, snapping back to the present as the magic of the future still blinded my eyes.

"What did you say?" Ddraig Boruc said, his reverie broken at last.

Startled, I repeated what I had said, and started to explain what I had just Seen. Once I had finished, the old dragon slowly walked over to me and placed his paw on my head. I could feel magic beneath his scales.

"Then maybe you will be the one to break our exile at long last. You are dragonkind's greatest hope now, Azlak," the ddraig said, taking his paw away once more.

"But why? Why me?" I asked, recoiling away from the ddraig. I simply could not believe his words, even if they echoed those Esperance had said to Kaz and me. 'Find the third dragon', she had told us. Ddraig Boruc had already denied that he was the dragon we sought, claiming he was from another era and not one for the future.

For my whole life I had been the Laxtal omega, the least important member of the clan. Knowing that I was actually Nixan had not changed that. No dragon could go from that position to holding the hopes of our entire species on their wings.

"Esperance has chosen you. She has seen something in you that no one else has. You have an obligation now to her, and to all of us," Ddraig Boruc said. I still didn't know what he was talking about, but I was sure he wasn't about to explain now. I was sure it had something to do with the eight runes I had Seen in my vision, but what they were or did was quite beyond me. The leopard rune I had found beneath Laxtal had been completely bereft of power or magic, yet it had been there with the others in the vision, and it had felt powerful.

I was saved from having to ponder the mysterious events of the future by Isikian's return. The Nixan was frantic, and he kept his wings extended even as the tips knocked and scraped against the cave entrance.

"I've found him." It was all the Nixan needed to say. Moments later the three of us returned to the sky, using the few clouds as cover against watching human eyes. One thing we had learned from our observations was that humans rarely looked up. For some reason, they didn't expect any dragons to attack them from the skies, and that gave us a distinct advantage. Even if one happened to catch a glimpse of us, from this height we would look like hunting birds.

Just why they had that confidence wasn't apparent. We had seen no defences against an aerial assault, nor any way of detecting us. But, for whatever reason, they seemed perfectly at ease.

Isikian led us towards a cluster of large tents at the far end of the expansive camp, close to the cliffs. From this high it was hard to make out individual humans, but the Nixan was confident this was where George was. I paid careful attention to how far we had flown from our little hideout, so that when the time came to fly in at night, I would be able to return here without having to rely on my eyes. Once the sun sank below the horizon, we would have just the humans' campfires to guide us.

We did not risk flying any lower to discover if George carried the Axinstone with him. We simply had to trust that the human would not want to let the precious rune out of his sight. As we turned around and started to fly back towards our cave, I noticed a small patch of utter darkness amongst the tents. It looked like something had sucked away all the light, for I could see nothing within the void, not even light from nearby fires.

I pointed this out to Ddraig Boruc, hoping he would know what it was. He sucked in his breath and started to fly that little bit faster. "Kernow has allied with a necuart," the old dragon said in a strained whisper that the wind threatened to blow away. Though I wanted to ask him what that was, his face returned to a pensive look, and I knew I wouldn't get another word out of him for some time to come. I had to wonder how much the ddraig lived in the past, lost in his own memories, oblivious to the present. Once I had lived like that, a slave to the future before I had managed some control over my magic. It was a dangerous place to live.

Isikian took the opportunity to quietly slink off and hunt before evening fell. There was precious little wild game in this part of the wilds north of Nixa, especially with the devastation the humans had caused. Some rabbits at least must have remained, as we saw fresh evidence of their presence. They wouldn't provide much meat, but they would give enough to sustain us through the night.

The Nixan wasn't gone long before he returned with three rabbits. Isikian and I both devoured ours hungrily, but Ddraig Boruc was slower with his eating as he continued to mumble and mutter his thoughts.

"If ever you see what looks like a tall, pale human, you are to fly away as fast as you can," the Vatrean eventually said, looking down at the dead rabbit at his paws and starting, as though he hadn't even realised it was there. He tentatively pawed at the soft flesh of the rabbit. "Do you understand me? These creatures will not hesitate to destroy you, if you're lucky. If you let yourself get caught by them then nothing will be able to save you."

Isikian paused in his eating, blood dripping from the scales on his chin. "What are these things then?"

"They are necuart; creatures of darkness and cold. They rarely emerge from the shadows of their barrow-cities in the Twilight Fields, for which the rest of Farenar is often grateful. They are powerful foes, and at least one of them is here," the ddraig explained. He ripped off a chunk of rabbit meat and slowly chewed, pondering over his next words. "Where there are necuart, there are grave bats. We will need to be very careful indeed tonight."

"Grave bats?" Isikian dared to ask.

Ddraig Boruc shuddered. "Nasty things. Bats as big as a dragon. They have a vicious bite and will obey the will of their masters without question. I haven't heard of any coming this far north for a very long time. Not since the cataclysm, at least."

"How come we haven't seen any yet?" I asked. I glanced outside, half-expecting to see shadows flickering across the light. Nothing came.

The old ddraig furrowed his brow, clawing limply at the rabbit at his paws. "Perhaps they have only just arrived to bolster our foe's army. But they are nocturnal creatures, just like their masters. They will only come out at night."

"Exactly when we need to go out," Isikian muttered, pointing out the obvious issue. Avoiding the grave bats and the necuart would be problematic. Our impossible task had suddenly become that much harder.

Nervously we waited for night to fall. From beyond the hills came the sounds of humans shouting and calling. It sounded like a celebration was underway; some festivities lasting long into the evening.

We struggled to stay awake as the air cooled. To try and stave off my tiredness I stood guard just outside the cave. A strong wind blew from the north, bringing with it every scent of the camp. Cooked flesh was by far the strongest smell. I had never understood the human need to sear everything they ate with flame, as there was nothing quite like the taste and texture of freshly-killed meat, nor the warmth of their blood.

It looked like the night would be a clear one, and I wasn't sure if that was good or not. Some clouds would have provided us some cover as we flew over the camp, but the stars were shining brightly, giving us more light to see by. It was a difficult compromise, and I could not make up my mind on which I would have preferred, no matter how long I thought about it.

Then the first grave bat flew overhead, and I shrunk down as low as I could against the ground, not daring to make a sound. It was every bit as terrifying as Ddraig Boruc had said. The bat's furred body was a little larger than a dragon's, and its leathery wings were at least eleven feet wide. Even from this distance I could see its sharp teeth and claws. I had no doubt that it would be a formidable enemy, a fighter every bit as tough as even the strongest Axaatl warrior. If it had seen me, it showed no interest in me at all.

Three more bats flew overhead before Isikian joined my vigil. Ddraig Boruc came out soon after, and together we waited for the noises from the camp to die down enough to risk flying over. That didn't come until long after the last of the sunlight had disappeared below the horizon. The moon would not rise for a while longer. Starlight was all we had.

Finally, the time came for us to take to wing. We flew silently and low to best avoid the marauding grave bats. There were a few human guards on the camp's perimeter, but it wasn't difficult to bypass them as again none of them even seemed to pay any attention to the sky. Whether it was incompetence, overconfidence, or both, I wasn't sure, but I couldn't believe they weren't expecting any attacks from above. Their only enemies here would be dragons.

There were enough campfires still lit that could see where we were going, though the smoke made my eyes water as we flew overhead. Only a couple of humans still wandered around, all of whom appeared to be patrolling guards. They were all armed with the new guns we so greatly feared, deadly weapons that would kill us from incredible distances. Our scales couldn't protect us from such devices.

Towards the far end of the camp was the location of their largest tents. They offered little in the way of shelter in comparison to the sturdy structures that the humans built their cities with, but they seemed a lot more spacious than the cramped tents barely large enough for a dragon to spread their wings in. I had no doubt that we would find George in one of these, and we came down to land behind the largest tent of them all. It was three times the height of a human at its tallest point and looked wide enough for ten dragons to stand side-by-side, wings outstretched.

The stench of humans was everywhere. It pervaded every surface, obliterating any hope I had of picking up any other scent. Relying on my hearing and sight, I stood guard while Isikian and Ddraig Boruc searched for a way to enter the tent. They scratched around the bottom of the canvas walls, hoping to be able to get in beneath, but there was a fabric floor in the way. It would have been easy to tear through, but if possible, we wanted to get in and out without being detected.

Gradually we edged around the tent until we found the main entrance, pulling aside a piece of the canvas that allowed us to slip inside. It wasn't completely dark, but there was very little light to see by as we slowly crept forward, taking care not to bump into anything. Through the gloom I could just make out a large table that dominated the middle of the tent, with a few dozen storage cases located around the edges. There didn't appear to be anyone in here, and nor could I feel the radiating magic of the Axinstone.

Ddraig Boruc leapt up on to the table and started searching through some of the papers left there. I joined him, leaving Isikian to stand guard by the entrance. I could hardly make out anything written on the paper through the darkness, but the ddraig didn't seem to be so hindered. I heard him muttering to himself as he read some of the documents. He didn't linger on anything for long, so I didn't think he found anything important.

As my eyes adjusted to the darkness, I began to make out more of what was in front of me. There were a few maps around, some showing places I didn't recognise, but others of the draconic territories. None were as detailed or complex as the map gifted to me by a couple of humans in Kernow. It had been a wonderful gift, helping us reach George's castle just off the coast of Trevena. It had been in Nataik's possession when we had left Nixa. I mourned the Xigax ness, just as I did the precious map.

On most of the maps were a series of markings I struggled to decipher. The red circles and arrows were easy enough to see, but there were a lot of annotations on the sides written in black markings that I was unable to properly read in the darkness. As the ddraig poured over them, I trusted he was able to glean any important information from them.

Whatever the Vatrean learned, he kept to himself as he silently gestured with a twitch of his wing for us to move on. We quickly stalked across to the next tent, keeping alert for any nearby sound. Nothing was approaching us, and once more we quickly found our way inside. Though once again I failed to feel any pulse of magic from the Axinstone, this tent looked more like what we were after.

My memory of the laboratory where we had initially claimed the Axinstone was understandably hazy, given the immense battle we had fought with Human-Nixans and Nightwings, but this tent reminded me of that place. There were several strange machines all connected to each other with a complicated web of wires. What powered these machines this far into our territory, I had no idea.

Again, Ddraig Boruc was eager to look around, running his paw over many of the machines as he passed by. Unlike with the maps, the mass of metal was all meaningless junk to me. I had no idea what anything in here did, but once more Ddraig Boruc's actions were all confident and assured. I trusted him to know what he was doing.

The ddraig summoned me over with a gesture of his wing. Without a word, he pointed to a small glass box that looked vaguely familiar. It took me a moment to place it, before realising it looked almost identical to the device that had held the Axinstone in George's laboratory in Trevena. I was quickly able to open it up. Though it was empty, I could feel the residue of magic inside the container. The Axinstone had been here. We weren't far away.

Now that I had detected a sense of the Axinstone's magic, it didn't take long for Isikian and me to find the whispering trail it had left in the air. I couldn't be sure when they had taken it away, but the sensation was a couple of hours old at least.

Cautiously we made our way through the camp, the magical residue leading us far away from the larger tents. Three times we almost ran into a patrolling guard, but each time we heard them coming and could shrink into the shadows before someone saw us. The cold was starting to sap our strength, but our reflexes were still alert enough to any danger. Beyond keeping all my senses alert for approaching humans, I didn't pay any real attention to where I was going, not until I felt a paw on my tail. Only then did I look up and see what lay just ahead.

A wall of darkness faced us, a blackness so intense that I could see nothing through it, as though a physical barrier existed there. Light from the campfires flickered on the grass until, like a solid boundary, darkness replaced the light. Slowly I crept forward, reaching out with a paw to touch the darkness. Nothing resisted my movement. My paw vanished into it.

The air was so cold here, and it chilled me to the bone. I shivered and pulled my wings a little closer to my body, trying to conserve as much heat as I could. This had to be some form of magic. The temperature had dropped too quickly to be natural.

Ddraig Boruc came up to my side as I pulled my paw back into the flickering fire light. "Necuart are close by," the ddraig whispered softly, confirming my suspicions. The pale men must be guarding the Axinstone, for the magical trail led right into the heart of the darkness.

I did not hesitate. Had I done so, I wouldn't have been able to maintain the courage I needed to walk on into the pitch darkness. My eyes were useless. I could see absolutely nothing, not even the end of my muzzle. I blindly blundered on, hoping I didn't walk into anything or anyone. A sharp pinch on my tail told me one of the other dragons had taken it in their mouth so we didn't separate.

It almost felt like I wasn't moving at all. The unseen grass beneath my paws felt the same with every step. The air was getting colder too. I was sure that if I could see it, my breath would be frosting into a cloud of vapour. No sounds reached my ears, but I couldn't shake the feeling that somehow, something was watching us through the impenetrable darkness.

The darkness shifted. Like clouds parting, a crimson glow began to emerge through the shadow. The light burned my eyes as it pulsed. With it came a wave of such intense power that I staggered forward, tearing my tail from the grip of the dragon behind me. A second burst of magic radiated out, but this time I was prepared for it. Suspended in the middle of the darkness was the Axinstone, shining like a beacon in the void.

A cold voice sung out from beyond the gloom. "Three little dragons, stumbling through the night. Are they going to die? I think they might." Though the voice was light and musical, I could easily detect the icy malice behind the words. I was in no doubt whatsoever that this was the voice of a necuart. I forced myself to ignore him, trying to block him out as he continued to sing threats towards us.

I took another step forward and suddenly the darkness lifted completely. There was a ring of light surrounding the Axinstone, held aloft on an ornate pedestal of silver and gold. I could see no sign of the singing necuart. Behind me, Isikian and Ddraig Boruc emerged blinking into the crimson glow.

Isikian made a move for the Axinstone, but the ddraig flung his wing in front of the Nixan, holding him back. "Wait. This isn't as easy as it looks," the old dragon said. Under his direction, the three of us spread out around the circle of light. I could feel the power of the Axinstone's magic on my scales, but I wasn't about to disobey Ddraig Boruc's warnings and leap forward yet.

"What now then?" Isikian hissed from the far side of the pedestal. He pawed at the grass, eager to move forward. The singing had stopped. It felt like we were all alone, a small sphere of light amongst the never-ending darkness. I tried to keep my eyes on the Axinstone in an attempt to ignore the terrifying void. The cold air was starting to get to me now, my wings drooping slightly from my sides. I didn't know how much longer my endurance could last.

I closed my eyes as I reached out with my magic to the warming touch of the Axinstone. Even that was not enough to quell the chill in my blood, but the golden light of eternity still opened out in front of me.

I Saw quick flashes of the future. They came at me so quickly I could barely understand them. Just one thing was clear. I knew what I needed to do to get the Axinstone. After that, I would have to rely on the present, not the future.

"When you get the chance, fly to safety," I whispered, hoping that Ddraig Boruc was close enough to hear me and the creatures in the darkness could not. "Get back to Laxtal as quickly as you can and warn Ddraig Anzig about the necuart. I will get the Axinstone."

"Are you sure?" the Vatrean ddraig said.

I wanted to shake my head. I was far from sure. "I've Seen a way," I lied. The future was anything but certain. So much risk to take. But it was the only chance we had.

My eyes opened. The magical connection to the Axinstone severed. A pocket of darkness separated from the rest, forming into a vaguely human shape that towered over us. Pale skin and red eyes shone from the darkness. The necuart grinned wolfishly, long fangs extending below his lower lip. He stood between Ddraig Boruc and Isikian. Though the Nixan backed away, the Vatrean dragon held his ground.

"So, my little dragons, after the Axinstone are you?" the necuart said, extending his pale, spindly hands outwards.

"What do you care?" I retorted, doing my utmost not to quail in fear. If I wanted the right future to emerge, then I needed to goad the necuart away from the pedestal. His eyes met mine. There was a cold fury there, but also a calm, measured curiosity.

The necuart chuckled, a sound like steel scraped across rock. "I care, dragon, because George asked me to guard it for him. It would not look good on me if it were to disappear without good reason."

"And you serve the human George?" I asked, finding courage to speak where I thought there was none. Behind the necuart, I could see Ddraig Boruc's frantic movements, gesturing with his wing for my silence. I ignored the Vatrean. This was what I needed to do.

"Serve? No dragon, I do not serve him. He offered me terms that were beneficial to me. That is all. I have no allegiance to the human but for one of mutual benefit," the necuart said, folding his arms across his chest.

"And… and what terms can we offer you to let us take it?" I stuttered, ignoring Ddraig Boruc's continued attempts to silence me. The old dragon was urging me to turn and flee. Isikian had already gone, vanishing back into the darkness.

The necuart laughed again. "You seek to bargain with me, dragon? You wish to negotiate terms for the Axinstone?"

I nodded quickly. "Yes, yes. Anything you ask for, I shall provide," I said, bowing my head and spreading my wings in a sign of submission.

The necuart took a couple of steps forward, taking him level the pedestal. He extended his hand out towards me. "Anything?" he crooned. "Even your blood, dragon? If I asked for your blood and your service, would you give it to me?"

"If that is what you ask, then that is what I offer."

Ddraig Boruc leaped into the air behind the necuart, but pale figure was more aware of his surroundings than he seemed. He spun around and struck Ddraig Boruc mid-flight, sending the old dragon sprawling. The creature leered at me, the ddraig ignored once more, a hungry gleam in his eyes as he pressed his finger against my face. I shivered at the ice-cold touch of the necuart's finger against my scales.

"No. That is not enough. There is nothing a dragon can offer me that I desire, since I already possess the soul of a brethren," the necuart said, gripping my jaw and lifting me into the air. I dangled uselessly, my legs unable to find purchase on ground or necuart, my mouth effectively sealed shut by the creature's powerful grip. He hissed in my ear, his long fangs touching the scales on my neck. "You aren't even worthy of my time."

The creature tossed me away, bouncing across the ground a few times before coming to a rest by the wall of darkness. Dazed, I tried to get back up to my paws. At the second attempt I made it up, shuffling my wings to make sure I hadn't hurt them in my fall. The necuart regarded me coldly for a few moments, before turning to face my companions, moving a few long strides away from the pedestal.

They had already gone. The necuart hissed in annoyance, but that turned into a howl of dismay as I used his distraction to lunge for the Axinstone, plucking it from its pedestal. Power surged through my paws as I evaded the necuart's grabbing hands. I flicked out at him with my tail, catching him across the jaw as I passed, giving me just a moment to escape.

Magic pulled at my mind. Tantalising glimpses of the future tempted me, offering their insight. I clamped down on my magic as best I could. It would only be a distraction.

Blindly, I flew through the darkness, desperate to get away from the necuart. I didn't know what he was capable of, or when I would be safe from him. I had no idea where I was going, or where Isikian and Ddraig Boruc had gone. All I cared about now was escaping the ire of the necuart, to find my companions and keep the Axinstone from falling back into the hands of the pale one.

Shrieks filled the darkness. Screams that were not human or draconic. The grave bats were coming. As I emerged from the darkness and into the camp, I saw them filling the sky. There were hundreds of them, and I quickly trimmed my wings to glide towards the closest tents. The sounds of human activity were louder now. The whole encampment was starting to wake up as the bats and necuart set off the alarms.

Free from the unnatural darkness, my body started to warm up slightly, though I could still feel a cold chill in my tail. I glanced back. The necuart melted out of the darkness, easily keeping pace with me without any exertion. He gave chase as I twisted my body through the narrow gaps between the tents. The guidewires that supported the canvas threatened to throw me to the ground every time the edges of my wings caught them, but somehow, I remained in the air.

"You will not get away with the rune, dragon," the necuart said as he bounded after me, his feet barely touching the ground as he ran. He was not far behind, almost close enough to reach out and grab my tail. Above my head the grave bats continued to swarm, slowly descending. I was running out of options.

Giving up on my wings, I dropped to the ground and ran, holding the Axinstone in my mouth. My jaw quivered with the raw magic emanating from the stone, but I wasn't about to let it go. Golden light sparked from my paws with each step. Small flashes of the future burst before my eyes. Bloodshed. Screams. Pain. Death. All were coming for this place. I had to ignore it all.

I used my smaller size wherever I could, darting under tables and chairs, kicking over as much as I could to throw obstacles into my path and slow the necuart. Nothing worked. No matter what I did, he remained just behind my tail.

I turned another corner, only to face down four waiting humans. The necuart behind me snickered. He had seen what I already knew. I had nowhere left to run. The creature was behind me, the humans in front. Grave bats covered the sky.

I needed no magic to tell me I had no way out. No chance of escape. I lowered my head and spread my wings, submitting to the humans as I placed the Axinstone at their feet. The necuart loomed behind me, covering me in his shadow. I tried not to think about his hungry red eyes.

One of the humans stepped forward. His eyes were as cold as the necuart's. Though I had never seen him before, I knew exactly who this was. "George Symons," I said with a growl. This was the human responsible for the invasion on draconic territories, and I was completely at his mercy.

The human ignored me for the moment, addressing the necuart instead. "Have you broken our agreement?"

"His companions got away, but foolishly left the rune for this one," the necuart said bitterly. I didn't dare glance back at him, fearful of what I might see there. The sight in front of me was bad enough. George had raised an eyebrow in thought, tapping his cheek with a finger.

"You're lucky this time. Your failure did not lead to the rune's loss. Go and find the others," George said, snapping his fingers at some humans by his side and spinning on his heel. "Bring the dragon and the rune. Rico will want to hear about the situation."

A human seized me in their hands.

I was a prisoner of George Symons.

# CHAPTER FIFTEEN

**Ellian**

"We know the humans aren't moving anywhere, so they're waiting for something. We don't want to linger long enough for whatever that is to arrive. We have tarried and dithered for a week already. That is a week for them to gain further numbers," Alaron said.

The wyvern was having a hard time convincing Anzig, who was the only one refusing to allow the dragons under his control to fly from the lair. Representatives of all the minor clans had submitted to Alaron's command. Hyantl, commander of the Axaatl forces had also agreed to the wyvern's proposed course of action, as had Ddraig Krateos for Nixa. James McArthur had pledged his support from the humans who had arrived a couple of days previously. Only Anzig remained, but he refused to leave the safety of our lair.

We had gathered on the hill above the gorge so Kyrus and James could join us. The inner passages of the lair had proven too small for the gryphons to navigate, and we doubted the clan would be happy with the presence of another human within the caves. There had been resistance enough to their arrival. Marin and Vinzent had been the most vocal in their protests, but as of yet a physical confrontation had been avoided.

"We know this land. We should wait for them to come to us," Anzig countered, attempting to stare down Alaron.

"Then we wait for them to grow stronger!" Alaron exploded, slamming both wings against the ground in his frustration. His claws tore up the earth. "They wait because they wish to destroy you. If we attack early, we catch them at their weakest."

Prince Kyrus clicked his beak and stepped between dragon and wyvern. His pristine feathers rustled in the wind. "We have no evidence to suggest the humans will target Laxtal. If we wait for them to move, we may well be waiting until spring and summer have come and gone and we begin a new year."

"Our agreement with Esperance will not keep us here for so long. We have other business to attend to elsewhere," Alaron snarled. He edged forward to stand beneath the gryphon so he could continue glaring at the ddraig.

Anzig arched his back as he faced the wyvern. "I will not risk the lives of my clan on such a hopeless attack," he said. He was on the verge of attacking Alaron before I stepped between in, wary of the gryphon's great talons. Ddraig Krateos too moved forward to place himself before the Laxtal ddraig.

"You speak without thinking, Anzig. We waited for our human allies to get here, but that is when we should have flown," Ddraig Krateos said sternly. The Nixan pushed past me to stand directly in front of Anzig. "You risk more lives by staying here. The wyvern speaks the truth. We cannot allow the humans to gather their full strength, for we give them time to finish their task. We don't know what their goals are. They might be gathering forces to attack, at which time Laxtal will fall just as Nixa did. Or we are simply giving them the opportunity to work their magic on the land. We have no cause for delay."

I hung back from the Nixan, inching towards Alaron and Kyrus. I feared Anzig's continued refusal to act would lead me to a decision I didn't want to make. I knew what we had to do to have any hope of survival, and my cousin was firmly taking the exact opposite of that. We simply had to fly out.

Ddraig Krateos and Anzig started to argue, and once more I was afraid my cousin would attack. Muscles in his back twitched, likely a futile attempt to spread his absent wings. Then the Nixan quietly said something I could not make out, but it was enough for Anzig to fall completely silent.

"I do not need help from you," Anzig growled in response to Ddraig Krateos's unheard statement. He barged past the Nixan to glare at Alaron. "I made no agreement to Esperance that lost control of my dragons. I make the decision on what Laxtal does, not you."

Prince Kyrus fluttered his wings and chirped. I could feel his gaze on me. I knew what he expected me to do. Anzig could not be the leader Laxtal needed right now.

Hesitantly, I stepped forward. My heart fluttered in my chest as my cousin's wild fury turned to me. "Anzig, please listen to them. They are right, we can't stay here and wait for the humans to come to us."

Anzig's claws tore through the dry grass. "So, it's true then, is it? You think yourself a better ddraig of Laxtal than me?"

I blinked in surprise. "That isn't what this is about. We need to fly and face this threat before our force breaks apart. You must know that it will be difficult to hold so many clans together if we continue to sit idle."

Anzig scoffed. "Fly? And how do you expect me to do that?"

Involuntarily, my eyes flicked to his back. I quickly looked down again. I didn't want him to think I taunted or mocked him. "You can travel with James. They must travel on paw. They will take you. They can help you."

I knew immediately I had said the wrong thing. Anzig's eyes flashed with anger, and he hissed with such venom that I stepped back. "I don't need help," he spat. "Not from you. Not from any dragon. If it must be this way, then go and fly to your deaths. I am going to go and take what I need."

"Anzig, please…" My pleading was cut short as my cousin lifted his paw. For one terrible moment I thought he was about to strike me. My horror only worsened as he turned his claws to his own scales.

Anzig ripped through the scales on his foreleg, spilling blood onto his paw and wetting the ground. A hushed silence fell as dragon, gryphon, and wyvern watched as Anzig lifted his bloody paw and placed it on my brow. I didn't dare close my eyes, even as the hot and sticky fluid dripped onto my muzzle.

"Blood of the ddraig who came before," Anzig snarled. He held his paw to my head still. "You are Ddraig Ellian of Laxtal now. May the clan prosper under your rule."

"Anzig, don't do this. Please," I whispered.

He dropped his paw and turned away, his tail almost whipping me across the muzzle. "It is already done. Good luck, Ellian. You're going to need it." He didn't look back as he limped away. No one dared to follow him.

Anzig was ddraig of Laxtal no longer. That power now belonged to me. Once before I had been ddraig, before Tsona had deposed me. Now that power was mine once more, and I sincerely wished it was not. Anzig was my cousin, and I was loyal to him, but I had to accept now that he was a weak leader for a time like this.

The grey wyvern regarded me with a critical eye. "So, Ddraig Ellian. What is it going to be? Will Laxtal join us?"

I looked up at Kyrus. The gryphon had warned me I would need to become ddraig if I wanted to do what was best for my clan. That had now happened, but I don't think either of us could have expected Anzig to voluntarily step down. Now I had to be the leader both the gryphons and the wyvern could respect.

There could be no other answer. Not after what had just happened. "We will fly."

Alaron wasted no time in making arrangements. "James, I want you to take your men and leave straight away. You'll have to travel by foot, so it'll take a lot longer for you to get there. Leave behind one of your slate communicators so that we can keep track of your location. Kyrus has experience using them, so give it to him.

"Ddraig Krateos, I want a full report on what each of your dragons can do. I want to know how many healers you have, how many have offensive magic, whatever. Anything they can do, I want to know it. I also want to know the area where the humans have camped. It is closest to your territory, so I need to understand how defensible an area it is, and where we can best shelter overnight.

"And Hyantl. Make sure every dragon is ready and able to fight. We're not going to have any opportunity to rest, so they need to be prepared. Brute force won't be enough to win this battle, but it could go a long way. That's going to be your responsibility. Any questions?"

There were none for the wyvern. As one we all deferred to his judgement, and Ddraig Krateos, James, and Hyantl all left to prepare those under their command. I knew that soon I would need to do the same for Laxtal. I would need to announce myself as ddraig. There would likely be protests. No one from the clan had actually witnessed the exchange of power, and I doubted Anzig would consent to being publicly humiliated by announcing it to them. Perhaps his blood on my face would be enough. I could only hope they would take the word of Kyrus or Alaron that the exchange had occurred.

I knew challenges would come. Yalle and Marin had not been too supportive of my rule previously, and as for Vinzent... the dragonet still turned me cold whenever I thought of him. I had trusted him as a potential mate, and he had spurned that with his harsh words of rejection. He had called me weak. Now I could prove him wrong.

"Are you ready for this, Ddraig Ellian?" Alaron asked me.

"I have no choice. I must be ready," I replied.

The wyvern nodded once. "A good answer, ddraig. Get your clan prepared. We will leave at first light the day after the next." He did not wait for an answer, before shuffling away to find space to launch into the air. Though he appeared a little awkward and clumsy on the ground, once his immensely powerful hind legs launched him into the air, he was perfectly graceful. In his element, he could easily outfly and out-manoeuvre any dragon that dared challenge him. Even the gryphons struggled to match Alaron.

Kyrus stood by my side as we looked out over the flatlands. My territory. But for how long? Would these two days be my last chance to look down upon Laxtal? Anzig had been right in one respect, we were risking the lives of many dragons. Our clan would be decimated, as would those who had pledged numbers to our cause, but it was our only hope.

"I do wonder if your cousin realised that I carried Alaron on my back when we flew here," the gryphon mused, clicking his beak in a manner I had come to recognise as laughter. "He uses his injury to justify every flaw in his character. I wasn't going to tell him that, of course. He was the weakness in your clan. I didn't want to carry him, but it is curious to note that he never even once asked."

"I think it would have hurt his pride to request such a thing from you," I said quietly. "Even walking on paw with the humans would have been a humiliation."

Kyrus chirruped loudly in mirth. "Pride? He is a wingless dragon. He should have precious little of that left."

"He is still my cousin," I replied, pawing the soft grass. I did not want to hear such insults towards him, even if I acknowledged his removal from power had been necessary.

Kyrus bowed his feathered forelegs and spread his wings. "You're right, I apologise. I just say what any gryphon would feel in a similar situation."

I growled, but I still accepted the gryphon's apology. Shouts from below pierced the relative silence as Hyantl ordered a few hundred dragons through more manoeuvres. There had been some early protests from a few Laxtal dragons about taking orders from an Axaatl drake, but those had quickly been quelled after some physical confrontations with both the Axaatl commander and Anzig. Ever since losing his wings, he had not lost a fight. I had only witnessed a few of them, and I had watched on with confusion. Anzig had never held an imposing physical presence. He had always been small in stature and generally preferred to avoid direct conflict.

It wasn't that he had suddenly become a much better fighter, but it seemed that everyone he fought had lost their desire to attack. Anzig had done something to terrify the clan into submission that affected the mind of every last dragon. I doubted I would be able to demand the same terrified respect, but I hoped I wouldn't need to.

Kyrus soon flew off to make arrangements with the other gryphons. I knew my duties were with my clan, but I left to seek out my brother. He would want to know what had just occurred. Mulner had been largely keeping to himself since arriving in Laxtal. He had worn himself out completely in his flight here, attempting to fly throughout the night in his urgency to deliver his message, but he had yet to recover his strength, which alarmed me. A couple of days rest and basking in the sun, wintery and cold though it was, should have been enough time.

I found him at the far end of the gorge, at the narrowest, deepest part as it weaved its way towards the distant mountains, hidden in the deep shadows. The wound on his neck was yet to heal. He insisted he had flown into a tree, though he could not specifically remember such an act. I was not convinced. It looked more like a bite wound to me, but this he had vociferously denied.

I wasted no time in telling him everything that had happened, that I was now ddraig of Laxtal once more. He was surprised, but he smiled as he held me close, holding his wing around me.

"I'm so proud of you, little sister," he said. His voice was hoarse and quiet, little more than a pained whisper.

"You feel cold. Why aren't you in the sun?" I asked, pulling out of his embrace to place my paw on his forehead. His scales felt like ice, as though he hadn't been in the sun all day.

"It hurts my eyes. I can't see in the light," he whispered, stepping away from my touch. His yellow eyes seemed paler than usual, a whiteness to them I had never seen before. "Ellian, I think I'm getting sick. I think something about this place disagrees with me. I should never have come back."

"Let me find Kaz for you. Wait here and I'll bring the healer," I said. I waited only for my brother's affirmative response before bounding into the sky. I would not sit idle and watch Mulner fall into illness, fading away just like our parents. In Kaz, we had access to a healer of far greater skill than any our clan possessed. If he was unable to determine why my brother was so cold and blinded by the light, then no dragon could.

I found the Nixan healer in the central chamber with Haeraig Zeena, along with a few other Nixans. Brushing aside questions from some Laxtal dragons, I interrupted Kaz and begged him to come to the surface with me. My mate's twin asked his haeraig permission to leave, not spreading his wings until she nodded her head.

As we flew back up through the lair, I explained why he was required. Kaz said nothing in response, his eyes dark in thought.

Mulner was lying in the shadows when we returned to him. He barely even responded as Kaz landed by his side, the healer taking care not to land on his outstretched wings. Only the smallest patches of light landed on my brother's extended membranes, certainly not enough to warm his body.

I hung back as Kaz got to work, not wanting to get in the way of the Nixan as he moved around my brother's body. To my eyes it looked like he was doing little more than placing his paw against random points on Mulner's head, chest, and wings, but I convinced myself to put faith in the healer's abilities. Kaz paid particular attention to the wound on Mulner's neck, which was still leaking a small amount of blood. The wounds were two days old. They should have closed by now.

For ten minutes Kaz worked; small crackles of orange light emanating from his paws as they moved over Mulner's scales. My brother twitched and whimpered pitifully, but otherwise didn't seem to be aware of his surroundings. There appeared to be no change. Not even the bite wound on his neck showed any signs of healing, and when Kaz took a couple of steps back with his eyes narrowed in confusion, I knew the news wasn't good.

"I don't understand. There's a different magic in his blood that's causing this, but it's nothing Nixan. It's something I've never seen before," the healer said. He rested his paw against his muzzle as he thought.

I hung my head. Becoming ddraig should have been a joyous moment in my life, but instead it was bringing me nothing but heartache and pain. Not only was I sick with worry about the state of Anzig's mind, but now my brother suffered with an illness not even a Nixan healer could identify. They were two of the closest dragons in my life, along with Airil. I didn't want to lose any of them.

"Unless…" Kaz pondered, breaking into my dark thoughts before stopping again.

"Unless?" I pressed. If there was anything that could help Mulner, I would take it.

"The Laxtal healers use herbs as medicine, is that right? We have always known the limitations to our magic, so sometimes we are forced to use natural medicine too. There is one plant in particular that seems to suppress magic. If your healers have any hutynnu flowers, then it may help stop the magic," Kaz explained, spreading his wings.

"I don't know what that is," I replied. I had never heard of hutynnu flowers before. The brief spark of hope was in danger of extinguishing already.

"I'll find some for you," Kaz said, taking to the air, weaving his way down through the gorge. He was soon out of sight, and I was alone with my brother once more. I lay on the springy heather by his side, listening to his gentle breathing. High overhead I watched the comings and goings of dragons of many different clans. There were those from every western clan here and, but for a few Laxtal protests, everyone worked together. Historic disputes between clans were put aside for the time being, and every day our numbers swelled as ddraigs released more and more of their numbers. It felt like we would soon have every western dragon in Laxtal.

A few dragons had even reached us from the eastern clans. Not everyone agreed with Ddraig Tsona and his draconic allies. About fifty had come from the tiny Clan Fentra alone, on the far borders of Xital. An emissary had also come from Xigax, formalising their support to our cause that Ddraig Aranat of Axaatl had promised. The emissary regretfully told us no army was coming. Axaatl and Xigax worked together to challenge the draconic armies Xital had mustered. This war didn't just challenge Laxtal and Nixa. Anyone who opposed Ddraig Tsona was now feeling his wrath.

How long we could hold this alliance together was another matter entirely. Those old rivalries could be put aside for now, but what would happen to our alliance should one dragon say the wrong thing to another? Alaron was right for many reasons. We needed to fly out, and soon. The humans would only get stronger, and we risked getting weaker with every passing day.

It would fall on my wings to prevent that from happening. I stood beside Ddraig Krateos as one of the leaders of our defence against Tsona and the humans. As ddraig of Laxtal I needed to be out there preparing our forces to fly out, but I simply couldn't leave my brother alone. Nothing else mattered, not until Kaz returned with the hutynnu flowers. Only then would I be able to worry about such concerns.

Until then I would wait, the shadows hiding me from the dragons that flew overhead. If anyone was looking for me, I heard nothing of it.

Mulner seemed to fall asleep. His eyes were closed. He breathed slowly, his lips occasionally parting in a silent snarl as though he was in pain. I wanted to rest my paw on his chest, but I didn't want to disturb him. If he was asleep, then surely some rest would be better than nothing, even if he was in pain.

When Kaz finally returned, he was carrying a bunch of small, red flowers in one paw. They looked freshly picked, the green stalks still covered in a little mud. In the other paw, he held a round slab of grey stone. As soon as he landed, he ground up the flowers against the stone with his paw, until all that remained was a rough powder.

Gently, Kaz eased open Mulner's mouth, before slowly sprinkling the powder on my brother's tongue. The healer held Mulner's muzzle closed as he attempted to spit the powder back out again.

"You have to swallow it," Kaz said, keeping a firm grip on Mulner as he started to thrash in an attempt to throw the healer off. Eventually he succumbed to the Nixan's wishes, and with a disgusted expression on his face he swallowed the powder. Only then did Kaz release him, and Mulner wasted no time in sticking his tongue out, his paw wiping away any leftover residue.

"That was disgusting," he growled, glaring at the Nixan.

Kaz shrugged his wings as he brushed his paws clean. "It should stop the magic harming you. Give it a few minutes and you should be able to return to the light and give you a chance to warm up again. Later, I will try to heal you again."

"Still doesn't change the fact it was disgusting," Mulner muttered. He furled his wings and slowly rose to his paws. He was unsteady, but that would be more due to the cold than any lingering magical effects.

"Are you able to look after him, Kaz?" I asked the Nixan, ignoring Mulner's hurt glare at my insinuations that he needed someone to mind him. Already it seemed my brother was starting to improve. Kaz's hutynnu flowers had been working just as he had expected. Now I needed to turn my attention to the larger matters that plagued the clan.

"He will be safe under my watch, I assure you," Kaz said, sweeping his wings wide and bowing.

Assured that my brother would be safe, I spread my wings and kicked off into the air. I already knew where I would be going – back to the central chamber to announce Anzig's resignation of his duties, and that I was now ddraig in his stead. I would be pressed to announce a haeraig too, but there were precious few I could trust with that sort of power. Once he had recovered, I would speak to Mulner about it. If he intended to remain in Laxtal, then I would need no other alternative.

The central chamber was packed to capacity, as it had been for almost every hour of every day since the influx of dragons from other clans. As had been their habit of late, Yalle, Marin, and Vinzent were near the centre of the cavern, not far from Haeraig Zeena and a group of surviving Nixans.

Yalle looked up as I landed on the raised dais, and the albino bounded up after me, Marin and Vinzent following just behind. "Have you seen the ddraig?" the albino growled. His eyes flicked to the bloody stain still between my eyes.

"You're looking at her," I replied coolly, meeting his eyes and waiting for him to lower his challenging glare. "Anzig has stood down as ddraig, leaving control of the clan to me."

Yalle and Vinzent both ducked their heads in respectful acknowledgment my new rank deserved. For a moment, I didn't think Marin would respond, before he slowly bent his knees.

"Very well, Ddraig. Perhaps you will care to explain the rumours that we are to be vacating the lair on a foolish mission north," Marin said tersely, completely lacking the respect required when addressing the ddraig of the clan.

"They are not just rumours, Marin. Every dragon capable of flying and fighting will join us as we seek to eradicate this human threat once and for all. Alaron believes that we will never have a better time to strike as the humans will only continue to gather in strength. This could well be our only hope," I replied, keeping my voice level as I fought to suppress my annoyance at his rudeness.

I revelled as Yalle's pink eyes widened in fear, an effect matched by Marin. I doubted the two had been attending the lessons the Axaatl warriors had been putting on since their arrival. Conversely, Vinzent had dug his claws into the dust that lay on the cave floor.

"It is suicide. The wyvern does not know what he is proposing," Marin hissed, but I brushed aside his concerns with a flare of my wings.

"It is our last hope," I repeated, before looking away from the growling dragon. He no longer concerned me, and I felt safe in turning my back. Unlike what those from my clan had given me, Ddraig Bakucic wasted no time in bowing his head and offering his congratulations on becoming the clan's ddraig. He asked no questions about the circumstances in which I had taken over from Anzig, for which I was glad. I had no desire to embarrass my cousin further.

I shared a few quick words with the ddraig. Haeraig Zeena soon joined us, allowing me the opportunity to ask if her father had already come down to pass on Alaron's plans. The Nixan ddraig had, which was probably how Yalle had learnt of the intentions to fly out.

"Vinzent," I barked, addressing the silver dragon for the first time since he had broken my heart. He cautiously approached me, keeping his head low the entire time. Of the three dragons who had been making attempts to gather power within the clan, Vinzent was the only one I remotely trusted. That didn't fill me with confidence.

"I need you to ensure every able-bodied dragon in the lair – Laxtal and otherwise – are warned that they need to be ready to fly at first light the day after next. No one is excused, except for parents who must stay behind to look after dragonets," I said, a stern glare in the direction of Yalle and Marin. I would have to pay particular attention to those two to make sure they joined us.

Vinzent bowed his head again, no sign of the old affections that had been present in our every interaction. There was no emotion in his voice at all. "Of course, Ddraig."

I watched him walk away, starting to spread the message through the clan, with many heads turning in my direction as the word slowly rippled outwards. Soon every dragon present would know that our time was almost up. For better or worse, we would meet the humans that threatened our territory and fight them for control of this land.

Though evening was some time away, I felt the need to retreat again for a short while. I hadn't yet had the chance to let my mind settle and think things over. I instructed Yalle to send Airil up to my chambers when he was next seen, before flying up to the caves behind the firepit.

I paused at the chambers that had only briefly been where I had sheltered. Now I was free to continue on and call the ddraig's chambers mine. I hesitated on the threshold. Anzig may still have a few possessions of his own there, and without the assistance of a Nixan he wouldn't have had the opportunity to come here to clear them out, unless he had risked the climb again. Even so, I succumbed to the temptation and pushed past the thin veil that divided chamber from passage.

A flash of silver burst in front of my eyes.

"Now this is interesting," an unfamiliar, metallic voice said, making me leap into the air in fright, a strangled squawk escaping my throat. "You didn't even need to sleep here, and yet my mind can touch yours."

Frantically, I looked around for the source of the voice, but I was completely alone. No one else was here with me, and the passages behind me were empty too. I caught movement in the corner of my eye, and slowly my gaze drew up to the alcove above the fire, where the silver statue had always sat.

The statue moved. Its silver head turned so it could look at me with blank, featureless eyes. I was too scared to even move as it uncurled its body, leaping down from the alcove in one fluid movement. Its body shone amber in the firelight but reflected nothing of its surroundings.

"I must say, Ddraig Ellian, I was not expecting to feel your mind so soon," the statue said, pacing around me with her long, serpentine body. Only my head moved as I tracked her progress around the chamber. She was certainly a ness, I was sure of that, but no statue of solid metal should be able to move as she did. I had to wonder what magic was at work.

The ness grinned, revealing many small, needle-like teeth. "You are more willing to accept I am real than Anzig ever was. He never really believed what his senses were telling him, no matter how much I tried to convince him."

"Anzig can speak to you?" I asked, forcing myself to move once more. I tentatively reached out with a paw, hesitating just before I touched the statue's silver scales. Already I could feel a powerful warmth emanating from her metallic body.

"Only when he was ddraig. His mind is already fading fast from mine," the ness said with a sad shake of her head. She edged closer to me, pressing her body against my outstretched paw. She felt like metal, not of scales and flesh.

"What are you?" I asked her, drawing my paw away from the strange feel of her body.

"I am Mushussu, a fragment of the guardian that once protected dragonkind. I am the shard that ensures the safety of the Laxtal ddraig, which is now you," she replied proudly. She lifted her head, chest swelling without breath. "My magic is not what it once was, though just perhaps things are starting to change again. I feel strength returning. What that may mean I cannot yet say but know this. If you sleep within this chamber overnight, I will be able to protect you from most harm for the next day."

I lay down amongst the pile of furs and rugs that had once belonged to Astar. "That protection will not last long," I said, looking up to the statue. "We will be flying out in a few days to meet our fate with the human army."

The guardian stood in front of the smouldering fire. Though she glowed brightly, the light did not reflect in her silvered scales. "I will do my best to protect you for as long as possible, but until the magic of the guardians is restored, there may be little I can do."

"And what will it take to restore you?" I tilted my head, changing the angle I looked upon the guardian, intrigued by her shiny scales that reflected nothing of the chamber. Some kind of shadow danced over her, one that related to nothing I could see.

Mushussu smiled sadly. "Undoing the events of the cataclysm will take a special dragon with a powerful fate. Perhaps it may be you, Ddraig Ellian. That remains to be seen."

I pawed at the bed of rugs. The scent of Anzig was so strong here, it was hard to believe that this place was now mine. My mind was still buzzing with the fact that the guardian even existed, but there were already so many questions that I wanted to ask her.

"I do not know where he's going," the guardian said. I blinked in confusion, unsure what she had been responding to. She shook her head and frowned. "He didn't tell you he planned on leaving? I thought he… aah, no. He never did, did he?"

"Leave? Why would Anzig leave?" I asked in horror, leaping up to my paws. My tail thrashed, distressed that I had not realised my cousin would be leaving the clan completely. I had thought he would still stay around. This was home for him. There wasn't anywhere else for him to go.

The guardian hissed. "He has had mixed feelings ever since Astar died. The last few days have simply been too much for him. The attack on his wings came dangerously close to breaking his mind. The necessary training from his father and sister only made him ever more vulnerable to this."

"Sister? He doesn't have a sister."

Mushussu blinked a few times. "He never told you that either," she said dully. She turned away from me and unleashed a low stream of words I did not understand. She sounded furious, and her tirade ended in a shrieked crescendo. Her wingless shoulders slumped. "I apologise, Ddraig Ellian. I am not usually so lax with your predecessor's secrets. The magic that bound me has weakened, though that should not be an excuse. Normally, I would be restricted from what I can say, forbidden by a greater force of magic than I possess not to reveal any secret held by a predecessor without permission before they passed on power. Now that I have begun, I suppose I should reveal Astar and Anzig's greatest secret. Please, you must understand that they kept this knowledge hidden for a reason, and though it will no longer have the impact it once would have held, it is up to Anzig to reveal the truth."

I sat back down and listened numbly as Mushussu told me about Anzig's true parentage. He was not the son of Astar, but of Ddraig Krateos. I could hardly believe it. The ddraig of our clan had been a Nixan, after all the protests over a Xital ddraig in Tsona. Of course, I understood the need for continued secrecy; there would be dragons after Anzig's scales for deceiving them, even if he had now fled the clan. What was more, Azlak and Maznar were his siblings.

"I need to see him," I said once Mushussu had finished telling me about Anzig's great secret.

"He… he has already gone," the guardian said, closing her eyes and bowing her head. "I can only just reach his mind still. He left with… he left with his sister? I'm sure it's Maznar he's left with. And there's another. A Nixan. Airil, I think his name is."

"Airil?" I yelped. Why would my mate have left with Anzig? It simply didn't make any sense. There was no way Airil would have left the lair without even telling me where he was going.

"I am sure it is him," Mushussu said, placing a conciliatory paw on my shoulder. I was tempted to shrug off her unfamiliar touch, but instead I found myself leaning in to rest my head against hers.

We stayed like that for a few moments. I had tried to come here to ease my mind, but I had only had more worries piled on top of the existing issues. Was this what it was like to be the ddraig of the clan? If that were so, then I would not shirk away from my responsibilities. It would take more than just a few setbacks to defeat me. I was sure Airil would return when he could. He was likely only doing Anzig a favour, taking him somewhere his wingless body couldn't carry him. I would not worry myself with anything I had no control over.

I trusted Airil. He would not do to me what Vinzent had done.

# CHAPTER SIXTEEN

**Mulner**

The light still burned my eyes, the heat making my scales itch. I mentioned none of this to Kaz, not wanting the healer to worry. The Nixan had been sure the vile tasting flowers would cure my ailment, but they had done little to ease the pain. I endured the suffering, resisting the urge to retreat to the shadows once more. The warmth was doing little to energise me, failing even to chase away the chill that permeated my blood.

It was this place. Laxtal was a curse on my life, and I had been foolish enough to return. The great beasts had scared me enough to leave my quiet refuge and now I was suffering the consequences. I had watched my parents die here. Now I would join them in death.

Once Kaz believed I was beginning to recover, he left me alone to attend to his duties. There weren't any other dragons nearby, the swollen numbers of the clan whipped into a frenzy by the change in leadership and the order to prepare for a flight north. However, there were some gryphons preening in the shadows of some oak trees. They lay amongst the golden leaves on the ground, cleaning and perfecting the set of their feathers. I moved over to join them, not out of any desire for company, but for the need to share the shade they lay in.

There were a few chirruped welcomes, but by and large the strange feathered and furred creatures ignored my presence. The magic that ravaged by body dulled any curiosity I felt towards the gryphons. I was aware I was probably being foolish in not telling Kaz the full extent of my condition, but I couldn't face the constant hassling and harrying from the healer, nor from my sister. She would have her own concerns now that she was ddraig once more.

Out of habit alone, I spread my wings across the leaf-strewn grass. There was no sunlight to absorb in the shadows of the trees, but once they were unfurled I didn't bother exerting the energy required to fold them against my sides again.

"I thought dragons liked lying in the sun," one of the gryphons commented, looking up from her preening for a moment. I sent her a withering glance. Her burnished bronze feathers seemed to shine, even when no direct light struck them. I couldn't help but stare at her, even though it made me lose much of the aggression I had been trying to muster.

The gryphon, seemingly aware of my rapt attention, shook her head from side to side, causing her feathers rustle and shimmer. I noticed she didn't have a crest of feathers around her neck like some of the others had. It must have been a male trait amongst the gryphons, a difference between the genders that dragons did not share to such an extent.

"Enjoying what you see, are you dragon?" the gryphon asked, rising to her paws and slowly ambling over towards me. I tried not to feel intimidated by her great height, far larger than any dragon could ever hope to grow. They dwarfed even the Axaatl dragons. My mouth hung open, but I was unable to project any words. The gryphon chirruped in amusement. "You can admit to it you know. It won't be any shame on you. We are quite magnificent."

"I've seen better," I replied, finding my voice at last. In truth, I could not recall seeing anything looking so pristine and perfect. She didn't have a single feather out of place, and on her hind legs her fur was perfectly groomed. There was no sign of the coarseness I frequently saw in the fur of wildcats.

The gryphon chuckled. "Then I should wish to see this bastion of immense beauty, for it must be great indeed to outshine a gryphon."

"Then you do not look around you enough, for every dragon far surpasses a gryphon for beauty. The shine of scales is far greater than the dull lustre of feathers or fur," I replied, watching her carefully as she lay down just in front of me. Her head was still slightly higher from the ground than mine had I been when standing.

The gryphon's eyes sparkled in mirth as she brushed a feather down with her beak. "You amuse me, dragon. As if any of your kind could match a gryphon for beauty." Once more she laughed, a musical chirrup that drew the momentary attention of some of the other gryphons. "I honour you with my name, Jesara."

"And I am Mulner. It is a pleasure to meet you, Jesara," I replied, surprising myself with my sincerity. It was the first time I had had an intelligent conversation with something that wasn't a dragon. Humans had proved a dull alternative, full of frustrating asides and a general lack of intelligence. This gryphon, though arrogant, seemed capable of a decent conversation and I was glad of her company.

Jesara inclined her head, crossing her feathered legs in front of her body. "If you'll forgive me for commenting, Mulner, but you have a shadow behind your eyes. Have you been touched by magic recently?"

I covered my eyes with my paw. Neither Ellian nor Kaz had noticed that, so was it something that just the gryphon could see? It could be no coincidence though, and there was little point in denying it.

"I don't know what caused it. Not even a Nixan was able to determine it," I said quietly, still hidden behind my paw.

She surprised me with a gentle touch against my scales. The gryphon's taloned paw was large enough to engulf my head, but she softly brushed my paw away so she could look into my eyes again. Though her touch was light, I didn't resist her at all, nor did I stop her as she ran a claw along the side of my muzzle.

"I think I understand what it is. A dark creature has influence over you, but I know something that should be able to resist it," the gryphon said, her claw under my chin lifting my head up.

"I have had hutynnal flowers," I said, shuddering as I recalled the vile taste once more.

Jesara shook her head, her neck feathers ruffling up. "This is no flower. If you're able to fly, I can take you to our apothecary. They should have something to help," she said brightly.

I groaned and rolled onto my back, tucking my wings against my side. I did not feel like I had the energy to take flight, but the gryphon had other ideas entirely. I squawked as she picked me up in her talons, hugging me close to her chest as she beat her powerful wings and lifting into the air. Whereas before her touch had been gentle, now it was firm. One taloned paw wrapped around my neck and shoulders, while her other forepaw held my tail tight, preventing any movement at all.

Unlike dragons, who preferred to sleep underground, the gryphons had shown no aversion to resting beneath the stars, only desiring shelter during the occasional downpour of rain. They had a large gathering just to the east of the clan, at the bottom of the steep hill that led to the gorge. Around two hundred were lying around in the sun, with a further fifty taking shelter beneath some trees. Jesara fluttered down on the edge of the small woodland.

One gryphon called out as Jesara landed, crying out in their strange, musical language. His eyes fixed on me. I tensed as Jesara released me, sending me sprawling across the ground. I looked up in fear at the hundreds of gryphons that surrounded me now. Their avian beaks looked particularly sharp, a predatory gleam in their eyes. Had I been wrong to trust them?

Jesara chirped back to the stranger, standing over me protectively. The two seemed to be having some sort of debate, but I was unable to comprehend their words. After a few moments the other gryphon took to wing and flew off, while Jesara took a step back and looked down at me. I couldn't help but feel the two had been fighting over their prey, in much the same way two wildcats vocally scrapped for the best pickings.

"Ely is going to find the apothecary. Trust me on this, they'll be better able to cure you than any Nixan healer," the gryphon said. It seemed I had been wrong. The gryphons hadn't been arguing which one got to devour me first. In my relief, I didn't answer. As she stepped back, the sun had shone down on my face, sending needles of pain through my eyes. I squinted them shut and crawled forward towards the shadows of the trees, not stopping until I felt the cool shade on my scales.

It was not long before two gryphons descended from the bright sky to land nearby. One of them I recognised as Ely, who immediately slunk off to the sun-drenched plains, but his blue-feathered companion was a stranger I had not seen before. The cobalt colouring on their feathers was uneven in places. Some patches were faded, and I could see flecks of bronze in spots. It took me a moment to realise what I was seeing; the gryphon had stained their feathers blue.

The feathers around the stranger's neck rose as they noticed my curious gaze. "It is not yet complete. I am finding it hard to find the correct berries to complete the dye," they said, nervously tapping the grass with their talons.

"I am sure it will look quite beautiful once it is done," I replied. I was quickly learning that flattery was the best way to get a gryphon to do what I wanted.

As I expected, my comments managed to placate the gryphon, and they bowed their head in response. To be fair, the iridescent blue feathers on the front half of their body made them stand out from the others, a welcome change from the prevalent browns, coppers, and bronzes. They actually did look quite pretty.

"I honour you with my name, Seri. Ely said you needed healing, but failed to provide information beyond that, but he did pique my interest in you. I've never treated a dragon before, and I feel as though

I shall enjoy the experience," the azure-feathered gryphon said. I didn't know if it was just an aspect of their avian faces, but the glint in their eye looked quite sinister. Had I had the strength, I would have attempted to fly away, but as it was I could do no more than lie there, prone on the dry grass.

Jesara seemed to know more about my condition than I did, and she explained my symptoms to the apothecary in a language I could follow. There was one word though that I did not understand, and the gryphons both repeated it multiple times. They were concerned that a creature known as a necuart had captured me. When Seri inspected the wound on my neck they squawked in shock. That was all the evidence they needed to confirm their theory, and the apothecary quickly flew off to acquire her medicines.

"It is as bad as I feared," Jesara said as we waited for Seri to return. She cleared a small area of broken sticks and leaves before settling down, her eyes constantly watching me. "When a necuart bites, it doesn't inject venom, but magic. While there is no cure to a bite, we do have things that will slow and suppress the effects of their magic, if we have caught it early enough. When were you bitten?"

"I don't know. At least two days ago, I think," I said, holding my head in my paws, trying to ignore the ache in my legs. I had no recollection of obtaining the wound on my neck. I had barely noticed the wounds until Ellian had pointed it out, so I could have gotten it any time before then. Surely though I would remember such a thing happening. The fact that there was no cure to this terrified me. I didn't want to live the rest of my life unable to bask in the sun.

"Amnesia is common with necuart bites," Jesara said, keeping her voice level as her eyes scanned the sky. "Can you recall a pale man at all?"

A pale man. Like a half-forgotten dream, I recalled the pale figure I had seen in the distance, the night I had attempted to fly to Laxtal in the dark. I repeated that to the gryphon, and she nodded her head.

"That was a necuart. If it was only a few days ago, then we still have a chance of suppressing this," she said, smoothing out some of her feathers as she spoke. "If there is any chance of stopping this, then Seri will find it. They are the best I know."

"They?"

Jesara's piercing eyes met mine. "They. Seri is neither male nor female. They considered using the same pronouns as the culvari jinna but decided that would be inappropriate. So, they."

"I see," I replied, not understanding at all. I did not have the energy to query what a culvari or a jinna was. I glanced up to the sky, trying to spot Seri's azure feathers, but could see no sign of the apothecary.

There were so many dragons in the sky now, of all different clans. They flew in a v-formation, with an Axaatl dragon at the point. It was a formation for war. A few gryphons flanked the dragons, whether watching or assisting I could not tell at this distance.

Perhaps wisely, Jesara didn't try and press me for any further information about how I was feeling. I was doing my best to ignore the prickling feeling that plagued my scales, and the stabbing pain in my eyes. Even the shadows were becoming too bright for me now. I didn't think it would be much longer before the light would force me to return to the caves below. Only in the total darkness of the underground did I believe I would be comfortable. That was no place for a dragon to stay for long.

When Seri returned, they carried a large leather satchel in their forepaws. They gently placed this on the ground before properly landing. Out of it they pulled several strange devices, most made from glass or metal, but some of stone. I couldn't even begin to guess at the function of any of them, but the gryphon handled them with familiarity, placing them down in what looked like a set order and pattern. Next came a variety of herbs and plants. One held most of Seri's attention; a small white bulb with a pungent smell. They set aside three of the strange bulbs, as well as several sprigs of rose and hawthorn branches.

I watched Seri intently, using their movements as a distraction from my aches and pains. By my side, Jesara resumed her grooming, seeming to pay little attention as the apothecary worked.

Seri started to explain what everything was, stumbling over some of the names as they searched for the term in a language I would understand. The white bulb was garlic, they told me, which had helped to ward off necuart for centuries. Rose and hawthorn also lessened the impact of the magic.

Just like Kaz had done with the hutynnu, Seri ground up the rose and hawthorn in a stone dish, using a few of their metal devices to cut and mash the branches. They then sliced up the garlic and placed it in an odd container, which after a couple of minutes squeezed some clear juice out. They added this to the mixture of ground plant matter, then mixed it all in with a liquid derived from fermented grapes, until eventually a thick paste clung to the edges of the dish.

"I'm… I'm not going to have to eat that, am I?" I asked in revulsion. This looked much worse than the hutynnu flowers.

"I'm afraid so," Seri said, wiping the excess paste off their talons onto the grass.

They pushed the stone dish a little closer towards me, and I wearily forced my legs into action, dragging myself up to my paws. I took a couple of unsteady steps forward until I stood right by the dish. I wrinkled my nose at the smell. This was not going to be pleasant.

I tried to eat the paste as quickly as I could. For the most part if was soft and easy to swallow, but occasionally my teeth crunched down on a small bit of rose or hawthorn. The taste was bitter, but surprisingly not as bad as I had feared. I wasn't about to lick the dish clean, but I was able to consume most of it before I felt like retching.

Seri placed their talons on the back of my head as I stood still, breathing heavily. I tried not to bring it all back up again. "Breathe deeply, dragon. The feeling will pass," they said softly, before whispering some arcane words in their native tongue.

"Will that be enough?" I panted, in between swallowing down a mouthful of bile.

"It's too soon to tell," the apothecary said, gently moving their forepaw down my back. My scales tingled with their touch, a welcome respite from the needles that had started to fade already. "You may need another dose if the necuart was particularly powerful, but I'm hopeful you should start feeling the effects already."

"I think I am," I gasped, a shiver running down my spine. Whether that came from the gryphon's touch or the effects of the medicine, I wasn't sure. Either way, it was proving more effective than Kaz's earlier attempts.

The gryphon apothecary chirped in pleasure as they started to put away the unused devices and ingredients, breaking the contact between us. "You'll never be fully cured as long as the necuart lives, but if you eat a branch of rose every month it should hold the magic at bay. You will also need to stay away from the necuart responsible for injecting you with their magic. Close contact can erase my work," they warned. "Ideally, I would want to keep you close by for a few months at least, so I can keep a close watch on you, but that would mean you would have to come back to the Aerie if we defeat the humans."

"Where is that?" I asked. I had thought myself knowledgeable on the lay of the land around the draconic territories, but I had never heard of the Aerie before. Then again, I hadn't even known gryphons had existed until a few days ago.

"A long way from here," Jesara said, breaking free from her preening to answer. She pulled me back and held me under her forelegs, keeping me sheltered from the sun. "It is our home. You must cross the distant ocean until you reach the windswept coast and towering cliffs of the most beautiful land imaginable."

"There are pristine woodlands and mountains that glow in the setting sun," Seri added. They lay down in front of Jesara and idly pulled some berries out from their leather satchel, organising and counting them even as they spoke. "And that is before you even reach the Aerie itself. It is the home of our species and the nest of Queen Hera, the mother of our Prince Kyrus."

"The Aerie is a spire of glimmering rock," Jesara said. She lifted her head and looked to the sky through the canopy. "Some say it reaches the heavens, though I have been to the highest chambers. It does not quite go so high, but it is still magnificent."

Seri chirped. "It is a land so perfect that even the gods refuse to leave."

I scoffed and shook my head. "If it was so perfect, then why did you leave?"

Jesara's forepaws tensed. Her talons pricked at my scales. "It was a difficult decision."

"For you more than most," Seri said. They leaned across and lightly touched their beak to Jesara's cheek. "She left behind her mate and nest. The eggs will likely crack before she returns home."

I lifted my head and tried to ignore the stab of pain behind my eyes from the sudden movement. "Then, why?"

The gryphon's feathers rustled. "Because if we do not stop people like this, then who is to say if they will turn their attention to the Aerie next? Prince Kyrus believes this is important, and so I do as well."

I looked down at my paws and fell into silence. How important was this? Thanks to the apothecary's medicine, I wouldn't need to avoid the sunlight, but how else would the necuart magic change me? I was convinced this wasn't all over yet, and there would be further consequences of my stupid attempt to fly through the darkness. If I had shown a little more patience that night, this would never have happened. And had it all been worth it? My news had barely been worthwhile. The existence of the monstrous dragons had already been known. The only thing I had been able to provide was their number was greater than they had initially realised.

The two gryphons no longer seemed to be talking to me. Instead, they were having a debate amongst themselves over which part of their homeland was the most wondrous. Seri believed it was the Aerie, and that no one could believe otherwise. Not only did it possess physical beauty, but it also held a spiritual wonder and importance that placed it far above anywhere else.

Jesara disagreed. She believed it was the Caves of a Thousand Stars. She appreciated the Aerie, what gryphon didn't? But that was also the obvious choice, and she thought that more of the territory should get the appreciation such wonders deserved. Every gryphon that stepped inside the caves were taken aback by the sheer beauty that met their eyes. The outer chambers sparkled with gems of every colour, creating a permanent rainbow of dazzling light. Deeper in, the stone walls had become polished and shiny by ancient forces, creating natural mirrors. In the glittering light, a gryphon could see themselves reflected in perfection, a creature of utter magnificence that shone with the light of the gods.

Seri respectfully conceded that Jesara had a point, but the apothecary refused to alter their opinion. The gryphon territories were like a perfect golden crown, but the Aerie was the glorious gemstone that attracted and delighted the eye. The Caves of a Thousand Stars, though a wonder in its own right, was only there to complement and enhance the Aerie.

Once they had settled their debate, or at least agreed to disagree on the matter, Seri checked on me again. They stared intently into my eyes, and I did my best not to look away when they did so. They also checked the bite wound on my neck, which had stopped hurting at last.

"I think it's worked," they chirped.

Jesara lifted her legs, allowing me to crawl out from beneath her. I certainly felt stronger now, and as I spread my wings, I felt no aches or pains. I was still unsteady on my paws, but I hadn't basked in the sun for several days now, nor had I hunted. It was little wonder I was weak. The gryphons understood this.

"Go rest in the sun for a while, Mulner," Jesara said as she stood up. She shook off the dirt and sticks that had stuck to her feathers, brushing the more determined pieces away with her beak and talons. "Seri can watch over you while I hunt for us."

Though once again I disliked the notion that they needed to watch over me, I appreciated the gryphon's offer to hunt. I didn't feel strong or alert enough to hunt even a witless rabbit.

The backdraft from Jesara's wings as she took off almost bundled me over, but somehow I remained on my paws and staggered out into the sunlight. I winced as the light struck my scales, expecting to feel the prickling burn on my back, but it never came. Collapsing on the warm grass, I spread my wings and closed my eyes in bliss, the evening sun's light warming my wing membranes in a moment.

Lying protectively by my side, the apothecary renewed their efforts in preening their feathers. Beneath their blue feathers I could see their naturally coloured bronze ones. They seemed a little embarrassed by them again, as I could just make out a pink flush on their cheeks.

"You wouldn't happen to know of any mulberries or blueberries that grow near here, would you?" they asked, pausing their grooming for just a moment. I shook my head, and they clicked their beak in dismay. "I didn't count on there being so little familiar plant life here.

I had hoped to replenish my stock, but I have yet to find anything that I need. I shall have to learn the local produce before leaving, I think. There could be something here that is more effective than at home."

"But significantly less beautiful of course," I said wryly. I had not intended the gryphon to take my words seriously, but they chirruped happily and agreed with me. I couldn't feel annoyed with them though. It was because of their efforts that I was already feeling so much better, as well as I had been feeling in days. They had done what Kaz had not, and I was grateful for that.

When Jesara returned, I had something else to be thankful for. She carried a whole deer in her forepaws, which she deposited on the ground in front of me before landing and licking her paws clean of blood. The smell of fresh meat was as energising as the sun's light, and I needed no invitation to tear into the warm flesh.

Once I had eaten my fill of the choice meat, I fell back to the grass with a contented sigh. Jesara dragged away the half-eaten carcass, flinging it deeper into the woods for the wildcats to consume.

I looked around at the hundreds of gryphons who shared this part of the plains to lie in. Barely an hour ago I their mere presence had terrified me, but now I felt comforted. They were free of the hatred that seemed to be consuming Laxtal at the moment, and in many ways, they seemed to be the far superior species compared to dragons. Of course, I wouldn't actually tell them that. They probably already believed it, and they didn't need me admitting it to fuel their vanity. I couldn't even dislike them for that. At least they provided an intelligent conversation. I could only hope they didn't look down on me the way I did on humans.

As the sun made its slow passage down towards the horizon, I lay in silence with the gryphons. I daydreamed about what I would do if I survived the upcoming battle. The temptation to fly with Seri and Jesara to the Aerie started to grow, and not just because the apothecary wanted to keep track of the necuart magic in my body. I wanted to see this beauty with my own eyes.

Our number was too great to fit in the central chambers now, so Ellian had summoned the clan outside. She stood above the gorge with Prince Kyrus by her side. Her purple scales shone in the morning sunlight. The rest of the clan watched her from the lower slopes. There had been some murmurings of distrust towards the gryphon's presence alongside the ddraig, but none had raised them directly to my sister. High above soared Alaron, the wyvern impatiently waiting for us to take to wing.

The gryphon had offered up some device to enhance Ellian's voice, and they were trying to set this up whilst the horde of dragons and gryphons waited in restless anticipation. The sun had only just breached the horizon, but there wasn't a single dragon attempting to bask in the morning light. Everyone was alert as the fires had burned hot and bright overnight in preparation for this. A final feast of salted meats had been enjoyed in an attempt to calm nerves, but I doubted I was the only one who hadn't slept.

"Dragons of Laxtal, allies and friends," Ellian's voice called out, far louder than she would ever be able to project naturally. Neither wind nor distance would be able to drown her out, thanks to the strange technology Kyrus had placed before her mouth. "For too long we have sat and waited for the humans to come to us. Nixa suffered for it, though we are glad some survived to warn us of their errors of judgement. We will not make those same mistakes. We will fly out and meet this threat as we have always done, with tooth and claw.

"I know many of you will be afraid. I would be lying to you if I said we are certain to win. These humans will try and kill us all, down to the last dragon, but we will not give in. Until they kill the last of us, we will not stop fighting. That is the Laxtal way. That is the draconic way. Allies of Laxtal, we fly to war. We fly to the deaths of our enemies, or to our own destruction. There can be no turning back now. One way or another, this war ends now. Are you with me?"

A deafening roar greeted Ellian's words, the likes of which I had not heard since Astar's great speeches, not long before my father had succumbed to illness. This was a passionate roar, one that spoke of the clan's desire to rid their land of this human threat. It was not free of the wavering fear though, and to me that concern was healthy. My sister was right. We had no guarantee of success, and even if we were to defeat the Kernow army, it was likely many of our number would die. It could even be after our decimation that Xital's forces could descend upon our weakened clan and easily pick off the remainder of our number. We were about to embark on a futile gesture of resistance, simply because there was no other alternative beyond waiting patiently for our deaths. Even Ellian's biggest dissenters in Saya and Marin had finally come around to her viewpoint.

There was nothing left to say, and Ellian spread her wings to the continued, resonating roars.

My sister, the ddraig, was the first to take to the skies. Behind her flew a thousand gryphons and over ten thousand dragons. It was the largest army Laxtal had ever mustered.

I doubted it would be enough.

# CHAPTER SEVENTEEN

**Azlak**

My cage gently swung in the breeze.

I had not been bound in any way, but my cracked and chipped claws were testament to how strong my prison was. For hours I had tried to escape to no avail. I hadn't even marked the metal bars that confined me. There was no chance to get out, the bars too close together to squeeze through. Even the surface beneath my paws was impervious to claws, as firm and metallic as the rest of the cage.

Humans did their best to ignore me, as I did with them. Given I was in the centre of the camp, in the middle of a large open square between the tents, this was not an easy task. The movement was almost constant, with activity and noise bombarding me from all angles. I soon took to hiding behind my wings, trying my hardest to block out the noise, but it was never enough.

A few dragons were present as well, though not as many as I feared. Mostly, they were from Xital. I recognised others from clans east of Xital, traitors who had allied with the humans. Those dragons, more even than the humans, put on a great show of ignoring me. Their eyes resolutely fixed on anything other than me and my cage.

Hours passed and turned into days. I could feel the Axinstone close by, its magic teasing me with dreams of freedom, but not once did I See any way to escape. Perhaps there wasn't one. If I Saw nothing of the future, did that mean there was none for me to experience?

One thing I could not comprehend was the lack of military presence this deep into the encampment. Hardly any humans who passed carried weapons. Then there were the strange sounds. Ferocious buzzing and whining frequently pounded my skull, often paired with wood splintering. Hammering of wood and stone greeted my ears from all directions, but rarely the clash of steel or the firing of guns I had expected as the humans readied themselves for war. I didn't understand it, despite the amount of time I had to do nothing but sit and think.

Then there were the regular pulses of magic. Some of them came from the Axinstone, a dizzying blast of invisible magic that scrambled my senses. During those times, I squeezed my eyes closed and struggled to get a grip on my magic before I lost myself to the future. But that was not the only source. Other waves of magic, similar in feeling but coming without the tantalising glimmer of the future, came from beyond the camp, closer to the nearby mountains.

It hadn't taken me long to recognise the shape of the peaks. Most of the unknown magic came from a place very close to the cave we had sheltered in on that first night back east of the mountains with the Axinstone. I thought back to the strange things we had discovered in that cave, least of all the massive statue of a dragon reared in pain.

The humans were doing something strange in the mountains. I almost longed for one of them to talk to me. Perhaps they would give away their secrets. None came close enough to test my resolve to engage them.

I waited for the cover of darkness, when the camp was quieter. I traced a claw along the ridge on my paw. I knew I could call out to Kaz so he would know of my capture, but I chose not to. It would worry him, and he would do something rash to try and free me. Short of an army, I knew I would not escape. There was only one choice. I squeezed my paw and thought of Esperance.

The slate beneath my scales vibrated. A few moments later, the shape of Esperance's head formed out of the air.

"Azlak, do you have information for me?"

My throat dry, I shook my head. "I've been captured by the humans. I don't know what they plan on doing to me, but they've been keeping me locked away."

Esperance's brow furrowed. The golden markings across her face flared brightly, even through the slightly fuzzy image imposed on the air. "I am half a world away, Azlak. Even if I could help you without breaking the laws that bind me, I would never reach you in time."

I bowed my head. I had feared that. My paw remained clenched around the slate, but I allowed myself to slump against the bars. "The humans are experimenting with magic. I can feel it often, but I don't know what they're doing with it yet. If I can learn something, I'll let you know."

I almost released my paw. Esperance spoke before I could. "You will need to use your ingenuity to escape. I believe you will find a way. I don't choose anyone to act as my envoy. There is a spark within you that I admire. Do not think yourself helpless."

"I will try."

The image of Esperance faded into the night. I blinked a few times as my eyes adjusted back to the darkness. I would get no help from Esperance. If I was to escape, then I would need to do it all myself. Struggling not to let despair take hold of me, I curled up and tried to ignore the stench of humanity around me.

The next day passed in just the same way, with no human coming to take me. My chances of escape looked equally remote, with no way to break through the bars. As another evening started to fall, I saw a shadow detach from the gloom around it. Like a ghost from the past, Maznar strutted forward from beyond the far row of tents. Unlike everyone else, she did not ignore me.

"Oh, brother, have you been a naughty dragon, to get locked up like that?" the spectre said. She showed all her teeth as she grinned, her red eyes gleaming in mirth.

"What are you doing here?" I hissed. I slammed my shoulder against the bars of my cage in another desperate attempt to escape, but the metal was too strong. If she was here, then it could mean only one thing. She had betrayed us just like Xital had done. We had been wrong to trust Nightwings.

Maznar put her paw against her chest. "Why, I'm making sure our brother gets what he deserves," she said. "He has been wronged, and now I have come to fix that."

I froze in horror as I caught sight of two more dragons emerging from the shadows. Anzig and Airil were here too. My mate's twin stumbled as he walked, his eyes vague and uncertain.

"You said we'd go straight to him," Anzig growled. With his paw, he impatiently scuffed at the muddy ground, Airil repeating the exact same gesture.

"Of course, brother. I wouldn't have you wait for another moment. I just thought it amusing to see the all-knowing seer captured like this," Maznar replied with a flick of her wings. "George will see you soon."

My tail lashed against the bars of my prison. They were going to see George? I didn't understand. How could I have failed to See this? Anzig's sorrowful eyes started to drift away. I bashed the bars to keep his attention.

"Wait, please." I hated how much I pleaded. "He won't help you, Anzig. He'll use you and betray you. They all will."

Anzig bared his teeth. "Help? No. I would accept no help from a human, but I will make him give me what I need."

I shook my head as I stepped back, tail pressing against the other end of my tiny cage. "He won't."

The spectre chuckled. She touched her wing against Anzig's bare back. "How little he knows," she said, eyes gleaming red as she kept staring at me. "Come, brother. We will prove this seer wrong. George will give you exactly what you need."

She bounded on, heading right for one of the largest tents. Anzig and Airil followed behind her without even another word towards me.

"Anzig, please, listen to me. Airil!" I called out, rattling the bars of my cage, but to no avail. Neither responded. My brother didn't even care about me. Whatever it was the spectre had promised, nothing else mattered to him. I would have hoped nothing bad would come from it, but if they were going to see George, I couldn't imagine anything good was about to befall them. I squeezed my eyes shut, trying to summon every scrap of my magic for some desperate way to See an escape. A glimpse of the future.

*Fire. Fire and ash and smoke that rose high enough to blot out the sun, casting all in a choking shadow. The ground scorched bare, stripped of plants and life. Bodies smouldered where they had fallen, still and silent.*

*A horrific, mechanical groaning echoed over the crackle of flames. Amongst the tattered ruins of a canvas city was a towering, charcoal black structure. Belching out smoke and flames, the machine was an amalgamation of technology and magic, pulsing with raw power. An unstoppable weapon that fuelled on the lives it snuffed out.*

*And yet, amongst all the death spewed out by the monstrous machine, three dragons staggered forwards, walking ever closer to it.*

*One gold. One blue. One indistinct and blurred. Their tails entwined around a blazing stone of crimson fire. Three dragons. Three fates.*

A vision I did not wish to witness. There had been the third dragon Esperance had spoken of, but they had appeared hazy and unfocussed to my vision. I did not know who they were, and nor did I know what the strange machine had been, but surely the city of canvas was this one. Just what was it the humans had here?

My isolation didn't last for much longer. A group of four humans emerged from the tent that contained all the scientific equipment and moved towards me with some purpose. At the same time, I felt a huge wave of magic from behind them. They were experimenting with the Axinstone again, and I didn't like the timing of the humans coming for me.

They unlocked my cage. Before I could lash out at the closest human, he pushed my head down with a leather-clad hand. The glove was resistant to tooth and claw, leaving me powerless to resist the iron grip of the four as they slipped a band over my muzzle. They laughed amongst themselves as they carried me back to the tent.

"They never understand the gift we're giving them," one of them said.

Another round of raucous laughter followed. "This one will, soon enough."

I tried to argue with them, to demand how they believed they were helping us, but I couldn't speak through the elastic around my muzzle. All I could do was growl furiously, but that only made them laugh harder.

There were about a dozen humans in the tent. I couldn't see any dragons, but George was present, standing by the machine that held the Axinstone. By his side was a strange human with faded red markings across his skin. A prickle of magic tickled my scales as I looked in his direction. Something was unusual about him, something nagging constantly at the back of my mind. George turned on his heel as my captors placed me on a cold table, each of my limbs tied down tight and secured against the underside of the table so I couldn't even twitch.

"So, dragon, are you ready to witness what I am doing here?" the human asked. He patted me on the head, a condescending gesture I could do nothing to prevent. I growled again, and once more laughter filled my ears. It was not George's voice. I was able to see the man who laughed was the marked stranger. His laugh was cold and cruel.

George's grip tightened around my shoulder. "You should be honoured. You are about to witness the absolute peak of human advancement. In time, more of your kind will come here without the need to be muzzled, but alas, you have proven to be… difficult."

Unless it were the thralls of Tsona and his traitorous allies, I saw no reason any dragon should willingly approach George. No one else would be so foolish. Except for my brother, I realised. I could not see him inside the tent. Wherever Maznar had taken him, it was not here.

Robbed of my voice, I was unable to speak my mind to the human. Not once did he look me in the eye, so even my furious glare was wasted on him. I knew I was utterly powerless, but I also vowed that if afforded the slightest opportunity, I would use it to create as much havoc amongst the humans as I could.

George turned his back on me momentarily, but a quick test of my bonds confirmed that any escape was impossible. The sound of machines powering up filled me with a cold dread; an emanating dull hum set my ears on edge. I thrashed against my bonds once more, in a desperate, futile attempt to escape whatever torture they had prepared for me.

"Try to relax, dragon. It will make everything so much easier if you do," George said as he turned back around to face me. In his hand, he held a large syringe, a long but slender needle extended towards me. A single drip of a clear liquid dripped from the end. I could already feel the heat of the magic emanating from the fluid within. This was human magic, a corruption and taint from the Axinstone's draconic power.

I eyed the needle warily, trying to growl out my protests, but I was unable to get any comprehensible noise past my bound muzzle. The needle touched my scales at the base of my wing, and I thrashed my body as much as my bonds would allow.

George recoiled, before slapping me with the back of his free hand, ceasing my thrashing immediately. Though the blow hurt, the human winced and shook his hand. My scales were hard enough to injure him too. The victory was small though, and the human brandished the needle once more.

"If you keep on thrashing around like that this will snap. I can't imagine the pain that will bring to you," George growled. My eyes widened as I shook my head. I had no desire to have the thin piece of metal break beneath my scales.

This time as the human approached, I remained as still as I could, closing my eyes as his shadow loomed over me. I flinched slightly when the needle pressed against the soft flesh beneath my wing and couldn't help but scream into my gag as the human pushed down. For a moment, I thought I could feel the fluid spread out through my body, the foreign substance cooling and numbing my wing and side.

Sensation started to return a few seconds later, but I kept my eyes firmly shut as I breathed heavily through my nose.

Someone loosened my bonds slightly, still not enough to escape, but I was able to shift my legs slightly to find a more comfortable position. I slowly opened my eyes, momentarily blinded as a bright light shone right at me. There were three humans just in front of me. One was George. By his right shoulder was the strange human, with a third just behind him.

I squeezed my forepaws tight, so tempted to cry out mentally for Esperance or Kaz. I was not able to speak, but if I opened communication with them, then perhaps they would see the situation I was in. I resisted that urge. If Esperance could help me, she would have done so already. There was nothing Kaz could do for me, either. I was beyond any help. Slowly my paws uncurled again, opening out to face upwards.

The strange human pushed forward, shoving George to the side before grabbing hold of my right paw. He sliced its bond with a slash of a previously hidden knife. His hand gently rubbed the raised scales on my paw, outlining the mark of the pebble beneath my flesh.

"Not this dragon," the human said abruptly. His eyes narrowed as he looked up at George. "You use this dragon, and you risk involving Ehran. We are not ready for that yet."

"We had a deal, Rico," George said, reaching out to touch the other human's shoulder, but Rico recoiled and pulled away, his hand moving away from my paw as he did so. I had not made a habit of letting humans touch me, but this one felt different to any other. There was an inner heat to his body that ran far hotter than usual. Magic coursed through him.

Rico thrust a finger towards George. "Yes, I know. I gave you the means to run these experiments, but there must always be limits."

George also took a step back and folded his arms across his chest. "We had a deal," he repeated.

"And that deal is off if you use this dragon," Rico replied. His eyes sparked red for a moment as he smiled. It was not a friendly gesture. Even his pale markings darkened, a pulse of red light flowing through them. "This one has been marked by Esperance. If you make an enemy of this dragon, you make an enemy of her. And I am not ready to face her. Not yet."

"Now listen here –" George started to say, before a call on the other side of the tent interrupted him. One of the attendants by the rows of machines summoned him.

"We're getting some strange sensor readings here."

"What?" George snapped, turning and rushing towards the person who had interrupted him. The other human moved across with him, leaving Rico alone with me. I stared up into his red-flecked eyes. They burned with a passionate fury. I would have fled right then if I could. This human hated me with a passion I could not understand. His hands twitched, as though he prepared to throttle me right there.

The strange human leaned against the table to lower his head to my level. "I don't know what their magic is going to do to you," he whispered, each word trembling as though bursting with rage. He glanced over to George and sneered. "With Esperance's magic in your body, it will not react how they intend. The results could be… interesting. I wish I could stay to see it, but I have no desire to get involved in their mistakes. Either they will draw Ehran into this conflict, or they will not. I don't care either way. I have all I need from them. We will meet again soon, little dragon, I can assure you of that. And I want you to do one thing for me. You will pass on a message to Boruc. I know the bastard is still alive, so you will tell him that I am still here and I will finish what I started. Do you understand me?"

I stared into the human's hate-filled eyes. I nodded once.

Rico gripped my jaw in his hand, squeezing tight. "Good. I will make you regret ever coming out of your egg. It will be most enjoyable to see you all suffer."

With that the human shoved my head back to the table. He turned to leave, silently slipping out of the tent. No one paid any attention to his departure, with everyone else concentrating on the machines. With my now-freed paw, I tugged at the bonds restricting my other limbs, but my claws were unable to tear through the sturdy material. It was a few more minutes before anyone turned back to me, by which time I was feeling an unsettling sensation spreading out from my stomach. It burned within me, more intense even than the magic of the Axinstone. A feeling of bile in my throat made me want to gag, but with my muzzle still bound shut I could do nothing but grunt. Something must have attracted the attention of the humans, as out of the corner of my eye I saw them approach me again.

"It's starting," one of them said. It might have been George. I wasn't sure. "Take him outside."

Hands roughly grabbed me as my bonds loosened further. I made no attempt to shake free. My limbs felt numb and listless, though in my chest a great energy was burning. I was barely aware of my captors placing me on the grass outside. The humans retreated out of my limited field of vision. I was free of my bonds, but my wings failed to respond. All I could do was squirm slightly as the heat within grew.

My scales itched as the grass shifted beneath me. A scream tore itself loose from my throat. A scream I had heard before, from within a tin mine upon a rocky headland. It felt like liquid fire had replaced blood within my veins. I arched my back, muzzle pointing to the sun as the fading echoes of my shriek bounced around my mind. The bright light that pierced my eyes was nothing to the pain erupting from every scale.

Reaching out with one forepaw, my claws dug into the earth, gouging out deep ruts in the soil as I struggled to rise to all fours. It took a few attempts, but I finally stood, panting from the exertion. Slowly I opened my eyes to look at the humans who surrounded me in a loose circle. There were more of them now than had been inside the tent. They were all waiting. I wasn't sure I wanted to know what for. Then I saw them. The traitors. Maznar and Anzig. The ness I had rescued, and the dragon I had once called ddraig. They stood in the shadows of humans. My brother and sister. The family I had longed so hard for. Now they gloated at me. Airil stood beside them, a vacant expression on his face.

I snarled at my brother, spreading my wings wide and showing off what he could not. His fear fuelled the magic within me.

My shoulders snapped and lurched forward, almost throwing me back to the ground before I caught my balance again at the last moment. Bones cracked and flesh shifted, my claws digging deeper into the ground as my paws expanded. Scales burned with golden light as flesh bubbled beneath. My tail felt heavy behind me. I thrashed it, trying to understand the sensations it gave me. Something heavy smashed, canvas wrapping around my tail. Only vaguely was I aware of the ever-growing distance between my eyes and the ground.

My shadow twisted on the ground. A deep roar escaped my throat as my wingspan stretched until I could feel tent canvas brushing my wingtips. Humans and traitorous dragons alike shrunk until they were nothing but pitiful creatures before me. Even the tallest human was shorter than my knee. I snarled again at them all, but they were not afraid of me. None of them stepped back in fear or cowered in terror. Only my pathetic, wingless brother showed any signs of panic as he scampered behind the ring of humans.

A growl rumbled from the back of my throat, a deep noise that vibrated through my paws and into the earth below. Still the humans weren't intimidated, not even as I flexed my wings, showing them the full potential of my span. The burning that permeated my flesh and scales no longer felt painful. Instead, I recognised it for what it was. Pure magic. Sheer power.

One human separated himself from the rest to approach me. I snarled as he came forward, his hand extended out towards my muzzle. In his gloved hand was a small shard of rock, emblazoned with a burning dragon's head.

The Axinstone called out to me. An insidious voice whispered in my mind. *"Obey. Obey. You will obey my every command."* It spoke the human's mind. The voice failed to overwhelm a fierce buzzing in my paw. I shook my head to clear my mind.

"Why?" I growled, my voice as deep as gravel. Why should I obey this pitiful human? I could swat him aside in an instant, should I wish. As it was, I revelled in the first moment of panic I saw in the human's eyes.

"You will obey, dragon. You are mine now," he said, his small voice frantic. He held the Axinstone out further, so that its heat started to burn at my muzzle.

"No," I snarled. There was nothing this human could do to me. I could feel his magic in my mind, but every time he sought control my right forepaw vibrated. Each time, I pushed him out. He was powerless against the magic he had given me.

"Why isn't it working? Rico? Why isn't this working?" the human cried out to his companions, but there was no answer from them. I covered the ground between us in half a step, pressing my muzzle against his chest. Terror was evident in his eyes as he gasped out in desperation. "Nightwings. Get Nightwings."

The name triggered a memory. A monstrous ness in the night. Memories flooded back in an instant, and with it, awareness of what I had become.

I roared in George's face, sending him cowering into the dirt as I beat my powerful wings. The Axinstone escaped his grasp, and instinctively I snatched up the tiny shard in one paw before kicking off hard. I eased into the air despite my now-massive bulk. My scales felt hot as I soared over the mass of tents that made up the human encampment. Desperate voices in my mind begged me to return, but I felt no compulsion to listen.

As I flew away with the Axinstone the pleading whispers in my mind grew fainter, and with them, any threat of control. The humans were losing their grip on the shard's powers, and any hope of holding sway over my mind.

I would not be their monster. I was not Nightwings.

I didn't know how far I flew, but I was long out of sight of the encampment before I came to rest, sheltering in the lee of a small hill. The sun was soon to set, casting an amber glow across the land. A small stream flowed by. Tentatively I approached the stream's many pools, fearful of what it would reveal.

My shimmering reflection stared back up at me from the uneven surface. My scales were not the complete black of Nightwings. They were still golden. My face still normal and just how I remembered it. Only I towered far taller than any dragons that had ever been. I was four times the height of a human at least, and proportionally even longer than I had been before. I looked back to the tip of my tail. It must have been at least forty feet away.

Was this what the humans were doing with the Axinstone? Were they creating monsters from dragons? But what had gone wrong with me? I remembered the voice in my mind. It had tried to control me, as they had controlled Nightwings, but something had prevented it. I lifted my forepaw up, tensing the powerful tendons in amazement. I could feel such immense power in every muscle beneath my scales – it both scared and thrilled me. And there, beneath my palm, was the slate Esperance had given me. Was that what had saved me from human control?

I unfurled my other paw, where the Axinstone had embedded between my scales. The shard was so small in my paw, but if anything, I had become more aware of its intense, radiating power. Perhaps now the humans could no longer create monsters such as Nightwings, and… I hesitated with my thoughts… and now myself. I looked towards the setting sun, tempted to fly to it, to keep on flying west until I left draconic lands. In my new form I had no place amongst my kin. I was nothing but a monster and did not deserve to remain in this land.

My wings slumped to my side, and I rested my head against the ground. I had done what we had set out to do – I had taken the Axinstone from George's hand, but at what cost? Somehow, I had to return the tiny shard to Boruc and Isikian so they could return it to Ddraig Krateos, but I couldn't let them see me like this. They would flee the moment they saw me, believing me to be the same evil Nightwings had been. And continued to be, I reflected silently. My sister had willingly returned to George's side, and now with Anzig alongside her. Airil had joined them, but I could not believe my mate's brother had gone willingly. But then, I would not have believed Anzig would betray his species like Tsona had done, but the evidence to the contrary was overwhelming. Something had lured Anzig to the humans. Something Maznar had promised him.

I feared for the state of Laxtal. If the ddraig had abandoned the clan, then what would that leave behind? Even with the Axinstone back in draconic paws, we would need to be at full strength to defeat the human threat. We could not hope to succeed if we remained divided.

I growled my frustration to the darkening sky. Come the morning I would start the search for Boruc and Isikian, if they had even stayed, so I could return the Axinstone to them. There would be no way I could hide my size from my companions. I could only hope they would not flee on sight of me.

As I curled up on the open ground, a new concern seeped into my mind. An unsettling sensation in my stomach warned me of my growing hunger. I looked down at my massive body. A rabbit or even pheasant or two wasn't going to be enough. I vaguely recalled flying over a herd of deer not too far away. I picked up their scent, before wearily spreading my wings in preparation to take to the air once more.

With the Axinstone secure in my clenched paw I began my hunt.

# CHAPTER EIGHTEEN

**Ellian**

I was surprised at how little opposition I faced from my order to fly north. Not only was the clan showing acceptance towards me as ddraig, but they also appeared to trust my decisions without question. Not to say there was total support, but all the opposition had come from the expected areas; the dragons who had been high in favour when Astar had been ddraig. Saya and Marin had reluctantly joined the massive army, forced to join us or else face the humiliation of remaining behind, and the declaration of incapability that came with such a decision. Even my fiercest adversaries would not risk such a black mark on their reputations.

Only a small number of dragons remained behind. The very young and the very old lingered, with a few parents of the dragonets also staying to ensure the safety of those who could not look after themselves. Everyone else flew in my slipstream, following me just as I followed Prince Kyrus and Alaron.

We had flown all day before finding a place to rest for the night, though our progress had not been as great as we had hoped. Organising so many dragons had proven a difficult task. Finding a place to rest before sunset had been even harder. Our only shelter was beneath the canopy of a forest, with nothing to protect us from the wind and cold. I had curled up with Kyrus, the gryphon's fur and feathers providing some warmth. My wings were still fresh, ready to fly again come the sunrise, but the cold threatened to undo most of that energy. Would we be in a fighting condition by the time we reached the human army?

I spent most of my evening with Alaron and the draconic leaders as we tried to work out a plan of attack once we came upon the camping human army. We didn't expect to be able to catch them unawares, as we were sure they would detect our presence well in advance of reaching their location. However, we hoped that if we moved fast enough, we wouldn't give them much time to respond to our assault.

I had hoped for a quiet night, resting between Kyrus's feathered forelegs, but Mushussu's presence arose within me. Her voice was little more than a whisper.

*"Remember, Ellian. Once you sleep this night, then you will lose my protection. I cannot keep you safe in the battle that is to come."*

I sighed and stretched out my forelegs. I knew already I would not be able to respond to her, the magic that bound the guardian also prevented me from speaking of her to another. That also restricted any conversation I may wish to have.

*"You may not be able to speak, but I still know your thoughts. There is not much I wish to say, other than a little advice. These humans are not necessarily what you believe them to be. There is conflict within their camp. Different beliefs are making it difficult for them to decide what to do. Some desire extermination, that much is true. But that is an exploitation that does not represent their true ideals. If you are smart, you may be able to use this discord to your advantage."*

I kneaded the soft ground, my claws easily ripping through the soil to dislodge a few bugs that scurried away for better shelter. I had known not all of the humans believed in our extinction; James McArthur was proof enough of that. But I had not known that belief spread wider than James's small group.

*"I do not know how strong this belief is, but it may be enough that they will surrender with a show of force, or if you manage to defeat the human responsible for this."*

I could only just hold back my snarl. George. This was the human we needed to target.

Mushussu's smugness drifted through my mind, even from such a distance. *"You would be wrong. George has his own plans, yes. And they are corrupting, but he is not the human who will see dragonkind destroyed. I have had enough contact with Anzig's mind to learn what he has been told by his sister. His insights have been truly fascinating. George will corrupt and control dragonkind, so he is still a threat to you. But it is the human called Rico who is the true danger. I wish I could tell you more about this human, but all I know is his name and his purpose. Destroy this human and you will have a chance."*

Rico. I had heard that name before. In my imprisonment in Xital. Was this the human who controlled the army? It would be important information to take to Alaron in the morning. The guardian had given me good news.

*"You are welcome, Ellian. I will leave you now. I wish you the best of luck in this coming battle, and I hope to feel your mind against mine once more. With no clear line of succession following you, this may be the last contact with dragons I have. I do not want that future."*

A shiver of fear ran down my back and into my tail. The emotion did not solely come from me. Then, quite suddenly, my mind was my own once more. She was gone. I hoped to feel her again.

I sleepily gazed into the nearby flickering fire, hoping that now I would have the chance to rest as I desired. Before I had the chance to even close my eyes, shrieks and snarls distracted me, emanating from not too far distant. With a weary groan, I rose to my paws, knowing that I would need to investigate the confrontation, and to diffuse the situation if needed.

Kyrus didn't move as I shook some stray twigs off my wings, the gryphon's head tucked under his wing as he slept. A few other dragons had woken at the sounds of fighting, though none seemed as eager to move through the trees and find the cause.

Shouts started to echo more loudly throughout the trees, and it only took a moment to recognise the voices. I knew I shouldn't have been surprised to hear Marin and Vinzent causing a ruckus, but I had hoped it wouldn't come during the first night of travel. By the sound of it, they were unhappy taking orders from a dragon who wasn't their ddraig. I hurried on, not wanting the situation to escalate.

Were it not for the many small fires carefully lit in pits of dirt, I would never have negotiated my way through the dark forest. As it was, I had to be incredibly careful not to walk face-first into any trees. The darkness was oppressive, and the cold air did nothing to clear the sluggishness from my mind.

Vinzent and Marin were both stood next to one of the firepits, wings flared as they stared down at the dark form in front of them. Though it was hard to see in the gloom, the silhouette was distinctive enough to recognise the shape of Alaron. The wyvern showed no sign of backing down from the two dragons as I stepped forward into the firelight, the shouted accusations dying on the tongues of Vinzent and Marin as they saw me.

"What is this all about?" I hissed towards the two dragons, whose bravado diminished in my presence. They slowly folded their wings against their backs, turning their eyes from me.

Neither dragon seemed willing to answer me, so I turned instead to the wyvern, ducking my head in respect. If the Laxtal dragons needed any reminder who their commander was, then a show of submission to the wyvern was necessary.

"Some of your clan have no concept of respect, Ddraig Ellian," the wyvern growled. His tail thrashed in his anger, the vicious barb at the tip scratching the nearest tree. His powerful wings flexed against his sides. "They need to learn who their superiors are."

"You are not my superior. You are not my ddraig," Marin snapped, flaring his wings again and stepping forward, Vinzent at his tail. Their subservience melted into the night at the sound of Alaron's accusations.

"I am not your ddraig, that is true, but whilst you are a part of my army, you will listen to and obey my every command," Alaron hissed.

I positioned myself between the wyvern and the dragons, making sure they couldn't easily get at each other.

Marin was not impressed by Alaron's response. "I do not take orders from anyone outside my clan. You have no right to control me."

This time I intervened, advancing on Marin, making the older dragon back away. "He has every right to control you. He is your commander, and you will obey him because I have ordered you to. That should be enough," I snarled, staring Marin down before I turned my gaze to Vinzent. The dragon refused to look away for far longer than was polite.

"I do not listen to cripples," Vinzent said, moving his eyes from me and on to the wyvern.

Silence fell and I turned cold. Alaron pushed me out of the way so he could stare down the silver dragon, muzzles barely an inch apart. "What did you call me?"

Marin's confidence fled him, and he made a hasty retreat from the wyvern, but Vinzent held firm. Grey wyvern and silver dragon stood nose to nose, neither refusing to stand down. I knew that if I did not intervene, the situation would only escalate. I had to lay down my authority or I would risk losing the confidence of Marin and Saya, and those like-minded.

"You will submit and apologise to Alaron," I growled at the dragon, but he shook his head, parting his lips and revealing his teeth in disdain. An open display of insubordination that he enhanced with a slow and deliberate spread of his wings.

"I will do no such thing. I will not sit idle and watch as dragons are led to their deaths by a weak cripple," Vinzent said in a low growl, every word carefully chosen as he continued to stare down Alaron, who bristled in rage. I wanted to cover my face with my wing.

"Weak? Cripple? You should show some respect, unless you're willing to back your words with tooth and claw," the wyvern responded, thrusting a clawed wingtip into Vinzent's chest.

"Vinzent, don't," I protested weakly, but he completely ignored me. Even Marin watched on in fear, barely able to keep his eyes on the feuding pair. Saya was by his side, her head held high. There was a small audience growing in the darkness now, both gryphon and dragon watching on with curiosity as Vinzent foolishly accepted Alaron's challenge. It was not often two dragons fought to resolve a dispute. There was a morbid intrigue at the possibility of spilling blood. I could not help but hear the whispered words of excitement, predictions made about who would win. Few favoured the wyvern.

Vinzent made the first move, attempting to strike the wyvern's wing, but Alaron easily evaded the strike, darting to his right with a fluid movement that belied his usual lack of grace on the ground. The wyvern's tail lashed out, striking his opponent on the shoulder with a loud crack. He struck with the blunt end of the barb, not piercing the scales.

Alaron followed up with a strike from his wing. His claws raked across Vinzent's nose.

With a pained yelp, Vinzent leaped backwards, out of range of Alaron's tail and claws. A few drops of blood dripped from the tip of his muzzle. The confidence that had been in his eyes seemed to drain away as he warily circled the wyvern.

Again, the dragon lunged. His teeth snapped on empty air, the wyvern easily evading him. Vinzent knew how to fight. He was strong and powerful, but he could not get near Alaron. No matter what he did, he failed to lay a single claw on his opponent. He lashed out wildly, losing all form as he leaped forward with a snarl.

When Alaron's assault came, it was brutal and swift. I couldn't keep track of his movements, his wings, tail, and legs all used to strike and block with alarming pace. Yet he never used the weapon that looked the most dangerous. The barb at the tip of his tail remained clean of blood. He didn't need it. His teeth sunk into Vinzent's shoulder, who howled in pain and humiliation. His wings were already torn and bleeding as he struggled to free himself from the wyvern's jaws.

Vinzent eventually found his mark, raking his hindclaws down the side of Alaron's leg. The wyvern hissed as he threw Vinzent away. The dragon landed awkwardly and rolled over onto his back, and for a moment I thought he may have broken his wings and was already defeated. Alaron must have thought so too, as he paused to stand over his foe.

"Are we done yet?" the wyvern snarled, spitting out some of Vinzent's blood.

Striking out with his tail, Vinzent grabbed hold of Alaron's standing leg and tugged him to the ground. The wyvern fell with a surprised squawk as the dragon scrambled to his paws. In a flash, Vinzent was on top of his opponent, trying to reach the wyvern's throat with his teeth, but always held just out of reach by the grey's wings.

Not for one moment did Alaron look concerned. His strong wingarms held Vinzent away as he took a moment to position his legs against the dragon's chest. With a powerful lunge, Alaron tore down Vinzent's flanks, his claws slashing twin wounds down the dragon's sides. Silver scales shed over the dirt, stained red by blood.

Only then did Alaron use his tail fully. The barb struck out, moving almost too quick to see. The sharp point punctured Vinzent's scales with ease.

Once more, Vinzent screamed in agony, rolling away from Alaron, but this time the wyvern was not about to let him go. He pinned down the dragon with his clawed wing, pressing down hard on his throat.

"Will you submit?" Alaron growled. The fight was over. Vinzent hadn't stood a chance against the wyvern.

"I will not," Vinzent said through gritted teeth, fighting through the clear pain.

Alaron snarled, pressing his muzzle against the dragon's. His tail slowly lifted, the barb waving so that the dragonet would easily be able to see it. "My poison is already in your blood. Submit now and you shall get the antidote. Know that untreated, it will be fatal."

Vinzent growled. He spat in Alaron's face.

The wyvern tightened his grip on Vinzent's throat. His barbed tail lashed dangerously close to the dragon's scales, threatening another dose. "You wish to keep on fighting?"

"I will not submit to a cripple," Vinzent retorted, weakly pushing against the wyvern's chest.

Alaron looked to me. He asked for permission. My body cold, I nodded my head. There could be no mercy for this.

"So be it," Alaron said, releasing his grip on Vinzent. The dragon looked surprised, raising his head slightly, only to be struck hard by the wyvern's wing. A loud crack rang through the air. Vinzent fell back to the ground, his head at an odd angle to his body.

Calmly, Alaron moved away from the motionless body of his adversary. Blood dripped from the wound on his leg, but most of the crimson that stained his scales came from Vinzent. The dragon who could once have been my mate. I tried to feel some shock or horror that I had just watched him die, but I felt nothing. It was not just the cold night air that sapped my emotions.

"Anyone else questioning my authority?" the wyvern snarled, glaring in particular towards Marin. The dragon quickly lowered his head and backed away. Any resistance he had towards Alaron's command had been convincingly eradicated.

With an odd feeling of detachment, I watched as a gryphon came forward with Saya to carry away the lifeless dragon. The ness could not keep her eyes off the body of her son. I did not look away until his silver form disappeared into the gloom.

"I am sorry you had to bear witness, Ddraig Ellian," Alaron said, breaking me from my reverie. He limped over to me, carefully avoiding putting pressure on his injured leg.

"You should see a healer about that," I said distantly. Shock at the events I had just witnessed, coupled with the increasingly cool temperature, my thoughts were becoming increasingly sluggish.

Alaron looked back at his leg, flexing it tentatively as he leaned on his wings, before gently placing it back on the ground. "I suppose you're right. But you should rest while you can, Ddraig Ellian. I can deal with any further dissenters if necessary."

I nodded. Despite the action and drama that had played out before my eyes, sleep was proving to be a compelling option. I would have a better opportunity to think matters through when exhaustion didn't fog my mind.

Despite his injuries, Alaron escorted me to my claimed spot of the forest. Kyrus was still lying in the exact same position I had left him in, with his head tucked beneath his wing. I doubted he had even realised I had left.

After bidding good night to the wyvern, I curled up again in Kyrus's waiting forelegs. My last thought was of Airil, hoping that wherever my mate was, he was safe. Then sleep took me, and I rested at last.

News of Vinzent's dissent and resulting death had spread noticeably by the time I woke. Kyrus roused me with a loud chirrup just as the morning sun breached the horizon, and soon the dawn chorus of gryphons started to wake even the deepest sleepers. The gryphon prince flew off to start the morning hunt, leaving me to find a patch of sunlight. I didn't know if it was just a result of sleeping away from the shelter of the lair, but I certainly noticed the cooler air of winter as I tried to find a warm spot to bask in. I knew I would not have long to warm up before Alaron called us up into the air again.

"Is it true what they're saying, Ddraig?"

The intrusion startled me, but when I looked up, I saw only a sombre Yalle. The albino bowed his head. For a few moments I stayed in silence, ignoring Yalle's question as I looked out through the forest at the many dragons and gryphons all waking up together. It was remarkable, seeing so many dragons from different clans able to put aside their differences and sleep together. It gave me some hope to erase the troubles of the night.

Yalle spoke again, and I realised I had not answered him. "Did the wyvern really kill Vinzent?"

There was no anger in the albino's voice, only sorrow. It did not sound as though he blamed the wyvern for the young dragon's death. I didn't feel the need to hide anything from him. I explained the night's events, leaving out no detail. I shared the insults told and the arrogance shown. It was for my benefit too, sorting out my own thoughts on the situation. Even still, it barely seemed real, as though it had been little more than an uncomfortable dream.

"It must be so hard on you" Yalle said eventually, placing a consolatory wing around my body. I tensed, but for now made no attempt to shrug off the albino's touch, just tilting my head in confusion. "So sad indeed, losing your mate and brother in one night."

Now I did push Yalle away, spinning around and snarling at him. "Vinzent was not my mate. He never was, and I never had any… wait, brother? What's happened to Mulner?"

Yalle took a couple of steps back, his head bowed right to the ground. "My apologies, Ddraig. I thought you would have been informed by now."

"Of what?" I snapped. A shiver of fear ran down my spine, fearing the worst for my brother. Had he too been involved in a fight last night and lost? I couldn't lose my brother so soon after finding him again.

"He deserted, Ddraig Ellian. He and two gryphons. They fled just after sundown."

A bittersweet relief swept through me. "So, he's still alive?"

"As far as I know, Ddraig," Yalle replied, bowing lower and spreading his wings over the ground. My mind raced. My worst fears allayed slightly, but I was still deeply troubled. Though Mulner was still alive, I knew he was not the type of dragon to abandon his duty without a good cause. There had to be a reason behind his sudden departure, but I didn't understand why he had mentioned nothing to me.

"Did anyone see them fly off? Or talk to them just before? There had to be a witness, right?" I asked Yalle, who simply nodded in response. "Then I want you to bring them to me. And find Kyrus too, if you can. He should know about this as well."

With a little reluctance, Yalle flew off to do my bidding. I hoped to be able to get some answers from the dragon the albino returned with.

While I waited, a few dragons nervously approached and offered their sympathy for Vinzent's death. Each time I aggressively denied the suggestion that I had been at all close to him before he died. It shocked me how the clan's perception could be so inaccurate. I had not held any close feelings towards Vinzent ever since our banishment from Laxtal under Tsona, and I thought I had been obvious about it. I had also not made any attempt to hide my affections for Airil, but apparently the clan had ignored this. After snarling for the sixth time that Vinzent had not been my mate, I slumped on the ground and spread my wings, waiting for Yalle to return.

To my annoyance, it was not the albino who found me next. Instead, it was Marin who landed close by, a dragon and gryphon with him.

"Yalle said you were investigating your brother's desertion," the older dragon said. He fluttered his wings as he landed, tucking them tight to his sides. He kept his head held high. "I was the first to witness them. I overheard their conversation. This Nixan was there as well."

The grey dragon who flew with Kyrus was vaguely familiar, but I couldn't immediately recognise him. He was Nixan, that much was clear. His short horns were so much like Anzig's, a feature I couldn't believe I hadn't noticed before. The signs had all been there, but I shook my head. This was not the time to think of him.

A flutter of feathered wings caught my attention.

"I heard there have been deserters, Ddraig," Kyrus said, almost before his front talons had touched the ground. His beak clicked in what I took to be annoyance. "Do we need to fear them going to the humans and warning them of our plans?"

"My brother was amongst them, Kyrus. An insult to him is an insult to me," I snapped at the gryphon.

He ducked his head in apology. "Please forgive me, Ddraig. I meant no disrespect to you or your kin. I was not aware your brother was involved."

I accepted the gryphon's apology, before turning back to Marin. "I want you to request Alaron's presence here too. He should know the situation," I demanded of the older dragon.

"I'm not your messenger," Marin replied sullenly.

"But I am your ddraig. Do not forget your place," I warned the veteran drake, flaring my wings at him. He shrank in on himself, accepting the rebuke. He spread his wings and took to the air, quickly returning towards the trees. I glared after him until his wings disappeared amongst the foliage. I would not forget his continued insubordination towards me. After all of this was over, if there was anything left of Laxtal left to rule, I would need to do something about the dragons who still postured for control. Marin remained a disrespectful threat. I hoped Saya would no longer be a concern, now that her son was dead.

With Marin out of sight, I returned my attention to Kyrus and the dragon in his shadow. Then the Nixan stepped forward, and I immediately remembered where I knew him from.

"Ddraig Ellian, my name is Inilta. I flew with your cousin to recover the Axinstone," he said, bowing his head. I waited for him to continue. "I do not know what Marin claims he overheard, but I thought you would need the truth from me. Your brother asked for my advice last night. He was after information on magic and on our old lair, though he did not say why. There's nothing left in Nixa but ghosts, but I think that was where he intended to fly."

Kyrus clicked his beak. "And the two gryphons who flew with him, did they honour you with their names?"

Inilta ducked his head towards the gryphon. "They did. Seri and Jesara were their names."

Kyrus paused to smooth down a feather on his neck, his eyes half-closed as he worked. "Your brother will be safe, Ddraig Ellian," he said, pausing in his grooming for a moment. "Seri is my cousin, and Jesara one of their closest friends. They would not have flown on some foolish errand. Your brother will come to no harm, I can assure you of this."

Though Kyrus's assurance did not completely calm my worries, I had no choice to believe what he was saying. I couldn't fly off and chase Mulner down; I had too many duties here to leave. I looked to the northern sky. If the Nixan had been correct, then my brother was somewhere that way, on his way to the ruined lair where the clan of magic had once dwelt. What had attracted Mulner and the two gryphons? I sighed. It was a question I doubted would have an answer, not until my brother returned.

Wingbeats soon heralded the arrival of Alaron and the return of Marin. While Kyrus continued his grooming, I informed the wyvern of the departure of my brother and the two gryphons.

"Mulner has been too long away from the lair," Marin declared. "He barely thinks like a Laxtal dragon anymore. It is no wonder he has abandoned us."

I growled at the older dragon. "You will mind your words, Marin. Unless you know specifically why my brother took flight, you would do well to avoid spreading rumours about my family."

Marin opened his mouth to speak. His eyes flitted across first to Inilta, and then to Alaron. They lingered on the spiked barb on the wyvern's tail. He closed his mouth again.

Alaron stepped forward, moving between me and Marin. The wyvern had attention only for me. "I trust your faith in your brother. He will not betray us, so our flight may still go unnoticed by the humans for another day at least. Prepare your dragons for flight, Ddraig Ellian. If we hold our pace today, then we should reach the heartlands of Nixa before sunfall."

I shivered. Beyond Nixa, we would begin to close in on the last known location of the human camp. There were not many sunrises left before we would face our foe in battle. Despite the morning sunshine warming my wings, I felt cold. How many more sunrises did I have left?

I tried not to think about that.

When Alaron's call came a short while later, I took to wing. Several thousand gryphons and dragons followed.

Our final charge was soon to begin.

# CHAPTER NINETEEN

**Mulner**


"For the last time, would you please tell me why we're flying off on this foolish mission?"

Once again, the gryphons ignored my questions. Ever since leaving the army behind just after sunset, they had deprived me of any and all answers. It was beginning to feel like I was being held captive until no longer of any use. Neither Jesara nor Seri were willing to impart what information they had learned from the Nixan, instead choosing to speak amongst themselves in their own, avian language. The only time they spoke in a language I could understand it was to warn me not to turn back.

It was a struggle to keep up with the gryphons. Their greater wingspan allowed them to cut through the air with ease, and I had to push hard just to keep in their slipstream. I had tired quickly, and it hadn't been long before I had given the gryphons no choice but to land and rest for the remainder of the night. Once morning had come though, it was straight back into the air. They hadn't even afforded me the luxury of basking in the sun. I had forced my cold and aching wings to support my weight. Somehow, I had stayed aloft.

And still I didn't know why we had to fly to Nixa. There would be nothing there but ruins and corpses, and even if we did find something, it would surely be too late to make any significant contribution to the war. I was not looking forward to reaching our destination, but they ignored my pleas to turn around. In the end, my only option was putting my head down and following the two feathered and furred creatures. They would not let me turn back.

Finally, as the day was starting to wane, we began to descend to the ground. I wondered where my sister was. Would she arrive in Nixa before the sun's last rays fell beneath the horizon, or would the wyvern commanding the great army find somewhere else to shelter? I had rarely flown through Nixa, but I recognised enough to know we weren't far away from the former lair of the clan of magic. We settled at the bottom of a wide, sheer-walled valley that separated two hills. Where the ground wasn't rocky, there was a thick layer of springy heather. It would be a cold, but comfortable place to rest for the night.

"I think it's time we gave you an explanation, dragon," Seri said, once we had landed. Their dyed blue feathers glinted in the fading sunlight as they clawed at the heather, kneading it in much the same way a wildcat would. Jesara remained standing as she looked out to the setting sun.

"It had better be a good one," I hissed. I had left my sister behind, my clan and my friends, what few of those I had. If I ever saw them again, they would want to know why I had abandoned them so suddenly. If I couldn't justify my absence from the clan's decisive few days, then I may as well never show my face in Laxtal again. I would be an outcast once more.

"Do you remember what Inilta told us?" Seri asked as they lay down in the indentation she had made in the heather. I resisted the urge to lie down too. I knew that if I did so, I wouldn't get up until sunrise, but I still wanted my questions answered.

"Something about a gryphonstone? It didn't sound powerful to me," I replied wearily. From what Inilta had been saying, it wasn't something that warranted immediate investigation, but Seri and Jesara had been abrupt in their decision to leave after learning of the Nixan artefact.

The apothecary nodded, their steely eyes staring into mine. I couldn't hold their gaze for long. After just a few seconds I had to turn away. As Seri remained in thoughtful silence, I moved over to join Jesara in staring up to the darkening sky. Perhaps the bronze-feathered gryphon would be more willing to answer my questions.

"You don't understand, do you?" Jesara asked before I had the chance to speak. She hadn't looked down, her focus still on the sky.

"I don't," I said. I didn't want to admit my confusion, but if I were to understand then certain sacrifices were necessary. "How can this gryphonstone be so important to you?"

"It's not."

Seri's terse reply stole the breath from my lungs. I swung my neck around to glare at the apothecary, but they coolly returned the stare. They ruffled their wings as they shifted around in the heather, getting more comfortable. "It's probably just some tablet that's been looked after for generations. I doubt it has any true magic about it."

"Then, why?" I whispered, bowing my head. It looked like I would be an outcast after all, sent on a wild hunt for a useless piece of stone. The birds were barely any better than the humans.

"It wasn't important, but you are. It was imperative we got you away from the others," Jesara added. She rested her talons against my back, gently stroking between my wings.

I shivered at her touch, but something still wasn't making sense. Why was it so important I left Ellian and the others behind? This time I did not admit my confusion. I was sure an explanation was forthcoming anyway. If there wasn't, then I would fly back to my sister.

"I saw your eyes flash red for just a moment when you were talking to your sister. We had to get you away from her. Far away," Jesara explained. Instinctively I held my paw up to my muzzle, one claw resting against my closed eyelid, but naturally I could feel nothing different.

"Are you sure it wasn't just the fire?" I asked, my voice weak with fear, knowing that the gryphon wouldn't make such a mistake. I had never heard of anything like that happening before. My heart went cold as I thought of the necuart that had bitten me. This had to be related.

Jesara slowly nodded, as though she knew exactly what thoughts were racing through my mind. "It seems we were a little premature in discounting any influence from the necuart. It must be more powerful than we realised. There is still a chance that it could control you, and through you, learn of our movements and betray us to George. We couldn't risk that happening. You had to be removed from anywhere that could provide your necuart with information."

"I would never…" I protested, but Seri interrupted me from where they lay.

"Willingly, no. But this creature might seek to dominate your mind completely. Once done, there would be no recovery. The thrall of a necuart has no willpower to resist their master. If it had asked, you would have killed your sister without any hesitation," the apothecary warned. My body felt I had fallen in icy water. I couldn't allow that to happen. Perhaps the gryphons were right in bringing me out here, if I could be such a danger to my sister.

"Is there any way to stop that happening?" I whispered, holding my head low and staring at the pink heather flowers. I could never allow myself to see another dragon again. My life would be one of loneliness unless I could find a way to rid myself of the necuart's influence.

"There is just one. The necuart who did this to you must die, but that is not possible for you to bring about. Come on, I'll explain on the way," Jesara said, beckoning for me to follow her on paw. A shadow fell over me as Seri loomed behind my tail.

"On the way? To where?"

Seri laughed, a musical sound like the cry of a morning bird. "You've forgotten already why we came out here? We're going to Nixa to find the gryphonstone." They nudged me with their taloned forepaw, pushing me to start walking.

"But you said it wasn't important?" I protested. The nights were getting colder. I had no desire to do anything but to sleep through it and wait for the morning sun. I certainly did not want to explore the open grave of untold thousands of dragons. I was not one to believe in ghosts or spirits of the dead, but with every step I took towards the Nixan lair, a sense of dread rose within in my chest.

"Compared to making you safe, no, it's not important," Jesara explained. She walked on my right flank, while Seri took a place to my left. There would be no chance that I could get away from them, should I desire to turn back or stop. "But by all accounts, the lair itself contained huge amounts of magic. While we're here, it would be foolish not to investigate it, just in case we find something that could help our friends. Even a gryphon needs help, from time to time."

Seri chirruped in laughter again. "You, maybe. A perfect gryphon would never ask for help, but if some were offered, then perhaps they would take it," they said. I thought I could detect a little fear beneath their words. Were they scared for what we might find in Nixa, or of the vicious battle we now seemed likely to miss?

The rest of the walk was largely silent, with just a few chirps and squawks passing between the two gryphons in their own language. I noticed they kept looking over their shoulders, but every time I caught a glimpse of the dark sky between their wings, I saw nothing. The thin moon was not far from following the sun below the horizon, providing little light. It soon took all my focus not to trip over any rough patches of grass and bracken. Placing one paw in front of the other was increasingly difficult when I could barely see the ground in front of me. The two gryphons seemed to have it much easier, the only sounds they made were the gentle ruffle of their feathers and the soft rustle of the grass beneath their assured steps.

As we started to climb the side of a hill, I became aware of another noise reaching my ears. Wingbeats. Something was following us. Judging from Jesara's sudden hiss, she had heard it too. I was immediately reminded of the giant bats that had flown across the night sky just before I had fallen into the eager mouth of the necuart.

Though I searched the sky, I could see nothing. The gryphons, with their far superior eyes, were quickly able to find what I could not. "It's a lone dragon," Seri whispered. I could hear their wings spread as they crouched, ready to spring to flight if needed. "It seems to have come from Laxtal, judging by its direction."

"It's definitely alone. If it comes to a fight, we will win easily," Jesara added, before whistling loudly to call the stranger down.

The gryphons' feathers bristled as the wingbeats grew louder. Whoever it was, they had heard Jesara's cry. Finally, a dark shadow moved across my vision as a slender green dragon flew just overhead, coming crashing down to the springy ground a few feet away.

"Cinson? What are you doing here?" I cried, slinking beneath Seri's legs to get to my friend.

"You know this dragon?" the apothecary asked, speaking over a low moan from the Xigax dragon.

"He's been one of my closest companions for a couple of years now," I replied, gently lifting Cinson's head off the ground. He didn't appear to be hurt, just tired and cold. Behind me, the two gryphons shifted around and talked amongst themselves, but I paid them no further attention. For the moment, I just had to worry about making sure Cinson was alright.

The Xigax dragon's eyes fluttered as he groaned again, slowly heaving himself off his chest and back to his paws. "I'm glad I found you. I thought I'd gotten lost," he said, resting his head against my shoulder as he tried to find his balance.

"What are you even doing here?"

Cinson shrugged and backed away. "I saw you fly off. I needed to make sure you were safe, and that you weren't being held captive." One of the gryphons clacked their beak in annoyance at that but didn't interrupt.

"I'm safe. It was everyone else who wasn't," I sighed. I wondered if I should send Cinson away, but the thought of having draconic company was too tempting. At least if I was in danger falling into the necuart's control, the two gryphons would easily be able to overpower me and prevent me from causing harm.

"What do you mean?"

I looked away, ashamed. I had barely even spoken with Cinson since he had flown off from our home without me. For one of the few dragons that I could call a friend, I had been distant with him ever since I returned to Laxtal. Some of it was because of my recovery from the bite, but it was still inexcusable. I owed him better.

Sensing the gryphons' impatience, I decided to tell Cinson everything that had happened as we walked. Though the Xigax dragon was exhausted, he kept pace with reasonable ease. He didn't ask any questions as I explained the reason for my flight, instead just padding by my side in silence. Only once I had finished my story did he speak.

"You know, there is a legend in Xigax of a creature like you described. They are men of darkness and cold. They live in the frozen wastes of the distant south. I always thought they were a scary story told to hatchlings, but maybe it's true." Cinson paused, looking up at the two silhouetted gryphons. "Just like the skycats were just a legend, but now we're walking with two. Maybe all our legends and stories are true after all."

"What's next? A firebird to shoot across the sky?" I asked with a laugh. A divine creature said to bring luck and fortune to any who saw one. How we could use one of those about now, but of all our stories, that was the least likely.

"We have stories of firebirds too," Jesara said, her voice distant as she stared up to the sky once more, as though searching for the mythical creature. "But I have never seen such a thing. Their feathers are rumoured to be almost as fine as a gryphon's."

"A legend, nothing more than that," Seri said firmly, before they bounded to the top of the hill we were climbing. A soft glow was coming from somewhere beyond the crest of the hill, slightly illuminating the gryphon's dyed cobalt feathers. They crowed out in triumph. "This though, this is real magic. Come and see."

Jesara leaped forward without any hesitation, but Cinson and I were more cautious. We were about to look down upon the death of an entire clan. I wasn't sure I wanted to see what the intervening time had done to all the bodies. More so I didn't lose face in front of Cinson, I crested the hill and looked down at what remained of Nixa.

Four other low hills formed a rough ring around the Nixan lair, but where there had once been a gentle slope in the interior, there was now a jagged chasm spewing forth what appeared to be pure light. For the most part, it was a gentle glow, but here and there were sparks of almost blinding intensity. It seemed to dissipate into the night sky almost as soon as it left the ground.

"Magic," breathed Seri. "What did I tell you? There was something worth coming to find here."

"Raw, uncontrollable magic though," Jesara said, stepping up to the side of her fellow gryphon. "There isn't much we can do with this lightshow. There might though, be something we can use inside."

"Inside?" I yelped, fear releasing my tongue before I could still it. Once more I had revealed a weakness to the gryphons. I glanced across at Cinson. I was somewhat reassured to see that he was making no effort to hide his terror either.

"What's the matter, dragon? Scared of a little light?" Seri taunted over their shoulder. The apothecary was already on their way down to the edge of the chasm, not even waiting to see if anyone was joining them.

"It's not just light though, is it? I'm not Nixan. I don't know what that would do to me," I said quietly, averting my eyes from the two gryphons. All my life I had heard warnings about the dangers of magic, that no one could trust it, and only Nixans could wield it. I wasn't about to walk into a chasm unleashing what was probably powerful magic. No matter what hit I would take to my pride.

I felt a claw twist in my heart when Cinson took a few uncertain steps forward, before bounding to catch up to the two gryphons. The Xigax dragon dared what I could not, and the three of them approached the lip of the chasm together. They were all bathed in the magic light, their scales and feathers luminescent. Then they were gone. One step forward and the magic engulfed them. Not a trace of them remained, and still my paws would not carry me forward or back. I could neither follow nor flee.

"Cinson?" I cried out, desperate for some response, but just silence greeted me. My wings flared uselessly by my sides, a futile gesture as my hindlegs refused to kick off to push me into the air.

*"Weak."*

I leaped into the air, the sudden voice providing my limbs the impetus to move. I frantically looked around, but I was completely alone. The magic that came pouring out from the old lair illuminated nothing living. Nothing living, and nothing dead either. For the first time, I noticed how bare the ground was. What had happened to all the bodies that should be here? I suddenly realised I didn't want to be alone. If something had come to remove the dead Nixans, I didn't want to be around to see it come back.

Crying out Cinson's name once more, I ran forward to the light, not stopping until I felt its warmth all around me.

The ground fell away beneath my paws, and sudden darkness consumed me.

Shadows swirled as I padded through the darkness. There was no discernible source of light that I could find, but somehow, I could still see. The soft, grey light simply was. No sound reached my ears, not even my own pawsteps, which fell on a surface I could neither see nor feel. All I knew was that something held me up with my wings furled, and I saw no reason to question further.

I didn't know how long I walked for, mind blank and no destination to aim for. I simply walked, because it was better than standing and doing nothing.

*"Weak dragon."*

One paw in front of the other. Again, and again. No need to stop. No need to think.

*"Submit. Submit to my will."*

Wings fluttered. A gentle breeze growing into a harsh wind. Shadows and smoke gusted into my face, forcing me to hide behind a wing. The air was bitterly cold and yet an intense heat poured into me. It seared through my veins, liquid fire burning every scale.

*"Weak, pathetic creature. It's only a matter of time before your mind is mine."*

My steps faltered.

"No."

*"Resistance is useless, pathetic creature. You can't escape."*

The light vanished, leaving me in total darkness. The wind remained, and I kept my wing shielding my head. Searing heat and bitter cold warred within me. I slid back in an airless gale, whatever formless ground I stood on offering little grip to hold my position.

*"Give in. Why bother fighting?"*

My hindpaws struggled to find something to push against, trying to slow my gradual slide backwards. I would not give in to the creature that was holding me here, the necuart that threatened to control me. For the safety of everyone I cared about, I could not let him win.

*"SUBMIT!"*

Something hard pushed against my tail. That was all I needed. I tensed my hindpaws against whatever protrusion had appeared there and pushed with all my might.

*"I said..."*

The wind faltered and died.

There was silence, and I emerged blinking into the light, my wings outstretched as I fluttered to the ground. The air was cold, but naturally so. Embers of heat lingered within my muscles, though they began to fade quickly.

"Glad you could join us," Jesara said wryly, staring down at me with amusement in her eyes.

The gryphon was standing with Seri and Cinson. They were all looking at me, but I could recognise no confusion or fear in them. They had not witnessed what I had. The darkness and that awful, cold voice had been in my mind only. Had it even been real, or had I imagined the whole thing? I shuddered. It had felt real.

For the first time I took in our surroundings. We were inside Nixa, that much was obvious. The small antechamber was white rock, all of which glimmered and shone with magic that poured towards the surface above our heads. The roof had been torn away in the explosion that had decimated the clan, but I could not see the dark sky beyond the intense gleam of magic.

But for the destroyed roof, there was only one exit to the antechamber. A narrow tunnel led out to what I assumed to be the main chambers. Following Jesara's lead, that was where we headed. The two gryphons were only able to make it through by crouching down almost so they were shuffling through on their knees, wings tucked as tight to their bodies as they could manage. I heard them complaining to each other in their avian language, and the moment they were through to the other side they started grooming their displaced feathers, making sure everything was perfect once more.

That allowed us a few minutes to stare in awe at the sight that greeted us. Though it was empty and lifeless, the sheer size of the Nixan lair took my breath away. The shattered ceiling was close, but it was the floor that was almost terrifying. I could barely even see it; it was so far away. It looked far enough that I could dive in freefall for a couple of minutes and still not hit the ground.

Once again, there was no trace of any bodies, with only the faintest lingering smell of death on the otherwise stale air. The whole place felt sterile. Even with the ruptured ceiling, no scents descended from outside. I heard no sounds, no drip of water or chirp of bird. But for the four of us, nothing moved in Nixa. And somewhere not too far away, my sister could be settling down for her last night alive. If nothing else, I had to make this worthwhile. There had to be some reason for me abandoning Ellian to her fate.

So that we could better find this artefact the gryphons sought, we decided to split up in order to cover the expansive lair. I headed straight down to the distant floor with Cinson, while the two gryphons started exploring the upper echelons. I didn't know what I was looking for, though Jesara assured me I would recognise it once I saw it.

As expected, it was a long way down to the floor. I could see reminders of the devastation that had befallen the clan everywhere. Where fire had not scorched the rock, there were scars left behind by debris that had fallen from above. Massive chunks of rock had been torn from the walls, revealing the small chambers where dragons had once lived.

We landed amongst the rubble that littered the floor. Some chunks of stone were larger than my body. I couldn't begin to imagine how many dragons had died there, crushed when these massive chunks of rock had blasted from the ceiling and walls. It would be a long time before the lair was suitable for life again.

"Which way, do you think?" Cinson asked, his quiet voice deafening in the silence of the lair. I was aware of his every movement, my senses picking up every minute scratch of his claws against the rock floor or rustle of his scales as he idly swished his tail.

"I don't know," I replied. Whereas Cinson deafened my senses, my own voice was quiet and distant to my ears. I gestured my head in an almost random direction for the Xigax dragon to explore. I didn't trust myself to be near him, and I quickly started to move away. There was a shadow on my mind again, and I didn't want to be close enough to harm him in case I lost control.

Thankfully, Cinson didn't attempt to argue with me, and he darted off towards the part of the lair I had suggested, slinking through the rubble with sinuous ease. I turned away and headed off in the opposite direction, not once looking back.

"Not again," I growled under my breath. The shadows receded slightly.

I rounded a corner and the debris thinned out a little, though a deep fissure ruptured the floor from wall to wall. It looked like an audience chamber, with a raised podium looking out over the cracked floor. There was one thing that immediately caught my eye. Amidst all the chaos and destruction, there was one piece of order looking distinctly out of place. A statue of a silver dragon stood proudly atop the podium. It looked oddly familiar, but I couldn't recall where I could have seen it before. I took a couple of leaps to land by the statue's side, nosing against it as I tried to work out how it could have escaped the destruction around it. There was no way it could have survived unscathed, but here it stood. I wondered if whoever, or whatever, had cleared the lair of the dead had left it behind.

The statue was warm to the touch, but as I gently prodded it, I felt no movement or life. I didn't know why I had expected otherwise. This was the clan of magic no longer. I didn't expect anything magical to happen within these walls. The silver figure was slightly smaller than me, and unusually serpentine, lacking any trace of wings. Not even dragons like Cinson looked like this.

I looked back. I couldn't see Cinson anywhere. He must have gone into another chamber beyond the rubble. Would I even get the chance to be with him in the future? Would I be too much of a danger to other dragons, with this monster at risk of controlling my thoughts and actions? The shadows crept over my mind again, seeping into my thoughts.

In sudden, inexplicable anger, I knocked the statue over, wincing as I struck the firm metal. I stared as it seemed to take an eternity to fall, eventually striking the stone ground and sending shockwaves reverberating through the massive chamber. I couldn't move as the blank eyes lit up with a cold blue flame.

"Foolish, little weak dragon," a voice hissed, seemingly emanating from the silver statue yet, at the same time, from nowhere. Slowly, impossibly, the statue began to right itself. Limbs of solid silver bent and shifted before my disbelieving eyes. Only once the thing was looking right at me was I able to take a step back. Tendrils of shadow started to emerge from the shimmering surface of the dragon.

"This can't be real," I said, shaking my head as I tried to back away, but something was preventing my retreat. I was stuck, unable to move.

The chilling voice snickered as the statue advanced. With every step it made the darkness surrounding grow deeper and stronger, until I could see nothing of the surrounding cave. It was just me and the statue.

"Are you ready to submit?"

I arched my back and hissed, lifting one forepaw off the ground, ready to strike if the statue came any closer. It completely ignored my terrified attempts at aggression, and it swatted my paw aside with ease. I tried to retaliate, striking at it with my other, weaker forepaw, but the statue didn't even react as my claws raked down its shoulder.

"You will be mine, dragon. There is no way to escape it."

"I will not give in," I snarled, once more lashing out to no effect. The statue didn't so much as recoil as my claws struck it repeatedly. I took a step to one side, and though the statue didn't move the shadows that surrounded it reached out and enveloped me. I could see nothing but shapeless forms moving through the darkness, and no matter how many times I spun around and lashed out, my claws only tore through the air.

The shadows taunted me, calling me weak and pathetic. Neither tooth nor claw had any effect on them as they swirled around me. Small fragments of shadow solidified into ghostly echoes of dragons with burning red eyes. Three of them advanced on me, and I couldn't help but think the end was coming. I could do nothing to fend them off. I closed my eyes. They were still visible.

A shadow touched my tail.

I reacted on instinct, spinning around and lunging, feeling flesh against my teeth at last. I opened my eyes to shadows, but hot blood filled my mouth. The shadows could bleed like any dragon. I tore into my foe, not giving them a chance to fight back before I subdued them. This was my chance to defeat the shadows, my one opportunity to free myself of their influence.

The shadows though, only snickered. The cold laughter sought to paralyse me, to fill me with dread at what I had just done. I loosened my jaws. There was a soft thump as my foe fell to the ground.

Then the shadows fled from my eyes.

I knew straight away I would never forget the betrayed agony in Cinson's eyes, nor the ragged attempts to draw in breath. His blood already stained the stone floor, a great pool spreading out and washing against my paws. There was little left of his throat, a gaping wound I had created. I could not save him. I had killed him.

"I… I'm sorry," I whispered as the light in my friend's eyes faded. His gasping breath failed. My friend, my faithful companion since my exile, was gone.

He was dead by my own teeth.

Grief threatened to overwhelm me, but before I could let it, I made my choice. I knew my mind could easily break. I could have snapped and given in to the shadows, but instead I felt stronger than ever against them. My mind hardened and filled me with fiery resolve. The demons in my head would suffer for this. They would be the next to die.

# CHAPTER TWENTY

**Azlak**

I could not sleep. The longer the night went on the more restless I became, until I had no choice but to rise from my attempted slumber. I could feel the chill of the early-winter night, but it had no effect on me whatsoever. I felt like I could fly as far as I wanted and not have to worry about the cold sapping my strength. That thought alone gave me the sense of incredible freedom, but as I looked down at the distant ground, I had to wonder at the cost of it all.

Taking care with each step, I slowly paced back and forth, trying to work out where I could go now. Unless I could find a way to rid myself of the humans' magic, I knew I would never be able to fit in amongst other dragons ever again. A life of exile was not an attractive proposition.

At the back of my mind, the presence of magic was a constant reminder of the Axinstone, safely nestled beneath a nearby bush. I never strayed far from it, though I doubted anything would have the courage to approach. It wouldn't do to have risked so much, only to lose the Axinstone due to a moment of negligence.

My senses were so much stronger now, especially my eyesight in the darkness. Before, I had barely been able to see beyond past my own muzzle once the sun had gone down, but now I could pick out so much detail in everything. I could make out individual leaves on the trees on the far side of the nearby stream. The gentle flutter of an owl's wings reverberated in my ears, as well as every chirp and screech from the insects and rodents scurrying through the undergrowth. It was overwhelming. The cold, dead nights were suddenly alive.

I squeezed my eyes shut and tried to block out the multitude of sounds around me, but to no avail. There was just too much. An intense heat built up in my throat, and I lifted my head up to the sky and roared. No sound escaped though, and instead a strong burning sensation escaped my muzzle. I opened my eyes in time to see the last licks of flame dissipate into the air.

"Fire?" I whispered, stunned by what I had just done. According to legend, there were once dragons who could breathe fire. Not the modern Nixans who could manipulate fire, but dragons who could truly create flames within their body and breathe it like air. None had existed for centuries. If they ever had. I thought the stories to be just myth, a fabrication passed down through the generations. The oldest tales told of dragons capable of incredible deeds, acts that no living dragon could hope to emulate. Perhaps until now.

Just what was it the humans were doing to us?

A crack of thunder tore through the night, but the sky was clear of clouds. In panic, I crashed to the ground and curled around the bush where I had hidden the Axinstone. A dragon's wingbeats followed soon after, tired and unsteady. They approached from the north, slowly getting closer.

Frantically, I looked around, but there was nowhere for me to go. I was too massive to simply hide. Though I knew no other dragon could possibly harm me, but for Nightwings, it was the reaction I was bound to receive that terrified me. I did not want to be this monster.

A small blue dragon came into view. His flight was uneven and several times I thought he was about to fall but somehow he kept going. For a brief moment, I thought it was my mate, before remembering the loud peal of thunder. It had to be Airil.

I stayed as still as I could, hoping that with his lesser eyesight, Airil would just fly straight past me without noticing. There was to be no such luck though, as his strength gave out. He plummeted from the air and slid along the ground, coming to rest just a few feet away from where I lay. He made one futile attempt to drag himself up to his paws before flopping motionless to the ground.

For a few more minutes I remained frozen, barely daring to move in case I woke Airil, or worse, accidentally hit him. Just one of my paws was almost as large as his body. I dreaded to think what sort of damage I could inflict. With great care so I didn't make much noise, I edged a little closer to my mate's twin, aware of every movement I made. Gently I wrapped my foreleg around his prone body, before covering him completely in my wing. The magical heat from my body would be enough to warm him until the sun rose.

Until then I would just lie still, one eye on the Axinstone and the other on the sky. Morning would bring a whole host of problems, but if I was able to explain myself to Airil then at least he could return the Axinstone back to Ddraig Krateos. That would be one less thing to worry about.

Throughout the rest of the night, nothing of interest flew by. I thought I could hear one of the grave bats, it was so quiet and far away that I was not concerned. Apart from a lone owl, nothing came close until the sky started to lighten with the approaching dawn. I was still no closer to working out what I was to do with myself; the restless night had not afforded me answers.

Movement against my leg warned me that Airil was starting to rouse, and I carefully furled my wing to allow the first of the morning light to strike him. I could only hope he would react kindly to my new appearance, as there was little that I could do to prevent him leaving. He could be gone in just a thought.

I couldn't look at Airil as he slowly started to wake up, scared of seeing the inevitable fear in his eyes once he opened them. The small weight against my leg was my only assurance that he was still with me. Absently I toyed with the ridge in my paw, desperate to talk to Kaz or Esperance, but I wanted to delay that meeting as long as possible. I could not bear the thought of my mate's terror at my appearance, and I doubted Esperance would be able to help me. She was far away, further south than any dragons had gone for generations uncounted.

"So it wasn't a dream?"

The small voice by my side was surprisingly calm, not laced with fear as I had anticipated, but still I couldn't look down at Airil. I was ashamed. Tainted by human magic. He should be scared.

"Not a dream, no," I replied sadly, staring down at the grass.

"I was there. I could see it all, but I couldn't… I don't understand. How could Anzig do that to me? It should be impossible," Airil said, panic rising in his voice. I could feel him stand, his weight pushing off my leg, only to hear him collapse back to the ground again. I chanced him a glance; too weary to remain standing, he had fallen in a heap, his wings spread out to take in as much sunlight as he could manage.

I figured there was nothing for it but to reveal the secrets that I had learned. Nixa deserved an explanation. "Anzig is my brother, and Maznar our sister. Ddraig Krateos is our father. We're all Nixans," I said soberly, swinging my head away before Airil thought to look up. I didn't want to see his reaction to that revelation. It was hard enough trying to come to terms with it myself. At least he had not yet fled in fear. That was something for which I could be grateful.

A brief spell of silence fell between us. I didn't push Airil to keep talking, content instead with the little bit of quiet. I could feel him moving around by my side. He felt so weak and vulnerable against my scales. Perhaps if Airil's reaction was anything to go by, I wouldn't need to be so worried about what other dragons might think. Even so, I would need to find some way of reversing the changes the humans had put upon me. Practically, I just could not stay like this. I would never be able to fit in one of the lairs. Wherever I ended up, Laxtal or Nixa, would be too small to accommodate me in this form.

Airil finally broke the silence. "How are you still, well, you? All the other dragons like this have been controlled by the humans, haven't they? Nightwings was."

I turned my paw over, claw tracing along the ridge beneath my scales. "I think it was something to do with this. Esperance put magic into your brother and me. That magic protected me. It allowed me to resist their control and break free from it."

Airil paced around me, leaping over my tail. I struggled to keep still, not wanting to surprise him with any sudden movement. Even a flick of my tail could cause him a lot of harm. He stopped when he returned to my front. He looked up at me, eyes wide. "You could probably have flown back to our army already. Why did you stay out here? Not that I'm not grateful for you looking after me during the night, but you could have gotten much further from the humans."

This time I did move. I slowly lifted my head and spread my wings to their full extent. Even though I made no effort to take flight, I could feel the air beneath my wings pushing up at me. This body was meant to fly, despite its size and weight. I gripped the ground with my claws. "Look at me, Airil. Do you think anyone is going to want to see me? They'll scatter and fly. Even Kaz. I don't know why you haven't."

Airil scoffed. He placed a paw on my foreleg. He showed no fear. "If I know my brother, then Kaz is not going to be afraid of you. He will see you just as I do. The same seer you always were. Maybe even better."

"What do you mean?" I asked, looking down at the Nixan. I didn't like the wide, mischievous grin on his face. I slowly rose to my paws, awkwardly shuffling away from Airil. He bounded up to his paws as well, much more energetic now that he'd had a chance to warm up. He had to run to keep up with my slow walk, darting between my legs much to my annoyance. I had to be so careful where I was placing my paws, constantly looking down as I wasn't comfortable with my co-ordination in this body.

"You know. More of you. I think he'll like that," Airil said, leaping ahead of me and heading down towards the stream. I chose not to answer him but followed him anyway towards the water to take a drink. The silence hung between us again. I closed my eyes as I tried to work out what we needed to do now. I reached out with my mind to access the future and…

And nothing.

"I can't See. My magic isn't there," I cried out, leaping backwards and arching my back, wrapping my tail around my legs. My breath came in short gasps as I tried to push out with my mind again, desperate to see something of the future, but I Saw nothing. Despair washed over me. For the first time since I was a young dragonet, I was blind to what the future held. Unwanted tears formed in my eyes.

I wasn't aware of Airil's presence until I felt his claws on my shoulder. He placed his paw on my neck as I struggled to calm myself, but the panic only grew. Of all the things that could happen, this was one of the worst. There were times when I had hated my magic and what it had done to my life, but never had I wanted it gone. It was too much a part of me, and without it I felt a part of my identity had withered and died.

My wings flared, though what I planned to do or where to go didn't occur to me. I didn't know what to do, and only Airil's sharp claws stopped me from taking flight.

"Azlak, listen to me," he repeatedly said, digging in with his claws between my scales as best he could. I managed to control my breathing and close my wings again, lowering my head to the ground as the Nixan's words broke through at last.

"I don't want to be without my magic," I whimpered, displaying weakness I knew would seem absurd in this powerful form. I pawed at the ground, trying not to think about the void within me where my magic should lie. My claws gouged out deep tracks in the grass. Small pools of water from the stream quickly filled them.

There was only one dragon I was sure would be able to help me work out why my magic was gone, but I didn't want to face Ddraig Boruc in this situation. At the same time, I was pretty sure I didn't have any choice. Without any advice from the experienced dragon, I feared I would be stuck like this, destined to live alone for the rest of my life. Either that or return to the humans and beg them to reverse their magic. I would have to be desperate indeed to willingly fly back towards George. I was not my brother, believing the lies told to him by Maznar. The humans would not help me. They would not give me what I demanded.

I looked back at Airil, comforted by the concern I could see as he raised his paw up to my neck. His acceptance of me helped to make the decision I faced that little bit easier. I would have to go and find Ddraig Boruc again, if he had lingered around after being chased away by the necuart.

There would be no way Airil would ever be able to keep up with my flight, so after he retrieved the Axinstone from its hiding place, he leaped onto my back. He took refuge between my wings, digging his claws between a couple of scales for grip. It was uncomfortable, slightly restricting the movement of my wings, but it was the only place he could go without tiring himself out with his magic. Once he was securely in position, I beat my wings a few times to make sure he wasn't about to fall off, before kicking off hard.

Flying was so different now, a wholly new experience that I enjoyed despite myself. The speeds I could reach were phenomenal. I could never have imagined such a pace to be possible as the landscape passed by in a blur. I could just about hear Airil shrieking from my back, whether in fear or thrill I couldn't be sure. Perhaps even a little of both. Though I had no idea where to start the search, I covered what would once have been an hour of flying in little over ten minutes. I saw or heard no sign of the human army or their allies through the day, for which I was thankful. It seemed they were not spending any of their resources to search for me.

More through luck than anything else, I managed to find the small cave we had sheltered in before my capture. The scent of my former companions was cold, but I sent Airil in anyway, just in case they had left me behind some token to indicate where they had gone. I waited outside with an eye on the horizon, wary of the relative proximity of the humans. I could hear their movement when the wind was still, on the very edge of my hearing.

The Nixan was only inside for a couple of minutes before he emerged again, a small slab of stone in his paw. Markings were engraved on the stone, but they written in a language I couldn't read. Thankfully Airil had already been able to determine what they said.

"I think Ddraig Boruc knew I'd be with you. This is written in draconic, and there are but a few dragons who can read it now," Airil said hesitantly, running his claw over the engraved markings. "It says they stayed a few nights, hoping to rescue you. After feeling the Axinstone being used, they flew south, to join up with the army he hopes is flying from Laxtal. He hopes you are safe, and that you escaped with the Axinstone."

"How could he have known?" I asked, turning my head to look south. Perhaps it was my imagination, but now that I knew which way they had gone, their scent seemed stronger that way. With nothing else to do this close to the human army, we were soon on our way again. Once Airil was secure on my back, I spread my wings and launched into the sky once more.

Whether by fate or fortune I picked up a stronger scent of Ddraig Boruc and Isikian after less than an hour of flying south. There were other smells close by too, unfamiliar ones I had no experience of. It put me in the mind of a wildcat, but I was sure it was something completely different. Almost obscured by the strange scents was one all too familiar. Dragons. Hundreds upon thousands of them. Laxtal's army was close. Kaz would be amongst them. Dual emotions of fear and longing stabbed through my heart.

We weren't far from Nixa when I finally caught sight of the two dragons ahead. I knew I couldn't get close to them, not without them attempting to flee. I sent Airil on ahead, before spiralling down to the banks of the river that marked the northern boundary of Nixa, where their territory gave way to Clan Reneza. With a loud crack like thunder, Airil was gone, taking the Axinstone with him. I was alone once more. There was nothing now to stop Airil meeting up with Ddraig Boruc and Isikian and flying on to the Laxtal army, leaving me here in my isolation.

I rested on a rocky promontory that pushed out into the river, my wings draped out more in habit than anything else. I no longer needed to draw in the sun's heat for energy, my body could do that by itself. I had expected to feel the need to eat more often, but I didn't even need to do that. I could not tell what sustained me now.

Looking down at my reflection in the river, I rolled my head back and forth. It was amazing how similar I looked to the reflection I recognised. Only my eyes were different. They were still gold as they had always been, but they were now infused with magic; flecks of amber and white sparking beneath the surface. They were fascinating and terrifying at the same time. Like the fire I had breathed the previous night.

The sun was starting to sink low to the Sxinix Mountains and I was beginning to feel sure Airil had abandoned me. It would have taken him an instant to return, but I hadn't seen a single dragon fly overhead. Only the occasional bird had flown by, hunting for their prey and oblivious to the conflict that was sure to come. I almost longed for their innocence, to be free of the worries and concerns that plagued my mind.

Finally, just as I was starting to lose hope, I heard the gentle flutter of a dragon's wings. I turned my head to see Ddraig Boruc land nearby, with Isikian close on his tail. While there was fear in Isikian's eyes –

like me, he had witnessed the full fury of Nightwings – Ddraig Boruc showed no terror at all. I could only see fascination and wonder there.

"Now this is a sight I never thought I would see again," he whispered, reaching out with one paw as though he meant to touch my muzzle.

"Again? You've seen others like me?"

"Apart from that ruffian that tried to kill Ellian and me, not for a very, very long time," Ddraig Boruc said, pulling his paw back and staring at it.

Isikian shuffled his wings. "And… they have no control over you?"

I shook my head. "None. They tried, but without the Axinstone they have no chance. Something stopped their magic. I think it might have been Esperance's slate," I said. I looked down at my paw where Esperance's magical item roughed my scales.

Ddraig Boruc noticed the focus of my gaze. "With something that powerful in your possession, I'm not surprised even the Axinstone failed to break that magic."

I nodded. If that was so, I was even more thankful to Esperance. She had saved me from servitude under human control. Isikian looked only slightly reassured by that, his wings still partially unfurled. I wanted to do something to comfort him, but I was scared that if I made any movement towards him, then he would panic and flee. I looked back to Boruc, focusing on the older dragon for now.

"There was a human there. He said you knew him. His name is Rico."

Ddraig Boruc hissed and shook his head. "The name is not familiar to me."

I looked around me, taking care that there was nothing beneath my paws as I settled in place, lying down amongst the grass. Even still, I was so much taller than either of the two dragons. "He said he wanted to finish what he started."

The older dragon met my eyes. "Could it be… No, he wouldn't be involved in this. He wouldn't do this to you," he said, gesturing with a paw to my enhanced self.

"Will you be able to fix it?" I asked, trying not to let my voice descend into desperate pleading.

Ddraig Boruc was silent, his wings wrapped tight around his body as he looked to the ground. I barely dared to move as I waited for his answer, and Isikian did much the same. The Nixan's eyes were wide as he stared at me.

When Ddraig Boruc looked up again, his eyes were bright. "I think so. I know how the human magic works, so I should be able to remove it. Once it is done though, I will not be able to reverse it."

I closed my eyes. There was nothing I wanted more than to return to normal and to feel the comforting touch of my magic, but one thing held me back. By stealing the Axinstone from them, humans had lost access to Nightwings and their other creations. I was the last one left. "I could be of use, couldn't I?"

"I won't force you into any decision, but yes. I can imagine you could be of great use," Ddraig Boruc said slowly. He looked up to me and met my eyes, holding them without any challenge. I was still forced to look away.

I growled softly. "Then, until this is all over, I shall stay like this."

Ddraig Boruc placed his paw on mine, his small weight barely noticeable. "You are doing a brave thing Azlak. If only I had been as brave as you, then my son... then he... this may never have happened."

The old dragon sighed and said no more, turning away and hunching his shoulders as he sat by the river. I shared a brief, inquisitive glance with Isikian, but we both knew not to interrupt Ddraig Boruc's silence. For the ddraig of such a minor clan, he was a dragon with so many secrets, but we respected him enough not to press him to reveal what he knew.

Isikian moved a few steps closer, his wings fluttering as they threatened to unfurl completely. "Airil has gone straight back to Ddraig Krateos to return the Axinstone. And to warn them..."

"To warn them of me," I said, completing Isikian's sentence for him. The Nixan nodded, turning his face from me in embarrassment. "I am not a monster."

I didn't know who I was trying to convince.

# CHAPTER TWENTY-ONE

**Ellian**

Our horde of dragons and gryphons flew without rest through the day. As a ddraig, I flew towards the front of the army, keeping wing just behind Ddraig Krateos and Alaron. The wyvern was a powerful flyer, showing no sign of weakness as he soared from thermal to thermal. Only Kyrus had made any real attempt to communicate with me during the flight, but I had remained quiet and largely chose not to answer the gryphon's questions. My mind was still trying to catch up on the events of the previous night. I still couldn't believe that Vinzent had died, and my brother had fled.

I had seen Saya briefly before we flew out. Though I knew the ness had seen me, she refused to look in my direction. Many times, she had challenged me or Anzig through her son. With him gone she had lost so much of her power within Laxtal. For now, she was no longer a threat. I had no doubts that if we all survived this war, she would find some other scheme to wrest more power from me.

More than anything I wanted Airil by my wing, but no one had seen him since Anzig had abandoned the clan. Maznar had seemingly gone with them, as she had likewise become scarce. The strange black ness worried me. I knew I wasn't the only one who didn't trust her. I feared she had filled Anzig's head with lies. About me. About the clan. Why else would he leave us behind at such an important time?

Every time I looked back at the force we had gathered, I couldn't help but feel a swell of pride. Most of the dragons were here because of my efforts. I had been the one to fly through the clans, recruiting numbers for our desperate cause. Thousands had answered, and still more trickled in all the time. Nomads continued to join us, more coming almost every hour. And high above the dragons flew the gryphons, keeping a close watch on any possible human movements within the area. They were Azlak's doing. I marvelled at the seer. I would never have thought he would be so important to us all.

Not until late afternoon was there anything to distract from the monotony of one wingbeat after another. Starting out as just a speck on the horizon, something started to fly towards us. A few gryphons squawked to each other as they tried to determine if it was friend or foe approaching. After a few sharp orders from both Alaron and Kyrus, we let them come, as they flew alone and without any support. It would take just a moment to destroy them if they turned aggressive.

I quickly recognised the slender form of a Xigax ness. Her sinuous body almost seemed to swim through the air rather than fly. She warily approached us, her eyes wide as she searched through the first few ranks.

"Ddraig Astar?" she called out hesitantly.

Upon hearing that name I moved to the front to fly alongside Alaron. "Astar is dead. I am Ddraig Ellian of Laxtal. Fly with us," I said, inviting the Xigax ness to my side. She introduced herself as Zuris, one of the commanders of Ddraig Nunahra's armies. She asked if we could land and speak properly, as the news she had was too important to say on the wing.

With Alaron's permission, I began the call to land. There were many thankful cries at the unexpected relief, and gradually our horde descended upon what was once southern Nixa. Given how close it was to sunset, we quickly decided to settle for the rest of the day, and a hunting party went out to the famed hunting grounds of Nixa. If it was to be our last night before we reached the human forces, then at least we would eat well for it.

There wasn't much in the way of shelter around; we were on the borders of the Nixan plains and a long way from any large forests. There were a few caves in the low hills, but certainly not enough to shelter our immense numbers. Most would have to sleep under the stars once more, but we were still far enough away from where the humans camped to risk warming fires.

While we waited for the hunters to return, I sent a messenger out to find James McArthur and our allied humans. They had to be close by, and it would be useful having them around, in case they had discovered anything on their slow journey on paw.

With a tired sigh, I joined the other leaders in one of the small caves to hear what Zuris had to say. Kyrus settled down to preen his feathers back into perfection, with Alaron sitting by his side. The wyvern's eyes were alert while we waited for a fire to be lit. Ddraig Krateos was quick to join us, though for once he did not come with his daughter. I was also surprised to see Ddraig Metrus of Eltee, who I was not aware had joined us. She ruled a minor clan between the borders of Nixa and Laxtal, whose lands we had passed over in the morning. She must have joined us then. The ddraigs and haeraigs of the other minor clans in our alliance also sat around our private fire.

Zuris stayed close to my side as we waited. She could not keep her eyes on Kyrus for long, but if she was afraid of the gryphon, then she hid it well. I could also tell she had noticed Alaron's unique anatomy, but thankfully she had not commented on that. I doubted the wyvern had much patience for someone implying he was a cripple, not after his display against Vinzent.

"So, what have we all gathered here for?" Alaron asked, staring down the Xigax ness who quickly looked away.

"Xigax was attacked by a force of dragons, led by Ddraig Tsona," Zuris said, slowing raising her head again, shuffling her wings against her back. "I think Xital underestimated our strength, as with the assistance of Axaatl, we routed them after just a couple of days. We believe a few of the survivors, including Ddraig Tsona, fled to join up with the human army on the northern border of Nixa."

Kyrus paused his preening and chirruped. "How many survivors?"

"No more than five hundred," Zuris replied, staring with wide eyes at the gryphon, who had returned his attention back to his feathers. "About five hundred more were too injured to fly. They were captured and are being held in Xigax. Haeraig Ilibela was being interrogated by Haeraig Cheiala when I left."

Alaron stepped forward, ducking his head in a rare sign of respect. "And can we expect any assistance in clearing the humans from your lands?"

"That is why Ddraig Nunahra sent me. It is my understanding that Ddraig Aranat pledged his dragons to your cause, with the expectation that Xigax would remain in this alliance. I am here to confirm that this is the case. Axaatl and Xigax will join you in battle," Zuris replied, showing all her teeth as she smiled. "My ddraig wanted to deal with the prisoners before taking to wing with our army, minus a small guard to remain behind. She is perhaps three days behind me with five thousand warriors from both our clan and Axaatl. We will see these humans gone."

"Five thousand?" Ddraig Metrus whispered to me in awe. It was not just the stunned response from a ddraig used to smaller numbers, for I had to agree with her. A force that strong would destroy almost any draconic clan that stood in Xigax or Axaatl's way. I could only hope that the humans would find them just as unstoppable, especially when added to our numbers.

"This could change things drastically," I said, keeping the eye of Alaron and then Ddraig Krateos for a few moments. "You will not find a better clan of fighters than Clan Xigax or Clan Axaatl. If they have annulled the threat of Clan Xital, then perhaps this isn't an unwinnable war. I do not know if we can risk delaying the attack, but if we can hold our ground for two days then the arrival of Ddraig Nunahra and Ddraig Aranat could decimate the humans."

Alaron lowered his head in thought. "You are right. Delaying the attack would only risk losing the chance to ambush the humans, or it may give them the opportunity to strike at us unprepared. We cannot delay, unless we find their defences are stronger than expected. But I hope your faith in Xigax and Axaatl is justified."

Ddraig Krateos growled. "An army of Nixans would be their equal. If the humans hadn't resorted to such dirty tactics against us, we would have torn them from the sky."

I chose not to say anything. I knew Ddraig Krateos would still be hurting at the loss of most of his clan, but the truth was he had allowed the humans access to his clan all too easily. If the might of Nixa had been what he boasted, then the humans should never have had that chance. Wisely, no one else spoke up against Ddraig Krateos either.

"We would be grateful for your numbers. You may find a place to rest and feed your fill when the hunters return," Alaron said, bowing his head once more towards Zuris.

The Xigax ness thanked everyone present, hesitating slightly when she came to the gryphon, before making her retreat to take advantage of the offered hospitality.

Ddraig Bakucic was the first to speak after she left. "I propose that we should send out fast fliers in the morning so that we can get an understanding of the landscape around the human camp. If these scouts learn that it would be better to delay our attack until Ddraigs Nunahra and Aranat arrive, then we will preserve our strength and save lives."

Prince Kyrus chirped. "I can arrange that. Gryphons are faster than dragons, and we can fly at night. I can have that information by morning."

"Please do, yes," Alaron said. He bowed his head to the gryphon and sat back on his hindlegs, wings wrapped around his torso. His barbed tail slapped against the ground a couple of times. "Once I get an understanding of the landscape, I will be able to develop a strategy, but it will likely be a case of keeping the humans occupied until Ddraig Nunahra and Ddraig Aranat can reinforce us. Unfortunately, I can't see any way of avoiding large numbers of casualties. The humans have superior weaponry that can bring down both dragon and gryphon. The ammunition coming out of Kernow in the last few years seems targeted specifically for dragons, which worries me."

Prince Kyrus clicked his beak. "We have little magical support as well. From what I understand, Kernow has a higher number of magic users compared to other human nations. If they have offensive capabilities, then we leave ourselves vulnerable to them."

My eyes flicked across to Ddraig Krateos. His gaze was low, staring resolutely at the dried leaves scattered across the grass. How we could use a full-strength Nixa.

Ddraig Bakucic drew in his breath, swelling his chest as he looked around the group with no fear or deferral. "I am willing to lay down my life if it must come to that. I am sure that every dragon here will do the same."

Alaron flicked his tail again. "I will do my best to avoid unnecessary losses, but until I know what defences the humans have, I can offer no guarantees. As the ddraigs and haeraigs of these clans, I hope you are prepared to send your dragons into battle, knowing many of them will not return."

I closed my eyes as I nodded and accepted the wyvern's warnings. I had to be willing to sacrifice hundreds of dragons who looked up to me as their leader. I had to be sure I could live with that responsibility, that shame.

We were all relieved when we got the call that the hunters had returned, giving us a chance to forget our worries for a little while. The hunters had killed an impressive array of creatures, from small birds to massive deer almost as large as a gryphon. Once again there was more than enough food to go around, and once they had taken their fill, dragons and gryphons alike started to settle down and take in the last of the evening sun.

I was looking forward to the same when a loud crack pierced the calm air. It was a sound I could not fail to recognise.

"Airil!" I cried, instantly leaping into the air, searching desperately for the source of the noise. It didn't take me long to find him, a speck of blue against the darkening sky. Once I had seen him, nothing or no one would get between us, and just seconds later we were embracing mid-flight.

"I missed you so much," I said, resting my head on his shoulder as his wings took most of our weight. Slowly we started drifting towards the ground, to an empty patch of grass near one of the many fires that had sprung up.

"I'm so sorry. I had no choice," Airil said, releasing me for just a moment as we landed, before holding me tight once more. I noticed he carried something in his paw, but that didn't matter for now. We curled up by the fireside together, his wing enveloping me as he hesitantly started to explain where he had been. He told me how Anzig had taken control of his mind, forced him to take my cousin and Maznar to the humans.

"I got to feel some of his thoughts when he controlled me," my mate whispered, his head bowed. "He thinks the humans can give him his wings back. Maznar told him they would listen to him, that they would give him what was taken."

I shuddered and tried not to think too much about Anzig. I didn't want to know about what he was doing with the humans. The mere thought sickened my stomach. "How did you get away?"

Airil leaned into me. "He got distracted. I was able to use that to escape when his magic weakened. I don't know what they plan on doing to him. Whatever promises Maznar made to him, he seems pretty convinced that the humans are his best help now."

I closed my eyes, trying not to let the horror of Airil's news overwhelm me. I had known Anzig was suffering from the loss of his wings, but I could never have realised it had come to this.

"That's not all, though," Airil said slowly. He held out his forepaw, and for the first time I saw what he carried. It was the Axinstone. Somehow, he had it, though I was sure it was still in Haeraig Zeena's possession. "Azlak went with Ddraig Boruc to take this back from the humans. We don't know when they stole it again, but it must have been sometime after Anzig gave it back to us. Azlak though, he was captured. They... experimented on him."

"Experimented? How?" I whispered, completely ignoring the precious stone Airil held in his paw. That was not relevant to me.

"Remember that massive dragon at the beacon?" Airil asked. I nodded silently. I would never forget. "They turned him into one of those, but," he said, suppressing my whimper of fear with a gentle touch of his paw, "he resisted their magic. They didn't get to his mind. He's completely free of their control, and he stole back the Axinstone as he escaped. I should take this back to Ddraig Krateos, but I wanted to feel you against me first. I don't want to leave your side ever again."

I tried to process what Airil was telling me about Azlak. He was one of those ferocious monsters now, but completely out of human control? I was sure my eyes lit up slightly at that news.

"He's coming here? Azlak?" I asked. Already I wondered how his presence would help shape and change Alaron's plans. If we had a dragon like Nightwings to protect us, then that could save many lives before Axaatl and Xigax came to finish the humans off.

"He should be here tonight. Ddraig Boruc thought it would be prudent if I came ahead to warn that he was an ally, and not to be feared," Airil said with the hint of a smirk. "He is quite… intimidating when you first see him."

I could imagine and I shuddered at the thought. My only other experience with these monstrous human creations had been utterly terrifying. It would be hard to dispel the notion that Azlak was an enemy.

Airil sighed and rose to his paws. "I should take this to Ddraig Krateos. Will you wait for me here or come with me?"

Though I was weary from my flight, I was not about to let Airil go from my sight so soon. He smiled as I stood up. We spread our wings and took to the air together.

I marvelled at the display of force that spread out below us. Hundreds of small fires flared to life, around each gathered large swathes of dragons, each trying to get the best spot closest to the heat. There wasn't much mingling of the clans that I could see, especially from the Laxtal dragons. There was a clear divide between those from my clan and our neighbours, something I was a little upset to see. After sheltering so many dragons in our lair, I had hoped that this fear would have diminished somewhat. The minor clans seemed quite content with each other's close presence, so why couldn't we be the same? Even the towering Axaatl dragons lay amongst those from Lilisxi and Eltee.

Beyond the horde of dragons lay the gryphons. I wasn't sure if I would ever be fully used to the presence of the feathered and furred creatures, but having them nearby gave me a feeling of confidence I knew I wouldn't have otherwise felt. They needed no fire to keep warm, and from the look of it most of them were preening their feathers or already sleeping. I tried to find Kyrus amongst them, but the heir to the Crown of Golden Feathers was nowhere I could see. But then all the gryphons looked quite similar to me, with most sharing similar gold and brown feathering, so he could easily have been down there with his kin.

Of course, he could have volunteered himself to scout the human army. If any gryphons had already left to spy on the humans, then they were already well beyond the horizon.

Ddraig Krateos was with the sorrowful remainders of his clan, less than a hundred dragons remaining of what was once the most powerful clan amongst dragonkind. Even Xital had feared their strength, but now there was hardly anything left, reduced to just clanless refugees desperately fighting for a home. *Even if we somehow won this war, would they have anywhere to go? Would they be able to rebuild their lair in Nixa?*

I was glad to see Alaron had remained with Ddraig Krateos, the wyvern and Nixan in deep conversation when we landed. They stopped talking before I was able to overhear what they were discussing. Without any hesitation, Airil placed the Axinstone on the ground in front of his ddraig, bowing his head as he backed away.

Ddraig Krateos reached out in shock for the Axinstone. He moved slowly, holding the precious shard of rock in one paw as though he barely believed his eyes. His mouth moved, but no sound reached my ears.

Likewise, Alaron stared at the Axinstone with wide eyes. It took him several attempts to speak, with just a couple of splutters escaping his mouth at first. "This? This is the artefact that was lost?" the wyvern whispered. He turned to glare at Airil. "Does Esperance know about this?"

"I… You would have to ask my brother, I don't know," Airil stuttered. He failed to meet the eyes of the wyvern, but he was spared further interrogation from Alaron by a joyous call. Kaz had heard his brother's voice and had come bounding across from the sprawled Nixan dragons.

Not even giving the brothers time for a reunion, Alaron urgently asked Kaz the same question. "I don't think we ever discussed the Axinstone with Esperance. It was never relevant to her."

"Never relevant? Dragon, this is the most relevant discovery in hundreds of years," Alaron hissed. The wyvern started pacing back and forth, at one point reaching out with a wing to touch the Axinstone, but a growling Ddraig Krateos quickly rebuffed him and took the stone further away from the wyvern's reach. "We had no idea Bri'An's Rune was being kept in these parts."

"You have it confused for something else," Ddraig Krateos growled. "The Axinstone has been in Nixan possession for hundreds of years, up until the humans stole it. It is not this rune you claim it to be."

Alaron puffed out his chest. "I am not mistaken on this. I would never confuse the rune for something lesser, and Bri'An's rune hasn't been seen since the cataclysm, so the time period fits," he said. He looked up to the sky as he continued to stalk back and forth. "The sightings of these larger dragons have got me thinking. I would love the chance to study one up close."

"You might have your chance," I said, moving forward half a step, just about resisting the urge to quail back once the wyvern's fierce eyes fixed on me. I quickly explained everything Airil had told me about Azlak, turning to my mate and pleading for help when I stumbled and faltered. Thankfully he was able to provide much more information than I could, and he even held Alaron's eye for a few seconds longer than I could manage.

The wyvern's eyes grew steadily wider as he learnt of Azlak. His pacing had ceased as he stared with absolute attention at Airil. Even Ddraig Krateos was unable to tear himself away from what my mate was saying. But then, Azlak was his son, wasn't he? Of course the ddraig would want to know what had happened to the seer.

"Come fetch me when he's here, will you?" Alaron asked.

A nervous grin spread across Airil's muzzle. "You don't think you'll see him first?"

For a moment I thought Alaron might cuff Airil with one of his powerful wings, before simply batting him gently on the shoulder. "Yes, of course, dragon. Come find me anyway. I plan on distracting myself for a while. You have all given me much to think about."

Before anyone could question him further, Alaron launched himself into the air, beating hard with his wings as he quickly ascended. I watched him bank away and disappear in the direction where the gryphons had settled down to rest.

Though we tried to warn as many as we could, there was still significant amount of panic when Azlak first flew overhead. I couldn't say I blamed them at all, as I was barely able to contain my fear and I had forewarning. Mercifully few took to wing; those that did were quickly shepherded back to the ground by the calmer gryphons. Most simply cowered low, shielding their heads with their wings. I hoped we would have the opportunity to correct that behaviour, should Nightwings or any of the other enhanced dragons face against us in the coming days.

Azlak settled down a little distance away from everyone else, and once I had sent someone out to fetch Alaron, I reluctantly took to the air. With Kaz and Airil flanking me, I was the first to approach the golden monstrosity of a dragon.

"Azlak?" I called out as I got closer.

"Haeraig Ellian?" Azlak rumbled, bowing his great head towards me. I noticed every movement he made was slow and careful. He looked like he was trying hard to be aware of where he put his paws and tail. "No, it'll be Ddraig Ellian now, won't it? Anzig betrayed us all."

"Tell me everything you know, Azlak," I said, nervously settling down with Airil.

As Azlak started to talk, Kaz slowly approached his mate. The seer looked scared for a moment, before Kaz lay down amongst his massive forelegs. Azlak let out a contented purr before he started to explain all that had befallen him. Not long after, Ddraig Boruc and Isikian returned, flying from the same direction Azlak had arrived. The elderly ddraig kept his silence as he listened to Azlak's tale, and we were soon joined by Ddraig Krateos and Alaron. At first I thought the Nixan carried the Axinstone, but then I saw I was mistaken. It was a similar rune, one that Alaron gazed at with absolute awe.

"What I don't understand," the wyvern said once Azlak finished his report, "is how this human has access to such lost magic. Not since the cataclysm has this sort of power been seen. Bri'An's rune alone couldn't have done it, surely?"

"I can't explain it. I don't think any mortal can," Ddraig Boruc replied. The Vatrean had shown no fear or shock towards the wyvern. If anything, he seemed almost familiar with Alaron. "But perhaps we can make educated guesses based on where we are."

Even Alaron blinked in confusion, no one responding to the elderly dragon's declaration. "You may need to explain yourself," the wyvern said, speaking what I was sure everyone had been thinking.

Ddraig Boruc fluttered his wings. "It was in a cave near the human camp where the cataclysm began."

Alaron stepped back. His tail twitched. "Are you saying they might be tapping into some of that magic? How would they even know how to do that?"

"I don't know. It raises many troubling questions, and the sooner we learn the answers, the better," Ddraig Boruc said. He lowered his head and tucked his wings and tail tight to his body.

"I'm not sure anyone cares about how this is being done," Ddraig Krateos growled, interrupting before Alaron could respond. "All we need to do is work out how we can stop him."

Azlak slowly glanced at each of the gathered ddraigs and the wyvern. "He has many allies. Dragons flock to his cause, though I can't imagine why. Humans we know about, but other creatures too."

Ddraig Boruc lifted his head again, but his wings remained tucked close. "It is the necuart we must fear the most. Of all George's allies, it is they who will be the most deadly. We have only seen the one so far, and we must hope that is all the human has been able to sway. Even so, the numbers of grave bats this necuart can control is immense. The bats alone could outnumber both gryphon and dragon."

"We do not fear bats," Ddraig Krateos snarled.

Alaron sent the Nixan a withering glare. "You should."

Ddraig Krateos scoffed and turned away. He muttered something under his breath but offered no rebuke to the wyvern. My brother had warned me about these bats. I was inclined to side with the wyvern, for they sounded like terrifying creatures indeed.

Our impromptu council once again had to wait for an interruption. A small commotion had broken out not far away. Many dragons had suddenly taken to the air again, screeching and squawking as a dozen gryphons tried to get them back to the ground. It didn't take long before I noticed the reason for the disturbance. Surrounded by a phalanx of Axaatl dragons were two humans. One was James McArthur, and the other a woman I only vaguely recognised.

James waved in greeting as he approached. "It is good to see you again, Ellian," he called out. He then looked up at Azlak and put his hands on his hips. Ddraig Krateos and Alaron continued their discussion about the grave bats, but my focus remained on the humans.

Azlak squirmed under the attention of the human, unable to meet his gaze for long. "Do I remind you of her?" the seer whispered, his voice so soft despite his great size.

James nodded, glancing across at his partner. "You do. Sophie here worked with Nightwings more than I did, but I was her handler for a month or so a while back. She was a wilful creature even back then, before George first used his magic on her."

"How is it done?" I asked before I could stop myself, curious to know how a dragon could become such a beast, but also terrified to know the answer.

"George kept that a complete secret," the woman said, bending down onto one knee to speak with me. "I think only two or three others know how he's managed to do it. There's very few he trusts with any of his secrets, let alone this one."

"Sophie's right. All we know is that without the Axinstone, George won't have the power needed to sustain the restoration," James added. He stayed up on his feet, even when he talked directly to me. I had to crane my neck up just to meet his eye, which he never returned anyway. His eyes were always flicking away to look at something new.

For a moment I thought Ddraig Boruc had something to add, as he flared his wings and pawed at the ground, but he held his silence. I was sure he had more information than he was letting us know, but I respected his silence for now. All the same, I planned on questioning him later on what he knew. Every scrap of information we could gather would be crucial.

With Azlak's permission, Sophie and James started to inspect the seer in greater detail, lifting a paw and checking his scales and musculature. The human woman even clambered up onto Azlak's back, making the seer wince as she stepped over his wings. The two were clearly familiar with a dragon of Azlak's size, and I watched on with curiosity with Alaron, Airil and Kaz by my side, the wyvern ignoring Ddraig Krateos's continued complaints for the moment. I didn't know what the humans were looking for, if anything, but they inspected every inch of the seer's body, much to his embarrassment.

The sun was starting to brush against the Sxinix Mountains in the west when the humans jumped down from Azlak's neck. Sophie patted the seer's leg. "You are perfectly healthy. The restoration worked exactly as it should, despite the lack of control George had over you. We found with Maznar that after her first restoration, she lost access to her innate magic. This returned after a few days, and the loss became less frequent with more restorations."

Azlak's shoulders slumped, his wings draping across the ground. "Thank you. That is a relief."

The human patted him again. "I don't think there's anything more we can say right now. Nightwings was used more like a beast, so I doubt you'll want insight into how we trained her."

Azlak growled and shook his head. The two humans took a step back at his aggression, which even caught the attention of Ddraig Krateos and Alaron.

"We'll discuss this more in the morning if you need to," James said. He put his arm around Sophie's shoulders and gently led her away from the enhanced seer. "We can only dream of wings like yours. Walking all day is quite exhausting, so if you'll excuse us."

The two humans lifted their hands in farewell and began to retreat. They soon disappeared into the growing dusk.

Alaron and Ddraig Krateos retired shortly after. It still sounded like they were arguing over the strength of the enemy, and what we could expect to face over the coming days. I didn't know why Ddraig Krateos seemed so eager to debate the wyvern, when it was clear that Alaron knew far more about the world than the Nixan. Their voices lingered long after their tails faded into the darkness.

After sharing a few quiet words with Azlak, Ddraig Boruc took to the air and left us too. Wanting to give Azlak and Kaz a little privacy, I put my wing over Airil and guided him back towards the camp. As we walked, a few dragons came out to meet us. Most whispered words of support and of hope, but few asked the questions I didn't want to face just yet. They asked what our chances were, if any of us would survive the coming days. I tried to respond with optimism, but in my heart, I knew that many of these dragons would not live. Even in victory we would lose so many. My head sunk. How could I lie to so many and tell them that everything was going to be alright when I knew what was waiting for us?

Just when my resolve was starting to weaken, Airil's wing reached out and touched mine. So long as I had him by my side, I knew I could be capable of anything. Every lie I told hurt me deeply, but I knew that each one was necessary. That was the life of a ddraig, I was beginning to learn; when to tell the truth and when to lie to protect my clan from the knowledge that would destroy them.

But sometimes, I knew I still needed to preserve a little time for my own selfish needs. I glanced across at Airil, a smile on my muzzle as a desire grew within me. If this was to be the beginning of our end, then I wanted to live it without regret at what could have been. No matter how much of it I had left, I wanted to pledge the remainder of my life to the Nixan at my side.

In his eyes I could see that same desire, and he reached his paw out to touch mine.

The crackle of Airil's magic filled the air until I was aware of nothing else. It was time to go somewhere private, where no prying eyes could interfere.

The rest of the night belonged to us.

# CHAPTER TWENTY-TWO

**Mulner**

I felt sick.

The demon inside my mind was getting stronger, I was sure.

We had burned Cinson's body, cremating him as per the tradition of our clans. Jesara had lit the flames with a small flint lighter, similar to ones the humans used. The fire had burned bright, searing my eyes and imprinting the vision in my mind forever. My only true friend, dead by my teeth. There could be no redemption for me now, but still I refused to give in to the darkness that threatened to overwhelm me.

It would be so easy to give in, but I had to hold on. For the sake of the gryphons by my side, but most importantly, for the sake of my sister. I would be a threat to her for as long as the necuart prowled these lands. Until he was gone, I could not succumb to his darkness. I could only hope my mind was strong enough to resist. Already I had failed. I could not afford to do so again.

The night was old, having fallen to complete darkness while Cinson was still alive. Finally, the two gryphons had curled up by the fire we had built near the glowing chasm that fell into Nixa. The cold didn't bother me, and the firelight burned my eyes, so I sat some distance away, staring up at the distant stars. I looked for the patterns we had learned to recognise since almost the day we hatched. There were some who claimed that in the stars we could read all the stories of the past, but there would be none that told a story like mine. No dragon had fallen to darkness like I had.

The insidious whispers in my mind had quietened down for now, but I knew they would return. Once they did, I knew I would be a threat to anyone around me, and I could not risk that happening again. I had no choice. I slipped away into the darkness without a sound, trying my hardest not to look back. Jesara and Seri would be better off without me to endanger them.

It was the second time I had flown in the darkness, and this time I flew without fear of the cold. Now I embraced it. It gave me strength. The light of the stars was enough to navigate with, guiding me north and west. There was only one thing left for me to do. Only one way I could break this curse. I had to kill the necuart who had done this to me, and there was only one place I was going to find it. I knew infiltrating the human army should have filled me with terror, but all I felt was cold calm. I would either succeed or die. There was nothing else to it. Succeed or perish. And if, in doing so, I could help my sister by weakening her enemy, then all the better.

I lost track of time as I flew. Feeling no weariness, I was surprised when the eastern sky started to brighten with the coming dawn. Using the sun's position, I corrected my course and continued to fly north. That was where these humans were. That was where the monster in my head resided. I would not stop until I found them.

There was no sign of the draconic army as they flew north. My flight through the night would have put some distance between us. I knew I would arrive first. I could use that advantage to slay the necuart before Ellian was in danger. Resolve gave strength to my wings.

Throughout the day, I flew hard. The expected weariness did not come, nor did I feel any hunger. I couldn't be sure if that was my determination to succeed, or some foul aspect of this monster's magic in my blood. I could feel his presence on occasion. A sickness on my mind when the necuart looked through my eyes.

*"You are coming to me. Good."*

The sun touched the mountains. The underside of the clouds turned pink as evening began to descend. The land below me was empty, with no sign of dragon or human. This army had come a long way from the Nixan lair since its destruction.

Wingbeats rustled behind and above me.

I had no time to react before talons encircled around my body.

Though I struggled, the talons had too strong a grip on me. I couldn't twist enough to lay claw or tooth on them. One claw pressed down on the back of my head, preventing me from even looking up. Without knowing the identity of my attacker, I was immediately put in the mind of one of those monstrous dragons created by human magic.

My attacker made no noise as they began to descend, dropping into the long shadows cast by the mountains as the sun set behind them. I was set down on the ground gently, but the talons continued to press down on me to stop me from moving.

I did not expect to hear Seri.

"You gave us a real chase there, Mulner," the gryphon said. They leaned down, curved beak finally coming into view, just a scales-width from my face. "We didn't think you would fly so fast."

"Let me go," I growled, claws digging into the ground as I struggled to free myself. The gryphon's grip only tightened.

Jesara swooped down to land just in front of us. "We can't risk that." Her talons flexed.

Seri chirped in agreement. "We know you may not fully be in control. If there is a gap in your memory, then it is because the necuart is controlling you. He is likely summoning you to him."

I growled again. There were no gaps in my memory. I recalled everything, even though I longed to forget. I knew what my best friend's blood tasted like, how his eyes looked as the life faded from them, betrayed and confused. Those were memories I longed to purge. It all remained painfully clear. The necuart's influence had confused me, guiding me towards evil actions, but nothing controlled me. I almost wished for that excuse.

I stopped my struggle and slumped to my belly. My wings were still outstretched, pinned in place by Seri's talons. "He isn't controlling me," I whispered, not expecting the gryphons to believe me.

Jesara lifted my head with a gentle touch of her talon. I trembled as that sharp claw pricked against my scales. She forced me to look into her eyes. I didn't dare turn my head away, fearing what that talon might do if I did. Her vivid green eyes narrowed as they burned into me.

The gryphon chirped and released me, stepping back. "He tells the truth. The necuart is not controlling him, at least not for the moment."

Seri was slightly less willing to believe their companion. The blue-feathered gryphon did not release their grip on me, keeping me pinned to the ground. "All the same, why did you flee? We have promised to help keep you safe and to protect you from causing harm to your sister and her army. Why do you fly towards them again, if not at the call of the necuart?"

How much could I tell them? I kept my eyes low as I worked things through my mind. Perhaps even speaking my plans would mean the necuart would know them. But I also knew that if I remained silent, then the two gryphons would not let me from their sight again. I needed to say something.

"I didn't fly because the necuart commanded it." I growled as I gained a bit of confidence, the declaration warming my blood as I spoke it into truth. The creature did not command me. I was in control of everything. "I flew because I chose to. I'm not flying to Ellian, but I am going to help her in the only way I can. This necuart is a threat to her. I am going to kill him."

Jesara squawked and jumped back. Her feathers fluffed out. "This is madness."

Seri's grip slackened. I used the opportunity to squirm away, tucking my wings to my sides in the hope that the gryphons would not feel like they needed to pin me down again. I doubted I would be able to outpace them anyway.

"It is the only way," I said, pacing over the grass between them. I could feel their eyes on me, their eerie unblinking gaze proving too powerful for me to meet. Was this what the humans felt when I looked at them? I didn't like it.

Seri settled in the grass, lying down with their forelegs crossed. They fluttered their wings a couple of times to get their feathers right, before tucking them tight to their sides. Even though the gryphon lay down, they were still taller than me, managing to look down with those piercing yellow eyes. Their gaze was so strong that I slowed my pacing until I came to a stop in front of them. Jesara lay down just beside them.

"I appreciate your heart, Mulner," Seri said, once all was still around them. "You seek to destroy a creature who is a danger to your sister. Killing the necuart would swing the balance of power towards the dragons. But you are not capable of doing this. It is not a matter of desire or skill, but one of magic. Once bitten, you are simply incapable of striking against your master, no matter how much you desire it. This is simply the way of the necuart's magic and it has never been broken."

A deep rumble settled in my chest, sending heat through my body to chase away the chill left by the necuart's magic. "Then I shall be the one to break it. Or I shall die trying."

Seri shook their head sorrowfully. "You will only throw your life away needlessly. There will be other ways you can help your sister. You just need to stay away from this necuart."

"Why do you choose to do this? Anyone else could kill this necuart and free you from his grip. Why must it be you?" Jesara added.

"Because I killed my best friend!" The words exploded from my mouth before I could stop them. White hot fury burned at my eyes, searing my scales. And yet, despite the anger, I found myself frozen and unable to move. I choked back on the anger, settling like bile in my stomach. Neither gryphon said anything as I struggled to contain my breathing, bringing my voice down to a quieter level.

I hung my head. "I killed Cinson. It was my teeth that did it, no matter who or what controlled or influenced me. No one can deny it was my teeth in his throat. Because of that, this creature must pay. And it must be me."

Jesara clicked her beak. "Mulner, this is pointless." She fell silent as Seri lifted their wing.

"You understand that you plan on doing something that no one has done in thousands of years," the cobalt gryphon said. Their eyes pierced through me. This time, I forced myself to meet their gaze.

I tucked my tail between my hindlegs. "I have to at least try. I owe it to Cinson."

Seri sighed, a whistle coming from their curved beak. "Very well. I think you are being foolish and should fly as far from this necuart as you can, but if you are determined that you must try, then I will help you get inside the camp."

Jesara chirped something in the gryphon's own language. Seri responded, the two exchanging a quick and high-pitched conversation in words I had no hope of understanding. Whatever argument they were having, Seri appeared to win, as they lifted their head a little higher, eyes twinkling brightly in the fading sunlight.

The bronze-feathered gryphon clicked her beak. "I don't know why I'm agreeing to this, but yes. We will help you. We will get you inside the camp, but from there it will be up to you. We will be too conspicuous. No other gryphon will have allied themselves with these humans, so you will be alone. I wish there was advice we could give to help you succeed."

I bowed my head and said nothing. It didn't matter if the gryphons doubted me. I could not fly away from this necuart. No matter what they thought, I would kill this creature and save my sister. The necuart would not harm any more dragons that I cared about. Cinson's death would be the resolve that allowed me to achieve the impossible.

"We shall fly out in the morning," Seri said. "Can we trust you not to fly away again before then?"

I would be foolish to ignore the offered help. Though my wings itched, eager to be in constant movement towards my goal, I sat down and forced myself to stay still. "I won't go anywhere."

The two gryphons chirped happily. While I remained sat still, they prepared a simple camp for the night, clearing aside some branches and preparing a fire beneath the shelter of the trees. It would not be much, but it would keep the wind from us once the sun had set. They refused to let me help, so all I could do was watch their movement as they worked.

Once they had prepared our camp, Seri pulled me close. They got me to lie between their forepaws, where their feathers could keep me warm through the cold night, in case the fire was not enough. I doubted I would need either, not with the cold magic running like ice through my blood. I did not turn down the offer, though. It would be nice to share the night with someone, even if it was a creature as bizarre and unusual as a gryphon.

As the sun finally set behind the mountains, Seri and Jesara began to sing. They told me the songs were about great warriors of the distant past, going to war and achieving great victories. I didn't understand a single word.

The swooping melodies of their trilled voices soothed me. Despite my best intentions of staying awake through the dark and cold night, my eyes soon drooped. With my head resting against Seri's forepaw, I soon sank into a dreamless sleep.

As promised, we left early in the morning, not long after the sun rose. My wings ached as we took to flight. I couldn't tell if it was the effort I had put in the previous day, or part of the affliction the necuart had imparted upon me. I mentioned nothing of it to the gryphons, forcing myself to keep up with the pace of their wings.

Early in the afternoon, I caught sight of our target, a dirty smudge on the horizon. The city of canvas spread over many miles. Even from a great distance, I could hear the activity within the settlement. Of Ellian and her allies, I could see no sign.

Following the lead of the gryphons, I dropped to the ground far enough away from the camp that the humans would not see us. We landed behind the shelter of a thin band of trees that snaked along the brow of an elevated ridge line of hills.

I was eager to hurry through the forest towards the camp, but Jesara stood in front of me to block any thought of approaching just yet. The gryphon peered through the thick trees, ears twitching. "There are patrols. None near us just now, but we won't have long."

"Then let's hurry," I said. I attempted to push past the gryphon, but Jesara stopped me by stamping her forepaw down in front of me.

"Wait," Seri chirped. "This might be your only chance to get in without being detected. You need to take the opportunity while they're unguarded."

I clamped down on my urge to leap forward and sprint away from the gryphons. They would not let me do anything without their permission. I had to accept that they were in control of the situation, as much as that burned at my gut. To use up some of the energy that twitched through my muscles, I pawed at the ground. "Then how do I get in? Their weapons mean I can't fly over their defences."

The gryphons were silent for a moment, before Jesara spoke. "I will see what you need to get past. Wait here for me." She chirped something else to Seri in their musical language. She then hurried away, moving with a silence and grace that surprised me, given her size. It was not long before her dappled feathers and fur blended in with the shadows and I could see her no longer.

Temptation flickered through my mind. With only one gryphon guarding me, perhaps I could make my escape and flee into the human encampment. I quickly reconsidered when I noticed Seri's eyes fixed on me. They were not going to give me the opportunity to get away.

I recognised the look in their eyes. I interrupted them before they even managed to open their beak.

"I'm not going to reconsider. I have to do this."

Seri clicked their beak. "I understand your determination. I just wish there was more we could do to help you. A necuart is a dangerous foe, even ignoring your unique situation. Do not underestimate this enemy."

My lip curled into a snarl. "Perhaps the necuart should worry about underestimating me. If it is true that no one bitten by a necuart has killed one, then he won't expect my attack until it is too late."

The gryphon chirruped softly. "Perhaps. But maybe it is best not to speak of your plans just now. Try not to think about them, if you can. I do not know the hold the necuart has over your mind. It is possible he may learn your plans should they be too strong in your mind."

I flicked my tail. How could I avoid thinking about my intentions? It seemed an impossible task, especially as I had nothing else to occupy my mind. All I could do was wait for Jesara to return from her scouting mission.

I tried to focus my mind on something else. Anything else. Closing my eyes, I listened for sounds from the camp. The humans were loud, patrolling through the mass of canvas tents with little thought given to stealth. When their encampment was so vast, there was little reason for it. In the distance, far from the boundaries nearby, I could hear a familiar sound. Construction. Just like the humans led by James McArthur, these humans were building something. The screech of their tools was distant, but almost constant.

Something nearer caught my attention. A sound and then a smell, completely unfamiliar to me. It was not a dragon, nor a gryphon. It wasn't even human. Several things moved through the undergrowth of the forest, away from us and towards the encampment. It was hard to determine how large they were, as they moved with near-perfect stealth.

I opened my eyes to see Seri was also aware of the strange beings moving through the trees. At least, they looked in the same direction where the faint noises came from. They pawed at the ground. "Do you smell them?" When I nodded, they continued. "Ailur. A species that usually lives a long way south and east of here, not too far from our homeland. I haven't known them to be in these parts for quite a few years."

"Are they friend or enemy?"

Seri clicked their beak. "I don't know. They could be either."

I tried not to think about the potential complication. Either the ailur would be a threat, or they would not. There was nothing I could do about them now.

It did not take much longer for Jesara to return. She emerged from the shadows as silent as the ailur. She chirped to get our attention, then gestured with a wing for us to follow her. I hurried forward, moving between the two gryphons as we finally began to draw near to my target.

The stench of humans was unmistakable as we approached the mass of tents, gradually becoming visible through the trees. Never before had I seen so many humans in the one place. I dreaded to think what their permanent cities were like, edifices of steel and stone, reaching up to the clouds but forever remaining bound to the earth. Humans had such a weird fascination with the sky, cursed never to experience the joys of flight. The skies were ours, but the reach of humanity was getting longer and bolder. Soon they would be able to pluck us from the air without leaving the ground.

Shouted voices overwhelmed each other as humans started to organise. I couldn't hear anything distinct, so I couldn't be sure if they had seen Ellian and her army. Occasionally I could see a human between tents, still so small at this distance. None of them were searching in our direction, so we continued unhindered through the dense undergrowth of the forest.

There weren't many birds or wildcats in the trees as there should have been. It seemed the humans' mere presence had scared most of them away. I could have used a snack before delving into the camp. There had to be something I could steal from the humans' supplies, even if it did mean having to endure the horrifically seared cooked meat the humans preferred. A growling belly would soon become the least of my worries.

A nearby bang startled me, my wings flaring and hindlegs tensing, though flight was impossible amongst all these trees. The sound hadn't come from the camp, but from deeper into the forest. Towards the scent of the strange ailur.

A shadow on my mind warned me of the presence of the necuart. Like a migratory bird knew where to fly for winter, I could tell exactly where amongst the masses of humans this cold creature was. The necuart's own magic that coursed through my veins would help assist his own death. I couldn't help but smile, baring my teeth to the uncaring foliage.

I had to ignore the magnetic pull in my mind for now. Jesara led us to the northernmost point of the forest. I could hear a river nearby, no doubt providing the humans with all the water and fish they could need while they waited.

The river was a boundary between the forest and the camp, much to my annoyance. The cold water separated me from the canvas city, with no clear way to cross without taking to wing. I was sure the humans had to have something they used; the idiot James McArthur and his small group had built a bridge within a week. This army had been sitting idle ever since they destroyed Nixa. They should have had plenty of time to construct whatever they needed, especially if they knew they weren't planning on going anywhere for this long.

As far as I could see in either direction, tents lined up right to the far riverbank. On the outer edge, the tents were all quite small, but I had chanced a glimpse at some of the larger constructs in the middle of the camp. Guards kept watch at regular intervals along the bank. Jesara flicked out her wing to the nearest group of guards, then melted back into the shadows.

"That is where you must go in," the gryphon whispered. She guided me beneath the trees again, away from any watching eyes within the camp. "We will provide a distraction to draw the guards out. Once inside you must try to look like you belong. Come. This way."

We crept onwards. I kept my wings tight against my sides to prevent them snagging on any overhanging branches, the gryphons having a bigger challenge than me to keep clean. Dry leaves littered the forest floor, a beautiful array of reds and oranges, down to the dull browns that had fallen earlier. They crunched beneath my paws, making silent movement impossible. Soon winter would be hitting with full force. It would be interesting to see how the humans would prepare against that. I feared what it might do to Ellian's army.

The trees grew more closely together the further from the edge I walked. Light was scarce. What few green leaves still clung to the branches still provided enough coverage to almost completely block out the sunlight. But that was not all that was up there. A gentle chittering drew my attention to the shadows that seemed to be moving. Bats. Hundreds of them. I knew they had heard us, but for now they didn't seem at all interested in descending to the forest floor. They clung to the branches close to the canopy, barging each other out of the way for space to settle. Not once did any of them fall, their massive claws gripped the branches tight. I could see from here how muscular their legs were, much more so than any dragon. Even an Axaatl dragon would be weak in comparison. Though the gryphons cast wary eyes up, they showed no fear to the bats. I tried to do the same.

I crept on, doing my best to minimise the sound I made on the dry leaves. The last thing I wanted was to arouse the wrath of an entire colony of grave bats. Thankfully they let us pass, with just a few angry shrieks to bother me. Perhaps they could sense the necuart's curse within me. Or maybe they weren't hungry yet.

Two more loud bangs alarmed me, a lot nearer now than before. It didn't sound like the construction that had been plaguing my small lair ever since James McArthur had moved in. If anything, it sounded almost like fighting. Had my sister come so soon?

We hurried on, quickly leaving behind the bats in their roosts. Jesara glanced back as she started to run. "I overheard the ailur. They are preparing to infiltrate the camp as well. We can use the confusion they leave to slip you in as well, Mulner."

I hissed in delight. "Then they are allies."

Jesara flicked an ear back. "I can't speak to that, but we at least share a common enemy. Hurry. It sounds like they've already engaged with the humans."

We soon reached the edge of a clearing. What I saw was unlike anything I had ever seen, and given the recent emergence of the gryphons, I was starting to wonder what else might be out there we didn't know about. Three dragons were in a small clearing, all Xitals judging from the crown of horns on their heads, but it what they faced that confused me. Resembling humans only in body structure but half the size, rust-red fur covered the bodies of the eight creatures, with black and white markings around their faces. Their long, fluffy tails arched right up over their heads. Their limbs were short, adding to their squat appearance. Each of them carried some sort of weapon in six-fingered hands. Half held swords, while the others carried what appeared to be slings.

Three large metallic structures had toppled to the ground. I couldn't be sure what they were, but they all leaked some foul-smelling liquid from several small holes.

Leading away from the clearing was a path towards the encampment. Already, more dragons were hurrying down the path, though there were no humans yet.

"Go, now," Jesara hissed. She nudged me with her forepaw, pushing me away from the clearing. "Go with fortune, dragon."

"May we see you again, Mulner," Seri added.

I lingered long enough only to dip my head towards the two gryphons. They both returned the gesture. Before I could reconsider what I was about to do, I leaped away, hurrying around the edge of the clearing and avoiding the path as I ran for the encampment.

A handful of humans ran past me, barely a wing-breadth away. They did not notice me in the shadows as they ran into the forest, weapons raised. But when I reached the edge of the forest, I saw that not all the guards had left their post. At least six more waited dutifully in position. Of course they would choose now to be disciplined.

I looked back as a pained shout erupted from deeper into the forest. That was my opportunity. I fought hard to hide the wide grin as I burst back out into sunlight. The skirmish had given me the perfect excuse.

I jumped across the river in one bound, using my wings to glide across to the far bank. Two of the guards saw me immediately, yelling and drawing their weapons.

"Ailur!" I shouted, trying to draw a sense of panic. "In the forest. They ambushed us. Hurry! There's too many of them!"

The guards didn't hesitate. Another dozen appeared seemingly from nowhere. I had to blink and stare, as they appeared to run across the surface of the river, barely making a splash. Then I saw, almost laughing. There was a bridge there, hidden just below the surface. I was almost impressed.

None of the guards looked back to see if I was joining them, so without a sound I slipped between the closest two tents. No one would confront me now. To the humans I was just another dragon; I doubted they would be able to tell me apart from the Xitals. If I came across any dragons, I simply had to claim I had abandoned my clan, preferring to ally myself with the indomitable human forces. Like Jesara had said, I needed to look like I belonged.

Progress was slow as I made my way through the tents. Though I was confident I would be safe no matter what, I still made the decision to stick to the shadows and stay out of sight. There was a lot of activity around, but it seemed most of the humans were still attempting to wake up. Few wore any armour or even carried any weapons, and many of them carried small cups of some steaming liquid. By staying in the shadows, I was able to observe a lot, but learned nothing from their behaviour. They truly were a curious species. Everything put me in the mind of James McArthur and what his humans had been building. It didn't feel like an army encampment.

As I paused to wait for some humans to pass, I thought I heard a noise from just behind me. I glanced back, but could see nothing there. A sense of unease was persistent though, a tingle at the base of my tail that I couldn't shake off. The feeling lingered, even as I scurried forward once more, following the magnetic pull in my head.

I was not prepared for the weight on my tail, or the arms around my belly. Pinned down, I could do nothing as I looked up into a pair of wide amber eyes surrounded by a mask of black fur. An ailur.

"Dragon prisoner of Selu now."

# Chapter Twenty-Three

**Azlak**

Dawn had come. A chorus of birdsong broke the silence. Few woke to the noise. I knew I hadn't been the only one to find sleep elusive. We had flown far the previous day, putting behind us the ruins of Nixa and towards the northern wilds where the humans had set up their great encampment. Ddraig Boruc was sure the place was deliberate, and something to do with the cave I had sheltered in with Anzig and our group on the way back from the human territory beyond the mountains. Why the humans would choose such a place was something no one but the old ddraig knew. He kept those secrets to himself. Not even Alaron had been able to pry more information from him.

Scouts had come and gone during the previous day of flying, with more still returning with the growing light. They were all gryphons, with none of the dragons capable of flying during the night. Though I no longer felt the chill sapping my strength, I had not joined the scouts, with the ddraigs refusing to give me permission. I had to remain on the ground with the rest of the dragons, restless energy coursing through my wings. That energy was something I would almost miss, once Ddraig Boruc restored me.

To my surprise, I received a summons to meet with the ddraigs and leaders. Taking care as I moved, I picked my way through the resting gryphons to the top of the nearest hill. The many ddraigs and haeraigs who had joined the Laxtal army soon joined me.

Prince Kyrus was the most alert of those present. His attention fixated mostly on his feathers, preening them back into position if they were in any way displaced during his rest. By his side sat Alaron. He grasped a ceramic cup borrowed from the humans in his clawed wing-arms, a hot black liquid spewing steam over his face. Condensation dripped from his scales as he sat, almost completely unmoving. He was muttering something to himself, too quietly for me to hear.

Ddraig Ellian and Ddraig Boruc were the last to arrive, fluttering down to the hill together. The two ddraigs dipped their heads towards Alaron and Prince Kyrus. The gryphon chirped and finally drew his beak away from his feathers. Despite all his work, I could not see a difference. He seemed satisfied, at least.

The wyvern drained the last of his drink, then looked up to the dragons and gryphons gathered around him. His claws tapped against the rim of his cup. "I will fly ahead with Azlak this morning to see this human camp. The scout reports have been invaluable, but there is nothing better than seeing it for myself. I will need Azlak for protection and for his knowledge of the area."

I did my best to stay still, suppressing the urge to lash my tail. "You want me, Alaron?"

The wyvern turned to look up at me. He showed no fear in his eyes, no sense of unease being in my presence. "George has given us a great gift in this form of yours. We would be foolish not to use it at every opportunity."

Kyrus chirped in agreement. "I will lead the rest of the force behind you. My scouts have indicated a good place to land, close enough that we can keep eyes on any human movements, but out of range of any fortifications they may have. Something about this situation unsettles me, though. We have seen little indication they are preparing for war. There is another objective here. One that we have failed to see."

"You're right," Alaron said, sighing softly. He ran his claws around the edge of his empty cup and stared down at the cooling dregs. "I hope all will become clear once I am able to see this camp for myself. We are missing something important, and I hope that won't lead to disaster."

The gryphon prince lifted a forepaw and clenched his talons. "Contact me the moment you discover anything."

I glanced over Alaron. I wondered where the magical slate was in his body. He didn't have a forepaw like dragons or gryphons. He gave no indication as he nodded once. "Azlak, prepare to fly out. I want to be there as soon as possible. Ddraig Ellian, prepare your dragons to fly after us. We may need to launch our attack immediately, so stay fresh on the wing."

"We'll be ready," Ddraig Ellian growled.

Was this really it? The humans were just beyond the horizon and our army prepared to face them. I stared north, towards the mountains. If I let the sounds of waking dragons and singing gryphons fall away, I could almost imagine the noises of that encampment. The clash of their hammers. The buzz of their saws. They were building something there. We needed to find out what and destroy it if we needed to.

At Alaron's instruction, I took to wing and let the magical heat in my body lift me from the ground. No one else followed, a relief from the previous day, when I had been at the front of the massive horde of dragons and gryphons. The thunder of wings had filled my mind, a bizarre sensation compared to the fear I had felt just two months earlier, when I had led Anzig and six other dragons across the mountains. The experience had been unsettling. Flying with just the wyvern promised to be a little more relaxing, despite our destination.

A group of returning scouts met us after about half an hour. They lingered long enough only to share a few quiet words with Alaron, before flying on to return to the bulk of the army. There appeared to be little information to please the wyvern, as he continued to fly and mutter to himself, constantly talking under his breath. At first, I thought he spoke to someone using his slate, but then I realised he growled both sides of an imaginary conversation.

With Alaron distracted by his internal musings, I kept on constant lookout for any aerial threats as we neared the human camp, but the sky was clear. There was no sign of any grave bats or enhanced dragons. Without the Axinstone, I hoped that the humans no longer had the capability to power the intense transformations – restorations, as James McArthur insisted on calling them. Despite the growing sunlight, I still feared some patrolling bats, but I saw none. The cold, wintery sunlight was enough to keep them away.

I shuddered as I caught sight of the camp on the horizon, in the shadow of the mountains. Even from a great distance, the sea of canvas reeked with the scent of humans. I quickly scanned over the camp, taking in the features I had not noticed in my hasty escape. While they had constructed most of the camp with the canvas tents, there were all sorts of wooden frames located around the outskirts, especially on the side facing the mountains. The larger tents, where I had endured the transformation into this monstrous beast, were much closer to the cliffs than I had realised. Several large, metallic towers rose just in front of the cave.

Hundreds of humans moved around the camp, climbing the wooden frames, swarming like bees on a flower. Their purpose eluded me, but Alaron appeared to take some understanding of what he saw.

The wyvern drifted closer to my head, soaring just in front of my wing. "Esperance chose you as an envoy. It is time to prove you are worthy of that honour. Land down there, by the gate," he said, flicking out his barbed tail to show me an empty stretch of grass between two forested areas.

I stared for a few moments, keeping my wings still and letting myself glide slowly. "There? It's in range of their weapons."

Alaron scoffed. "Just land, dragon. You need to be the voice of Esperance for this. They won't attack you, and I doubt they could even hurt you anyway. Your scales are much tougher now."

I did not feel reassured, but I still tilted my wings and aimed for the patch of clear space the wyvern pointed out. I kept a wary eye on the humans as I descended. Sure enough, the activity in the camp changed as I approached. Distant and quiet shouts became louder. The sounds of construction stopped, but the expected attacks did not come.

On the way down, Alaron quickly told me everything he wanted me to say. I struggled to remember it all, but the wyvern did speak the truth. Esperance had chosen me for a reason. It was time to prove her faith in me was accurate.

I almost stumbled as I landed, my paws scuffing against the ground as I failed to account for my larger size. I could feel the eyes of Alaron and the humans on me. I lifted my head and tried to ignore them all. Breathing in deeply, I let my chest swell with air and the hot magic that swirled through my gut.

With a deep roar that shook the trees, I unleashed that air and magic in a jet of fierce flame. Once the heat dissipated, I stamped a forepaw to the ground and bellowed my voice as loud as I could, doing my best not to stutter through Alaron's instructions.

"I am Azlak, voice of Esperance! I call upon the human George Symons to come forth and explain why he has invaded dragon territory, disobeying the treaty established by Ehran seven hundred years ago." I hesitated. No one responded. My claws sunk into the soft earth as I summoned the inner fire again, letting it swell and warm my body, stoking the vulnerable confidence. "Come out, George. Speak with us and we can avoid any further bloodshed."

Silence continued to greet my words. I took in a few more deep breaths while I waited.

"Give them chance to respond," Alaron said quietly. He lingered between my forepaws. "Invoking the name of Esperance has weight, even this far from Ehran. George won't be comfortable knowing her envoys are here."

I flicked my tail, safe from accidentally striking Alaron with it. "Does she really have that much influence?"

The wyvern chuckled. "You really do have a lot to learn."

"So everyone keeps telling me," I replied. I got no further answer however, as movement started to become apparent just beyond the gate. I watched warily as the only entrance in the low wooden wall creaked open. A lone human stepped through. It was not George.

I took a step back, taking care not to tread on Alaron. The human was the strange one present in my transformation, Rico. His pale markings were not visible this time, his skin bare and clean. The human moved with a swagger as he approached us, showing no fear towards me or the bristling wyvern between my paws.

The human spread his hands. "I knew to expect you, envoys of Esperance. You especially, dragon. I warned George that magic would not work how he liked. Just look at you now." He smiled widely, somehow his blunt teeth looking more ferocious than anything a dragon could manage.

Alaron stepped forward, his barbed tail lashing back and forth. "We are here to discuss why you have breached the treaty…"

Rico waved his hand and barked in laughter, interrupting Alaron. "Yes, I heard the big guy. Truth is, I don't care what you have to say."

The wyvern growled. "Bring us George. He is the one we wish to speak to."

"Can't help you there." Rico folded his arms over his chest. "George is too busy tinkering with his experiments trying to get it all to work again. That means I'm in control. Unfortunately for you, I'm a lot less reasonable than he is. George, now he might have gone home if you asked nicely. He might have realised that this was my plan all along, but you've fallen into the trap as much as he has."

Alaron moved forward a little more, stepping out of my shadow to stand halfway between me and the human. His tail stopped moving as he braced his wingarms against the ground. "Who are you?"

Rico's eyes flashed as he lifted his head. One hand reached up, fingers closing as though to grasp something at his throat, but there was nothing there. "So, the old bastard didn't tell you. No matter. Your end will come, dragon. Here. Soon. There's nothing you can do to stop it. Pray to your gods if you must. They can't help you now."

Alaron snarled. "Then it seems you are the danger here, and not George. On behalf of Esperance, I find you a danger to the peace of Farenar."

The wyvern moved faster than a diving falcon, leaping for the human in a grey blur. His tail lashed out, whipping for Rico's throat.

The strike never landed. Rico stepped aside and grabbed hold of the wyvern's neck with a speed no human should possess. In one fluid movement, Rico hurled the wyvern back towards me. Alaron was unable to correct his momentum before he struck the ground and rolled between my legs.

I leaped aside, chest swelling. Smoke billowed from my mouth as I advanced on the human. Even still, Rico showed no fear. He stood his ground and smirked, arm extended out towards me. In his hand was a small pistol.

A flash of light erupted from the weapon. Cracks like molten lava snaked up the metallic barrel, splintering the pistol even as searing hot pain burst across my muzzle. The flames in my throat died. My forelegs buckled and I crashed to the ground before I could reach the human. I dug my claws into the soft soil, trying to get up again, but the human didn't approach.

Char and soot blackened Rico's hand. He inspected the remains of his weapon with a disappointed glare. "Useless, like most of George's tech. No matter, I'll deal with you all later. Enjoy your final day while you can. I'll make sure you all suffer."

The human didn't give me the opportunity to recover. Even Alaron was too slow to catch him. By the time the wyvern staggered towards the human, Rico was already at the gate. He paused to wave, before slipping inside the encampment. In the time our conversation had taken place, guards had come to protect the gate and the wall, a dozen rifles aimed towards us.

My nose still buzzing from Rico's weapon, I reached out with a paw to shield Alaron from the marksmen. The wyvern lashed his tail and growled, but wisely began to retreat with me, getting out of range of the guards.

"Diplomacy has failed," Alaron growled. His breath hitched in pain as he limped away. "I had hoped they would be reasonable, but this man seems determined to go to war. The question is why. Why does this human seem so eager to fight dragonkind?"

I had no answer to that question. I doubted the wyvern expected one from me. One thought did come to mind. Had we been wrong to consider George as the main threat? Whoever this Rico was, he seemed the one most eager to kill dragons. I didn't think it changed much. We would still need to defeat the humans in battle, no matter who commanded them.

I looked back to the gate once more. The humans still lingered there, eyes on me. My tail curled. It wouldn't be long before I would return, this time as a weapon against the camp. I had no doubt that Alaron and Prince Kyrus wanted to use my size and strength. Now that I was here, fear began to trickle through me, replacing the magical warmth that this form possessed.

"Come on, hurry," Alaron said, breaking into my thoughts with his snapping tone. "Kyrus and Ellian will be here soon. There should be a good place to land just on the other side of these hills. We need to be ready."

With a sigh, I tucked my wings tight to my back and followed the wyvern.

A thunder of wings descended on the plains between the two forests. Prince Kyrus and Ddraig Ellian led the massive army that took up most of the sky, a show of force that would have been terrifying were it not for the fact I had seen what we faced. Even the incredible number of dragons and gryphons seemed inadequate to the human encampment on the other side of the hills.

The gryphon prince immediately approached us, eager to learn everything we had discovered. Ddraig Ellian and my father joined Prince Kyrus, though I could see nothing of Ddraig Boruc.

"A human called Rico is the threat," Alaron said, explaining what had happened as we led the gryphon and ddraigs up the hill so they could see the camp with their own eyes. "We tried diplomacy. We even tried to take him down while he was vulnerable, but he was stronger than I gave him credit for. We will have no choice but to fight."

We crested the hill. Distant shouts echoed across the plain as the humans mobilised their defence. They would have seen our great army land.

"This is no mere army," Prince Kyrus hissed. He squinted as he looked over the camp. "They're workers. This is a city they're building."

"A city? In our territory?" Ddraig Krateos growled. The Nixan crouched over the Axinstone. He flexed his claws, gouging through the soft earth with ease. "This land belongs to Nixa. They have no right to settle here."

"They defeated your clan in battle," the gryphon pointed out. He stood over the Nixan, easily dominating the ddraig for height. "Does that not give them the right?"

Ddraig Krateos growled, giving no answer to Prince Kyrus. I turned my focus back to the camp, trying to work out where most of the humans were keeping their numbers, and what tools they used to construct their new city.

"If they were only here to build, then we might have come to an agreement," Ddraig Ellian said. She stood between my father and the gryphon, but she stared unblinking towards the camp. "They have shown that they are not content with simply building new cities. Whether they want to experiment on us or kill us doesn't matter. We need to show them that we will not accept that."

"You speak truthfully," Alaron said. He looked across to Ddraig Krateos. "Will the humans be able to access the Axinstone from across the battlefield?"

The Nixan ddraig put his paw over the precious stone, as though a human was reaching out to grab it there and then. "No," he growled. "I tested it with one of McArthur's humans. If just one dragon was magically connected to the Axinstone, they were not able to reach its power. Only we will be able to use it."

"Good. We can't risk their wizards being at full strength. They're dangerous enough as it is," the wyvern said.

"What about that other rune?" Ddraig Ellian asked. She hesitated and glanced up to me. "The one Azlak and Kaz found beneath Laxtal?"

Alaron shook his head. "No, only Bri'An's rune has the power needed to fuel the change. The leopard rune is powerless by itself," the wyvern explained, before turning his focus back on the rest of the small group. "We attack while there's still some confusion. Azlak, you will go first. You will be largely invulnerable to their weapons. Ddraig Ellian, if you could please gather the other ddraigs and haeraigs. We will need to coordinate our attacks. To all of you, may the wind rise beneath your wings. Listen to my orders, and we might just yet survive this day."

"I'm ready," I rumbled, trying to suppress the terror that was welling up in my chest. I tried not to think about the weapon Rico had used on me, hoping there were no others like it. The tip of my muzzle was still itching.

"Go and make your final preparations and return here. This hill gives a good vantage of the whole battlefield. We shall command from here," Alaron said, turning and bowing his head to each of us, which we repeated back to him. As one, they all took to wing and left me alone. I looked out across the plains. Where there was now a few sparse trees and undulating grasslands would soon be a battlefield of terror and bloodshed. The forests and the river that bordered the human camp would run red with the fallen.

I wasn't ready for this.

The last few minutes went by far too quickly. Before I even knew it, Alaron had returned. Kyrus followed just behind him. At the bottom of the hill the gryphons had started to line up in ranks, a few of the higher in command walking through and inspecting everything from feathers to claws.

Behind the gryphons was Ddraig Ellian, leading her large army of Laxtal and Axaatl dragons. It was the full force Laxtal could muster. Though I no longer truly felt a part of that clan, I still feared the decimation that faced the dragons I had grown up with.

The other clans lined up beside the Laxtals, with Ddraig Metrus leading her clan alongside the gryphons. Clan Eltee would fly just behind me, forming the first line of assault on the human forces. Not one of those dragons showed any sign of fear, every single member of the minor clan holding their heads high with pride.

"On your command, Azlak," Alaron said, forgoing any attempt to give a speech to his army. Everything that needed to be said had been said. All that remained was death.

I spread my wings and behind me several hundred dragons did the same. Launching myself off the ground, I unleashed a powerful roar that reverberated through the air. Magic coursed through me as I beat my immense wings, closing the distance to the humans in just a few short moments. I swooped low over the tents a few times, searching for possible targets and giving the Elteeans a chance to catch up once more, as I had left them far behind already.

The humans panicked as they tried to organise, just a few lone shots fired up at me, the bullets ricocheting uselessly from my scales. From the corner of my eye, I could see the Elteeans approaching; I knew it was imperative I kept them out of the direct line of fire, or else they would be easy targets, picked from the sky with ease.

Inhaling deeply, I could feel magic swell in my throat, a fierce burning sensation that kept on building until I could no longer contain it. A ferocious spout of flame burst from my jaws, igniting a row of tents and sparking a few small explosions as the canvas and the contents it protected was superheated.

Twice more I passed over this small section of the camp, unleashing the flame of legend upon the defenceless humans. The Elteeans descended in my wake, tearing into the unprepared foe with tooth and claw before rising back out of reach. Before the humans could even arm themselves with their guns they were out of sight, falling on another group of victims. They moved with much greater agility than I was able to manage, but even the shots that struck my more vulnerable wings failed to do any damage.

From towards the centre of the camp I could hear sounds of barked orders. The humans were starting to organise. I gave a bellowed roar, ordering the Elteeans to begin their retreat.

As I did so, another distant roar reverberated back. This was no echo, and the sound was all too familiar. Nightwings had come. The spectre from the past had returned to her full glory; evidently the humans had still had enough magic left for one last transformation. Behind her flew an army of dragons, rising from the far end of the camp, close to the mountains.

Behind us, Alaron reacted, sending forth Kyrus's flock of gryphons. I led the Elteeans out of range of the humans' guns before turning around and waiting, halfway between the human camp and draconic forces.

I roared out a challenge towards Nightwings.

My sister answered the call.

The battle had begun.

# CHAPTER TWENTY-FOUR

**Ellian**

Our fate had come. Dragon fought dragon. Gryphons and humans prepared themselves to die in our wars. The army of George and Tsona faced us at last. We would drive them out of our lands, no matter what goals they had here.

By my side, Kyrus shrieked out orders to his gryphons, sounding like a hunting eagle diving on its prey. Only half of his gryphons had joined the battle. The others were in the forest, preparing for the next stage of our plan.

The gryphon force shepherded the humans back towards the gate, while dragons harassed those defending on the wall, preventing clear shots from the deadly guns the humans wielded. The air was a flurry of activity, with warriors on each side wheeling around each other. The Xital dragons were strong and resolute, not retreating a wingbeat even at the ferocious sight of gryphons against them. Those from my clan led the attack against the treacherous royals.

Through it all, Alaron was mostly silent. The wyvern stood impassively from his vantage atop the hill, staring down with unblinking eyes as human, gryphon, and dragon fought and perished in battle. When he spoke, it was only to pass a quiet order on to me or to Kyrus, which we relayed to our forces. I dug my claws into the ground as I watched Ddraig Metrus leading her clan towards the wall, scattering to avoid a volley of gunfire. Several dragons fell mid-stride.

"This isn't working," I cried to Alaron. My wings fluttered, almost lifting me from the ground. "We need to join the fight."

"No, hold," the wyvern snapped. He did not turn his head. "We have to give Ddraig Bakucic the opportunity to get into position. Their eyes must be on us while we flank them."

"They're dying out there," I protested. Reluctantly, I tucked my wings tight to my side again, but my claws still gouged deep trenches through the soft earth.

"This is war," Alaron replied in a harsh tone. "There is going to be death. Stay put Ddraig Ellian. Your time will come soon."

I bowed my head in submission, but I couldn't keep my eyes from the battle for long. Ddraig Metrus bellowed her commands loudly, taking control of the situation in front of the wall on the ground. Alaron had impressed on us that we needed to take the fortification before nightfall if we wished to succeed. The humans were resolute in their defence. If they were able to resist Ddraig Bakucic's flanking force, then we would struggle to take the wall from them.

High above the fight, Azlak circled with the great ness I could only assume was Nightwings. The two snarled at each other, few words exchanged as they descended into mindless hatred. The two were brother and sister, I had to remind myself, fighting on opposite sides. I wondered where the third sibling was, the dragon I had grown up believing was my cousin. Where was Anzig in all of this? I had seen no sign of him. Perhaps he had managed to escape to live in wingless exile, away from human and dragon. That might still make him the lucky one.

The main gate opened. From out of the sea of tents came reinforcements for the humans, geared in brown and green clothing and carrying several of the new guns. The old weapons didn't bother a dragon much, but these new ranged weapons were a thing to fear and respect.

Alaron had seen this movement too. "Ddraig Ellian, redeploy the Axaatl dragons to defend the centre from those newcomers," he barked out.

I raised my voice to project it across the battlefield. Hyantl, the commander of the Axaatl army, was on the left flank. I repeated Alaron's order to him. The large dragon bowed his head before growling to his warriors.

The Axaatls abandoned their flank, giving up on reaching the wall at that side, as they loped across the field. Their protection came from a handful of Nixan dragons who ran with them, looking pitifully weak and small next to their larger brethren. Airil was not amongst them. Alaron had other plans for my mate.

I kept my eye on the Axaatl warriors as they ran across the lines of battle. They sprinted hard, dodging falling dragon and gryphon as the human reinforcements got into position. I could just about hear the calls from the human commanders as they prepared their first volley of gunfire.

I winced as a series of explosions tore out from the human front line. The Nixans did their job though, diverting or blocking the bullets with their magic. By my count, only three Axaatls fell before they smashed into the humans, ripping and slashing with tooth and claw.

Stronger and tougher than the humans, it wasn't long before the Axaatls started to even out the casualties in the air, so much so the Xitals started to disengage and drop down to help their human allies. The wounded Laxtals took advantage of the reduced numbers to make a retreat to safety, where healers could begin their work.

A roar echoed from the trees away to our right. Taking initiative for himself, Ddraig Bakucic launched from the shadows to crash into the vulnerable flanks of the humans. His clan swept from the forest, pinning the humans between themselves and the massive bulk of the Axaatl warriors. I let out a low hiss of admiration and envy as Bakucic bloodied his scales.

I was sure this was not the full might the humans had to offer. Only about five hundred opposed the Axaatls, but we were sure many thousands more were safely holed up inside the camp. But the first victory was ours, as after barely twenty minutes there were no humans left alive on the battlefield. Led by Hyantl, the Axaatls took to the air to kill or chase away the remaining Xitals. That was over quickly, the Xitals shrieking as they fled back across the camp towards the mountains. Hyantl did not pursue them far.

"Kyrus, secure the fortifications," Alaron said, still as calm as he had been at the start of the battle.

The gryphon swooped to the air, shrieking his commands to his kin. Immediately, the remainder of his army rose from the forest, carrying felled blocks of wood. They flew for the wall, scattering the remaining humans who had dared to linger when the rest of their forces had retreated.

Dragons and gryphons landed on the wall together, quickly putting into position the carefully cut blocks of wood and using rope to secure them. It would provide us with shelter to hold the wall, our first paw into taking the camp from the humans and routing them across the mountains.

Of Nightwings and Azlak there was no sign. I had lost track of them in the chaos, though I could occasionally hear a muffled roar. They must have soared high above the clouds.

Ddraig Metrus could barely look up as the survivors returned to receive attention from the few Nixan healers we had access to. Her clan had suffered the most; already half their number lay dead.

Only those with serious wounds had the chance to see a healer. Those with mere scratches had to endure the pain until the battle was over. Even strengthened by the Axinstone, sheer numbers threatened to overwork and overwhelm the healers. About fifty gryphons were able to assist with healing, but few were as effective as the Nixans.

Alaron finally began to move, walking slowly down the hill and around the bodies of the fallen. I followed him, trying to avoid looking too hard at those dragons who had died already. Based on the horns, many came from Laxtal or Eltee, with almost as many Xitals.

Ddraig Krateos hurried towards us. He had survived the first skirmish unscathed. "That went surprisingly well," the Nixan growled. He looked back towards the healers as they started to spread through the landed dragons and gryphons.

Alaron jumped up onto the defensive wall that had once protected the humans. Now it was our protection from them. He bared all his teeth in a wide grin. "It is far from over. It has only just begun."

# chapter twenty-five

**Mulner**

The ailur held me in a tight grip. Their hands may have been smaller, but the strength they possessed shocked me. They had two thumbs on each hand. Perhaps that had something to do with their grip.

One hand pinned shut my mouth, while two others held my body as they carried me quickly and quietly through the camp. I would have feared they planned to give me up to the humans, but they kept to the shadows and stayed hidden whenever anyone came close. These ailur were not on the side of the humans.

When the ailur were satisfied where they were, they tossed me into a nearby tent and quickly pinned me down again. One hand pressed on the base of my neck, keeping my head to the ground. They knew how to handle a dragon. The deep growl that rumbled in my throat was all I could manage. It was a pitiful reaction.

The leader of the ailur, the one who had introduced herself as Selu, stood in front of me. Her arms crossed in front of her chest, and she tapped the floor several times with a restless foot. I got a good look at the strange creature. Her red fur stuck out around her brightly coloured clothes, which had several sparkling gemstones woven into the fabric. Black fur masked her amber eyes.

"You. Dragon. What you doing?" Her voice was sharp and rapid. "You ruin plan."

Another three ailur stood behind my interrogator. All three had aimed their slings at me. They may have been fighting the Xitals, but

I couldn't be sure if they were friend or foe. The enemy of my enemy was not always a friend.

"I am here to slay a necuart," I said slowly, staring into the eyes of the ailur who held me. Not once did she look away, her large eyes fixed on mine. So she wasn't like a human, who couldn't stay looking at one thing for a few seconds. The challenge lingered until I succumbed to the urge to blink.

"You lie. Tell truth," the ailur said. She lay one stubby black claw against my exposed throat. I wasn't willing to chance that my scales were tough enough to protect me.

"I am telling the truth. You saw my eyes. Tell me you can see the curse of that demon there," I snarled, trying to push the ailur off, but she was too strong. She had positioned herself well, out of reach of my claws and just too far away for my teeth.

Quicker than I could react, the ailur reached out and grabbed my muzzle, holding it tight. She roughly pulled my head to the side, exposing the healed bite wounds on my neck. Her nose twitched. "Dragon tells truth. Still don't trust. Why dragon ruin plans?"

"I did no such thing. I didn't even know you were here," I protested. I tried to flare my wings, but the ailur had too strong a grip to make room.

"Tchh. Dragon bring guards. Not ready. Blood on dragon's claws." The ailur pressed her claws harder against my throat. "Gryphons not enough to save."

"I didn't know. I swear. I didn't know you were here until I saw you in that clearing. I just used your distraction to slip inside," I spluttered, unable to move away from the furious creature.

"Then dragon help fix. Dragon come. Dragon Selu's now." The ailur snapped her fingers at one of her companions and pointed at me. "Bring."

The ailur released me, and before another one could lay their hands on me I bounded up to my paws. "Help fix what?" I demanded, placing myself between the ailur and the canvas flap leading outside. "What are you even doing here?"

"Dragon silent. Or dragon muzzled," the ailur snarled. I noticed she had a roll of tape in her hand. I quickly snapped my mouth shut. I didn't want to give her the opportunity to use it.

We all emerged back into the sunlight. The group of ailur completely surrounded me, staying too close to my sides to spread my wings to take flight. I wouldn't be able to go anywhere before they stopped me. They had trapped me without bonds. I couldn't help but feel begrudging respect for their skill. I had to wonder where they had learned it. Dragons had not come across a race like the ailur before, to my knowledge, but they knew how to capture one.

The ailur moved in absolute silence, their padded feet not making any noise against the grass and mud. I struggled to match their pace, but every time I moved a little too slow the ailur on my tail gave me a firm hit to hurry up.

When we paused for a moment, it allowed me to come up to the side of the lead ailur. "You said your name was Selu?" I asked her, keeping my voice low.

The ailur waved the roll of tape at me. "Dragon silent," she hissed. Her nose twitched. "Yes. Am Selu. No questions now. No words."

Keeping a wary eye on the tape, I fell once more into silence as Selu led on. She seemed confident about where we were going, expertly avoiding human eyes with such proficiency I had to wonder if something more was keeping us hidden. We were moving right through the centre of the camp, not far away from where I was sure the necuart was residing. I doubted the monster would be active at this time; Jesara and Seri had been quite adamant in saying the necuart were only comfortable during the night.

More than once I was sure a human was about to look at us as they walked by, but each time their eyes just seemed to slip past. Some sort of magic had to be at work, but none of the ailur seemed to be doing anything to obscure us from sight.

Just as I was beginning to wonder anew what the ailur's plan was, Selu thrust out her paw, calling us to a halt. We were close to the base of the cliffs. In front of us was the largest tent I had seen so far, with several spires of metal reaching above the canvas. Thick wires connected the narrow spires with the ground and the cliffs. There was a lot of activity in front of the tent, busier than any part of the camp I had seen so far. Was this really our target? Whatever skill or magic the ailur had used to get this far would not be sufficient to go much further.

The ailur knew what to do. Those behind me slipped away into the shadows, vanishing far quicker than was natural. I blinked several times, but there was no trace of the ailur at all. Some sort of magic protected them. I shot a quizzical glance at Selu, but she just stared back at me with her wide amber eyes. She held a finger to her lips before gesturing down with her palm. Hesitantly, I crouched down, waiting for her next signal. There were so many questions I wanted to ask, but with so many humans around I couldn't speak. I may be hidden from their sight, but I was sure they would be able to hear me still.

If a signal came, I must have completely missed it, as Selu suddenly hissed at me, waving me forward. I could see no discernible difference in human activity in front of me, but the ailur was aggressive in her gesticulation. I was to advance.

I took my first steps out into the open, expecting a human to cry out and see me, but it never came. With a quiet hiss, a thick cloud of choking smoke filled my vision, obscuring absolutely everything from view. I could hear humans panicking, some coming perilously close to colliding with me as they blindly searched for the cause of the smoke.

Selu guided me through the haze, her paw on my wing. She appeared only as a dark shadow in the gloom. I wasn't sure how she was able to find her way, but she led us through the acrid smoke and into the massive tent, where the air was still clear.

What met my eyes was unlike anything I had ever seen before, even amongst James McArthur's small colony. Several strange machines took up much of the space in the tent, all with a purpose that was completely unknown to my mind. Thick beams of wood supported the great weight of the canvas tent, like the skeleton of a great beast the humans were slowly constructing.

Dozens of wires led from the strange machines, through an opening in the far end of the tent, which led through to a dark cave in the cliffs. Many of those machines had bright screens illuminating the darkness, displaying bizarre symbols I couldn't understand. A vast stack of rippled metal sheets piled up on one side of the tent. Behind that was a dull, obsidian machine that was constantly vibrating. I couldn't even begin to comprehend what I was seeing.

There weren't any humans inside, but there were plenty of sounds around the outside of the tent, and from inside the adjoining cave. Selu grabbed hold of my wing and dragged me forward. "Quick now. Little time."

I gasped in pain, but aware that humans were just outside, I managed to keep my protests quiet. I hurried along after her loping gait as quickly as I could manage towards the centre of the tent.

"What are we even doing here?" I hissed. A sharp jolt of pain speared through my wing as the ailur pulled me beneath the machines on the far side of the tent, near the vibrating obelisk that made my scales itch.

"Dragon help Selu. Dragon destroy experiments. Selu destroy bad machine," the ailur snarled, extending her arm towards the machines, her eyes lingering on the towering obsidian pyramid beside us.

"What experiments?" I asked, following where she was pointing, but I still couldn't understand what I saw. These machines were unlike anything I had seen before. What did any of the bright screens or whirring noises mean?

Selu put a finger to her mouth. "Hush, hush. Stay hidden. Wait."

I bit down on my tongue and did what the ailur asked. I remained in the shadows and stayed still, though what she waited for was not clear to me. Outside the tent I could hear the conflict: raised voices of both pain and panic, as well as the commands of leaders trying to establish control. Whatever the other ailur were doing, it was creating a lot of chaos. But here inside the tent, all was calm. But still Selu did not move, her hand resting on my wing.

Footsteps echoed from the tunnel of canvas that connected the tent to the adjoining cave. The pressure on my wing increased, and I shrank back into the shadows, unsure if the ailur magic would still be enough to keep us hidden.

A dozen humans charged down from the cave. Most of them carried those new kinds of weapons, the guns that we had received so many warnings about.

"What is going on out there?" one of the humans bellowed. He was one of the few who was not carrying a weapon.

"The dragons have started their attack, sir," another replied. "They have started to assault the eastern walls."

I lifted my head. Ellian was already here? I didn't have any time to waste, but here I was with Selu to destroy some experiments? I barely suppressed the growl of irritation.

"Get me Rico. He needs to sort out this mess," the bellowing human said.

Selu tightened her grip on my wing and started to pull. Reluctantly, I hurried after her, away from the humans as they lingered by the main entrance of the great tent. She led me down the vacated tunnel. The human's reply followed me down there. "I believe he's coordinating the defences. His way, George. He's commanded for no mercy."

A shout of frustration echoed through the tunnel. "We're too close for this. Come with me."

I glanced back in alarm, but the humans were not returning. Instead, they were getting quieter as they went out into the fray. I picked up my pace in response to Selu's tight and unrelenting grip on my wing.

We emerged into a massive chamber, only partially illuminated with dozens of electric lights attached to the stone walls and from small metal poles rising from the floor. Thick wires and cables criss-crossed between them, with several thicker ones stretching out into the darkness towards the middle of the cave. To what, I could not see. A strange energy crackled in the air.

There were no humans in the cave, though their stink was everywhere. I couldn't escape it, even if I breathed through my mouth. Many of them had spent a lot of time in this cavern, but there was another smell beneath it. Older and deeper. It was almost like a dragon, but infused with stone and something else I couldn't identify. It was as unsettling as the feeling of the air.

Selu's nose quivered, like she could also pick up on the same scent. She bared her teeth and hissed. "No time left. Dragon. Hurry. Take," she said, rummaging through her pack and taking out a small black cylinder. She pointed into the darkness, following the cables on the ground. "Find power. Destroy for Selu."

I shook my head. "I don't know what that looks like."

Selu clicked her tongue and rolled her eyes. "Go. See. Can't miss it. Don't harm statue."

I stared at the ailur, still not understanding what she meant, but I got the impression she wasn't about to explain any further. Tentatively, I took the offered device. It felt like a strip of charcoal and nothing more.

"Careful with firestick. Very hot. Don't burn scales. Turn on here," Selu instructed, pointing to a small button on one end.

I shifted my grip and squeezed. A burst of searing heat roared from the tip, scorching the stone and leaving a black char. I almost dropped it in shock.

"Careful dragon. Firestick dangerous. Now go. Selu has own thing to destroy," Selu said, slapping me on the shoulder and pointing back to the tunnel of canvas. Large sheets of metal blocked off the rest of the cave mouth, creating only one small entrance. The only way back out was into the large tent.

Wondering what I had gotten myself into, I unfurled my wings and kicked off. I didn't lift too high from the ground, just enough so my wingbeats did not touch the rough stone floor. I didn't look back as Selu scampered in the opposite direction to complete her sabotage. I was alone, with no knowledge of what I was meant to be doing.

The darkness was not complete. In the distance, more lights flickered. A ring of poles held more electric lights, circling around what I first thought to be a column of rock. Then I realised it was no mere block of unshaped stone. Someone had sculpted it in a deliberate way. This was the statue Selu spoke of: a great and towering dragon lifted onto its hindlegs; face contorted into a snarl of anger. No. Fear. The great dragon was terrified and preparing to flee.

What a strange statue.

Still, this must have been what Selu wanted me to find. I lowered my eyes from the terrified visage of the statue to see the mess scattered around its paws.

More machines. More wires. The humans loved this stuff. It would give me great pleasure to destroy some of it.

I landed and quickly got to work, using the firestick to slice through as many wires as I could find, pressing the heated end of the charcoal device to burn into the beeping machines. Red lights started to flash. I destroyed those as well.

Nothing escaped my attention. Everything that looked human-made, I set the firestick on. Metal melted and ruptured, sparks flying as wires and cables severed beneath the fierce heat of the firestick. I left nothing intact, both inside the machines and out.

Without knowledge on what I was destroying, I couldn't be sure about the damage I caused. I didn't even know if I destroyed the right things. I simply tore through whatever I could and hoped that Selu would be content. Once everything around the statue's paws was a smoking ruin, I cast my eyes around for anything else I could destroy, for I still couldn't hear any sound of the humans returning.

My attention drew up to a pair of cables that dangled from the statue, plugged into a couple of the ruined machines. I looked up, following the cables until I noticed what I had missed before. The cables attached to a strange hood or cap that slipped over the statue's head. Small sparks of golden light still flitted out from the hood, quickly disappearing into the darkness. I grinned and spread my wings again. The ailur did need a dragon for this.

I powered my wings up, through the smoke that burned at my nose. Finally, I was able to rid my senses of the stench of humans, but this acrid scent was no better. I gagged as I angled to the side to get out of the column of rising smoke, fluttering my wings as I reached the statue's grimacing face. I struggled not to think of the monstrous dragons I had seen in my territory. This statue was about the right size for them, but they couldn't be related. The stone used to craft this statue looked ancient, yet still somehow not at all weathered.

I landed on the muzzle of the statue, hindpaws scrabbling for balance. I found no purchase on the surprisingly smooth stone, until I finally found some balance by digging my claws between a couple of scales. The firestick buzzed in my paw, even before I activated it. An irritating sneeze built up deep in my throat but refused to come any further than that. The air was thick and hot, choking at my lungs. I could barely breathe in it.

The firestick sputtered as I held it over the leathery hood that cowled the statue. More sparks erupted from the cabling coming from it. The sparks were gold and silver and many other colours, some of which I had never seen before. I couldn't help but breathe them in, choking on them as their heat warred with the chilling cold that sapped at my strength. It took all my strength just to keep my paw on the firestick and burn through the leather, hoping that I did not damage the stone beneath.

The air grew thicker. My body burned, vision swimming. The colourful sparks swirled around me, forming indistinct patterns as they enclosed my body.

My paw started to slip. The firestick flickered off for a moment. Then the cowl tore and fluttered away. In an instant, the air snapped back to normal. My senses returned and the heat faded as quick as extinguishing a fire. I gasped, sucking in several deep breaths. My heart raced, like I had been flying at full speed for hours.

A human screamed. Close by.

Feeling a strange weakness go over me, I fell from the statue and only just managed to open my wings in time. My shoulders strained as they took my weight, and I managed to swoop into a glide before hitting the ground.

Three humans ran from the canvas tunnel. One carried a gun. The other two wielded knives.

I flicked my wings to bank to the side, but there was no other way out. They had me trapped in here.

A stone whistled through the air and struck the gun-wielding human in the head. He crumpled.

His companions turned on the spot. Too slow. A second stone and then a third zipped from the tunnel and knocked them both down.

I fluttered on the spot, not daring to approach. Then I saw a shadow melt from the darkness beyond the lights. Selu. In her hand was a sling, a fresh stone bouncing in her hand. The other ailur emerged behind her, protecting their leader's blind side. They all wielded slings as well.

Selu grinned. "Dragon done?"

I nodded. My throat was hoarse, but I forced the words out. "Yeah, it's done." At least, I could only hope it was. The ailur did not make any moves to check.

"Come. Hurry, dragon."

Whatever the ailurs' exit strategy was, they were already putting it into effect, Selu slapping something against her arm as she ran. I kept close, knowing they were my only hope of escaping with my life. If the humans caught me, I was as good as dead. So much for sneaking in to kill the necuart.

Once we emerged from the tent, the ailur ran without detection, despite the masses of humans that were running in the opposite direction. The destruction of the machines in the cave had attracted attention from all parts of the camp, it seemed. Even a few traitorous Xital dragons were amongst those drawing close.

We managed to find a small, isolated tent for temporary shelter. A multitude of aromas struck my nose. I recognised some of the scents from James McArthur's colony, the variety of food they cooked like bread and cured meats. None of it interested me, but one of the ailur started to raid the various containers. Another of the ailur had an arm injury, and while he received treatment from his companion, Selu took me to the side.

"Dragon did good," she said, a wide maniacal grin on her furry face as she took the firestick from my paws. "Might need dragon all the time."

Selu accepted an apple from her companion, but when she offered me the same I refused, wrinkling my muzzle up at the green fruit. I didn't know how humans could stand such vile things, but Selu munched through it with her amber eyes lit up in pleasure.

"Why are you even here?" I asked. It was a question that had been nagging at my mind for a while. When the gryphons had come, there had been no mention of any ailur for allies.

Selu blinked. "To destroy experiments and weapons. Human too close to truth. But use truth in bad way. Must be stopped."

"But who sent you?"

Selu gnashed her teeth and grinned. "Human have many enemies. Selu's master have many allies. Chronicler control like great web. Dragon doesn't even know is caught on it. One string tugs," Selu paused as she flicked my leg, "and the rest will answer. Selu friend of dragon. Nothing else important."

I snorted, but Selu didn't appear ready to elaborate on her motives. I could only hope that she was being truthful, and that she fought for the same allies.

"Can I count on you to help with my task?" I asked instead, realising I was going to get no more out of her.

Selu held up her hands. "No, dragon. Selu will not fight necuart. Dragon's task is for dragon alone. Selu must report to Chronicler. Warn master of terrible weapon humans possess. Beyond Selu's skills to destroy."

"I helped you though. Why would you not offer the same in return?"

"No. Dragon almost ruined plan. Dragon redeem by helping. Selu owe dragon nothing," the ailur snarled. She clenched her fist, and for a moment I was sure she was about to hit me. Then she tugged on something on her glove, and to my horror she faded from sight until nothing but a shimmer remained.

I spun around, but the other ailur had already disappeared. I was alone once more. Unleashing a snarl, I knocked aside some of the food the ailur had dropped. They had left me in the middle of an army of humans on high alert after we had destroyed their machines. Selu had not made my mission any easier, but as I closed my eyes and tried to re-find the magnetic pull to the necuart, I was pleased to realise it was not too far away.

If I could avoid detection, then perhaps I would still be able to fulfil my goal. The chaos that had spread amongst the humans could become an advantage.

The darkness in my mind grew ever blacker. The time for distractions was over. Either the necuart was going to die, or I would. It was time to meet my fate.

I used the chaos of Ellian's arrival on the edges of the camp to move quickly through the sea of tents without anyone seeing me. Despite the carnage I had caused with Selu, no one was looking for a single dragon. Not even one moving away from the eastern boundary, where the attacks from the Laxtal army came from. I was just another dragon to the humans. Even the Xital dragons didn't stop me. They didn't know an enemy when they saw one. Pathetic.

A deafening roar filled the sky, soon answered by a second. A few moments later a dark shadow darted overhead. I glanced up in time to see the great spectre pass by, and it was all I could do to keep calm and not flee. There was the creature known as Nightwings, just as terrifying as the whispers from across the mountains told. She was like the statue in the cave come to life.

I had to forget the peril my sister was in. If the necuart still lived by sunset, then I knew my sister would perish. He could not survive this day, and I was the only one who could stop him. His dark magic could not defeat me, my mind still intact despite all he had inflicted upon me.

When I finally found the wall of darkness, I almost forgot all of that and fled. Sheer terror emanated out from the swirling gloom, a shadow that needed no source. The darkness was so absolute I doubted any light would ever be able to penetrate it. I trembled, digging my claws into the soft soil, my courage threatening to abandon me completely.

That was where I had to go though, and slowly I edged forward until my nose touched the shadows. Sudden cold permeated my whole body, sapping almost all the strength in me. The voice in my head, silent ever since leaving Nixa, awoke. A cold laughter filled my mind, drowning out all other sounds.

*"Little dragon has come to me?"* the necuart chuckled. I couldn't be sure if the voice was real or inside my head. I decided that it didn't really matter. I had to ignore it as best I could. *"How wonderful. I could use you, and you brought yourself all the way here."*

I didn't answer. I tried not to think at all, knowing that any thought was a weakness for my foe to pounce upon. I focussed on one paw stepping in front of the other. In the absence of light, I saw nothing, not even a shadow in front of me. I couldn't even be sure I was moving at all, and not just pacing on the spot.

*"Are you here to submit your will to me?"*

Again, I chose not to speak. Not to think. One paw pressed to the ground, wet away from the sun's light and warmth. Something brushed against me. Fur and leathery skin pushed against my scales. Chittering laughter bombarded my ears.

*"My bats like you. You will be a good ally to them."*

I growled as the bats moved away again. I could still hear them, their breathing booming in the total silence. Eyes gleamed red. Time seemed to pass inconsistently. A breath felt like a lifetime, yet an hour could have passed by in mere seconds.

"I have come to find you, yes," I whispered to the darkness. My heart constricted in my throat as terror threatened to overwhelm me. "Would you reveal yourself to me?"

The necuart laughed again as a cold wind blew against me. It bit into me, cutting through my scales and chilling my bones. I closed my eyes, for all the difference it did to my vision, and flung my wing in front of my face. That barely helped at all as I submerged into an icy dread. I could hardly breathe, and I knew then that the necuart was standing in front of me.

I stopped my blind pacing.

"I thought you were a little bigger last time. No matter. Soon you will answer only to me," the necuart said, his voice spearing icicles through my wing, which I tentatively withdrew from my face.

I looked up to see the cold figure from my nightmares. I could almost mistake him for a human, but his skin was as white as fresh snow, and his thin, almost skeletal form was too delicate for any

292

human. Then there were his eyes. They were as red as blood, and radiated a sense of malice that made me shiver more than the cold did.

"Are you ready to submit?" the necuart said, looking down at me with a wolfish grin. Two small fangs jutted out from beneath his top lip.

I gasped as the wound in my neck ached. I chose to keep my silence. Any words I could say he'd twist and throw back at me, using them to burrow his way into my mind. I could not allow him that opportunity.

The necuart snickered. "Still resisting? You think your mind is so strong, to keep me out, but let me tell you this, dragon." The necuart reached out with his hand, gently touching my scales with one finger. I almost hissed as the side of my neck went numb to his touch. "You all fall in the end. There is no escaping your fate. Struggle all you will, it will make no difference. Just give in and make it easy."

"I am stronger than you think," I whispered, knowing that at any moment the creature could attack, and then it would all be over. If the necuart didn't kill me, there was a ring of grave bats all around us. Three more swooped around overhead. I would not escape this alive. I knew that now. I had always known that. I just hadn't admitted it to myself. A deep determination rose in my gut, smouldering like a stubborn flame.

"Then you will be a powerful ally. But you are foolish to think you can resist me," the necuart said, withdrawing his finger. An angry buzz of sensation returned, like hundreds of small needles jabbed me all at once.

Visions streamed past my eyes. Darkness and shadows were all I saw, twisting and forming grotesque creatures. I didn't know whether they were meant to intimidate me, but I couldn't feel any terror. I felt nothing, merely blinking each phantom away. Neither of us moved, the necuart glaring down at me with his hand outstretched. There was anger in his red eyes, flashing before me between each of his phantasms. I could feel the shadows battering at my mind, but the horror of killing Cinson created a wall they could not penetrate.

The small embers of my resistance began to grow. Heat flooded through my limbs, chasing away the ice the necuart sought to put there.

I growled, keeping my eyes affixed on the cold creature, waiting for the moment he attacked, but still he stalled. He resorted only to his shadow tricks. I didn't know what he was waiting for. Did he still believe I would be his ally? His servant? Never.

Before he had a chance to recognise my intentions, I tensed my hindlegs and pounced for him, catching him unawares as my claws raked down his side. The necuart hissed as I leaped away, quickly spinning around as I landed so I continued to face him. Two deep gouges of red ran down his face, but I had missed what I had been aiming for: his cold, dark eyes.

"Fool of a dragon. I offered you power untold, and that's how you answer me?" he growled, the darkness looming ever greater beyond his shoulders. I could feel his voice in my head again, urging me to obey, but there was desperation there now. He no longer wanted me to obey; he needed it. He feared me. I had done what Jesara and Seri had said was impossible: I had wounded the necuart.

Fire roared through my veins, fuelled by the first small victory. Every last scrap of ice melted beneath the force of that strength.

Digging my claws into the soft earth, I tried to glare at the necuart in a way I hoped would be threatening. "You offered no such thing. I would have been your slave and nothing more. You offered me nothing," I spat, feeling pride in how the necuart narrowed his eyes coldly. I was annoying him; that much was clear.

He moved so quickly, I barely had time to react. The necuart jumped for me, hands outstretched as he grappled with me, pinning me down to the ground. I was just about able to roll onto my back, lashing out at his chest with my hindpaws. The creature howled in pain as my claws found their target, tearing into his vulnerable flesh.

The necuart backed away, and I was glad to see he was holding his chest in pain, his dark clothes stained with crimson. "You should not be able to do this. Why can I not control you?" the creature snarled, his already pale face turning whiter as his panic grew. The touch of his mind was as weak as the touch of his flesh.

All around us the grave bats fluttered and shrieked, a few of them swooping down to us, but none interfered just yet. What they were waiting for I couldn't tell, but they seemed reluctant to attack.

The necuart returned to his stalking, keeping his distance from me. He was wary now, treating me as a threat. Whatever control he had possessed over me was gone, just a small whisper at the back of my mind that I was able to ignore. That had been one of the few weapons he had that could harm me, and the creature knew that. Without that, the necuart was as weak as an unarmed human. I braced my hindlegs against the ground.

"Now, listen," the necuart said, raising his bloodstained hands. He had nothing left but pitiful pleas, but I was in no mood for mercy. I pounced.

The grave bats shrieked and swarmed as I tore past the necuart's timid defence, my teeth clamping around his vulnerable throat. I expected to feel claws tearing into my back, but still the bats didn't attack. They just watched as the necuart flailed, trying to get a grip on my back to throw me clear, but my scales were too smooth, his hands too weak.

Blood poured into my mouth, the taste of it making me growl and squeeze tighter. Flesh and muscle ripped beneath my teeth, the necuart's movements growing ever weaker until, with a final desperate attempt to grapple my wings, he fell still. I tore his throat away, a last gasp of air gurgling out with a spray of blood.

I panted, the voice constantly running at the back of my head ceasing. The silence of my mind was overwhelming, but it didn't last for long. A cacophony of voices poured into my skull, a high-pitched chittering that never ceased. I shrieked and looked up to the darkening sky, now visible once more as the necuart's unnatural darkness dispersed.

I had lost track of time. Many hours had passed, as night was almost about to fall. Over the voices in my head, I could hear humans nearby, shouting and yelling, adding to the maelstrom of noise that swirled around me. Gunshots rang out and the screams of human and dragon in pain competed with each other.

One of the grave bats landed just in front of me. We looked at each other eye-to eye, the bat shuffling awkwardly on his wings as he slowly approached. He chittered at me, and my eyes widened as I heard his voice separate from the cacophony.

"Master," the bat said. "Master."

"Master. Master. Master!"

The bats were chanting. Just one word bombarding my mind. Master. I was master. They were mine. Perfect. A cold smile spread across my muzzle. My tongue lapped at the blood that clung to my scales.

My eyes turned to the east, where the battle would be raging between dragon and human. My bats were eager for blood. Soon they would drink their fill.

I spread my wings and slipped away into the night. An army of bats followed behind me. There would be death beneath the light of the moon.

# chapter twenty-six

**Azlak**

We were evenly matched. Brother and sister. Our private battle took us high above everyone else, with all thoughts of helping our respective sides gone. Up into the clouds we twisted and turned, trying to rake each other with claws or scorch scales with fire. Neither of us could hit the other, just a couple of glancing blows that caused no serious injury. She had said nothing to me yet, no taunts or insults, just savage snarls and roars of anger.

I was sure she was holding back on me, pulling out of her dives at the last moment, unwilling to properly strike me. Only once we were above the clouds and out of sight of the battling armies below did she speak, and her words were not what I expected.

"Do you think they can still see us?" she asked, her expression softening as she pulled out of another attack, leaving me to parry at empty air. She hovered, wings beating slowly to keep her steady, while I circled around her, expecting a trap. She kept one eye on me at all times, but otherwise didn't move except for her beating wings. "You are my brother. I do not wish to harm you."

I growled, making sure to show off the numerous small wounds she had already inflicted upon me.

"To keep up the pretence," Nightwings said, answering my unspoken question as she stared down at the thick band of grey clouds below us. "Do you trust me, Azlak?"

"I would never trust you again," I spat, glaring at my sister. I would not let her out of my sight, wary of any sudden movements. She would not lull me into a false sense of security and then attack. Yet the lunge I expected never came, in fact she turned away and slowly started to fly from the battlefield below the clouds, heading away to the south.

"Will you follow, at least?" she asked, looking over her shoulder.

I hesitated. I knew I couldn't trust her, but I couldn't see why she would need to pull me away from the others just so she could try to kill me somewhere else. If she wanted to attack, then she could do so right away. A tiny seed of doubt formed in my mind. Perhaps she was being genuine, and she didn't want to hurt me at all. Reluctantly, I started to follow her.

We had travelled many miles to the south before Nightwings led me back beneath the clouds, over an hour of fast flight for regular dragons. We said nothing in all that time, leaving me alone to my uncertain thoughts. I wondered where she had taken me, but I soon recognised the great river in the distance that marked the northern boundary of Nixan territory. Everything was quiet and peaceful, with just the wind blowing through the long grass and the occasional chirp of an alarmed bird to disturb the quiet.

Once we landed, I expected Nightwings to start talking. Still she kept her silence. She lay in the grass, head held low with her tail wrapped around her legs. I stayed on my paws, alert and ready, constantly expecting an ambush. Even though I could smell no humans or other dragons in the area, I still knew I should be prepared.

"I guess I owe you an explanation," Nightwings said slowly. She pawed at the soft earth beneath her.

"You owe much more than just that, but an explanation will do for a start," I growled. I thrashed my tail behind me, smashing aside a small bush in the process. I winced as a few spiny branches slipped in between my scales, shaking them free and trying to ignore the smug smirk on my sister's face.

"You know some of the story, how the prime minister is spearheading a campaign to expand Kernow's borders. There's not much to the south, but this side of the mountains? To Kernow, this is empty land, with the dying remains of a once proud species scattered through it. To them, dragons are worthless, and are certainly not a threat, but there used to be respect there. I fear I changed that," Nightwings said, turning away and clawing at the grass.

"How do you mean?" I asked, a little tension slipping from my shoulders as I started to settle down in front of her. My senses were still alert for any danger, but so long as I stayed out of striking range of my sister, I knew I'd be safe enough.

"It was the Axinstone," Nightwings said slowly as the tip of her tail twitched. "No one knew about it until just a few years ago, and even then, it was only when I picked up on it in a Nixan dream. I explained it to George, and he was more excited than I had ever seen him. He kept on yelling about how it was the lost one of eight, but he never explained that to me."

"One of eight? That sounds familiar," I said, frowning as I tried to think of where I had heard something like that before, but I simply couldn't place it. I shook my head. It wasn't important for now. Instead, I needed to know just what Maznar had done to spark this war.

"I was sent to steal the Axinstone. I'd already suspected I was a Nixan and would be able to break through the defences the clan had to protect itself from outsiders," Nightwings said, closing her eyes and sighing. "It was all too easy. I even spoke with my… our father when I was there, but he never suspected a thing. I took the Axinstone and fled at night. No one ever knew it was me.

"When I took the stone back to Trevena, George was ecstatic. He was able to tap into the magic of it and do some incredible things, the greatest of course being this," she said, flaring her wings. Though I tensed, she made no further movements. "He said he was returning me to our former glory, and that I should be thankful. At first I was, but then, after a while I began to wonder what sort of monster he'd turned me into. Until he started experimenting on other dragons, there has never been any other dragon like me, or so I believed."

I wanted to reach out to her, to place my paw on hers, but I fought the urge. "How did you resist their control? It was only because of Esperance's magic that I was able to hold them back myself."

Nightwings shook her head. "They never had any need to control me like that. I always knew it was obey them or die. They had me under their thumb from the moment I hatched. Believe me, Azlak, I never wanted to do anything to hurt dragons, but I would have been killed had I not obeyed them."

Breathing out heavily, I looked up at the largely overcast sky, trying to work out what to do. There was a large part of me that wanted to believe everything Nightwings had said. I wanted her to simply be Maznar, to be my sister and the family I had craved for so long. But she was not my only sibling.

"What happened with Anzig? I saw you lead him straight to George," I asked, still not looking down at her. I could hear her shift slightly, just a gentle movement.

"He pleaded with me. I think he'd been driven mad with his injury, and being overthrown as ddraig was what finally snapped in his mind. He saw George as his only means for healing, as none of the Nixans could give him back his wings. He thought the humans might be able to do what the dragons could not. He wanted to take back the sky."

"No one ever worked out who attacked him. Did he ever tell you?" I asked with a sigh.

Nightwings paused. "He accused Vinzent, but I'm not convinced," she said quietly. "I don't think even he was too sure. The pain was too traumatic for him to remember."

"I just wish I'd been able to See it before it happened, I could have saved him," I said, trying to suppress that guilt. Though control over my magic was much better than it had been, it still wasn't perfect. I doubted I'd ever be able to predict every eventuality.

Nightwings hesitated. She pawed the ground. "There is something else. The prime minister has his motive for this invasion. George has his own. But there is a third human. A third goal. Rico is the one you should worry about."

"I've seen him," I growled. The human with the strange tattoos.

"Then you should know how dangerous he is," Nightwings said. She lifted her head and looked beyond my shoulder. "The prime minister wants land. George wants his experiments. But Rico will not rest until every dragon is dead. George has been trying to work against him, but Rico keeps getting more powerful. Prime Minister Brightwell will side with Rico. Kernow will see dragonkind destroyed unless we stop him."

"Then get George to help us. Maybe he should side with dragons for once," I said. My tail thrashed again, lashing through the remains of the destroyed bushes.

Nightwings sighed and shook her head. "Perhaps."

"If it's our only way to survive…"

My sister looked up. She lifted a wing to interrupt me. "You haven't recovered your magic in this form, have you?"

"No, why?" I asked sharply, glaring down at her.

Nightwings blinked. "No reason. Just curiosity. No other Nixan had been changed, so I wasn't sure if you'd react differently to me. I'm still able to access dreams even when I'm like this, but it took me a few weeks to be able to recover that magic. I'd imagine you'd be the same."

I scrunched up my muzzle. "I don't intend on spending many more days like this, let alone weeks. No matter what George might think, this is not how a dragon should be, and I will find a way to fix it."

Nightwings shrugged. "There are ways to do it, but nothing you or I would be able to do. It takes a very specific kind of magic," she said slowly, looking at something beyond my shoulder again. I turned my head to see what had attracted her attention, but there was nothing there. Just a couple of birds in the distance, two eagles out hunting.

"So where do we go from here? We need to defeat Rico, but will the humans try to control you if you come back? Will you keep fighting for George even if that weakens you against the real threat?" I asked, uneasy about being away from the battle for so long. I knew we couldn't just sit around and talk, as much as I wanted to understand more about what George had done.

"No, one of us has to defeat the other," Nightwings said, rising to her paws. I quickly followed her, taking a cautious step back. I didn't like the growl that had slipped into her voice.

"Stay here then. I can claim to have defeated you, there's no one around to witness it. I go back and help defeat Rico, then you're free to do whatever you like," I said urgently, taking a few more steps back, my hindpaws crunching over the bush I had destroyed with my tail, crushing it completely. A few spines dug into my paw.

"I'm afraid it's not going to be as simple as that," Nightwings said with a sad shake of her head.

I was about to question her when three near simultaneous cracks of thunder tore through the quiet. As the sudden scent of human wafted against my nose, I wasted no time to think about the betrayal, kicking off hard and spreading my wings and letting the innate magic in my body lift me into the air. Quickly beating my wings, I tried to put as much distance as I could between myself and the humans. My sister made no attempt to follow, and for a moment I thought I'd be able to get away.

One of the humans yelled just as I felt a spear of stabbing pain lance through my back and wings. I shrieked out in pain, my wings locked in place as I started to drift back down to the ground. Then I felt a strange pull against my body, like a paw had reached inside and was trying to tug out my heart. With no control over my body, I crashed back into the ground, sliding and coming to an undignified sprawl of limbs.

Three humans started to approach from all angles, not daring to come close but holding their hands out at me. They shimmered slightly as ropes of light snaked out from their hands to dig into my flesh. Once again, I cried out as that tugging sensation intensified. Though I was able to move again, it was all I could do to dig my claws into the ground and arch my head back in agony.

Beyond it all, over my own screams of pain, I could hear the cracking voice of Nightwings. "I am sorry, brother. But this is how it must be."

I could feel the magic coursing through my veins slowly diminish, the awesome power that had fuelled me fading to nothing, leaving me feel cold and weak. The ground moved beneath my paws, with claws digging deep gouges in the loose soil as they dragged closer together. Bone and tendon popped and snapped into new positions, my loud roars of pain getting quieter as my form shrunk down. The humans around me loomed larger, but still they came no closer, keeping their distance as I pressed my head into the ground. Gasping and shivering, I could feel unwanted tears forming in the corners of my eyes, before eventually the agony started to subside. When I opened my eyes again, I was much closer to the ground.

The moment I felt like I could trust my wings again I jumped back into the air, easily avoiding the lazy attempts by the humans to stop me, but this time I could hear the concussive thrum of Nightwings as she swooped into the air. In such an open space, I knew there was little I could do to outrun her, but I knew I'd never give up without a fight.

My wings felt so weak, claws and teeth so pathetic and small, the ground passing me by with such painful slowness, and it was just a few seconds before I felt Nightwings's shadow passing overhead. I quickly darted to the side, looking up and shrieking at the sight of her open maw descending towards me. I was only just able to roll out of the way, her wake almost dragging me down to the ground as she passed.

Without even looking to see how she avoided crashing, I hurried on, desperately flying north and beating my wings as fast as I could do generate some speed, but everything was so much slower without the magic pumping through my body. Now it was just blood and heat left to power me, and they weren't enough. I knew I'd be able to outpace any human, and I soon flew out of sight of the three who had changed me back, but I got the feeling my sister was simply toying with me. She hadn't made any more lunges for me, but was instead soaring high above me, tracking me with ease. Beyond her I could see that sunset was starting to approach. The lingering magic in my body would only warm me for so long when darkness fell.

Another loud crack reached my ears, a small shockwave making my wings tremble for a moment. Nightwings used that moment to dive again, letting out an ear-splitting roar that almost drowned out a familiar voice scream out my name. Once more, I rolled to the side before flaring my wings, quickly changing direction before Nightwings could react. She shot past just in front of me, flames licking out from her mouth in anger.

Two dragons were approaching in the distance, a glimmer of blue scales making my heart leap, before realising with a little disappointment that it was not my mate, but his twin. With my weakened vision I couldn't quite make out who was lingering just behind, before catching a flash of sunlight on faded grey. It was the old Vatrean ddraig.

I heard Ddraig Boruc cry out, and below me Nightwings shrieked in anger and pain. Fearing she still pursued, I didn't look back until I reached Airil, who had been hovering and waiting for me. Wondering why he wasn't trying to flee, I chanced a glance back, only to see Nightwings writhing on the ground. In the far distance the three humans were trying to catch up, but I saw a thin stream of magic that was pouring out from the massive ness's body, my eyes following it to the outstretched paw of Ddraig Boruc.

"How?" I whispered, but Airil's paw tugged against mine.

"No time for that," the Nixan said, beating his wings backwards and trying to pull me through the air. Though it seemed Ddraig Boruc had neutralised Nightwings for the moment, there could still be more humans in the area. I turned and started to flee with my mate's brother, back towards where the Vatrean was hovering, eyes narrowed in concentration.

Behind us, Nightwings diminished much like I had just done. She clawed at the ground as though trying to stretch herself back out, but with a high-pitched wail she was soon little larger than me, and still the humans had yet to reach her.

With a sharp gesture from Ddraig Boruc, the ribbon of magic that connected him with Nightwings severed. He held out a paw to the Nixan. "Now, Airil," he said, his voice rumbling with power.

I felt Airil's paw touch my side, and suddenly everything went black.

# Chapter Twenty-Seven

**Ellian**

Though we took the defensive wall, further skirmishes came throughout the day as the humans struggled to take it back. Time and time again they approached, guns firing, but the additional fortifications the gryphons had constructed was enough to keep them away. It was all we could do to keep what we had gained, suffering more losses as evening began to fall.

Clan Eltee had taken most of the losses. Ddraig Metrus had fallen in the early evening, wrestling a human from the ramparts by herself. Her daughter, Kiarla, had taken command of what remained of her clan, the drying blood of her mother ceremoniously smeared over her brow.

As darkness fell, a new issue began to arise. The dragons were starting to tire as the temperature dropped. It would not be long before we needed to find shelter, and there would not be enough gryphons to hold what we had gained over the day. The humans, perhaps knowing this, had reinforced their attacks as the sun touched the horizon.

Alaron paced up and down the ramparts, pausing only to look down at the humans who tried to raise ladders to climb up, after we had destroyed or blocked the stairs they had previously used. On the inside of the wall was another wide clearing, a strip of empty land before the edge of the encampment. That took away some cover for the humans but gave them better range and accuracy with their guns.

I couldn't be sure what the wyvern thought of the situation. Prince Kyrus had been the only one he had spoken to for some time.

Hearing movement behind me, I glanced back, expecting Ddraig Krateos, but it was not the Nixan leader. I wasn't too surprised to see Keita approaching with her mate. I had sent her out earlier in the day to try and find Airil, as no one had seen him or Ddraig Boruc for most of the day. I could tell from her expression that she had been unable to locate my mate.

"No sign of them, Ddraig. Not even Kaz knows where they went," she said with a shake of her head. "My father is still searching though. He'll find out where they went eventually."

First Mulner had gone off unannounced, and now Airil, so soon after he had returned? I knew they hadn't abandoned me, but I couldn't help but feel saddened that neither of them had thought to let me know of their departure first. I wasn't too confident in Yalle's ability to find them, no matter what trust Keita put to her father.

"Last time anyone saw them was just after Azlak flew off with Nightwings," Okazuni added with a shudder. I imagined they thought they'd seen the last of that monstrous ness, and it wasn't hard for me to understand why they had been so terrified of her. She could crush a dragon beneath her paws with absolute ease.

"We'll find him, Ddraig Ellian," Keita said, dropping her head. I sighed, wishing I could share her confidence. My brother had yet to return to me either.

I noticed Okazuni tense as he looked over my shoulder. Quickly glancing back, it only took me a moment to notice what had caught his eye. Yelling out to Alaron and Kyrus to grab their attention, I pointed a wingtip at the growing cloud of darkness against the black sky. It was not just the humans we needed to worry about at night. A swarm of grave bats was filling the sky.

Kyrus yelled out orders to the gryphons, but few were prepared to deal with such a threat. Alaron tried to rouse the nearby dragons, but the wyvern was only successful in dragging a handful up to their paws, by which time the bats blotted out the moonlight. I couldn't help but think that this would be the end of our resistance. There were untold thousands of them and nothing the gryphons had constructed would hold the bats out for long, and that wasn't even considering those dragons who had nowhere to shelter but beneath the open sky. Even so, I would not close my eyes. I flared my wings, feeling Keita and Okazuni do the same. We would fight until our bodies refused to function, until the cold and our wounds forced us into our final sleep.

There was a shape up there that didn't belong to a bat. I peered up into the gloom, shocked to find it belonged to a dragon. I hadn't thought even the Xitals would have dared fly amongst the grave bats; Alaron and Kyrus had both warned us that grave bats refused to listen to any that weren't necuart and would kill anything else that approached.

In response to the grave bats, even the human attackers began to retreat, fleeing towards the safety of their tents. I could still see their shadows moving amongst the temporary structures.

Alaron managed to gather a force of about five hundred gryphons and a few dozen willing and active dragons, but the grave bats had started to soar above us, not making any attempts to dive down.

"What is going on?" Prince Kyrus hissed. The gryphon flared his wings, but at a sharp command from Alaron, he did not fly.

The dragon amongst the grave bats began to descend, leaving the terrifying creatures where they were to block out the moonlight. Hundreds of shadows danced across the bloody plains and the wall as the maelstrom of screeching bats whirled above us.

With my attention firmly on the bats, it took me a few seconds to recognise who the dragon was.

"Mulner!" I shrieked, immediately taking to wing, ignoring the cries of warning from Keita and Alaron. There was no one who would take the wind from my wings when it came to my brother. It was only once I got close to him that I slowed down, even backing away from him a little. There was something different about him, chilling and cold that didn't go away even when he smiled at me.

"You're safe from him now, Ellian. He can't harm you through me," he said quietly, his wings making no noise as he slowly spiralled down towards the wall, towards Alaron and Kyrus. The gryphon and wyvern stepped back as my brother finally touched down. Too nervous to speak to him, I took to the ground a couple of feet away, pressing my wings tight against my back and sharing a nervous glance with Keita, who quickly turned to the side.

"Is Ddraig Boruc here?" Mulner asked, swinging his head around the small group, searching for the elderly dragon.

I was about to shake my head when, incredibly, Ddraig Boruc stepped out from the gloom behind Alaron, who let out an undignified yelp of shock as the Vatrean walked past him. He was not alone either, with a restored Azlak pacing beside him, eyes milky white. Behind them both, to my relief, was Airil. My mate came around to wrap his wing around me as Ddraig Boruc started to inspect my brother.

"Something has happened to you, young one," Ddraig Boruc said, holding his paw against Mulner's shoulder, who remained completely still as the Vatrean prodded at him with a claw.

"I killed him. I killed the necuart who did this to me," Mulner said, baring his neck to the Vatrean, showing the two bite marks that were still red against his scales.

Ddraig Boruc leaped back like fire licked at his scales. "That's not possible," he hissed.

"The creature thought so too, right up until the moment I tore out his throat," Mulner replied with a growl, tensing his claws against the dirt.

The Vatrean ddraig shook his head. I had never seen him quite so agitated. "No, you don't understand. This isn't something that is rare, or shouldn't happen but can. This is strictly impossible. It can't be done. Never in history has a thrall even injured their master unintentionally, let alone killed them. The magic that binds the two forbids it, and to overcome that bond would take a strength not seen since the Cataclysm. I do not doubt your strength of will, young dragon, but you do not possess the power necessary for this."

"You don't believe me? Look above you," Mulner growled. We all looked up to the flock of grave bats that swooped around, none of them ever coming close to us, like some force held them back. Or someone's will. "I control them. They call me master now. The necuart is dead."

"That is… that is unprecedented. Only one other has ever been able to control the grave bats beyond the necuart. I was never sure how he did it, but he wasn't a thrall either. I… I don't think I've ever been as confused as I am right now," Ddraig Boruc said with another shake of his head, pawing at the wooden planks of the wall.

"I don't care what you think, Boruc, but what I'm telling you is true," Mulner snarled. He went to turn away before he paused, tilting his head as the cacophony of noise from the bats increased. It was as though he was listening to them, but I couldn't hear anything discernible in their shrieks.

My brother slowly turned back around to face Ddraig Boruc, mouth agape. "They know of you," he said, twitching his head up to the bats. He looked genuinely perturbed by whatever information he was getting from the screeching, chittering creatures that swooped and wheeled through the night air. The same was true of Ddraig Boruc, who took a couple of steps back.

"They should not be able to remember, it has been too long," the Vatrean whispered. His claws scraped at the wood beneath his paws again, leaving several deep gouges. "Come with me, if you would. I'd like to hear all of this in private." He looked around at those gathered, bowing his head in apology before kicking off into the air, showing no fear for the grave bats above his head, nor of the humans a mere gunshot away. Mulner touched wings with me before he followed

Ddraig Boruc into the darkness, the screeching bats following their new master away.

"What was that about?" Kyrus asked, clicking his beak and peering around the gathered group. I shook my head. Something my brother had said had alarmed Ddraig Boruc severely. I had never seen the old ddraig so disturbed before, but I certainly wasn't able to explain it. Neither the gryphon nor wyvern were able to understand it either, but all of us were sure that it had something to do with the bats that patrolled overhead.

Kyrus and Alaron soon moved away to continue their private conversation. Azlak used the opportunity to quickly approach me. It was strange seeing the seer back at his normal size, like I had forgotten just how small he had always been. Of course, he had been our greatest defence against the terror of Nightwings, and though it was good seeing Azlak free of the humans' magic, we had lost some much-needed protection.

As though he had read my mind, or simply understood why my gaze lingered on him, Azlak smiled and ducked his head. "Nightwings is no longer the same threat to us. I don't know how he did it, but Ddraig Boruc was able to remove the magic that had been maintaining her form, much like the humans did to me. Unless the humans recover the Axinstone, Maznar can never be Nightwings again," the seer explained, bowing his head to me.

"But what of Anzig?" Keita asked, stepping forward with Okazuni. "We've heard nothing of him since he left."

I sighed, glancing around at Azlak and Keita. We were probably the three closest dragons to the former ddraig, and yet none of us knew what had truly been going through the head of my cousin. Or who I had always believed to be my cousin.

"I don't think he's coming back," Azlak said sadly, looking down at his paws. "Losing his wings was a terrible blow, but I think his mind had already broken by then." Keita didn't appear to notice the small glance Azlak gave her, but I did. I had to agree with Azlak's unspoken reasoning. Whether she knew it or not, Keita's denial of Anzig by taking Okazuni as her mate had shattered Anzig's heart, and from then on, his mind had begun to unravel.

Keita held her eyes low to the ground. "I loved him once. I owe it to him to find him, and bring him home safely," she said, resting her head against her mate's shoulder.

"You will get that chance," Azlak said, turning his pale eyes towards her. "I have not Seen the outcome, but I think you will face him down, and you will try to reason with him. Just don't go seeking him out. He will come to you."

"You are a good dragon, Azlak," Keita said, breaking away from Okazuni and placing a paw upon the seer's shoulder. "I have wronged you greatly in the past, but I can see now that you care very much for your clan and your friends. I am glad to have flown with you."

"And I with you," Azlak whispered back, furiously blinking his eyes, but I could see that they watered. He was trying his utmost not to cry in front of us. If there had been any doubt in my mind that he was Nixan, then that doubt was gone now. I stepped forward to spare him a little embarrassment.

"We should all get some rest while we can. The humans seem scared to approach while my brother's bats are here. We should take this opportunity," I said, looking around at the small group, taking hold of Airil's tail in mine. Keita and Azlak remained huddled close to each other, and they both nodded in agreement. Azlak especially looked weary from a long day, and it seemed the pains of his transformation was troubling him. The seer's wings were drooping as he turned away, Keita lingering for a few moments longer before hurrying after him with Okazuni.

I rested my head against Airil's shoulder, feeling his comforting wing against my back. The cold was starting to make me weary. We left behind the wall, which the gryphons would guard overnight. We made our way back up the hill that overlooked the camp. I then turned and stood with Airil, staring out at the human encampment, listening to the quiet sounds of activity from across the blood-soaked plain. The defensive wall, so hard fought for, looked flimsy and weak compared to the size of the camp. At least the forest and steep valley walls to the north and south of our position would keep us protected.

Even as I watched, two forms broke away from the wall. The quiet rustle of Prince Kyrus's wings preluded the gryphon's arrival. Alaron followed in his wake. They landed in front of me.

"My warriors will keep watch tonight, but we don't expect any attack until dawn, not with your brother's bats patrolling," the gryphon said with a click of his beak. His eyes glanced up towards the stars, where the skittering cries of the bats sounded out into the night as they swooped. "He has provided us with some hope."

"Rest well, Ddraig Ellian," Alaron added, staring out towards the humans. "This was just a prelude to the coming storm. Tomorrow the real war begins."

I would be ready.

For the first time since the gryphons had come, dawn was silent. No birdsong greeting the morning sun. The quiet was unnerving, but I didn't want to break it as Airil slowly opened his eyes beside me. Slowly I rose to my paws, legs aching from the exertions in the cold the previous night. Glancing up, I could see the sky was clear and pink, tinged with blue towards the eastern horizon. There was no sign of the bats that had been patrolling the darkness. Likewise, there was no sight of my brother, but I vowed to find him amongst the horde of dragons that were slowly waking up.

Slowly, the muttering and groaning of tired dragons broke the silence. I shared a glance with Airil and started to walk. We didn't need to speak. We both knew where we had to go.

We picked our way through the sprawled dragons, few even looking up at us as we passed, let alone moving out of our way. I had to take extra precaution not to tread on any outstretched wings, Airil following on my tail as we slowly climbed uphill.

The eastern slopes were mostly covered in dragons, taking advantage of the first light of the sun, so our progress was slow. I didn't have the strength yet to take to wing, and my legs were heavy and unresponsive. My wings drooped from my sides by the time we finally crested the hill to look out upon the plains between us and the human camp. A garrison of gryphons stood watch on the wall, but as of yet there appeared to be no threat coming from the humans.

The gryphons had not been idle during the night, beneath the protection of the bats. They had cleared many of the bodies during the night, the remains of a bonfire still smoking away to the north. I bowed my head and closed my eyes as Airil settled down beside me. The worst was yet to come, I knew that.

A click and soft chirrup betrayed the presence of a gryphon. I opened my eyes and looked up to see Kyrus slump down nearby. For once, he didn't start preening, letting the few feathers sitting out of place remain so.

"A sombre morning today. We should mourn the dead, but our enemy will not give us such an opportunity. Already they will be preparing their defences," the gryphon said with a slow, sad shake of his head.

"Is that why you don't sing?" I asked him, voice timid against the continued quietness of the morning.

Kyrus bowed his head. "Fifty gryphons lost yesterday. I don't want to think about how many dragons perished. Too many to count, and today we do it all again. There is no joy in the morning, and that is why we don't sing."

"Then sing of the sorrow. Sing to mourn," Airil said. My mate stared down at the gryphon's talons.

"A song of sorrow?" Kyrus shuffled his wings and arched his head back. "We sing for joy, so there are few indeed of those. But I do know one such song, about a gryphon who longed to see home just one more time before he died. This far from the Aerie, maybe it is right to sing it."

For a few moments Kyrus remained silent, before he trilled out a few long, haunting notes. Twice more he repeated the same notes. On the third call over two dozen gryphons had joined in as they descended into a chilling melody of long, sad cries. I held Airil close as the sound buried itself into me. I knew then that for as long as I lived, I would never be able to forget the terrifying beauty of that song.

By the time the last few notes faded into silence, every dragon and gryphon had awoken. We were far from alert, but already some organisation was starting to filter through our ranks. Clans came back together, the few ddraigs and haeraigs creating order amongst the sleepy masses. Like the song, the mood was sorrowful, but I recognised a hardness beneath it. Everyone knew what was to come, what we had to do. Everyone knew that they were to risk scale and wing to defeat the humans. No single life was important if it meant we came out victorious. And that meant mine too. If I were to be a ddraig worth following, then that meant I would fight.

With a flutter of wings, Alaron landed just in front of me. It still shocked me how graceful he could move without any front legs, his wings partially folded at his side as he pushed his weight down on the small claws halfway along their length.

The wyvern growled softly as he looked out towards the encampment on the far side of the walls. "Yesterday we tested their defences. They are strong and determined. Their resistance will not be easy to break. Our only aim is to survive the day. If we still live by the time Clan Xigax arrives, then we still have hope."

"Then all must fight?" I asked, taking a nervous step forward. This was what I had been waiting for, the chance to prove myself a true leader by fighting with those I commanded. I would have it no other way, but I couldn't suppress the terror that welled up within me. Not even Airil's calming touch could quell that.

"No one can be held back," Alaron said with a nod. His clawed wings dug into the ground a little before he slowly spun around to glance at Kyrus and me. "I would have liked Azlak again to lead the charge, but we shall have to make do with what we have."

"Every dragon will fight to the last beat of their wings," I vowed, raising my head up.

"And every gryphon," Kyrus added. He had finally started to groom himself again, tucking his wayward feathers back into place with a disapproving cluck.

Alaron nodded, before turning to Airil. "Can you summon the ddraigs? I would like to speak to them all before we're forced into action. We shall meet on the wall. I hope I can also address the humans. We might still have the chance for diplomacy."

My mate quickly bounded away to carry out the wyvern's orders. Though my body protested the movement, I got up to follow Alaron down the hill, across the bloodied plains. The smell of death hung like a fog, pervasive and choking. It got no better as we reached the wooden wall and clambered up, a quick flutter of wings lifting us to the defensive vantage point.

We waited in silence for the ddraigs and haeraigs of the clans. Only the occasional clicks of Kyrus's beak disrupted the quietness between us as he resumed his grooming. I kept watch on the humans. There was some movement amongst their tents, but nothing close enough to raise the alarm of our sentries. We had secured one victory against them, but I was sure it wouldn't be long before they were fully prepared for a long day of war. Without the bats to terrorise them and keep them trapped within their encampment, they would soon cross the plains if we did nothing to stop them.

And thinking of the bats, I had to wonder where Mulner had gone. I had seen no sign of my brother at all, nor of the grave bats under his command.

"Has anyone seen my brother?" I asked. I simply spoke the question to the nauseating air, not expecting an answer in return.

Prince Kyrus paused in his grooming for a few moments. He stared down at me with one cold eye, then swung his head towards the nearby forest that bordered the southern edge of the encampment. "I didn't see him myself, but I was told the grave bats went to roost amongst the trees. I would assume your brother was amongst them," the gryphon said, before returning to his feathers.

I had to wonder if we would see Mulner again during the battle. He was no coward, I knew that of my brother, but I recognised that he would use any opportunity he could to avoid taking part in our conflict. He would roost with his bats, emerging only at night to protect what remained of dragonkind. I didn't blame him. At least one dragon would survive.

One by one, the various clan leaders started to arrive. Ddraig Krateos was the first, soaring onto the wall and settling on the other side of Kyrus. He barely even acknowledged me as he landed. He stared resolutely away from Alaron as well, his eyes only for the camp. Ddraig Bakucic followed shortly after the Nixan.

"It saddens me that it comes to this," the Lilisxi ddraig said, shaking his head as he put his forepaws on the temporary ramparts the gryphons had constructed. "We throw ourselves at them because they refuse to listen."

Ddraig Krateos glanced across. "Is this truly something to die for?"

Despite the difference in clan power between them, Ddraig Bakucic stared the Nixan in the eye. "It is. I'm not one to sit back and wait for the humans to come to me. I would rather die than see my trees burn around me. Today I shall fight, and I will die if I must. I would shame my clan were we not to fight."

"Bakucic is right. We will fight to the last beat of our wings."

I turned to see Ddraig Kiarla approach. She ducked her head towards me as she drew near. The Elteean ness looked weary, her paws dragging along the ground, wings not fully held up along her back. I knew she grieved as well. She had lost her mother the previous day. Some of her blood was still on the new ddraig's forehead. Eltee had suffered the worst of our losses and would likely take on even more once the battle resumed. Already there would be little clan left to rule.

I did not have the opportunity to respond. Alaron balanced on the edge of the ramparts, looking out over the humans. "Rico!" he bellowed; his voice projected far louder than I could have thought possible. "We give you one last opportunity to lay down your weapons and abide by the treaty of Ehran."

The wood just above the wyvern exploded as a bullet cracked through it. Alaron didn't flinch.

Rico stepped out from amongst the tents. He was alone, smoking pistol in hand. His voice projected just as loud as Alaron's as he shouted across the wide clearing. "We do not answer to you. We do not answer to Ehran. This is about finishing the work started by the cataclysm. There is no stopping us."

Alaron opened his mouth, a snarl twisting his muzzle. If he was about to say anything, then he reconsidered. He jumped down and looked around the gathered dragons. "I had hoped…" he sighed and shook his head. "Esperance would like to speak to this Rico so she can understand his motives. There is something about him I do not like."

"Other than trying to destroy dragonkind?" Ddraig Krateos growled. "If he is the threat, then we must do all we can to kill him."

"We will attack with three flanks," the wyvern said, seeming to ignore Ddraig Krateos entirely. "Ellian, you will lead the southern flank with Lilisxi and the humans. I will take the centre with Axaatl and the gryphons. The rest shall follow Ddraig Krateos to the north. Each flank will have an aerial and a ground force. Ellian and Krateos, I shall leave it to you to decide who will take command of those in your respective flanks."

"And what is our target?" Ddraig Bakucic asked.

The steely eyes of the wyvern fell on the Lilisxi ddraig. Bakucic did not waver.

"We take as much of this camp as we can. We force them back until they are forced to surrender," the wyvern growled. He batted his wingclaws against the wood. "They have every advantage right now. We must hit them hard before they can use that. Until our reinforcements from Xigax get here, we risk defeat with every moment."

"It will take great bravery," Prince Kyrus chirped. He teased at a feather before finishing his grooming. "We must survive this day so that Esperance can bring justice to those who have brought about this violence. Fight well, dragons. May the gods bring you fortune."

I shuddered. We would need more than fortune from the gods to survive. The plan was to trap the humans between tooth and claw, not giving them any chance to organise themselves. We would be relentless, throwing our full strength in and not stopping until we had nothing left. There would be no second chances for us. We had to survive another day.

We soon went our separate ways, Ddraig Bakucic following me as I headed back towards my clan so I could start moving them towards our flank. We didn't have long, so I enlisted a few dragons to start spreading the message to prepare to fly. Keita and Okazuni were willing to offer their wings, and I was able to convince a weary Yalle to assist his daughter.

I took a moment to scan the survivors of the first day. Saya and Marin were present and amongst the first to rise. I had been pleased that I had not had to deal with any further petty machinations from the former conspirators in Laxtal, though it was upsetting that it had required Vinzent's death to shatter their resolve. At the same time, I knew that their focus would be solely on trying to survive the next few days. I had no doubt that if there was a clan to return to, I would have to face their plots once more, especially as I was yet to name a haeraig. That would have to be a concern for another day.

Laxtal would be taking the flank closest to the trees Mulner had led his bats, I realised as I looked over the plains. I hoped to be able to see him before the chaos of battle overwhelmed us. Before long we were all ready to fly out, keeping low to the ground and descending into the thick forest. Behind me I had several thousand dragons, just over a third of our force.

Bats screeched overhead as they rested amongst the branches. None of them made any movements to attack us, though no dragon rose too close to them. They didn't share my trust that the bats wouldn't descend, and I could hear a few cautious mutterings behind me.

The ground was uneven under paw, rocky and sloping. The terrain had protected us during the night, providing a natural barrier that extended beyond the reach of the defensive wall the humans had constructed. It slowed our progress. I was sure the humans expected an attack to come from the trees, but we came across no defences. We could only hope that the joint attacks coming from the north and east would split the attention of Rico and his army.

I called a halt as we reached the agreed ambush point, close to the edge of the camp. We were close enough now to hear the humans, shouts and calls for order drifting through the trees. We didn't have long. James McArthur and his small band of humans weren't far behind us. He came forward to meet me, and I took him and a couple of dragons out towards the edge of the trees to better scout out our position.

As well as Ddraig Bakucic, Yalle, Marin, and Keita joined me, with Okazuni shadowing behind his mate. The only Nyrian present, Okazuni had chosen to join his mate rather than go under the command of Ddraig Krateos on the far flank. Airil had not been so fortunate, swept up with the other surviving Nixans. I tried to suppress my fears for him, knowing that he would be able to escape in a moment should he find himself in any danger. I had not yet seen any sign of Ddraig Boruc, so I assumed he had joined the Nixans.

From our vantage point, I could see no sign of Ddraig Krateos, nor of Alaron and Kyrus. The line of hills to the east blocked all vision of the gryphons, though I could just about hear the chirping voice of their leader. Even this far from the battleground of the previous day, the smell of death was still strong on the air.

"We shall attack hard and fast. As soon as Alaron and Kyrus engage, we shall fly for them. I shall lead from the air. Ddraig Bakucic, take your clan with James on paw," I said, not looking back at the dragons and human who stood just behind me. I didn't want to see the fear on their faces, nor let them know just how terrified I really was. It was all I could do to simply keep the emotion from my voice.

Rustling in the trees above me caught my attention. I glanced up, a little shocked to see Mulner stalking along a thick bough. He looked down at me and grinned, before leaping from the tree and spreading his wings to gracefully glide to the ground. His paws crunched down upon the crisp leaves that coated the forest floor.

"The bats rest. They refuse to fly beneath the sun, but if we get some clouds then I may be able to convince them to fight once more," he said, resting his wing over my body. He had eyes only for me, not once looking from my face yet never truly meeting my gaze.

"They have already done us a great service, by keeping the humans away during the night," I said, bowing my head. I could hear my other companions not far behind, perhaps wisely keeping their distance for now and letting me share a moment with my brother. The soft voices of Bakucic and James soon became indistinct mutters.

"Promise me you'll be safe, Ellian. Can you do that for me?" Mulner whispered, his voice cracking like I had never known it to do before. "I would hate to… Everything I've done, it's to keep you safe. To protect you as best I can. But out there, I can only do so much. While the sun shines I'm powerless to help."

I rested my paw on top of my brother's. I was sure we both knew that there could be no guarantees for my safety, or of any of the dragons behind us. My brother trembled and rested his head against mine. He felt so cold.

"I can try," I whispered, entwining my tail with his. "Just promise me the same. Promise me you'll stay safe too."

I didn't believe his weak smile. "Safe? I'm always safe, Ellian. You'll see. We'll both survive this."

I chose to ignore the lie.

# CHAPTER TWENTY-EIGHT

**Mulner**

I hated myself. How could I look Ellian in the eye and tell her I'd stay safe when I knew I was dying. The magic burned inside me. I could feel the agonising cold sear course through my veins, tearing me apart from the inside. As I watched her talk to James McArthur and the other dragons, I longed to tell her the truth, but I didn't want to add to her many burdens. Best I find a way to die with honour than give her false hope that I had defeated the curse I had so foolishly inflicted upon myself.

The bats called to me. Constantly, their whispers threatened to drive me to madness, urging me to roost with them and sleep the day away, but I knew I couldn't give in to that temptation. The moment I closed my eyes to rest would be when I would lose my mind and soul to this magic. Best to stay awake. Best to give Ellian all I could to keep her safe.

"Master. Come."

I shook my head and growled. The bats did not listen. They were relentless. They had not been satiated by their night flight, forced to patrol and keep watch whilst the dragons slept. They longed for blood, but refused to go out into the sunlight to fight the enemies I gave them. I could hear a few longing cries at the prey that lingered below their trees, but I firmly refused to allow that. I would not see the bats feast upon any dragon but for those that fought alongside George and Tsona.

Another call broke out from my bats, a fierce chittering that rippled through the forest. I closed my eyes and held my head in my paws, desperate to rid myself of their voices. In my distraction, I almost missed the movement coming from the camp. It was only Ellian's quiet call that alerted me to the human army that was starting to march. I quickly clambered up into the trees, claws scrabbling for purchase on wood as I found the best vantage point amongst the leaves, doing my best to ignore the cold chill seeping through my limbs.

I did not know how many humans came forth from the city of tents and into the strip of cleared land before the wall. There must have been eight thousand at least. Rank upon rank emerged, most on foot but some perched atop their machines of metal that roared out through the never-ending maze. All seemed to carry a gun at their hip, and a strange shield slung over their back. The sky filled with the remnants of Xital's draconic army, and once more I nudged a thought towards my bats to fly forth, but they sleepily ignored me.

Silence greeted our enemy. The humans advanced unchecked from the centre of their camp to stand in formation. I looked down to Ellian, but she stood with quivering wings, quite content to surrender the ground to our foes. She was waiting for something, and it wasn't until Alaron stood atop the wooden wall to the east that I understood what. Haloed by the rising sun, the wyvern emerged with a line of gryphons either side of him.

A call went out from the humans to halt their advance, and for a few moments the two forces stared each other down. Then a ripple ran through the gryphons, and as one they all launched into the air. A matching cry came from below, a rousing snarl from Ellian as she kicked off, leaping out from between the trees, a horde of dragons at her back. Half took to wing, the remaining half sprinting on paw and trying to keep pace with the fifty humans than ran in their midst.

I lingered back in the shadows, waiting for the commotion to pass, until I was the last dragon remaining. I looked back towards my bats, listening to their call to retreat and roost, but I shook my head. That would be the cowardly option. I was no coward. My wings flared and I soared out into the light, which felt like claws on my back. Our formation did not last long as a horde of dragons swooped towards their foes.

Volleys of gunfire tore through the air. Hundreds of dragons fell, but from my distance I couldn't see who. I thought I saw someone right from the front spiral down with a crash. I could only hope it wasn't Ellian. Then I saw her, lilac wings spread wide as she careened into the Xital dragons without a care for her own safety. She fought savagely, tooth and claw piercing scale, paying no heed to the blows she received.

Moments later, I heard the bugling call of Ddraig Krateos as his flank descended on the humans. I tried to avoid what I could, tail lashing out and fending off a few dragons as I attempted to find my sister amongst the chaos.

For a few minutes it seemed like we were defeating our enemy faster than they could kill us. Gunfire had ceased. Even those humans not distracted by the dragons on the ground had stopped shooting for fear of hitting the Xitals in the melee. Then the gryphons and Axaatls reached the frontlines, their superior weight crumpling the leading edge of the human army, but their numbers were immense. They soon started to push back.

Alaron was a maelstrom of fury, his apparent awkwardness replaced with astonishing grace as he lashed out with wing and tail. Blood splattered and stained his grey scales already. By his side was Kyrus, feathers still perfect even as he gripped a shrieking human in his powerful talons. The human fell silent. The gryphon moved on to his next prey.

I felt claws against my back. Spinning quickly, I threw the dragon clear. A bronze Xital ness snarled at me. She already had blood on her claws, but I could see her wings trembled with the effort of keeping herself aloft. Whether weakened by injury or sickened by the conflict, I couldn't be sure, but nor could I succumb to a moment of pity. I struck hard and fast, teeth latching around her throat before she had chance to resist.

Hot blood poured onto my tongue, the ness choking through my grip. I growled and squeezed harder, ignoring her claws weakly battering against my chest. Then she fell still, and I flung her down to the distant ground, her limp body striking the head of an unsuspecting human. I could feel blood dripping from my mouth as I snarled, furiously seeking someone else who dared challenge me. For a few moments I felt restored. Blood warmed me, but the longer I remained still the stronger the chill pervaded my body. I had to keep moving. Keep fighting. Keep killing.

It was tough to tell ally from foe in the chaos of battle. Not every dragon I fought was Xital with the distinctive crest of horns atop their head. Many eastern clans had followed Xital, swayed by the ruling clan's guile, especially by the words of the treacherous Ddraig Tsona. If there was anything I could do before the magic within my body consumed me, it would be to see that pitiful excuse for a dragon dead.

I lost count how many times claws raked down my back. I felt no pain despite the blood that dripped between my scales. Nothing could be as agonising as the magic freezing from within. A terrible fury descended upon me, desperate to do as much damage as I could before my strength faltered. Of Ellian I saw no sign. As far as I knew, she could already be dead, but that would not stop me. If I could not keep her safe, then I would avenge her instead.

A definite shift was taking place in the fight. Slowly the dragons started to drift closer towards the ground, guided down by the Xitals who kept gradually sinking towards their allies. Though I noticed it, I was powerless to resist the general movement, more roars doing nothing to get anyone to ignore the diving dragons and keep away from the flashing blades and piercing guns the humans carried.

On the ground, the humans had fortified their positions, using the tall shields they carried to interlock into a strong wall. Small holes between each shield allowed them to shoot through, and they were seemingly tough enough to withstand even a gryphon's talons. They were vulnerable only from the air, but with the efforts of the Xital warriors, fewer were attacking the humans from above.

With a snarl, I took to paw a little distance away from the fight to gather my breath. The ground was thick with the wounded and dead, and I tried my hardest to block my nose from the scent of the deceased.

"You fight well."

I turned to the voice, narrowing my eyes towards the small Nyrian dragon who fluttered down next to me. He had been a companion of Anzig, I knew that much. Okazuni. I couldn't recall ever having spoken to him before. I grunted in response, keeping my eyes on dragon above and human on the ground. A flash of blue feathers caught my attention. I flicked my wings as I saw Seri fighting off a couple of Xitals, their cobalt colouring as perfect as ever. As always, Jesara was just a few wing lengths away. They had survived the attack on the ailur. As much as I wanted to see them and fight by their side, I thought it would be unwise to approach them. Instead, I turned back to Okazuni.

"Have you seen my sister?"

"Ddraig Ellian? She was with the wyvern last I saw her, somewhere over there," the Nyrian said, pointing with his wing towards the boundary of the camp. I still couldn't see her, but the fighting was fierce there, with the sound of gunshots ringing out with alarming regularity. Gryphon, dragon, and human all fought there, not far from the river that flowed by the forest.

Shuffling my wings against my back, I started to prowl forward, keeping a wary eye above me. Okazuni hurried forward to walk by my side, though he didn't offer any explanation to his presence. I was thankful of that, but also of his company. I knew he would watch my back. No one would catch us unawares.

I tried not to look at the bodies that we passed, not wanting to risk recognising any of them. Okazuni had given me hope that my sister still lived, but those who had been a part of my small clan I had beyond Laxtal's borders were still precious to me. Every one of them I cared for, and I didn't want to see them dead in a war that should never have concerned them. Should never have concerned me. Not for the first time I wondered if I would be facing death if I had just stayed back and waited it all out. For a moment I bowed my head and closed my eyes, trusting Okazuni to be keep alert to approaching danger. I would not see another dawn. It would have been nice…

I shut down those thoughts. Better to make use of what little time I had left. I broke into a loping run, avoiding human and dragon. Somehow, I knew that I would find both of my targets in the same place. I would save Ellian and I would kill Tsona. And a storm was brewing in the distant west, massive clouds towering above the mountains. Perhaps my bats would get to fight before night fell as well.

I found the enemy first, near the banks of the river, close to where we had first engaged. Ddraig Tsona was no coward. He was fighting with as much ferocity as any other dragon, his golden scales stained with the blood of his victims. He retreated only to soar into the air and roar out orders to his warriors, marshalling his forces and directing them into the weakest points he faced, clearing the path for the humans to open fire with their guns. I tracked him for a few minutes, keeping low to the ground and watching his movements. With a savage grin on my face, I realised that he was slowly approaching as the flow of fighting pushed him towards the river.

Crouching low on the banks, I waited. Okazuni was gone, lost again in the chaos. That didn't matter. I didn't want to get him involved anyway. This was between me and the Xital ddraig. Revenge for how he had treated my sister.

Tensing my hindpaws against the ground, I waited until he was within range. Silent as the bats I controlled, I pounced and knocked the Xital ddraig clean out the air, rolling and cuffing him with a paw before he had chance to react. I expected to feel the weight of other dragons on my back, but to my surprise I found there was honour still even in the midst of war. Combat was one on one, and if a dragon challenged another, then honour demanded that no one else intervene. Ddraig Tsona was my fight, and none would interfere.

Tsona's hindpaws smashed into my belly. I squawked and regained my balance, but Tsona was already on his paws. He circled around me.

"You challenge me?" he spat, standing tall with pride. Even though there wasn't much difference in height between us, he still managed to look down on me, yet never truly met my eyes. "Who even are you to challenge the only dragon who dared to forge an alliance with the humans?"

"I am Mulner of Laxtal," I hissed, using the clan I had not acknowledged for years before I even realised what I had said. "Ddraig Ellian is my sister, and I challenge you for her honour."

Tsona blinked. "Mulner, is it? Well, I shall take great pleasure in defeating you. And then I shall find your sister and kill her too for what she has done to me. Maybe then Laxtal shall bow to me as they rightly should," he said, sneering down at me. I kept moving, not letting him approach, always keeping him directly in front of me.

"I killed your necuart. You will not find me so easy a victim," I said, revelling in the moment of panic I saw cross his eyes. He suppressed it well, but I could tell from the flicker in his expression that he suddenly feared me.

"You killed… Ugh, pathetic. I always knew George was wrong to ally himself with such a sad excuse for a necuart," Tsona growled, dragging his claws through the dirt. I could see his hindquarters tense, ready to spring at a moment's notice.

I was ready for him, dropping to the ground and letting him soar right over the top of me. I lashed up with my tail, slapping him across the chest as he passed, but otherwise neither of us did any harm to the other. He landed and spun around quickly, barely giving me chance to regain my paws before he charged again. This time he bit down hard on my tail, gripping it between his teeth. I cried with pain, lashing my tail to free it from his grip, but his teeth sunk in between scales.

Tugging my tail, I lashed out at Tsona's face, grazing his cheek with my claws before striking his horns. He hissed in pain and released my bloodied tail, and for a few moments we both warily circled each other once more. My full focus was on him. Nothing else mattered.

"You can't win," Tsona growled, his eye twitching. I had come close to catching it with my claws, a thin red line passing within a scale or two of it.

"You scared of me, Tsona?" I taunted him, a small smirk on my face. I had rattled him, I knew that much. This would not be the easy fight he had expected.

He didn't answer me, instead feinting a lunge towards my right before twisting and lashing out for my left. I easily darted to the side, avoiding his claws, but not his tail as it struck my muzzle. I winced and snarled, shaking my head as I failed to grab it in my teeth. He was faster than I anticipated.

I didn't give Tsona chance to prepare his next attack, lunging for him, snapping at his limbs with my teeth as I tried to get a grip on him. He fought back hard, slamming into my chest with his shoulder to fend me off. I struggled to sink my teeth into the Xital, his scales sliding beneath me. But neither was he able to penetrate my scales, the two of us locked together, wrestling in a show of strength that found us equally matched. Whoever fell to the ground first would pay with their life and so we were both determined not to make that so.

My hindpaws dug into the ground as I resisted Tsona, pushing against his chest and trying to grab his neck in my mouth. I shrieked in pain as I felt his claws loosen a few scales on my shoulder, gritting my teeth and pushing back against the Xital.

We disengaged and circled each other again, both panting and limping slightly from a few cuts to our legs. I noticed he glanced out to a few of the nearby dragons, none of whom seemed ready to intervene. I doubted they would, not until I was about to strike the killing blow on their ddraig. I would have to make it quick if I wanted to succeed. Though I had not expected to defeat the necuart and live, this time I knew I had no hope of survival beyond this fight. I would kill Tsona with my last breath; I didn't need any seer to tell me that.

"Ready to give in yet?" I snarled, keeping my head held high. I wanted Tsona to think I was confident still. Then he did something I didn't expect. The Xital scoffed and turned his back on me.

"You aren't even worth my time," he said, flaring his wings and tensing his hind legs to kick off.

"Coward, stay and fight," I snarled, stomping the ground and digging up a clump of dirt in my claws. Tsona paused and turned his head to face me. He smirked but showed no sign of returning to our fight.

I heard the gunshot before the flaring of pain in my chest. It took me a few moments to even realise what had happened, by which time my legs trembled with the exertion of keeping me standing. Glancing down, I saw with detached disinterest the ragged bullet hole puncturing my right shoulder.

My right paw tingled and then went numb. Better than the stabbing cold.

I didn't even care that an honourless human had interrupted our fight. I just cared that I wouldn't be able to pursue the Xital dragon.

"You're dead, Mulner of Laxtal. It will only take a word," Tsona said, gloating over me. I hadn't even noticed him turn around again, but there he was, standing in front of me, wings spread to loom dark and imposing in my fading vision. "One word though, and you can live. Surrender to me and I'll see that you survive this day."

He thought I was harmless. In his hubris he thought I was already quelled and meek, surrendering and willing to give in. I doubted he even considered that I knew there could be no survival for me. Perhaps he thought I was about to keel over anyway, dying from the shame of defeat. He kept on approaching until his nose almost touched me.

"Your sister was just as easy to defeat," he said, brushing his teeth against my neck. "She may have shot me and left me to die, but I still lived. You can survive this too. Just give up this foolish fight and accept I have won."

I remained still, panting for breath, waiting for my opportunity even as I could feel my lifeblood draining from the wound in my shoulder. I felt numb and cold, as though the magic in my veins was slowly freezing me. As I weakened, it grew stronger. It was claiming me.

The Xital hissed as I remained silent. His teeth were bloody and exposed. "You are dead, Mulner," he repeated.

Tsona arched his head back to look up into the air. I didn't know whether someone called him, or if the chaos of battle momentarily distracted him, but I took the opportunity given to me. I lunged forward, ignoring the fierce protest my wounded shoulder gave. Tooth tore through scale, puncturing Tsona's throat and robbing him of his breath.

He struggled to free himself, but my grip was too strong. I longed to slowly squeeze the life from him, to hear him choke. To hear his attempted pleas, but I knew I didn't have time for that. The other Xitals would be on me in a moment.

I twisted, tasting hot blood in my mouth. Claw and wing battered against me, and I could feel more scales falling away beneath the desperate assault, but before he could dislodge me, I ripped upwards.

Ddraig Tsona staggered back, unsteady on his paws as he stared at me with wide eyes. His chest heaved, a futile attempt to draw in breath as I spat out the remains of his throat. I struggled to flare my wings wide, to show off my full size. I was almost sure I heard my wings snap as they unfurled. My body began to fail.

"I was already dead," I whispered. The once mighty ddraig slumped to the ground. The life faded from his eyes.

I expected claws. The wrath of Xital would surely fall upon me.

It did not come. A flash of blue darted in front of me. Large talons closed around my body, lifting me into the air.

My vision darkened. Magic tore through me, freezing each scale as though turning them all to ice. Even the blood that leaked from my shoulder was like a frozen slush, like snow on a spring morning.

I dangled from the talons, struggling to keep my eyes open. Thoughts scattered. Breaths came short and sharp. Limbs numb.

We passed away from the battlefield, away from the tents and over the forest. Gently, the talons laid me down on the ground.

"Healer!"

A gryphon's voice screeched. Vaguely I was aware of activity around me.

I blinked a few times. Slowly, a shape came into focus. Blue feathers. A familiar beak. Seri. Jesara loomed over their shoulder.

"We have you, Mulner. Just hold on a little while longer. A healer is coming," Jesara said. She held her taloned forepaw lightly over my belly, as though I had the strength to move. Seri nudged her aside and crouched beside me.

I swallowed around the taste of bile and blood. Sorrow filled my heart, even as my life oozed from it. My chest fluttered. "I would have liked to see the Aerie with you."

Seri cupped my head in their forepaw, talons soft and delicate against my scales. "We would have been honoured to show you."

I blinked slowly. The darkness lingered even when my eyes opened again. My chest constricted. "There is still so much…"

Seri touched a talon to my mouth. "You will see it all. In your next life and the lives to come after that. May your soul find the beauty it deserves."

A pained laugh forced its way from my throat. "Then I will surely be a gryphon."

Jesara touched her beak to my muzzle. "You fought well, great warrior. Be at peace and know your sister will be safe."

I managed a smile.

I had killed the necuart. I had killed Tsona.

Jesara was right. Ellian was that little bit safer now.

I allowed my eyes to close one last time.

Darkness took me. I was done.

The world cracked.

# CHAPTER TWENTY-NINE

**Azlak**

War was where futures died. I couldn't recall how many possibilities I had Seen emerge and fade almost as soon as I had sensed them. I had done what little I could, calling out to Ddraig Krateos with advice on how best to counter each threat before they emerged. It never felt enough. All around me dragons were dying. Selfishly, I turned my magic towards those I cared most about, seeking to protect my father and Ddraig Ellian from harm. Kaz never left my side, protecting me from the present while the future distracted me.

For all that I saw, one vision troubled me the most. It was unclear just what I was Seeing, but wings of metal flashed past several times, bringing death and destruction wherever they went. I growled and shook my head, trying to focus my magic on them, but nothing ever made sense. I Saw bursts of seemingly random images. Anzig showed up a few times, but I couldn't understand what I was Seeing. He was important, that much was for sure, but his decisions seemed to help both dragon and human, but I couldn't find the catalyst that would cause him to fall to one side or the other.

Keeping close to Ddraig Krateos kept me nearer to the battle than I would have liked, but I knew I had no other choice. If I were to make any difference, I needed to stay at my father's side. His booming voice was a constant, guiding the magic of the few Nixans left alive, as well as the dragons from the other clans left under his command. They obeyed him without question, and I latched my magic onto his fate most of all. I knew it would be his decisions that would have one of the greatest influences on the outcome of this day.

But no matter what I did, I could not find a way to keep him alive. Before sundown, my father would be dead.

I could have cried, but I knew my duty. I could not let my emotions get in the way of what we had to do. The longer my father lived, the greater an inspiration he could be to those around him, so it was all I could do to keep him breathing until the weight of fate forced me to accept the inevitable.

He would die to his daughter's claws. I had Seen it several times. Though each vision had been different, there had always been one consistency. Nightwings was there to kill him.

"Azlak! Do we help the gryphons or Laxtal?" Haeraig Zeena cried out, standing beside her father with wings outstretched. The two had cleared an area around them, both prepared to spring back into the action. The haeraig carried the Axinstone in a leather pouch slung over her shoulder, borrowed from one of the gryphons.

Quickly, I scanned ahead, noticing a group of a dozen gryphons pinned back by gunfire, a commandeered shell of human shields their only protection. Not far beyond was the Laxtal force, grounded by the pestering of Xital dragons and in danger of getting overwhelmed. I didn't need the magic to decide. I had seen Maznar amongst the Xitals. My father could not go anywhere near her.

"Help the gryphons, quickly," I replied, hoping that my decision wouldn't kill too many Laxtals. Almost immediately, Ddraig Krateos bounded across with Haeraig Zeena and nearly a hundred other dragons, diving upon the humans before they had chance to react. I closed my eyes and turned my head from all the death and destruction they inflicted at my words. It was almost too much for me to bear.

Once more, gunfire echoed throughout the clearing, and for one terrifying moment I thought I saw my father fall. But there he was, leaping up and sweeping aside four humans with a single wave of his paw, eyes ablaze with fury and magic. His power was immense. With the Axinstone nearby he was almost unstoppable. And yet unless I did something to stop it, he would die because of his daughter this day.

Kaz remained close to my side, protecting me from harm and warning me of the dangers of the present while I struggled to understand the future. I couldn't say how many times he saved my life, nudging me away from the worst of the fight, even protecting me with tooth and claw. It would have been safer for me had I stayed by the fortifications, but there I wouldn't have been able to communicate with my father and help shape the course of the battle. How I longed for Anzig. With him I could have stayed in safety, and through my brother's magic been able to reach anyone. But no one had seen him since I had attempted to speak to him in the human encampment. He loomed over my visions still, the shadow of his lost wings casting darkness on every choice.

Those choices I made hopefully led me towards a future where I could save my father, but the end of all my visions still saw him dying at the claws of his daughter. As Kaz kept me safe, I began to get more concerned. I had never known something to be so inevitable before, even amongst the chaos of battle, and that terrified me. There had to be a way.

Before long I found myself back close by my father, the Nixan ddraig's scales splattered in crimson. He'd lost a few scales in combat, with claw marks down his flank. Despite these, he showed no sign of pain, not even limping as he strode amongst the last surviving members of his clan. By his side was Haeraig Zeena, the ness also showing the signs of battle, her left wing held away from her side with the delicate membranes slightly torn.

"Azlak, where to next?" the haeraig called out, her eyes kept on the sky, wary of any possible threats from above. Our father stayed on the ground, flanked by his guard of dragons and gryphons as he struggled to tear a hole through the human defensive line.

I shook my head and closed my eyes. It was almost too much to keep track of. Trying to sort through the threads of time was making my head hurt; finding the right path was almost impossible. I Saw so many different futures, all hinging off so small a choice. I directed Ddraig Krateos out towards the forest, where my visions told me a fierce counterattack from the humans was about to commence. Something critical was happening there, but my focus on my father had blinded me to those events until now, when it was too late to See. Every future was mine to See, but my understanding of the present could never expand beyond my own two eyes.

"Follow the blue feathered gryphon," I gasped, finding one clear image from the visions. That gryphon was important, though I wasn't yet sure why.

With Kaz by my side, I followed Haeraig Zeena and the other Nixans. The gryphons carved a path through the Xital dragons. I tried to close my eyes and ears to the death and suffering all around. Trying not to think about how many deaths I had been responsible for, I trimmed my wings and kept Kaz's cobalt scales in sight.

What met us near the forest stunned me. With a load screech, the gryphons descended to defend a lone drake surrounded by Xitals. I was sure I recognised the besieged drake, but I couldn't get a proper glimpse of him as I descended after Ddraig Krateos and Kaz. The gryphons made short work of the Xitals, routing them after just a few short, bloody seconds. Something had crippled their morale.

The blue feathered gryphon grabbed hold of one of the dragons in their claws and quickly flew away. A second gryphon followed them, while the others remained to deal with the routing Xitals.

I stared at the body of a dragon lying motionless in the mud. His golden scales were much like mine, but it was the crown of horns that set him apart.

Ddraig Krateos bowed his head as he approached the golden drake, blood still leaking from a terrible wound in his throat. "So, here ends Ddraig Tsona," my father muttered, reaching out with a paw and easing the fallen dragon's eyes closed. I failed to feel any great sadness or loss over his death, only that I had failed to See or witness it.

I looked towards the retreating gryphons. Already they were too far away to see who the one with blue feathers carried. The slayer of Tsona would remain a mystery for now.

"We should push on our advantage while we can," Haeraig Zeena said. She moved past her father, but she did not chase after the gryphons and retreating Xitals. They flew towards the edge of the camp and the maze of paths between the thousands of tents. The humans had raised several wooden sentry towers quickly, even since the beginning of our assault. We would pay for any gains of territory amongst the tents with a lot of spilled blood.

"Wait, not after them," I said, distracting the haeraig before she could make her move. Nightwings was still amongst the Xital dragons, organising their retreat and into the safety of the camp. I did not want Ddraig Krateos anywhere near her. I needed to protect him.

*"Do you really think he will care for you?"*

The thought drifted through my mind, unbidden and unwanted. It took me a few seconds to then realise that the thought hadn't been my own. As soon as I was aware of that my whole body tensed, eyes wide as I stared down into the churned mud. My brother was in my mind. Whether he intended it or not, I caught a glimpse of his position. He was with George, hurrying through the tents from the back of the camp, closest to the cliffs. They came this way.

I shuddered and tried to ignore the touch of Anzig's mind. My father's attention was on me, awaiting clarification. "Humans are on their way. George will be amongst them," I said.

"George is coming here? He will not be pleased to learn of Tsona's death," Haeraig Zeena said. She started to move, as though to chase after the gryphons, then held herself still. I followed her gaze. More armoured humans began to emerge from the depths of the camp, approaching the fleeing Xitals and their gryphon pursuers. Just how many more of these humans were there?

Ddraig Krateos shouted, drawing my attention away. "There!" my father called, flicking out a wing to point down a different path in the camp. Even more humans. They wore less armour and carried fewer weapons. At their head was George. His face was red, streaked with ash and grime.

A whistling sound pulled my gaze up. My paws took a couple of involuntary steps back. A green scaled dragon soared directly above George's head, wings glinting unnaturally in the sunlight.

Multiple futures tore at my mind. I stood still, frozen between them all. Did we help the gryphons, confront George, or flee towards the safety of the open clearing and the wall?

A sneering voice bellowed across the battlefield, magically enhanced as it drew attention from dragon, gryphon, and human alike. "They have served their purpose. Execute them at will."

George let out an anguished cry and began to run back towards the centre of the camp. Down the other path, gryphon and dragon both cried out in alarm. A fresh volley of gunfire rang out. Draconic screams of agony followed as the humans turned on their allies. All around the camp, humans attacked dragons. Any dragon.

A cold chill ran through me, my mouth dry. How had I not foreseen this? I already knew the answer. I had been too focused on protecting my father. I had missed this betrayal.

"We should retreat," Haeraig Zeena suggested.

I nodded numbly. Something had shifted within the human army. A new direction. A new purpose. It had been Rico's voice that had changed things. Was that what Maznar had tried to warn me of? Did I dare believe that she might have been telling the truth?

"Fall back to the wall," Ddraig Krateos hissed. "I will meet you there. I must help them."

My father moved before I could stop him. He left his daughter and any support behind as he ran for the camp, towards the armoured humans and the doomed Xitals. Those who once pursued the dragons now helped them. The gryphons fended off the humans while the Xital dragons struggled to escape, so many killed already. Maznar was amongst them.

"Azlak, hurry," Haeraig Zeena called. I ignored her. I chased after my father, hurrying on paw after the Nixan ddraig. Whistling wings followed above me.

Most of the Xital dragons were dead already, gunned down by the humans who should have been their allies. They may have been our enemy, but for the moment, we had a common foe. With a bellowing roar, Ddraig Krateos leaped over the retreating dragons, his magic blasting out and knocking over several of the attacking humans.

Maznar was by his side in an instant. My heart skipped a beat. Nothing happened. She did not attack the ddraig.

Gryphons screeched as they did their best to protect the dragons. Talons slashed and beaks jabbed, puncturing armour with ease. But more humans were coming. There was always more of them.

"We need to retreat," Maznar called out. She wore a leather harness over her scales, several pouches filled with human devices and technology.

A couple of the gryphons looked towards Ddraig Krateos for guidance. The Nixan had eyes for me. I had no vision to help make a choice. With more humans coming, there was no time to reach for my magic and search the future. Could I trust her?

"Come with us." The words were like bile in my throat.

Gunfire peppered around us, missed shots throwing up explosions of dirt. The humans were finding their range.

I turned tail to run, hoping the dragons and gryphons were able to keep pace. More screams. More death. Paws thundered close behind.

Half a dozen humans stepped out from behind a tent. I had no time to react, not even to slow down.

A dragon plummeted from the sky, smashing into the humans. Wings of silver slashed and sliced, tearing through armour with the ease of a gryphon's talon.

"Keep going!"

I almost stopped anyway. Anzig turned to run by my side.

I managed to resist the urge to stare at my brother, my eyes fixed forward. The open plains were close by, where finally we could leave behind the tight and narrow paths of the camp. Where the humans would have better range to pick us off one at a time. But what other choice did we have?

All around me, dragons and gryphons were in retreat. Our army fell back, pushed out of the camp by the new ferocity and aggression shown by the humans. Alaron and Prince Kyrus bellowed their orders, echoed by Ellian and the other ddraigs.

For a moment I thought we all had a chance. Gryphons began to outpace me as we fled across the clearing. The wall loomed large before me, the towering edifice of wood a dominating defence that stretched across the wide valley.

I took to wing at the last moment, leaping high into the air. My claws scrambled at the wood for grip as I hauled myself over to the protection of the far side, where the human weapons could no longer reach me.

Anzig was not far behind me, sprinting with the Xital dragons and the gryphons who lagged behind their kin. Ddraig Krateos was amongst the last, the Nixan's attention almost exclusively behind him. His magic deflected bullets as they flew, flicking them aside with a mere glance of his eyes.

Maznar stumbled, her paws falling beneath her.

Anzig grabbed hold of the wall and looked back. His eyes widened and he cried out, leaping off the ramparts again. His silver wings extended wide as he dived for his sister – our sister. Ddraig Krateos also turned towards the stricken ness.

Anzig reached her first. He extended a wing like a shield, while Ddraig Krateos grabbed hold of the ness and lifted her back to her paws.

From the wall, Alaron bellowed commands, trying to build some organisation to the chaotic retreat. Prince Kyrus swooped to scatter a group of humans who had foolishly run ahead of their companions.

The humans did not advance all the way to the wall. They came to a halt in formation halfway between the fortification and the camp. The first row of humans dropped to one knee, with the row behind standing. They all carried guns, aimed for the stragglers who had not yet cleared the wall. Including my father and siblings.

Without thinking, I jumped from the wall just as the first volley fire pealed out. A series of deafening explosions disorientated me. Anzig kept his wings extended, protecting himself and Maznar. The air rippled around them as Ddraig Krateos's magic deflected projectiles away.

I grabbed Maznar and dragged her away from the shelter of Anzig's wing. I didn't even look at my brother, nor the miracle of his glimmering wings. There would be time enough for that once we were safe.

A human voice echoed through the clearing, commanding and marshalling the soldiers as they raised their guns for another volley. I grabbed hold of Maznar by her harness and hauled her away. I shoved her towards the wall. "Fly, quickly!"

The spectre leaped from the ground, almost clearing the wall without needing to beat her wings. A quick bit of lift and a scrabble of claws and she was gone.

I had no chance to follow her. There was a command to fire. A rippling explosion of light and smoke roared across the plains. Flashes of gunpowder crackled with human magic.

Anzig flicked up his wing. My father's paw lifted, guiding the bullets around us as they thudded against ground and wall. Sparks erupted from Anzig's wing, bullets cracking against the reflective surface.

Ddraig Krateos grinned, his fangs showing in a savage and silent snarl. His paw did not waver, eyes unblinking as he stared down the hundreds of humans. None of them could hit him.

Anzig crouched to jump, wings shifting position. Another volley of bullets peppered against him. Two ricocheted by my paws.

A third thudded into Ddraig Krateos's chest with a wet spurt of blood.

He fell without a word.

This wasn't how it was supposed to happen. I couldn't believe my eyes. There had to be a mistake.

Dimly, I was aware of someone shouting. Anzig. It was my brother who screamed at me. I couldn't make out the words. I could only stare at Ddraig Krateos, lying still on the ground. Hot blood pooling around his body.

Talons closed around me and the ddraig, lifting us both from the ground. Gryphons carried us over the wall before the next round of gunfire could rip through us.

Even as I was set down again, I was barely aware of anything around me. I thought I heard Alaron shouting above me, but none of his words were meant for me. Whatever was happening on the other side of the wall did not matter.

I put my paw on Ddraig Krateos's neck. He did not move. His heart did not beat.

Kaz pushed his way past me, hurrying up to the fallen ddraig. As he reached out and placed his paw on Ddraig Krateos, I already knew it was too late. My mate's magic sprung out from his paw, bathing my father in a gentle light and the deep wound in his chest started to close, but no movement returned to the Nixan's chest. No life returned to his eyes.

"Azlak…"

Maznar whimpered as she approached. She seemed unable to tear her eyes away from the body of our father.

She did not kill the Nixan ddraig. He had died because he had saved the spectre's life. The life of his daughter. How had I failed to see that in my visions? War confused the future and kept so much hidden from me. There was too much I did not understand, but one thing was for certain.

My father was dead.

Nixa had lost its ddraig.

# CHAPTER THIRTY

**Ellian**

We fought fiercely. Many dragons had given their lives for the cause. Our numbers were vastly depleted, and yet the onslaught of humanity never seemed to end. We had taken catastrophic losses, but so had Clan Xital and their allies. We had annulled much of the danger from above, but still the threat of humanity's steel and gunfire remained.

I couldn't recall how many times I had come within moments of death. Whether it was some Nixan enchantment or pure luck, I could never be sure, but every time I faced claw or sword, I was able to escape with no more than a small slice to my scales. I bled for our cause from wounds on my shoulders and legs, but I had not suffered any of the horrific injuries I had witnessed, of dragons, gryphons, and humans alike staggering away from the fight, desperate to receive the attention of healers. Those who had been lucky enough to survive so long.

Then the unpleasant voice boomed across the valley, and everything seemed to change in an instant. Every gain we had scrapped and fought so hard for over the day disappeared in less time it took to blink.

Dark storm clouds gathered on the mountains, obscuring the sun early and bringing about a premature dusk. I stayed on the wall as our desperate retreat ended, but the humans did not seem eager to approach the stolen fortification.

As the sunlight faded, a loud chittering began to grow from the forest in the south. Though I knew it was coming, I still could not prevent the fear from building in my chest as the first of the bats emerged from the trees. A great, screeching hoard ascended into the sky, further blotting out the dying embers of sunlight and casting dappled shadows across the bloodstained ground. Though I looked, I could not see my brother amongst them.

I kept on my guard, fearing the bats might change their behaviour. They remained high above the camp, whirling like a seething cloud to enforce the uneasy and unsettling stalemate between human and dragon. Wary of the bats, the humans began to retreat to their camp.

We had survived another day, but at what cost?

My wings ached as I held them against my back, longing to spread them out and catch the last few rays of sunlight before they disappeared behind the darkening clouds. I wasn't even able to keep my legs from shaking as I jumped from the wall. I needed to find Alaron so that I could finally understand the true damage of the day.

The wyvern was not far away, at the centre of a cluster of dragons and gryphons by the base of the wall. Voices were raised, competing with each other as well as the constant shriek of the bats above.

I barged my way into the circle of dragons, only to freeze in shock. Several Xital dragons stood with Alaron, their crown of horns distinct amongst the Laxtals nearby. Then I saw Maznar amongst them and the growl came quick and fierce.

A green dragon stepped across me, blocking the path to the diminished spectre. I moved to shove him aside before realising who it was. The snarl melted from my muzzle, replaced by slack-jawed shock. Anzig.

My eyes immediately flicked to his back, no longer bare. But he did not have his wings restored. Instead, there was a parody of them strapped to his body, secured by leather straps around his shoulders and underbelly. The new wings were metal and leather, with thin and articulated sheeting folded neatly to his sides connected to a clawed joint on the leading edge. Even accounting for the artificial material that made them, they were only a loose approximation of true wings.

The bile in my stomach grew bitter as I stared at them. If anything, they only emphasised the injuries Anzig had sustained.

Anzig spread his wings, the different segments of the artificial membranes moving smoothly against each other. "I took back the sky," he said breathlessly.

My tongue seemed swollen in my mouth, barely able to move it as I struggled to get anything out. "Anzig…"

Relief flooded me as Alaron summoned me with his harsh and demanding voice. I could avoid speaking my mind. I could look away from Anzig's wings.

"Ddraig Ellian, I'm glad to see you looking relatively unharmed," the wyvern said as I approached, lowering his head for a second. As always, Prince Kyrus stood close to Alaron's side. Almost everyone I expected to see was present, with Ddraig Boruc also standing near the wyvern. A tearful and bloodied Haeraig Zeena slouched next to Azlak and Kaz, though there was no sign of her father.

Alaron had not escaped without injury. He had broken one of his wingfingers, so he avoided putting too much weight on his right wing as he shuffled around. He'd also taken a claw to his neck, with a ragged line of broken and bloodstained scales from the side of his neck down to his shoulder.

Kyrus appeared to be unscathed, though he limped slightly with an apparent injury in his left hindleg. Blood blemished his feathers, and I could see a few red stains he had not yet managed to clean away from his claws. His beak clicked as he slowly looked around the gathered dragons, his eyes lingering on the Xitals.

"Can someone please explain why they're all here," I said, sweeping my wing out to gesture to the survivors from the royal clan, as well as to Anzig and Maznar.

Kyrus was the first to answer. "Ddraig Tsona is dead and the Xitals began to retreat," he chirped, not once moving his eyes from one particular Xital ness. "It seems after that, the humans turned on their allies. We believe Rico gave the order to attack and kill every dragon, not only those from our alliance."

"It's true," Maznar hissed. Her eyes were wet with Nixan tears. "I tried to warn you. George was not your enemy. Rico was. And now thousands are dead."

"What do we know about him?" Alaron asked. He sat back on his hindlegs, keeping his injured wing off the ground. By his side was one of his usual cups of steaming hot fragrant drinks, seemingly untouched for the moment.

Maznar growled. "He will stop at nothing to see us all dead. Every single dragon. Beyond that, no one really knows much about him. Not even George. The prime minister must trust him though, as it was Brightwell's orders to have him cross the mountains."

Ddraig Boruc spoke quietly. "I have my suspicions, which I will share with the envoys of Esperance only."

"This gives us an opportunity," Anzig said, stepping ahead of me to address Kyrus and Alaron directly. His metallic wings clicked as they twitched. "George still has allies over there. If we can reach them, then they can help us."

I growled. "Anzig…"

Haeraig Zeena snarled. "We are not going to seek help from them."

"What other choice do we have?" Anzig replied.

"Anzig!"

This time, the former ddraig hesitated. He slowly turned around, an irritated frown on his forehead. "What?"

"I am very happy to see you're still alive, but you are not ddraig any longer," I said, speaking quickly before he could attempt to interrupt me. I spread my wings wide and stretched out my neck, emphasising my height advantage over him. "Leave us. I will speak to you later."

Anzig did not retreat. He spread his wings to match mine, the metallic monstrosities reaching a greater span than before. "I have the sky back. I took it so I could regain my place. My rightful place."

"Do you still think it was about that?" I growled. I did not let myself back down. "You surrendered the clan to me. I am ddraig still."

The colour drained from his eyes, fading to a milky white. Perhaps I was wrong. Maybe Anzig could become ddraig again. His leadership might be useful. Later. When all of this was over.

"Anzig…" Azlak's growl got both of our attention. White eyes flicked back to yellow.

I took in a sharp breath as my thoughts became my own again. My muzzle pulled back into a snarl. "We do not have the time to debate this now, Anzig. I am ddraig still. Once we have survived, we can discuss what can happen to what remains of Laxtal. Until then, I trust you will respect my right to rule."

Anzig held my gaze a few seconds longer. Then he slowly started to tuck his wings to his side. He bowed his head. "Very well. But we need George's help. Only he can defeat Rico."

The former ddraig did not wait for a response as he turned to leave, his wings clicking oddly against his scales. Maznar scampered after him. They did not go to the Xital survivors, instead heading towards the forest on the southern edge of our refuge.

With a great effort, I bit down on the lingering growl. I wanted to denounce Anzig's suggestion again, but before I could, Ddraig Boruc spoke.

"With regret, I must agree with Anzig, if not for the same reason," the Vatrean drake said. He pawed at the loose dirt. "We don't need him to win this battle, but we do need to understand the process behind his restoration. This magic could prove crucial to how we survive in the years and decades to come. Put simply, we must know how he has been able to achieve this."

Alaron hooked his wingclaws into the handle of his cup, lifting it gently to his mouth. "I agree," he said, before taking a sip of his drink. "We can do nothing tonight though. Tomorrow, we must try to capture George alive so that we can question him."

None of the gathered dragons protested or complained. My tail thrashed in irritation as I looked around them. There was still one notable absence. "Should we not wait for Krateos before we start planning our moves tomorrow?"

"He's dead," Haeraig Zeena said. She took a deep breath to swell out her chest. "He died in the retreat. If there is anything left of our clan after tomorrow, then I will take the wylax and become ddraig." She gripped tight onto the Axinstone.

Judging from the lack of response to her words, the others had already known about the loss of Ddraig Krateos. Her news was like a physical blow to the chest. The Nixan leader was a terrible absence. His magic and conviction would be a great loss. "I'm sorry to hear," I said, unable to raise my voice much above a soft whisper that the cacophony of bats easily drowned out. So much death already. I barely had the heart to hear about more.

"We have some hope," Prince Kyrus said. His musical voice still sounded as bright and fierce as ever, though his grooming was far from its usual standard. Several bloodied and broken feathers jutted out around his face and mud smeared up his legs and belly. "Ddraig Nunahra sent a messenger through an hour ago. Wary of the grave bats, they did not risk flying to us near dusk, but they have made camp less than two hours away. The Xigax and Axaatl army will join us in the morning."

"Tomorrow is when we win this war," Alaron said. Whereas normally he was prone to pacing back and forth as he spoke, this time he remained standing in one place, hindered by his injured wing. "The humans know we are vulnerable, but they can't attack tonight while the bats protect us. We will strike them hard and with greater numbers than they expect. They failed to wipe us out today. Tomorrow, we will make them regret that."

"Rest while you can, ddraigs and haeraigs. See to healers if you need them," Kyrus chirped. His piercing eyes fell on me. He let out a little chirrup. "Ddraig Ellian, if I may speak with you privately quickly."

A sense of foreboding built in my chest as I followed the gryphon. The other dragons all began to slowly disperse, leaving the protection of the wall to the gryphon guardians and the screeching bats once more. The dangers from the bright lights of the camp meant we could not feel completely safe but, for the moment at least, we had an opportunity to recover.

The gryphon clicked his beak before speaking. "There is a gryphon who wishes to speak with you. Their name is Seri."

The name was familiar. It didn't take long to remember where I knew it from. "Is that the apothecary who flew off with Mulner a few nights ago? Your cousin?"

Kyrus dipped his head. "That is correct. They wished to speak to you directly."

The gryphon prince led me towards the edge of the forest, where the healers were tending to the wounded. Not far away was where the dead lay in their eternal rest, placed so the prevailing wind would not waft the scent of death and bonfire smoke across us. I forced myself to keep my head high and look towards the vast collection of bodies, dragon and gryphon alike. There were many hundreds, and those just the bodies we had been able to recover. I dreaded to think how many more lay on the far side of the wall.

The apothecary waited for us, pacing by the trees. Their bright blue feathers were distinctive even amongst the strange creatures. Bright yellow eyes quickly found me, and the gryphon bowed deep and low, front legs bending so much their beak almost touched the ground.

Prince Kyrus chirped something to Seri in the gryphon language, before making his quiet retreat. I was alone with the apothecary.

"Your brother came to us in a time of need," the gryphon said, keeping their head low. When finally they looked up, the black markings around their eyes were streaked down their blue feathers like the patterning had partly melted. They chirruped sorrowfully, a deep trill that fell into silence.

I already knew what the apothecary was going to say. A chill settled on my heart.

"I failed your brother, I am sorry. I cannot be sure if it was the necuart magic or the wounds inflicted by Tsona, or perhaps even a combination of the two. By the time I found him there was little I could do but watch his soul transition to the next life," Seri said. They slumped onto their haunches. "I know it will be of little consolation to you now, but he died a warrior's death. He killed both the necuart and Ddraig Tsona."

"He never wanted a warrior's death." My voice cracked to reflect my heart.

"May he find the peace and beauty he desired in the next life," the gryphon said.

I looked up to their bright yellow eyes. The words were sincere, I was sure of that. It did little to ease the pain I felt within. My brother had been out of my life for so long. I had gotten to enjoy scant weeks with him back. We had lost so much time together. How many more needed to die simply so that we could survive.

The gryphon twitched nervously, their wings shuffling against their sides. I struggled to swallow around my grief and instead tried to feel some measure of pride. My brother had died to save the lives of many, taking away two of the greatest threats against us. "Thank you for everything you did for my brother. You did your best to save him."

Seri bowed their head again. "Should there be anything you need from me, please call. I would like to make up for my failings to you."

"That won't be necessary," I said quickly, before holding back a choking sob that threatened to tear itself free. I took a deep breath. "But thank you. I appreciate the offer."

Seri chirped. Their eyes brightened a little, tufted ears flicking up. "If you'll excuse me now. I must see what help I can give to the wounded."

I stepped away and let Seri return to those who needed them. I stared at the gryphon as they left, blue feathers distinct amongst their brethren. In so many ways we were lucky, fortunate to witness such strange and helpful creatures such as the gryphons. But their presence was a necessity in our struggle to survive. No matter what happened the next day, our world had forever changed. No longer would draconic matters belong only to dragons. It would be foolish to think we could continue as we always had. What did that mean for dragons like me? The actions of a select few ddraigs had caused this war. Could we rely on the ddraigs of the future to avoid a repeat of all this pain?

I had no answers. I would find none in my own mind.

I was desperate for company to ease me through the grief. My brother was gone. Thousands of others had died in the last two days. And I was their leader, their ddraig. The dragon they trusted to keep them safe.

I tried to block my ears to the sounds of discomfort all around. Dragons whimpered and hissed as they tried to get comfortable, some crying out in agony as they waited for the overworked healers to reach them. So much suffering already and we expected them to go and fight again. I didn't know how I could do it, but what choice did we really have?

Time and time again I was stopped by dragons desperate to know if we had any hope of victory. Each time I replied in the same way. "We always have hope. Stay brave and we can triumph."

Hollow words. Was that really all I had to offer?

A familiar face was a welcome relief. Ddraig Boruc came to greet me, the old dragon looking as weary as I felt. He shielded me with a wing and walked by my side as we made our slow way through the crowd of dragons.

"I am sorry to hear of your brother," the Vatrean said. I did not question how he had heard of Mulner's death. "I hope he recognised that his actions most likely saved us all. Without the grave bats to protect us, we may never have survived the first night. They will follow his final orders until dawn at least."

I glanced up. The chittering screeches of the bats continued unabated. After a while the noise had receded into the back of my mind, but every time I focused on them, the cacophony returned full force. Those that did dive to the ground did so on the far side of the wall. I tried to ignore those that went into the trees with a body in their claws.

Ddraig Boruc led me to one of the many bonfires that had been lit. This one was close to the forest on the southern edge of our camp. Both humans and dragons sat around the fire. I was pleased to see James McArthur with them, wrapped up inside a sheet of warm fabrics and holding a metallic stick emanating light. In his other hand was a black device with a rainbow of colours around the edge. The human appeared weary yet unharmed. There were some unfamiliar faces amongst the humans, those who had not been in the group who had settled in Mulner's lair.

My attention lingered on James for barely a moment, as Airil quickly barrelled into my side. We embraced, my wings wrapping around him before we settled down together. Nearby, Azlak lay down with his head resting on Kaz's chest. The Nixan healer looked barely conscious, his eyes open but his wings draped across the ground.

No one spoke for a long time. I closed my eyes and listened to the crackling fire as it burned over the wooden fuel. The ashen smell of smoke was welcome relief to my nose, giving me the opportunity to ignore the scent of lingering death and blood.

The silence could not last forever. My curiosity won out as I looked through the calming flames towards the strange new humans. "Where did they come from?" I asked.

James McArthur looked up from his slate-like device. "It wasn't just dragons who Rico betrayed. There were more of us who didn't care for this extermination of your kind. Like there were Xitals who fled, so too did some of George's people. Scientists, mostly. But they wanted nothing to do with what Rico is doing, so Alaron and Kyrus allowed them to take refuge with us."

I stared at the strangers. Like the Xitals, I could not bring myself to trust them. For too long had they fought against us, enemies who would bring about the end of our way of life. A common enemy made them uneasy allies at best.

There were not many of them, but for every human that sided with us represented one fewer to fight. It was small consolation.

A healer soon came to us, giving the hope of relief from our wounds. Kaz tried to stand to assist the ness as she came around, but the Nixan simply smiled and placed her paw on Kaz's head. He instantly fell asleep at her touch, tail draped over Azlak's body.

I tried to refuse the healing, preferring for the ness to conserve her strength for those who truly needed it. However, she insisted. I was too weary to evade her, so when her paw found mine, I could feel the warmth of her magic seeping through my body. Scales renewed as the damaged flesh righted itself, all the little aches and pains I hadn't even been consciously aware of fading to nothing. My body felt rejuvenated, though my mind was exhausted.

"With your forgiveness, Ddraig," the Nixan healer said, bowing her head and keeping her eyes low. "I use the strength of those who can afford to give it up to complete the healing. That way we can see to more of those in need."

I nodded and gave the ness's paw a gentle squeeze before she pulled away. "Thank you. Your efforts are most appreciated," I said softly, before she retreated into the darkness to provide her services where they were next needed. After having my energy drained, I didn't know how much longer I would be able to remain awake. My eyelids drooped as my head fell back into Airil's body. His legs and tail wrapped around me, holding me close.

Though danger lay less than a mile away and our protection from above came from a horde of bats who could easily turn on us, I found that I could not resist sleep. My dreams were troubled. A black spectre with red eyes haunted them, but she never forced me awake. I slept through the night.

I woke to darkness. I couldn't see the stars beneath the trees, but dawn had certainly not arrived. Airil's chest rose and fell beneath my head as he continued to sleep. The unnerving red eyes from my dream continued to gleam from the darkness like a ghostly imprint leftover from my mind's eye. But that wasn't what had woken me up. It took a few moments for my cold body to recognise the warm hand resting against my side.

Blinking to clear my eyes of the afterimages of my dream, I could just about make out the outline of James's shadow in the darkness as he crouched over me. Only the light of his little communications device allowed me to see him at all.

"Huh? What's the matter?" I asked, fighting off the urge to simply fall asleep again.

"Alaron summoned us. The bats are starting to return to their roost before dawn," James said quietly, making sure I was staying awake before moving on to rouse Ddraig Boruc. The human carried a cup of hot, steaming liquid in his hand, smelling the same as those the wyvern preferred.

I dragged myself up to my paws, weak and unsteady as I tried to remain upright. Airil twitched his tail and curled it lightly around my leg as he slept. Temptation tugged at my mind to lie by his side again, but reluctantly I shook my paw to free it before taking a few stumbling steps forward.

Instead of delving deeper into the forest, James led us out towards the outskirts. With the trees less dense, some starlight started to shine down through the leaves, but it was still barely enough to see by, especially as the moon would have set sometime in the middle of the night.

Sleeping dragons sprawled out everywhere. There seemed to be no particular order amongst it either, dragons from different clans lay across each other without concern. Nixans lay with Lilisxi dragons, Laxtals with Axaatls. In their exhaustion and pain, none had worried about the boundaries that separated our clans. Saya and Marin lay together in what could almost have been a conspiratorial huddle, were it not for the deep snores that came from them both.

Dawn was just breaking as we slowly climbed up one of the surrounding hills. The wyvern was waiting for us at the summit, standing tall with no signs of the discomfort he had been in the previous night. His focus was not on the potential human city on the far side of the plains, but to the skies of the east, above the pink glow of the rising sun.

"If she doesn't come today…" the wyvern muttered, before slowly turning around to face us. I wasn't sure if we were meant to hear his words of doubt, but he showed no discomfort in knowing that we had overheard him. I bowed my head to him, and the wyvern repeated the gesture. "I trust you slept well, Ddraig Ellian and James McArthur."

"It was too short, but restful enough," I replied, looking up to the human beside me who nodded his assent. For once I was envious of his warm clothing, usually finding the strips of cloth and fabric pointless, but in the cool winds blowing down from the north they would have provided some warmth. I barely had the strength to even hold my wings up tight against my back. The first few rays of sunlight on my scales would be most welcome.

Alaron scratched at the ground with his claws as we waited for the others to arrive. Prince Kyrus was next, the gryphon already looking perfectly preened as though he hadn't even settled down to sleep. I wondered how long he had already been awake, just to get his feathers in place. Haeraig Zeena approached with Inilta by her side, a film of flames licking at her scales. When the Nixan haeraig, soon to be ddraig, settled down, Inilta approached the middle of the circle and placed his forepaws together on the ground. When he removed them, a spring of fire roared up, instantly hotter than any other natural fire I had known.

Like moths to the fire, Ddraig Bakucic and Ddraig Kiarla were next to arrive, both muttering quiet words of greeting before spreading their wings in front of the magical flame. There were still others to come, but Alaron wasn't willing to wait any longer.

"I have sent a messenger out to Ddraig Nunahra, instructing her to sweep in from the north. If she has remained undetected by our enemy then I am hopeful she can decimate their last resistance," he explained, looking around at the gathered ddraigs and other leaders. His eyes settled on me for a moment before moving away.

A paw settled on my tail for a moment, and I turned back to see Ddraig Boruc behind me. I moved to the side, brushing into Kyrus's softly furred hindlegs as I did so, to allow the Vatrean to join in the circle and rest in the firelight. He looked exhausted and seemed to be suffering from the cold more than anyone else.

In my distraction, I almost lost what the wyvern was saying.

"Our success today will depend on Ddraig Nunahra and her reinforcements. With their help we can overwhelm the humans, but that is not to be our only objective," the wyvern said. He paused to take a sip of his customary morning drink. "Ddraig Ellian, you will have a new mission for the day. You will take James McArthur and a small group of dragons and humans that I have selected for you. Your task will be to infiltrate the human camp and secure the safety of

George Symons. Prince Kyrus and I will coordinate the attacks to keep them from detecting you."

James sat down next to me and placed his hand on my back. His skin was warm to the touch. "With the information Azlak and Anzig have given us about their camp, I think I know where George will be," the human said.

"Then it is settled," Alaron said, as always holding our gaze for a few seconds. He even glared into the eyes of the human but seemed to find James's lack of focus an annoyance. "We shall strike in one hour. Sooner if the humans look in danger of attacking first. Use that time to warm up and energise yourselves. This is the day of our destiny."

I took a deep breath. The fate of dragonkind rested on us now. Win or lose, our lives would never be the same again.

# chapter thirty-one

**Azlak**

The sun barely made it over the horizon when my eyes opened. I had spent the night in Kaz's wings, enjoying what I feared could be the last night I would get to spend with him. I knew I had dreamed a lot that night, but frustratingly they remained elusive. Only flashes of meaningless images remained.

In my paw I could feel the indentation left there by Esperance's slate. The longing to contact her was starting to grow, desperate to hear her words. She would want to know whether or not we were able to win. But she would also be just as likely to chastise me for bothering her with such trivial things. I knew that while she would probably care about us, we were also beings lesser than her. If we died, she would find someone new.

Resisting the urge to squeeze down on my paw, I slowly rose from the ground, rousing Kaz as I did so. We would want to be energetic and warm as soon as we could, so we wasted no time in heading out from the forest. Despite the number of dragons gradually rousing themselves, the forest was quiet without the chatter of the bats above us. They must have found somewhere else to roost, now that the willpower of Mulner was no longer present to keep them here.

We were far from the only ones who found some sunlight on the crest of one of the many hills, wings spread out over the grass to take in some of the morning heat. Kaz lay down by my side, but it wasn't for a few minutes before I recognised who I had settled down next to.

Keita glanced across at me, but where she would have once recoiled or demanded I leave, instead she just gave me a tired smile. "What have you Seen for today?" she asked me.

I shook my head. "Not much. It's too intense for me to properly make out any one future. Too much is changing all the time," I said. I hadn't even tried to use my magic since waking up, too afraid of what I might See. "War is a dangerous place for a seer. If I risk looking too hard then I will witness every eventuality, every death that is to come. It is a terrible burden."

Once she would have berated me for my unreliable magic, but now she just nodded and sighed. "Shame. It would have been good to know at least," Keita said, before she yawned widely. On her other side was Okazuni, and before long Inilta joined us, who wandered down from the top of the hill where I could see the ddraigs and haeraigs gathered around Alaron. The Nixan greeted his brother halfway down the hill, the two of them soon joining us.

Keita. Okazuni. Inilta. Isikian. I closed my eyes as memories threatened to bring tears to my eyes. My travelling companions over the mountains. I was not the only one to be thinking of such things.

"We're missing three," Keita said in a small voice.

Okazuni put his wing around his mate. "We will honour Carlee and Nataik today and make sure their deaths weren't in vain," the Nyrian said, pressing his head to Keita's side.

"And what of Anzig?" Inilta asked. He looked up to the brightening sky as though seeking for my brother. I had seen no sign of him.

"He seems misguided," Isikian said. The emerald-scaled healer kneaded at the ground with both forepaws. He opened his mouth to speak, hesitated, then stared down and whispered what he had to say. "He has faced a lot of hardships recently. It is only natural that he has struggled to come to terms with this. The humans have promised him something he desired, and he believes he can get it from them."

"His wings," Keita mumbled.

"His clan," Inilta added.

We all looked up the hill, towards the ddraigs. Ddraig Ellian was up there, her lilac scales glittering in the early morning sunlight.

"We can still help him," Keita said, leaning back into Okazuni. I wondered if she was aware of how those sorts of actions had contributed to Anzig's decline, that her courtship of the Nyrian had been one of the breaking points in my brother's mind. I sighed. She had to know. She had as much as told me, but that she had not regretted her actions. Anzig had failed to declare his intentions towards her and had suffered the penalty for that. It should be no slight on Keita's wings that she had chosen her own happiness.

I remained silent. I was starting to recall fragments of my dreams, little pieces of the many possible futures that were constantly changing. It was hard to tell which actions would lead to which futures, but one certainty was Anzig. He was central to everything that would happen today. Was he the third dragon Esperance had tasked us to find?

"I wonder what they're talking about."

Isikian's words distracted me from my internal musing. He was still looking up towards the crest of the hill, where the gathered ddraigs and the other leaders were deep in conversation. I could hear none of their words, but it appeared the wyvern was doing most of the talking.

"Probably discussing just how they're going to send us to die," Okazuni muttered darkly. He was clawing at the ground, not looking up at anyone. Keita muttered something in his ear, something that I couldn't hear. It could have been some assurance that they weren't going to die, but I knew eyes would start to turn to me for that guarantee. It was one I could not provide. I despised not knowing the future, especially to determine the fate of those dragons who had become close to me. I felt like I owed the likes of Isikian and Keita the assurance that they would survive this day.

I didn't even realise I had gotten to my paws before I found myself walking away from the group, making my way downhill. Kaz followed me, though he respected my need for silence. His company was most appreciated though, and I reached out with a wingtip to brush against his side.

We kept on walking until we were out of sight of the others. The sun was a little brighter on the northern slopes of the hill, but we weren't out there to bask. There was little room for it anyway, as hundreds of dragons had flocked out to find the warmth after waking up in the cool darkness beneath the trees. It wouldn't be long before we would hear the call into action by Alaron and the ddraigs, so they wanted to be ready. Talk was scarce. A few looked up at us as we passed them by, but none met our gaze.

"I can't See a way to save everyone," I said once we were out of earshot from the resting dragons. I didn't look across to Kaz, not wanting him to see the pain in my eyes. He stopped and placed a paw on my dragging tail.

"You can't save everyone, Azlak. And nor can I. There were so many dragons I couldn't get to in time last night, or where I was too weak to do anything but ease their passing," my mate said, his voice dull and quiet. I turned around to face him, and for the first time that morning I truly saw him. His wings tucked right up into his side, making him appear small and timid. There was genuine grief in his eyes, grief for those who had died. I had been mourning those I hadn't even lost yet, and it made me feel so foolish.

"Oh Kaz, I'm so sorry. I didn't even think…" I started to say, but Kaz held up his paw to quieten me.

"It's alright, I understand. You're never fully in the present, are you?" he said, placing his paw on my shoulder. I rested my head against his and closed my eyes. If only I could just See a future for the two of us, I would feel much more comforted, but again the chaos of the coming events hid everything from me. If I could get my paw on the Axinstone, then maybe I would acquire the clarity I needed, but I knew Haeraig Zeena wouldn't be letting the precious stone from her sight, and the possibility of all futures at once scared me, especially this close to the promise of death.

I lifted my paw up from the ground and stared down at the small ridge beneath my scales, once more tempted to give the slate a squeeze. Kaz moved his paw from my shoulder to close over mine.

"She won't come. She has sent us her help. Everything else must be up to us now," he said, confirming the thoughts that had been running through my mind. We would get no help from Esperance. We had to earn that, and we had done nothing for her yet. This was something we would have to do alone. "We must be brave and stand together."

"I don't feel brave," I replied. Despite my words of weakness, I kept my head raised up. I wasn't ashamed to admit my failings to my mate.

"Then we pretend. That third dragon Esperance promised will make themselves known. Together, we will succeed," Kaz said as he placed his paw beneath my chin.

I shook my head and smiled. The third dragon was running out of time to appear, and still we were no closer to knowing their identity. As much as I willed for Esperance's prophecy to be true, deep down I knew that we were alone.

Our fate was on the horizon now. It would soon reach us.

We were to infiltrate the canvas city with Ddraig Ellian and a small group of dragons and humans. Our mission was to capture George and kill Rico. It all sounded so simple, but I did not need my magic to know that this was a foolish and desperate move. We hoped to succeed, rather than expected it.

I was glad for Kaz by my side as we silently slipped through the forest, now eerily silent without the massive colony of bats screeching in the trees. That alone meant we had to succeed today. We would not survive another night now that their protection was gone. Nothing would stop the humans from attacking while we were sluggish and slow in the cold night. We did not have enough gryphons left to keep us safe after the sunset.

Keita was just ahead of us, with Okazuni next to her, guiding her through the foliage. Even with his help, she still stumbled a few times as her paw caught a root or branch that she had not seen. Each time she did so, her head lifted as she looked towards the human camp beyond the trees and across the bubbling stream. There was never any indication the humans had heard us.

With Ddraig Ellian were the two dragons I was most conflicted about. Anzig and Maznar walked with the ddraig, my brother's new wings shimmering whenever he stepped through a patch of light. He frequently nudged against the ddraig, stepping ahead of her, or trying to direct her down a different path. Each time, she ignored him.

The former spectre still wore her leather harness. Though I had asked, she had not told me what she carried in the many pouches.

The humans and a small group of other dragons were behind me. I was wary around the humans, especially those who had made their way to our side of the wall during the night. Only James McArthur seemed truly certain of their allegiance.

Beyond the trees, everything was quiet. Alaron kept the combined army of dragons and gryphons behind the protective wall. On the clearing between the fortification and canvas city, the humans moved and got into formation, but the wyvern did not take the opportunity to attack. They waited, just as we did.

Once we got into position, all we could was hope the humans did not discover us early. Ddraig Ellian sent a few dragons up into the trees to act as spotters, searching for our signal to strike.

I took a deep breath and closed my eyes, teasing gently into the future with my magic. If I was careful...

*Anzig stood in front of George, metallic wings thrown wide. He snarled at the dragon in front of him, all while the human cowered in pain...*

*...lightning seared across the sky, ripping apart anything that got in its way...*

*Rico slouched against a toppled monolith of stone. He stared at his trembling hand, stained in blood...*

*Nightwings loomed over everything. Her eyes gleamed, reflecting the inferno in front of her.*

My claws gouged through the dirt as I struggled to return to the present. The visions had been oddly clear, despite being so scattered. How many of those were all part of the same future, or were they separate possibilities?

"Are you alright?" Kaz asked, placing his paw on mine.

My head twitched from side to side as I slowly opened my eyes to the present. We were still waiting.

"I am, yeah," I said quietly, not wanting to trouble my mate with the details of my vision just yet. I knew he could tell I was hiding something from him, but he didn't press me for more information.

A few leaves floated down to the ground followed by scattered branches. Foliage bounced off scales as eyes turned upwards. One of the lookouts was struggling to descend gracefully, the branches too close together to spread her wings.

Restless and nervous murmurs broke out amongst the gathered dragons and humans as the lookout landed next to Ddraig Ellian's side and exchanged a few, quiet words. We all knew what they said, even if none of us could hear the exact words. Ddraig Nunahra had come at last. Five thousand dragons from Xigax and Axaatl were preparing to dive into battle.

"We go on paw. Quickly now," Ddraig Ellian said, spreading one wing and gesturing to us all. Though some quietly complained that we weren't taking to wing, I understood the ddraig's reasoning. If we flew, we'd quickly leave the humans behind, and they would be providing us with protection once we closed in on the canvas city.

A few eyes turned towards the plains as we ran for the tents. Even from this distance, I could easily make out the sight of wheeling gryphons and dragons, looking almost like they were dancing through the air. The undulating ground hid the humans from my eyes, but I could hear their shouts and cries. And there, in the sky above, was a horde of dragons led by the serpentine Xigax ddraig. Their number appeared to be as great as what they promised. We could only hope it would be enough.

Like everyone else, I had to put them out of my mind and ignore them. We had our own task to focus on. The loud crack of gunfire forced me to concentrate on where I was going. A few straggling humans had spotted us. Our human guards had done their job, but someone would have heard the gunfire as our enemy fell. Stealth was no longer a possibility for us.

A quick glance back confirmed we had lost one of our number already. Whether dead or merely injured I wasn't sure. Though it clearly pained some of the humans to do so, no one stopped for him. If he was still alive, he'd have to fend for himself until he got back to safety. If dead, well there was nothing we could do anyway.

I stumbled a few times as we ran, trying to keep up with the impressive pace set by both the humans and other dragons. Okazuni, only slightly larger than me, had slipped to my side towards the back of the group. Our diminutive size didn't matter so much in the air, but on the ground our strides were so much smaller than everyone else's, that we were in danger of falling behind.

Though I knew where our target was, I stayed towards the back of the group. The humans took the lead, with Anzig and Maznar running amongst them. We headed deeper into the canvas city, towards the largest tents that backed against the cliff. Towards the machines that controlled the restorations George subjected dragons to. That was where we would find him, if he was still alive. That was where we hoped to find Rico.

We had a chance to catch up when the larger group struggled to make progress through the camp. The crack of gunfire and whine of bullets was never a pleasant sound, but it was better than losing touch entirely, left alone out here.

Diving behind one of the tents for cover, I huddled with Okazuni in a desperate attempt to seek protection from the latest round of gunfire. The thin canvas sheets would do little to prevent bullets ripping through, but at least the humans couldn't aim for us directly. It was small comfort.

James McArthur and his group of humans weren't hiding in the cover from the tents, instead kicking up any piece of furniture or sturdy structure to crouch behind. I caught a glimpse of those they were firing on; a group of about thirty heavily armoured humans. They were surely guards of some sort. We had to be getting close, if Rico had wanted to hold so many humans back from the front lines. It also meant they outnumbered us, and one at a time, they could pick off and kill our humans.

I closed my eyes and grimaced. There had to be something we could do, but I knew that if we left the shelter of the tents, their guns would rip through our scales with ease. Never before had there been a weapon so adept at slaying dragons. Had this been the result of George's research and experiments? Or was this Rico? It didn't really matter anymore.

Ddraig Ellian was not idle. She whispered some instructions to a few dragons around her. She then gestured to the rest of us, ordering us to follow her. Taking care not to make a noise, we all slowly crept away from the battle, taking a longer route around the sea of tents. I glanced back at James McArthur as we left. If he had seen us leaving, he didn't show it.

*The human crouched down over a badly wounded drake, who curled in on himself, grasping one foreleg close to his chest. James's hand came down on the dragon's chest. "A healer is coming, don't worry," the human said quietly.*

Maybe he would survive at least. I hoped he did. But I had to put him out of my mind, and not let those possible futures distract me from what was important. My magic was returning now that I had cleared myself from the immediate chaos of battle. If I could be of any help to the ddraig, then I needed to focus on our future and nothing else.

Anzig loped alongside Ddraig Ellian, his wings clicking with each small movement. His head swung back and forth as he scouted the way ahead, as well as each branching path between the tents that we passed. There were no other humans this far into the camp. They were all dealing with James or the army on the plains.

I could still hear the terrible sounds of gunfire behind us, punctuated by the occasional cry of pain. Sometimes those yells silenced suddenly and terribly. It took so much to keep my eyes open and looking ahead, resisting the urge to curl up and let the grief overcome me. I didn't know those humans. It wasn't even really their fight, but they were laying down their lives for us to succeed. If nothing else, I would do my utmost to ensure their deaths were not worthless.

Once Ddraig Ellian had led us far enough away from the fight, we changed our course again to aim towards the far end of the camp and the largest of the tents. The air grew thick with magic, crackling through the air like a brewing thunderstorm.

If there were still any doubts that this would be where our fate was decided, the moment we stepped from the shadows and into the clearing around the largest tent, our enemy stepped out to face us. Rico had one arm around George's waist, using the other human as a shield. His other hand gripped a pistol, the barrel aimed directly for George's throat.

"I knew you'd come," Rico said, smiling wolfishly. He pressed the tip of the pistol harder against George's throat and shoved the other human forward a couple of paces.

No dragon dared to move. Maznar snarled, her body tense and primed to pounce, but she made no move just yet.

"Is this supposed to be a threat? We don't care for this human. Alive or dead doesn't bother us," Ddraig Ellian said. She kept her head lifted high as she stared at the two humans. No others came out from the tent. I doubted Rico was alone. There had to be other humans close by, but it was hard to pick out fresh scents.

Maznar's snarl changed pitch to a hiss of despair. Her focus turned from Rico to the ddraig, tail lashing. I took half a step forward, closer to my sister.

Rico smiled wider. "Well, in that case then…" His finger moved to the trigger.

"No!" Anzig barked. He jumped in front of the ddraig and spread his wings. "You will not hurt him."

"You do not appear to be in a position to bargain, dragon," Rico said, spitting out the last word like an insult.

Anzig's eyes bleached white. His paws tensed as his brow furrowed. Then his head snapped back with a screech of pain.

Rico began to laugh. "Did you really think it would be that easy to control me? Foolish dragon!"

Maznar hurried to Anzig, protectively shielding him with her body while he recovered. I kept my focus on the human. Rico was unpredictable and dangerous. I knew he would show no mercy. He wanted us all dead.

The human's reinforcements arrived. Seven more humans stepped out of the tent, each clad in their protective clothing. They all carried a pistol like Rico's, which thrummed with magical energy. A few dragons stepped back, closer to the relative safety of the tents.

I flicked my eyes back and forth, taking in the positions of the humans. None of them trained their weapons on us, pistols held lazily at their hips. What futures were there for us? I longed for the Axinstone to fuel my magic, but its gentle warmth against my scales was too faint to draw power from. Haeraig Zeena carried it. She needed it more than me.

Human shouts came from behind. Familiar voices. James McArthur and his soldiers came to provide reinforcements.

My claws tensed at the ground. Perhaps it would not end here.

Rico rolled his eyes and shook his head. He grabbed hold of George tighter and dragged him back. "I see you are as stubborn as ever. I've had enough of your games."

George struggled to escape but seemed powerless to prevent the other human from pulling him back into the tent. He managed to get one strong elbow into Rico's ribs. He croaked out a command, voice hoarse and desperate. "Nightwings. You know what to do."

Rico disappeared behind the line of guards, who closed ranks to prevent any thought of following.

The black-scaled ness reached into her harness and pulled out a small, cylindrical device. On one end was a red button, which she held out in one paw for everyone to see.

"Maznar, don't…" Anzig whimpered. Our sister ignored him.

"It ends here," the spectre growled. She pressed the button.

A deep roar tore through the earth. Searing white light pierced my eyes a moment before a blast of hot air and ash blasted into me, scooping me up and throwing me into the nearest tent. A deafening peal of thunder ripped through the camp a moment later.

I no longer knew what was up and what was down. My head spun as dazzling after-images blinded me. Angry red smudges covered everything, and my ears rung with endless echoes of the explosion.

Human and dragon alike struggled to rise. I managed to do so, standing on unsteady paws.

Rock growled like an awakening beast drawn from slumber.

The cliff began to collapse.

# Chapter Thirty-Two

**Ellian**

I held my head in my paws as I struggled to regain my balance and composure. My ears rung noisily with the echoes of the blast. Dirt and dust coated my scales. I coughed and spat out some scraps of canvas that had gotten snagged on my teeth.

"What was that?" I hissed. My vision spun when I opened my eyes. I forced myself to stay steady on my paws, legs held wide for balance.

"Ddraig Ellian! Down!"

I gave no thought to Azlak's command. I fell to my belly as gunshots peppered around me. Heat scorched across my back as one bullet barely missed me.

Gunfire crackled all around me as James and his reinforcements engaged with the guards. I kept myself low to the ground, crawling away until I was amongst the other dragons. Anzig's metallic wing flicked out like a shield.

"Hurry, this way," Maznar growled. She slunk away, leaping behind cover whenever possible as she picked her way towards the great tent. Anzig followed her, but the other dragons all went in the other direction. Towards James McArthur and the humans.

For a moment, I was torn. Then I snarled and followed Maznar and Anzig. I needed to know what mischief they planned.

The armoured guards didn't see us until the last moment. Anzig leaped for the nearest human, claws and teeth not his only weapons. He moved his wings like Alaron, slashing with the clawed protrusions halfway down the leading edge. Maznar was his shadow, leaping on shoulders and slashing at vulnerable necks and throats, giving James and his soldiers the opportunity to press their advantage.

Then they were gone. Half of the humans were still standing, but Anzig and Maznar jumped behind them to hurry after Rico, leaving the remainder of the guards behind. I muttered a quick curse beneath my breath and picked my target. One human stood away from the others.

I braced my hindpaws and sprung, claws extended. I hit the human hard across the chest, shoving them back. In one fluid motion, I brought my hindpaws against their armour so I could use them as an anchor point, wings spread as I soared high beyond their reach.

The human yelled then fell silent to another round of gunfire. I did not look back. Not even at the draconic voices who called my name. I ran after Anzig and Maznar. They knew these humans. If they ran after Rico and George, then it was for an important reason.

I ignored the machines as I followed their scent, difficult to detect amongst the many smells of humans and the more recent blast of gunpowder. Despite this, it didn't take me long to pick up their trail. They had gone down a tunnel of canvas that, if my bearings were correct, went directly towards the cliffs. There was little light, so it was hard to see, and the air was choked with dust and smoke.

So dark was it that I bumped muzzle-first into a dragon before I even saw them.

Maznar growled. "We have company."

She was little more than a dark shadow amongst shadows, her outline indistinct as the dust from the explosion danced through the air. Beyond her, I could just about make out Anzig. He clambered over fallen rocks; great boulders torn from the cliffs to plummet into a haphazard pile. Stones skittered beneath his paws.

"I think there's a way through," Anzig grunted, giving no indication he had heard Maznar, or that he was aware of my presence.

More stones clattered down as he moved. His wings and claws scraped against a few of the boulders as he wriggled into a patch of deeper darkness. Maznar scampered up after him while I remained on the ground. Small chunks of rock battered against my paws as they dislodged above us. The entire pile of rubble groaned and growled.

"Anzig, be careful," Maznar called out. She had clearly recognised what I had. None of this was stable.

Thick stone muffled Anzig's reply. "I think I'm through." He then yelped and I heard scale and metal strike stone. A low groan of pain followed.

"Are you alright?" Maznar asked. She hopped up to the hole Anzig had forced himself through.

The rock growled again. A deep rumble vibrated through the ground and into my paws. The darkness shifted as the boulders began to fall again.

I jumped forward and grabbed hold of Maznar's harness with my teeth. I wrenched her back just as the passage collapsed with a horrifying smash. The ness screamed. Pressure resisted my pull. Then it released with a snap.

We rolled together on the grass, Maznar shrieking in agony when my weight pressed down on her.

A cloud of debris billowed over us and settled like an ashen cloak. I choked on the thick film of powdered stone, struggling to cough it all away to clear my mouth and nose.

Maznar groaned and kicked me off her, favouring her hindpaws. I rolled aside, flexing my wings as I stood to make sure they were still intact.

Torchlight burst through the darkness. Pawsteps hurried towards us. I spun around, teeth bared and wings flared, only to relax when I recognised James McArthur at the front of the approaching crowd.

The light swept across Maznar. She still lay on her back. She had broken her foreleg, crushed by the falling rocks. She breathed heavily, her eyes squeezed closed.

"What happened here?" James asked. His torch swung up to illuminate the rockfall. Anzig's passage had completely sealed. If we could not clear the rocks, then he would remain trapped in there with Rico and George.

"Anzig got through the rockfall. We should get back before anything else collapses, and Maznar needs a healer," I said, taking a wary step away from the collapsed cliff. A few loose stones continued to bounce and roll down.

James kept his torch shining on the collapsed rock. "Our targets?"

I flicked out a wing. "Both in there. They aren't getting out in a hurry."

We were all distracted by a new sound, coming from deep within the mountain. A low growl most unlike anything that had come before it. This wasn't rocks falling. This was rougher, more primal than that. It was a sound that set my teeth on edge and thundered through my ribs.

Maznar leaped upright, howling as her injured leg struck the ground. Her wings flared as she hopped back. "No, no they said they wouldn't…"

I trod on Maznar's tail to stop her retreating. "What? What is it?"

"Hellfire," the ness hissed. "A terrible weapon I hoped would never be used. Only a necuart can control it, that's why we had one with us. But he died, so the Hellfire became useless. It's designed to kill and destroy everything around it, but no human can control it, not even Rico. If he tries, he'll die. We all die. Every human, dragon, and bird."

I glared into Maznar's eyes, knowing how many times she had tricked us all before. The fear I saw there seemed genuine. I didn't believe any dragon could fake such utter terror. Her pupils were dilated and her mouth was hanging open. Her tail twitched so fast it was almost vibrating. No, she was being truthful about this. Reluctantly, I decided to trust her and I lifted my paw from her tail.

"How do we stop this?" I asked, addressing Maznar but also swinging my head around to look at Azlak, who lurked just beyond James. The seer shook his head and frowned, but I couldn't be sure if he was indicating his disapproval for trusting his sister, or whether he simply hadn't Seen any way to stop the Hellfire.

"I don't think you can." Maznar paused and stared fearfully at collapsed rubble as the fierce rumbling increased intensity. It shook the earth, making a few humans stumble and almost fall. The injured ness struggled to remain standing on three paws. "Call a retreat," she whimpered, her voice barely above a cracked whisper.

Azlak stepped up to my side. He glanced at my face before bowing his head. He showed no such respect to Maznar though, as he snarled down at her with unconcealed anger. "Is this another of your tricks?"

"No!" Maznar yelped, shaking her head vigorously. She trembled as she carefully balanced on three paws, keeping her injured leg tucked up against her belly. "I swear to you. I swear to Dirus. I swear to any god you would name. This is not a trick. We're all in grave danger, and we must fly. Everything within five miles of that thing will be obliterated. Nothing can survive the Hellfire. Please, I beg you. Fly before it's too late."

My tail curled up as I pondered trusting the treacherous ness. Azlak kept his head bowed low, unable or unwilling to contribute. Then I looked back to James. He nodded his head once.

"Alright. We'll trust you," I said. I could hear Azlak draw in a hissed breath, but he said nothing to argue with me. "If you can still fly, get yourself to safety. Azlak, you too. I'll pass the call to retreat. Make sure the message gets to Alaron as well."

We moved as quickly as we could while supporting Maznar. Back through the ripped and torn canvas tunnel and towards the large tent. Not all the guards had died. Some had been captured, tied and watched over by more of James's humans.

Almost as soon as we emerged into the sunlight, wingbeats approached. Looking up into the sky, I could see the Nixan haeraig diving to meet us, half a dozen gryphons flying with her, Prince Kyrus amongst them. She clasped the Axinstone tight in her paws.

"The humans are routing. They flee for the hills," the gryphon prince called out. "Has Rico or George been captured?"

James and Maznar explained the situation to the newcomers. I slowly turned and stared back at the cliffs. The deep growl grew stronger, becoming a deep and bone-shaking rattle that rose into a high pitch shriek.

"We're running out of time," I said. "Take Maznar and fly as far as you can. If anyone knows how to stop this thing, then now is a good time to start explaining."

Haeraig Zeena helped Maznar up into the air, but Azlak stayed on the ground with me. I narrowed my eyes at him, but still he didn't unfurl his wings. Then I noticed his eyes were white.

"I think we've already run out," he whispered quietly. I wasn't sure those words were meant for me, so I chose not to respond to them. But they put haste beneath my paws as I bounced away with James and his band of humans.

"There might be a way. If Rico can't control it, it will remain active until it literally explodes," one of James's commanders said. Sophie, I remembered her name was. Hot air was starting to blow out from cracks in the collapsed cliff. "Unless we remove the power crystals from it. There's a small hatch near the base that houses those crystals. If you remove those, the Hellfire has nothing to draw power from. Of course, you can't get close enough to it once the machine is on, and we can't reach it..."

"Are you sure?" I asked, eyes wide and wings partially unfurled as I readied myself for launch. A quick glance around confirmed that the other lingering dragons hadn't waited for my order. They were following after Haeraig Zeena already.

"We might get a chance if it brings the cliff down, but there won't be a big window of opportunity. A dragon might be small enough to get through, but I don't think we'll be any help here," James replied, before gesturing for his soldiers to retreat. Only Sophie remained behind, lingering with Azlak and me. Everyone else had fled. I didn't blame them.

Stone splintered. Deep cracks punched through the cliffs, dislodging ever more boulders to cascade down from up high, crashing into the massive canvas tent and ripping massive holes through the thick fabric. Support beams splintered and fractured as piece by piece, the tent shredded from the force of stone and the strength of the hot wind blowing from inside the cave.

That heat scorched my scales as once more a massive explosion shook the earth. Fragments of rock discharged high into the air, scattering over a wide area, forcing me to hide my head beneath my wings. Even those dragons who had already fled had to take evasive action, diving to the side to avoid the deadly rain.

From out of the remains of the great tent billowed clouds of black smoke charged with flickering red lightning. A dark shadow loomed in the haze. A tall, black structure of obsidian stone, twice the height of a human, began to emerge. A series of spikes ran around the circular top. From those spikes came the charged lightning. Flames licked at the hovering base as magical energy scorched away the grass and fragments of canvas beneath it. Shadow and smoke swirled around it as a column of crimson magic started to rise from the spikes.

Sophie directed my gaze to a small, white indentation near the base of the obsidian spire. "There, do you see it? That's the crystal housing unit," she said. It was right there, a tantalising target, but before anyone could react, a blast of hot air pushed out from the Hellfire as it started to drift towards us, a ponderous movement that gave the impression of being unstoppable. A loud, grating growl followed as a bright glow started to emanate out from the obsidian.

Sophie swore and held her arm up before frantically gesturing back. "It's powered up, we're too late. Run, as fast as you can!"

I didn't wait for Sophie to finish speaking, sprinting away and kicking off hard, powering my wings to gain some height. Azlak hovered in the air not too far away, and once he saw me ascending, he spun around and started to rise as well. I chanced one quick glance back down just as an arc of red light spiralled out from the sides of the Hellfire, ripping the remainder of the tent to shreds and setting some of the nearby structures ablaze. Any human and dragon still close to it fled before the devastating display of power caught up to them.

As the canvas fell away, torn apart by the fearsome energy emitted, the Hellfire gradually emerged. I yelled for Azlak to fly, a needless command as the seer was already straining his wings to escape as quickly as he could. Far ahead of us I could see Haeraig Zeena and Maznar flying together, and beyond them the few dragons who had been with us had almost reached the surviving portion of our army. I was sure they had to have seen the terrible awe of the Hellfire, but to my horror I noticed they were flying towards us, not away.

"No, turn around, turn around," I muttered beneath my breath, willing them all to start retreating and flying as fast as they could in the other direction. I did not want to witness what would happen should the arcing beams of magical energy strike anyone.

By the look of it, most of the Xigax dragons had survived, as had half of the gryphons. It was hard to tell just how many had lived through the ordeal, but it looked like a number fewer than two thousand that was still airborne. Far below, I could see some more dragons limping on paw, as well as the remaining humans running from the burning remains of their encampment.

The deep rumbling was getting louder as the lightning charged up around the Hellfire, sounding like rocks grinding over each other, but there was a new sound adding to the terrifying cacophony. A keening wailing was growing into a piercing shriek. Without stopping my desperate flight, I glanced back to see what the machine was doing. My eyes widened as I noticed it glowing with a fierce red light that suddenly exploded out in a shockwave of magic.

The air crackled as a circle of red light expanded out from the Hellfire, incinerating the tents it passed through before eventually fading. Nothing remained but ash, cinders, and scorched earth, the obsidian stone left standing in isolation. Once more the glow started to return as beams of light started to pierce out almost at random. One passed close to me, and I could feel the intense heat burn my scales.

Another shockwave launched from the Hellfire, but this one didn't remain on the ground. Instead, it arced up into the air, and I had to loop over it to avoid the magical blast. The air burned around it, the thermals it produced pushing up at my wings and making me quickly ascend ever higher. I yelled out a warning to Azlak, but he didn't even need to look back before he started to dive below it.

The wave of energy faded before it reached Haeraig Zeena and Maznar, but I could tell the two were struggling to maintain a level flight. I hurried to chase after them, worried that Maznar's injuries were slowing them both down.

I caught up with them just as they reached the army, led by Alaron and Kyrus. For the moment we were out of range of the Hellfire, but if Maznar was right, then that range would only start increasing as its power grew and the human that piloted it started to lose control. It had started moving, ponderously hovering in our direction. I didn't know how quickly it could move, but it wouldn't be long before it would be back in range of us.

"We have to shut it down. We're too close, we won't get the injured away in time," Alaron said, glancing back and down behind the hill where several hundred dragons huddled. A few healers wandered amongst them, but most were lying down, too injured to move. They only had a few minutes before they would be vulnerable to the Hellfire, powerless to defend themselves.

I bit my lip and twitched my tail. I could tell there was some truth in Alaron's words, but I wondered how many more would die if we attempted to assault the Hellfire. Apart from taking the power crystals, I wasn't even sure we could stop it through a show of force alone. But how could we ever hope to get close enough? There was no other option. We had to try, and I knew it had to be me to volunteer. I wouldn't send anyone else down there to take on the hellish device.

"I know how to stop it, but I can't get close enough," I said reluctantly. I didn't want to get any closer to the Hellfire, but at the same time I knew that if no one was able to stop it, then we were risking the fate of every dragon and gryphon nearby.

Alaron was about to protest, but an interruption from Azlak silenced him, the seer hovering just behind my shoulder. "I'll go with you, Ddraig. Kaz too. Together we might be able to do it. We would just require one thing." The seer turned to Haeraig Zeena, eying the shard of stone clutched protectively in her paws. "We need the Axinstone."

I expected Haeraig Zeena to protest, such had been her protection of the Axinstone ever since we had reclaimed it from the humans. Only her father had held it since. Instead, she surprised me by holding the precious shard out for Azlak to take. It crackled and sparked with magical energy as it changed paws.

We didn't have much time, but Kyrus found a moment to place a clawed paw on my shoulder. "Be safe, Ddraig Ellian. And good luck. May your feathers shine bright."

"May the wind rise beneath your wings," I responded, bowing my head in response to the gryphon. Then I turned my back on them all and trimmed my wings, starting to descend to the ground and the Hellfire. Azlak and Kaz followed behind me. I could only hope the seer would be able to See a way for us to succeed, for I couldn't see how we could survive this.

Under Azlak's guidance, we touched down just on the edge of the charred earth already caused by the Hellfire. The air was already so hot, making each breath difficult. I kept a wary eye on the machine, on the lookout for any more of the charged magic launching towards us, but most seemed to be arcing well above us, aiming for, but falling short of, the dragons still clustered up there. There were so many of them, it was taking an age to organise them all to start fleeing, or maybe it was simply because I was willing them to leave quicker, any movement they did make seemed painfully slow.

"Ddraig Ellian, I hope this doesn't hurt you, but wrap your tail around ours," Azlak said, nosing my flank and guiding me to look down at his tail, which he already entwined with Kaz's. The Axinstone sat snugly between them.

I blinked a couple of times before my eyes widened, realising what Azlak's idea must be. I nodded and wrapped my tail around theirs, pausing for a moment before resting my tail against the Axinstone.

My body burned as magic obliterated my senses.

# chapter thirty-three

**Azlak**

The magic of the Axinstone surged through me. With it held securely in our tails we slowly walked forward onto the charred grass beneath our paws. I had been worried for Ddraig Ellian when she had touched the Axinstone, fearful of what the magic would do to her. She didn't seem to be suffering, but she was taking a lot of heavy breaths.

I braced myself for the pain I knew we were about to endure. I had shared a couple of brief words with Kaz and the ddraig, warning them what waited for us. Kaz's magic was going to be crucial, the Axinstone needed to repair the damage the Hellfire was going to inflict on us. My magic would foresee the worst of the Hellfire's fury, allowing us to avoid harm. Or, at least, not dying before Kaz could save us. I wasn't yet sure what purpose Ddraig Ellian had, but in my first few visions of what was to come I had Seen her with us. She had a part to play still. I wondered if she was the third dragon Esperance had spoken of. Was her destiny one of those that would decide the ultimate fate of dragonkind? If not her, then I could see little time for another to emerge.

Almost without realising what I was doing, I squeezed my left paw around the slate buried beneath my scales. I felt it buzz as I took a few more steps forward, before Esperance's ghostly visage appeared before us. Her golden tattoos shone brightly. I couldn't see much of her surroundings, but she appeared to in front of a sheer cliff face, as I could only see rock behind her. Shadows moved, and the soft murmur of voices suggested that she wasn't alone.

"What is it?"

"In case we die, I wanted to say sorry for failing your trust," I replied, bowing my head to her. By my side, Kaz also ducked his head low, while Ddraig Ellian just stared at the floating image of the mystical human with eyes wide.

Esperance shifted her position, sitting up slightly and leaning forward. "If you die? What are you doing?" she asked, her brow furrowed in confusion. Her hands reached out towards us, as though she could touch us through the illusion of her magic.

"Trying to stop a Hellfire. We're the only ones who can get to it," I said, lifting my eyes up to look into hers. There was no challenge there, just an admiration of her golden eyes.

"You're doing what?" she demanded, a sudden urgency to her voice. Through the illusion I could hear a few cries of alarm as she stood up. "You will do no such thing, I forbid it!"

Kaz chuckled and shook his head. "It's too late for that, Esperance," he said. With Ddraig Ellian stood between us, I couldn't rest my head on his shoulder like I wanted.

"I'm on my way." Esperance's terse reply ended the conversation, the flickering sight of her face fading away. All I could see now was the obsidian tower of the Hellfire.

I knew that if Esperance were truly on her way, then she would have no way of getting here in time. Nothing could save us now but ourselves. If we failed, we would die, and with us most of the survivors of the draconic race.

Closing my eyes, I tightened my tail around the Axinstone, letting the magic from the shard of blazing rock infuse into my body. Threads of the future unravelled in front of me. Hundreds upon thousands of possibilities all centred on our actions of the next few minutes. Without the Axinstone I would have no hope of processing every future, every possibility, but each made sense to me now. Every branch of that golden and glittering future was clear. Every action, every reaction, had a consequence.

"Follow my every command," I warned the others. My heart thundered as I considered the prospect that I was ordering a ddraig, but I knew that we had no choice. I alone could See the consequences of our actions, and already I could See hundreds of ways that we would die. Thousands. I knew this would strain my magic to the absolute limit.

Slowly we walked towards the Hellfire, Kaz and I flanked Ddraig Ellian with our tails entwined around the Axinstone. The ground was hot beneath our paws, the air difficult to breathe. There was so much magic, I could feel it scratching at my scales, an annoying irritation that threatened to distract me from my visions.

Present and future intermingled. *Three dragons forced themselves forwards, the burning magic increasing around them as they approached the Hellfire. Spikes and protrusions spun around on the obsidian spire, controlled movements that directed a sizzling arc of energy towards them.*

"Down!" I cried, and just in time the three of us hurled ourselves to the charred earth. With an awful wail, the Hellfire's lightning speared through the air above our heads, scorching and burning away our scales. The agony was severe, until Kaz was able to summon the power of the Axinstone through him, his magic starting to soothe the pain and heal our wounds.

I could give no consideration to what was happening outside of the three of us. As much as I wanted to look back and see that the others were starting to escape, I knew I could not afford myself such a distraction. I also knew a lot of them would die. The power of the Hellfire was growing with every passing moment. The fiery blasts of magic scattered in all directions, not just at us. I could almost hear the pained screams, or were they the echoes of the visions I forced myself not to See?

Slowly the magical pressure built up around us, a constant burning sensation that blistered my scales as quickly as Kaz was able to heal them. The pain only got worse, never once diminishing. I could hear Ddraig Ellian whimper, and I glanced to the side to make sure that she was keeping pace. Crimson blood already stained her muzzle despite Kaz's best efforts, the scales around her mouth peeling away.

It was only going to get worse. We had only covered half the distance to the Hellfire, and the magical pain inflicted on our bodies would increase the closer we got.

We could fail in uncountable ways – one wrong step and a gust of powerful magic would obliterate us in an instant. One pain-induced stumble could be the difference between life and death. We had to keep moving.

The lightning crackled brighter, darkening everything else around us until all was black but for the magic of the Hellfire. A shadow engulfed the obsidian stone, so dark that I could see it only as a reflection of the crimson lightning. The ground burned with flame, both real and magical.

*Her paws closed around the crystals and the purest agony tore through her body. A peal like thunder cracked, an explosion flinging her back with wings pulled open, before she landed and rolled, clutching her foreleg to her belly. She screamed in pain, her throat torn raw...*

It felt like every scale ripped away from my agonised body, only to be rebuilt by Kaz's desperate magic. Each pawstep triggered unending pain as the scorched earth blistered into my vulnerable flesh. It was hard to focus, and even fuelled by the Axinstone, every next second was one in which we died, over and over again, each filled with more pain than the last. Yet still we moved. Still we breathed.

Golden branches of time flooded my vision. The future changed.

"Right!" I yelled, and the three of us dived to the side. Kaz yelped in pain as the edge of the arcing beam of light glanced his side. I couldn't see how bad his wounds were, but he resolutely stumbled on, gritting his teeth as he focused on his magic once more.

Ddraig Ellian was the next to stumble and cry out in pain. I hadn't even Seen anything to strike her, and for a horrifying moment I felt her tail loosen in my grip. If Kaz lost contact with her, then his magic wouldn't reach the ddraig. In the whirling maelstrom of magic we walked through, she would be dead in an instant.

One paw in front of the other.

One step at a time.

*The dragons launched into the air, spreading their wings as they attempted to fly, to reach the Hellfire quicker. It took only a couple of seconds for their wings to get torn to shreds, the fragile fingers of bone smashed to tiny fragments. They fell to the broken ground, writhing in agony as their tails separated...*

We couldn't leave the ground. The magical winds were too strong. On paw was the only way.

I tried to ignore the pain. Kaz's magic could not ease that. There was no respite. Scales tore. Eyes bloodied. Claws cracked and blunted. To stop was to die.

The Hellfire never seemed to get any closer. The maelstrom of light and magic grew more intense around the obsidian stone, dazzling my eyes and threatening to blind me completely. I was sure I could only still see because of Kaz's constant flow of healing magic. A deep, growling roar emanated from the monstrous weapon, a savage snarl that that sounded almost like a pack of angry wolves.

"Slower here," I said, warned by another flashing vision of danger.

"No, push on, please," Ddraig Ellian whimpered, trying to pull us ahead.

I pulled the ddraig back harshly by her tail, just in time as the burned earth in front of our paws erupted as the Hellfire's magic struck it. For a few moments I was blind, unable to see anything but crimson.

Whether after images of the magic, or blood in front of my eyes, I simply couldn't be sure. Maybe it was both.

"Listen to me," I growled as my vision returned, the words slicing out of my throat. We were close now, just a few feet away from the towering spire. I craned my neck, trying to find the small section the ddraig had pointed out before. It was there, about a foot up from the base.

At my guidance, we took slow steps backwards as the Hellfire ponderously moved forward. This close the sound of the crackling lightning diminished, instead replaced by the low hum of whatever power held it up off the ground. Beneath the obsidian, the air rippled and pulsed, charged with intense magic and heat.

I didn't dare unfurl my wings as I raised up onto my hindlegs, reaching for the small indentation. My paws fell short, barely able to even reach the Hellfire at all. With flight denied to me, I was simply too short. I growled and bit my lip, glancing across to Kaz. My mate was only a few inches taller and longer – he wouldn't be able to reach either. I knew what was going to happen. I didn't want it to happen, but we had no choice.

"It's up to me then," Ddraig Ellian said, her voice strained with pain. "Will it hurt?"

What was one more pain on top of the agony we suffered? And yet I knew Ellian's pain was about to be greater than anything I felt. Even still, I could not lie to her.

I swallowed a mouthful of blood. "Yes."

The ddraig did not pause. She lifted onto her hindlegs. Unlike me, she was able to reach the indentation.

As though aware what was going on, the Hellfire let out a savage snarl before blinding me with another ferocious blast of blood-red light. I staggered back, almost losing grip on Kaz's tail.

Ddraig Ellian shoved her paw into the indentation. Her body convulsed in pain. She did not scream.

With a loud clunk, the dazzling display of light ended.

An explosive shockwave ripped out of the Hellfire, throwing the ddraig back. Her tail tore from ours, knocking loose the Axinstone, sending the shard of stone to the blistered and blackened soil. The loss of magic chilled me, leaving me numb in shock.

My scales felt like they were all about to crack. Without Kaz's magic to heal me, small filaments of blood began to snake between them, dripping from almost every part of me. No matter what I moved, some new pain started to sting.

The Hellfire creaked and groaned as it tipped to one side. It fell slowly, striking the ground with one corner before toppling over. It crashed down and sent a massive plume of smoke and dust into the air. My wing covered my face to protect my eyes as I strained my ears for the sound of any life within the stricken weapon.

Metal screeched and something slammed. A human groaned, and as the dust began to clear I made out a shape moving against the obsidian. Somehow, Rico still lived. I had not foreseen that.

"Kaz, get ready." I got no response from my mate. Chancing a glance back, I noticed him sprawled out on the ground, his chest heaving for breath. Even with the magic of the Axinstone to sustain him, he had drained the last of his reserves in trying to keep us alive.

Ddraig Ellian was likewise lying prone, a bit further beyond my mate. I clenched my paws against the ground. It would just be me.

Rico crawled from the Hellfire, little more than a silhouette through the haze. His heavy breathing disrupted some of the smoke, sending it swirling through the air thick with ash and magic.

"You would dare get in my way, dragon?" the human snarled. He limped forward, stumbling over the broken remains of his ruined weapon.

I took a couple of steps back, keeping some distance between myself and the human. The ground was dry and cracked beneath my paws, every scrap of moisture burned away by the magical heat. My blood was all that moistened the crumbling dirt and blackened scraps of grass.

The human ranted as he jumped from the smoking husk of the Hellfire, sending out a cloud of ash as his feet hit the ground. "Do you really think you have stopped me? You have just made it worse for your wretched species. You could have all gone out in one go, but no. You made it more fun for me. I will throttle every last one of you if I must, my hands around your throats."

I stepped back again. Tendrils of the future tickled at the back of my mind, flashes of golden magic emanating from the Axinstone, which had fallen halfway between Kaz and me. I struggled to resist the allure of my magic. I did not need to See the future to know that Rico meant his words. His intentions were true. If I wanted to stop him, I needed to stay in the present.

"You know already, don't you?" the human snarled. He stepped out of the smoke. Muck and grime smeared over his face, doing little to hide where his skin blistered and peeled. "You already know what your destiny is. It was written hundreds of years ago. I am just here to finish the work that was started."

Distant shouts called through the haze and smoke. A whir of wingbeats soared high above.

Rico had eyes only for me. In his hand was a pistol. Red light snaked up the barrel.

I needed to keep him distracted. I needed to stay alive long enough for help to come.

"The cataclysm? Do you really think you will bring that again?" I growled. I lowered my body, legs crouched to get better purchase on the ground, ready to spring aside in a moment.

Rico laughed, cold and harsh. "The cataclysm. Unfinished business. It was a shame what happened then. There will be no mistakes this time."

The pistol clicked as Rico lifted it up. The barrel aimed directly for my head.

I took another step back. My hindpaw brushed against the Axinstone.

Magic flooded my mind.

Rico fired, then stumbled forward as a great weight crashed into his back.

I rolled to the side. The bullet, aimed for my head, clipped my shoulder. Agony punctured through me again, another distraction to the many scrapes and stinging pains from muzzle to tail.

The pistol clattered to the ground. I kicked it away, sending the weapon spinning across the dry dirt. It came to rest close to Ddraig Ellian's outstretched and prone paw.

Anzig's metal wings slashed at Rico. Dragon and human fought hard, both snarling as loud as the other. Claw and tooth gave Anzig an edge, but Rico had the advantage of size and strength. They both moved with incredible speed, Anzig scratching at the human before leaping away. Rico's hand closed around the air where my brother had been moments earlier.

I struggled to stand. My right foreleg ached even through the muted sensation, a numbing tingle spreading down from my shoulder.

I limped forward and spread my wings. Through the clearing smoke I could see that we had no help coming from the dragons and gryphons. One lone human approached from the cliffs. If we were to end this war, then we needed to stop Rico. Anzig would not be able to do it alone.

Ignoring the protests of my pained body, I jumped for the human. My teeth sunk into his wrist, tearing through flesh, filling my mouth with the tang of human flesh. There was a fierce heat to the blood as it dripped from my muzzle.

The human yelled in pain and tried to free his arm, but I used my weight to pull him back, my hindpaws on the ground. Beating my wings, I pulled myself back, dragging the human with me.

Anzig's eyes met mine. He nodded and pushed back off the human.

Rico lunged for my brother, swiping out with his free arm. He missed and almost unbalanced. My neck strained with the effort of keeping him still.

A shadow moved through the smoke. Two-legged and tall.

George emerged from the haze. A deep slash cut its way across his cheek. He lifted his pistol.

Anzig grabbed Rico's other hand and pulled the human back. His metallic wings spread wide, clawtips dripping blood.

"Is this really what it's come to?" George asked.

Though fear rose in my chest merely at the sight of the human, I kept my position. The pistol aimed at Rico, not me. For the moment at least, George was an ally. A way to defeat our true enemy.

"You know nothing," Rico spat. "You think this is the end? It is nothing more than the beginning."

George tightened his grip on the pistol. The weapon clicked and whined, the red lights down the barrel illuminating brighter. "It sure looks like an end to me."

Rico's fist clenched. His wrist bulged with power and strength, straining against my teeth.

A flare of bright light shone through the human. His blood burned hot. An explosion of magic scorched my tongue, ripping my teeth from his flesh. I rolled twice and landed on my belly, dazed from the impact.

Rico hurled Anzig at George. Dragon and human collided with a sickening crunch, both collapsing to the ground and falling still.

I struggled to my paws, legs trembling. My shoulder almost gave way beneath me.

Rico ignored me as he sauntered towards Anzig and George. His markings briefly flickered bright, before starting to fade again until they were almost imperceptible. He kicked Anzig aside. A wing spike had punctured deep into George's chest.

The prone human spluttered for breath. His arm weakly raised, but Rico easily plucked the pistol from his grasp.

"It is over," Rico said.

He fired twice. George's arm fell limp.

Anzig screamed as he struggled to rise. He could barely stand. His wings were askew, the leather straps holding them in place fraying. His tail lashed. "You just made a big mistake."

Rico didn't answer. He simply struck out, kicking Anzig square between the forelegs. My brother yelped and fell back, weakly striking back with claw and wing.

I limped after them, barely able to put any weight on my right forepaw. My wings protested as I spread them, desperate for some lift.

Anzig bit down on Rico's arm again. The human howled, but I could not reach him before he landed several powerful punches directly onto my brother's head.

Human and dragon both collapsed into a tangled heap.

I finally found the strength to rise from the ground, jumping for them in a wing-assisted glide. A muffled gunshot blasted before my claws dug into Rico's back.

I pulled Rico from Anzig. I froze when I saw my brother. His eyes were open and his chest heaved for breath, but he was losing a lot of blood from the gunshot wound to his belly.

Rico's boot kicked hard at my chest. My ribs cracked as I fell to my back, wings splayed across the ground. My eyes tore from Anzig to look up at the human, grinning widely. He pinned me down with his boot, squeezing down on my chest and restricting my breathing. His pistol aimed for me once more.

His malicious face would be the last thing I saw. How could I have failed to See this?

I kept my eyes open. If I faced death, then I would do so without fear or cowardice. There was only regret.

A gunshot deafened me. I did not flinch.

The expected pain did not come.

Rico's boot slipped. The human crashed to his knees, and then keeled to his side. Blood bubbled from his mouth. He still breathed, short and shallow gasps.

My eyes flickered across to see Ddraig Ellian still holding the gun she had fired in an awkward manner, using her two hindpaws to balance the gun and a forepaw to fire the trigger. She moved only to pant. Her eyes were wide open.

I staggered to my paws. Anzig draped across George's body, leaving behind a smear of blood where he had dragged himself towards the human. He struggled to draw breath.

I knew already that there was nothing I could do. Kaz had no energy to heal anyone, even if he was awake. Not even the Axinstone could save him.

Anzig reached for me. A trembling and bloodied paw touched my cheek. His mind fluttered against mine.

"I thought I was doing the right thing," he whispered. "What Maznar promised me… it was right. It was how we fix everything…"

His paw fell. His eyes stared beyond me, into the life that came after.

I could do nothing as my brother died.

Nothing could stop the tears from flowing.

# CHAPTER THIRTY-FOUR

**Ellian**

*I knew I dreamed, but I could not bring myself to wake.*

*I lay in the ddraig's chambers in Laxtal, unfamiliar yet comforting in their own way. The memory of Ddraig Astar still lingered there.*

*Even in my dream, my body was in agony. Ever since I had stepped within the radius of the Hellfire's horrific magic, I had burned. Not even a dream was safe from such terror. My paws felt blistered and cracked, my scales peeling and flaking away from my body.*

*"You were brave, Ellian. Braver than any dragon I can recall, and that is a great number of dragons."*

*I looked up at the voice. The silver statue of Mushussu uncurled herself from the usual nook above the fire. The guardian's presence felt real enough, and not simply an aspect of a dreaming mind.*

*"I didn't think you could talk to me unless I slept in my chambers. I'm not back there, am I?"*

*The guardian jumped down. "No, you are not. But something curious has happened. Draconic magic has escaped into the world again. Not much, but enough that I can touch minds with you. It is possible that every ddraig can feel the presence of their guardian."*

*I rose to my paws. My right forepaw felt strange, numbed where the rest of my body prickled with heat. "How?"*

*"That is still hidden to me," the guardian said slowly. She shook her head and turned to stare into the fire. "All I know is that dragonkind is changing, and there is still more to come. You hold in*

*your paws the ability to finish this. It will be your choice, Ellian. You have the opportunity to bring dragons to the attention of everyone in Farenar."*

*"Is that the right thing to do? What if that just brings more attention from people like George or Rico?"* We had barely survived them. If others turned to a weakened dragonkind, then I didn't know how we could defeat them.

*Mushussu rested her paw on mine. "It is the only way to fix what had been broken. Dragonkind is waking up to magic once more. You are but the first. With luck and fortune, you will not be the last."*

*I tilted my head. "What do you mean?"*

*The guardian smiled. "It means our destiny is not yet decided."*

I woke abruptly, torn from the dream that was not a dream. I took in a sharp breath. Pain needled at every scale.

"Ddraig Ellian, are you awake?"

I squinted open my eyes. I couldn't focus my vision at all, but I caught a glimpse of grey scales. It took a long time for my slow mind to recognise the voice as that of Alaron.

"I am. But I'd rather not be," I whispered, each syllable tearing open my throat. I could taste nothing but blood. Slowly I stretched out my legs, trying to ignore the blistering pain that went through me. Something felt amiss as I moved. I had hoped it had been nothing more than a horrific nightmare that had latched on to the horrors I had survived, but as I looked down, I knew what I was about to see.

Taking the crystal from the Hellfire had incinerated my right forepaw. Kaz's magic had not been able to heal it, but he had closed off the wound. My leg simply ended in a savage looking scar just below the joint. I was no longer whole. Just like Anzig had been.

"Ddraig Ellian?"

I had forgotten Alaron was there. The wyvern sat in front of me, his wings wrapped around his body. He had taken a few wounds himself, but nothing as severe as mine. The worst he had suffered was a deep gash on his neck. Healers had closed the wound, but the crimson stain on his grey scales remained.

"Are you alright?"

I shook my head. My body felt like it was slowly burning, but it was the absence of feeling from my right forepaw that disturbed me the most. It wasn't even like a numbness. It was a nothingness, and that was all I'd ever feel from there again. I told the wyvern that, admitting my weakness to him in a way I wouldn't trust most dragons. He listened to my long list of complaints in silence, keeping still until I finished.

"I don't know what we can do to help, but Ddraig Boruc wanted to look you over when you were awake. He seems to know things no one else does, so perhaps there's something in that old head of his that can help you," the wyvern said as he stood up. He placed one wing on my head, before he braced himself against the ground.

"Wait," I said hoarsely, stopping him from taking flight just yet. For the first time I looked around us. I was back behind the hill where we had taken refuge during the recent nights. There weren't many dragons or gryphons around, though I could hear more amongst the nearby trees. A small patch of burned and slightly smoking grass indicated where there had been a small, warming fire. The air was fresh with morning dew. "What happened?"

Alaron's face was grim. "We won, but barely. They fought bravely, even as the Hellfire was killing at random. Human and dragon and gryphon fell to that monster until eventually they surrendered. We haven't counted how many survived, but we lost most of our number. Thousands fell. I haven't seen so much death in many a year. The Hellfire was… well I just hope that was the last one, dragged out from some museum somewhere." The wyvern shook his head and sighed, settling back on his legs. "The important part is that we won. You saved the lives of the survivors. I would have given my wings if I knew it would save half the lives you saved."

"Anzig?" I asked, voice trembling. I knew what had happened. But unless I heard it from someone, there was still that faint hope.

Alaron crushed it with a shake of his head. "I'm sorry. We could not get to him before he passed to the next life."

I choked back a dry sob. "George? Rico? Azlak? What about them?"

"George is dead. Too bad, as we couldn't question him," the wyvern said. He lightly touched his wingclaws to my shoulder. "Azlak will survive. Like you, he needs rest to recover from his injuries."

I did not miss the fact that Alaron ignored one person. "Rico?" I pressed.

Alaron's tail lashed so hard that his venomous barb stabbed into scraps of canvas that drifted in the wind. "We could not find him. We were too concerned with making sure you and Azlak were safe. By the time we tried to capture him, he was already gone. We do not know if he got away by himself or if he was rescued, but we will find him. He will face punishment before the gods for what he has done."

A fierce heat burned through me. I had not been accurate enough. Rico was still alive. Next time I would make sure I killed him.

"Do not concern yourself with him," Alaron said, his words perfectly focused on my thoughts as though he had been able to hear them. "Rico will be hunted; you have my word. The gods know of him now. They will not sit idle."

I did not have much faith in the gods. I would prefer to deal with Rico with my own claws, but right now I had no energy to protest the wyvern's assurances.

The wyvern bowed his head. "Rest for now, Ddraig Ellian. There will be plenty to discuss in time, when you have recovered."

I watched Alaron fly away, then looked down to my leg. I would not fully recover from this. Nothing would get my paw back. I curled up, keeping my injured leg tucked up beneath my body so dragons passing by would not see it. A whiplash crack of air told me I wasn't alone for very long.

My mate nosed against my side before lying down next to me. He didn't say anything and nor did I. I didn't even move, but I could tell he knew I was awake. We didn't even need to speak to each other. His mere presence was enough to comfort me until I eventually uncurled and extended out my truncated leg for him to see. I expected him to wince or recoil, but instead he merely held his right forepaw against it. The one he was missing a toe from.

"You know you didn't have to go and out-do me on that," he said, a pained smile on his face. His eyes were wet with Nixan tears as he looked down at me.

I couldn't help it. I laughed. Despite all my worries and my pain, I laughed. Not even the spasms that went through my chest caused me to regret it. I leaned into my mate's side. "You're an amazing dragon, Airil. I love you so very much."

Airil rested his head on my shoulder, his wing spread over my body. "You're quite the amazing ness too. The saviour of the draconic species, some are calling you." I scoffed at the thought, but Airil just grinned. "And three paws or four, you're perfect for me."

Lying against Airil's chest, I asked him for more details than I had gotten from Alaron. He told me how dragon and gryphon had harried humans from the air, trying to avoid the bolts of magic that burst out from the Hellfire. I had witnessed little of the full power of the monstrous device, having been so close to it the whole time. Airil had seen the destruction it caused. Dragons and gryphons had fallen from the sky, some still shrieking but others killed the moment the powerful magic had struck them. Even on the ground, humans had perished in the same manner. The Hellfire hadn't discriminated between friend or foe. If we hadn't succeeded in shutting it down, there would have been no survivors, of that I was now certain.

Though the Hellfire had crippled the human forces, when I had eventually managed to shut it down with Azlak and Kaz, they had still rallied and made one last, desperate defence. Once again, fighting had been fierce, but it wasn't long before one by one the humans started to throw down their weapons. About three hundred of them surrendered, with a few hundred more estimated to have already fled, possibly with Rico. Our numbers were little more than that. Haeraig Zeena and Ddraig Nunahra were overseeing the imprisonment of the surviving humans.

Once the battle had come to a grisly and devastating end, most of the surviving dragons and gryphons had tended to the dead, with the few surviving healers seeing to the wounded. Human, gryphon, and dragon alike had all burned on a massive bonfire that had lit up the night. I was glad I had not seen it.

By the time Airil had finished, Ddraig Boruc and Prince Kyrus had joined us. I was pleased to see the older ddraig had survived completely unscathed, with no trace of injury on his aging body. The gryphon had yet to correct his feathers, nor had he cleaned the blood from his beak and claws.

"You did a brave thing, Ddraig Ellian," the Vatrean ddraig said, bowing so low that his head almost touched the ground. "There are few dragons indeed who would willingly walk towards an active Hellfire. I can not claim that bravery for myself."

"I only did what I felt I must," I replied. I nudged against Airil as I pushed myself up to a sitting position. I found it a little awkward only having the one paw to use, and I had to suppress a whimper of pain from the simple movement.

Ddraig Boruc nodded. His eyes were bright with curiosity as they danced over my body. With a couple of twitching steps like an excited hatchling, he approached me and placed a paw on my shoulder. "Let's have a look at you then and see what's troubling you."

The old dragon held his paw on my chest and closed his eyes, muttering a few unknown words beneath his breath. He remained like that for a while, and I struggled not to move away. I was unsure just what he was trying to achieve, but he seemed to learn something at least. When he pulled back, his eyes were wide.

"I think it's magic. Pure magic from the Axinstone. Somehow, it's infused into your body and is changing it," he whispered in awe.

"Changing me? How?" I asked. I couldn't help but glance back to look over my body, but I could see nothing different. Apart from my paw I was completely unchanged.

"Open your mouth for me," he said, looking in when I followed his instruction. "Move your tongue from side to side. Can you feel those?"

I did as he asked, feeling two strange bumps, just to either side of my tongue on the bottom of my mouth. I knew for certain I had never felt those there. Before I was able to ask what they were, Ddraig Boruc answered for me.

"Fire glands. That heat you can feel inside you? That's fire, Ellian. It's magic." Ddraig Boruc had to take a moment to compose himself as he twitched with excitement, his wings partially unfurled. "Magic is returning to dragonkind at last."

"Fire glands? You mean I can…?"

"Breathe fire? Yes, I think you can. Best not to practice here though. Wait until you've gotten your strength back for that," Ddraig Boruc said. His words sent my mind into a frenzy as I tried to work out the implications of what he had told me. Azlak had been able to breathe fire when George's magic had changed him, as had the other enlarged dragons, but beyond those others altered by the Axinstone, breathing fire was just a myth.

There were many questions in my mind, but I was only able to breathe out one word. "How?"

Ddraig Boruc pawed at the ground. "That I don't know. I can only assume it was a combination of different magics that triggered this change," he said as his eyes unfocused, a slight smile on his face. He muttered something in the old draconic language before patting me on the shoulder again.

Prince Kyrus didn't give me any longer to ponder the changes to my body. "We should address the survivors. I imagine there's still a bit of confusion amongst them as to what happens now."

I averted my eyes from the gryphon as fear welled up within me. "They'll see me like this though, weak and injured."

A paw gripped around my tail as Airil spoke. "They'll see you as someone who fought through any injury to save them."

"Your mate is right," Prince Kyrus agreed. "And you're far from the only one still bearing their wounds from yesterday. It will do them good to see their ddraig has suffered with them. Walk, don't fly, and meet us at the summit of the hill. This is something you need to get used to."

"But how can I walk?" I asked, trying not to look down at the stump of my right foreleg. Even though magic had healed the terrible wound, my purple scales gave way to smooth white scarflesh that still twinged with pain if I moved the leg.

"We'll be here to support you," Airil said as he nosed into my side.

Reluctantly I gave in to his suggestion and carefully lifted myself to my paws. Standing wasn't too bad, balancing on three paws with my tail extended. The first step though, almost sent me right back to the ground again, losing my balance as I tried to place my missing forepaw down to hold my weight.

I whimpered in pain and squeezed my eyes closed. A hot burning sensation flooded behind my eyes. Moisture tickled at my scales.

Airil gasped. "Are you… crying?"

I opened my eyes. My vision blurred. I blinked a few times, slowly clearing it. The moisture lingered on my cheeks. I flicked out my tongue to taste it. Salty. Strange.

Ddraig Boruc nodded, as though he had just seen something to confirm his thoughts. He did not share them with us.

I could only stand still, stunned. Only a Nixan dragon could cry. Only a Nixan could use magic. Now tears leaked from my eyes and magical heat burned through my blood. What did that make me?

Prince Kyrus whistled. "Come, Ellian. Your dragons await."

I slowly started to walk. Or, at least, hop. Each step was torture, but I did not flare my wings. I needed to learn how to move properly without my paw. I would not always be able to rely on flying.

With my injured leg held up against my body, I half-hopped forward with each step, struggling to keep my weight balanced far enough back whenever I moved my foreleg. My mate provided all the physical support I needed, giving me a shoulder to lean on and help me to adjust my steps.

By the time I reached the summit my three legs burned with the exertion. My head stayed low as I breathed deeply, and I ignored all of those gathered to collapse to the ground. I felt a paw on my back, and after a few moments a little energy started to pulse into me, radiating down from the paw and through my body. The aches in my legs started to fade.

"Thank you, that feels better," I muttered, taking a few moments to enjoy the sensation of not having any pain to worry about before I attempted to stand again.

"You're welcome, Ddraig," a voice said. I tilted my head before looking up. I had expected Kaz, but instead I saw emerald scales, not sapphire. Isikian, one of Anzig's companions. I was surprised to see him here. Looking past the healer though, I saw that Anzig's other companions had joined us. Keita and Okazuni huddled together with Isikian's brother, Inilta. Beside them was Azlak and his mate. I was even more surprised to see that they were guarding Maznar with Haeraig Zeena keeping a watchful eye over them. Haeraig Ilibela was another dragon I didn't expect to see. I had been under the impression Clan Xigax had captured and imprisoned her. I could only assume they had dragged her here to answer for the crimes of Clan Xital. Her white scales were dirty and stained with a little blood, while her green eyes stared down to the ground without once looking up.

Everyone else present was who I expected to be there. The various surviving ddraigs had come, as had Alaron and the gryphon prince. The wyvern gestured with one wing towards me that I could remain lying down as he started to speak.

"War is over. Esperance's debt has been paid," he said, looking around at the group of ddraigs. Prince Kyrus chirruped his agreement. "It is not for us to decide how dragonkind progresses from here, but we shall assist as the voice of Esperance to advise you."

Ddraig Nunahra was a slender ness typical of those from Clan Xigax. Her crimson red scales gleamed as she stepped forward. I had always thought the dragons from Xigax had their legs too far apart on their elongated and serpentine bodies, but if anything they turned this to their advantage in battle as their unique body structure gave them much more flexibility than any other dragon.

"Xital must never be allowed to rule again after what they have done to dragonkind," she snarled, her long neck twisting so that she could glare at Haeraig Ilibela, who cowered from the Xigax ness. "They have proven they can no longer be trusted to act as our leader."

Ddraig Kiarla was the next to speak. "And what of those clans who have lost everything?" she asked in a small voice. "My clan numbers twenty dragons now, plus a few hatchlings and their carers still sheltering in our lair. Clan Eltee is finished."

"Lilisxi may never recover from this either," Ddraig Bakucic added, his voice still proud and strong.

"We have also taken punishing losses," Ddraig Hyantl said, the big Axaatl drake puffing out his chest. "It would be difficult even for our clans to provide the support needed to ensure the minor clans survive. Should they not come to our lairs, rather than trying to continue with broken clans?"

Ddraig Nunahra flicked her tail. "For better or worse, we have space in our lairs now."

The Lilisxi ddraig growled, showing no fear before two of the most powerful dragons. "You would have us abandon the lairs we have held for generations? And for what, so the strong can get stronger with our numbers?"

"It was our strength that secured your survival," Ddraig Nunahra said. She pointedly turned her head away from Bakucic, ignoring his growling protests.

As they had promised, Alaron and Kyrus did not contribute to the discussion at all, keeping slightly behind the dragons and watching on as they argued. No one even bothered to ask them for their opinion.

Haeraig Zeena was the next to step forward. The Nixan glared at those who dared to meet her eyes. "Bickering will lead to nothing. It was this weakness that Xital was able to exploit. Only one dragon had the foresight to see this and she united the clans to fight as one. I would hear what Ddraig Ellian has to say."

Silence fell as eyes turned towards me. Everyone, even Ddraig Nunahra, bowed their head. I had not realised how truthful Prince Kyrus and Airil had been. They truly respected me.

With difficulty I hauled myself up to my paws and hopped forward. I hoped they did not look to me for grace.

I kept my silence as I looked around all those gathered. We were the ddraigs and haeraigs of the clans. Some of us wielded power through the size of our clan or through the history and prestige of our land. Others were from smaller clans, never given the opportunity to grow because of their more powerful neighbours. Were dragons like Kiarla and Bakucic really lesser than dragons like Hyantl or myself?

What about dragons like Tsona? Why was it that he got to fly dragons dangerously close to extinction, vulnerable to humans like George or Rico?

The answer was clear to me. I opened my mouth to betray the memory of every ddraig who had come before me.

"For generations, clans have divided us and kept us apart. Have these few days not shown us that when we fight as one, with one cause, we are stronger?" I said quietly, knowing that every last one of them was holding on to my every word. I turned my gaze to the wyvern and gryphon. "Prince Kyrus. Alaron. Do your species divide themselves as we have done? Squabbling amongst ourselves and hindering our very chances of survival?"

"We are several nations that do not always get along, much like the humans in that regard," Kyrus said as his cold eyes swept around the group of dragons. "But I certainly do not know of any species that split themselves off so drastically, and in such small groups, as dragons. It truly is an unusual way of living."

"And scrapping over the same piece of territory too," Alaron added. "It distracts from what is truly important for dragonkind. You ddraigs spend so long trying to out-do each other that you end up clipping your own wings just so long as your rival is hobbled more."

I nodded and glanced around at the other ddraigs and haeraigs. "I propose that we dissolve the clans." I had to snarl to silence a few of the immediate protests. "We dissolve the clans and we truly unite as a species. We've been too busy looking in at ourselves that we've forgotten there's a bigger world out there. We've been trying to fly against the wind. It's time for that to stop."

"What you're proposing… it would never be accepted," Ddraig Bakucic said. A few murmurs of agreement rippled through the other dragons. "I fear some ddraigs would never want to release the power they hold in their paws." Though his eyes never strayed from beneath my forepaw, I could tell who he was implying. It was certainly true that a select few clans held more power than others, especially amongst the ruling clans. With the ddraigs and haeraig of six of those clans present, it was a dangerous thing for Ddraig Bakucic to say.

The tense silence shattered with a barked laugh from Ddraig Hyantl.

"Three months ago we were gathered in Xital at the great council," the Axaatl dragon said. He paced around the circle of dragons, not once stopping. "We all listened as a Laxtal dragon gave us a mad proposal. Send a pawful of dragons into human lands and steal the Axinstone. We all thought it to be too foolish to work. And yet it succeeded. Now we listen to a Laxtal ness propose to dissolve the clans. Every bit as foolish as Anzig. But perhaps so crazy that it might work."

I blinked in surprise. Of all the dragons present, I had not expected support from Ddraig Hyantl.

Haeraig Zeena stepped forward, stopping the Axaatl dragon from pacing past her. "Dragonkind still needs a leader. There has to be someone to look up to and follow. Clan Xital was that before, but if we dissolve the clans, then who shall step up in their place?"

"Having a single ruler is what got us into this trouble to begin with," Ddraig Boruc rumbled. I was surprised at how little he was getting himself involved, but like the gryphon and wyvern, he was standing back from everyone else. His knowledge and experience from his long life would have been useful indeed.

Tsona had gathered power unchecked and unquestioned, even by his own clan as he had welcomed in human traitors. Such a situation could not happen a second time. We had to avoid giving one clan, one dragon, so much power.

Once more, all eyes turned to me.

"We form a council to rule. One dragon from this council can lead us," I suggested.

"Is that not what the ruling clans were meant to be?" Ddraig Bakucic said accusingly. I flared my wings briefly.

"In theory, yes. But Clan Xital simply wielded too much power that they could ignore whatever the ruling clans suggested. If we start anew, with the ruling ddraig unable to act without the council's support, then we eliminate the chance of another Tsona," I said, noticing a few nods replacing the snarls and mutters of discontent.

"And who would be on this council?" Ddraig Kiarla asked. She swirled her tailtip across the ground behind her, twisting up small blades of grass.

"Let them decide," I said, gesturing with a wing down the hill, to where I noticed from the corner of my eye a great crowd of dragons and gryphons were gathering. Though I knew they would not be able to hear us, still they gathered in curiosity to know what we said. "Give the council a year at a time, but if we don't think they're doing the best for dragonkind, a new dragon comes in to replace them."

"And the council would elect a leader from amongst them?" Haeraig Zeena said, her head tilted slightly to one side. "I think that could actually work. There would be some resistance, of course. But in time, everyone should come to accept that sharing the rule will be beneficial for all."

I bowed my head to the Nixan, thankful for her support. I had thought that she would have been most vocal against such an idea, and perhaps before Nixa had lost their home, she would have been firmly against it. Now it was a chance to restore some balance of power back towards Nixa, even if the clan itself wouldn't exist anymore.

"Then are we all agreed?" Alaron said, the wyvern coming forward to speak for the first time since I had directly addressed him. He looked around the group, who all nodded and confirmed their agreement to him. I felt a tingle flare through my body that wasn't magic. It was excitement.

Mushussu was right. I had the opportunity to change the future of dragonkind, and now my words had fulfilled that promise. I could only hope that I had made the right choice.

*"I cannot know the future, but I feel like you might have chosen wisely. My fractured selves have not felt this unified for centuries."*

Was this how Anzig had felt, all that time ago? I had watched him from my vantage point at the entry to the grand chamber in Xital with Keita as he had made his passionate plea for assistance to fight off the humans. He had been so proud then. How had it all ended in his death?

The wyvern had finished getting everyone's assent, even allowing Haeraig Ilibela and the other dragons to give their opinion. There were no arguments or counter-suggestions. Only Maznar remained silent.

"Then it is settled. For ease of transition, the first council will be the first to be appointed, not chosen. Every ddraig and haeraig present here knows what is expected of them, and as such should form the first council," the wyvern said, looking around with a stern eye. "I can trust you to select a leader from amongst you. I call on each of you to nominate another dragon to act as the leader of all dragonkind."

The wyvern turned first to Ddraig Bakucic, who responded without hesitation. "Ddraig Ellian."

Ddraig Kiarla was next, and her answer was the same. As was Haeraig Zeena's and Ddraig Boruc's.

By the time Ddraig Hyantl added his vote with my name it became clear who would be the chosen representative. Only Haeraig Ilibela hesitated. Every single dragon spoke my name. Alaron didn't even bother asking me my nomination. It mattered for little.

"Congratulations, Ddraig Ellian. As ddraig of a united dragonkind, I believe it's your responsibility now to address your dragons," Alaron said, bowing his head to me. It was a gesture repeated by everyone else present, even Kyrus.

I nodded and rose to my paws, holding my injured leg against my belly again. I hopped forward so I stood on the edge of an outcropping looking down. My heart skipped a beat in my chest as I saw how few survivors there really were. Only a few hundred dragons gathered below, about the same number again for gryphons. About a dozen humans stood amongst them. I noticed a few Xitals down there too, refugees from the betrayal by their former allies.

I knew that any victory speech would be in poor taste with so few surviving. It would feel hollow and unwarranted, so I didn't even refer to the battle we had just fought so bravely for. That wasn't what we needed.

"Today a new wind blows for dragonkind. One that will push us into a new era, where we don't hide away from the rest of the world. If you'll have me, I shall lead you all there, where we work together as one, and not have to worry about petty clan politics and rivalries," I said, my voice picking up in volume so that even the most distant dragons could hear me. I could tell I had them all listening to me intently. "Those who can still fly, take to wing and head to Xital. There we shall all decide the fate of dragonkind. Everyone shall have their voice heard."

I did not expect a strong response from my words, but I was surprised from the roars of approval from the bottom of the hill. Dragons from every clan rose to their paws and spread their wings. One by one, they all started to fly, leaving only the healers and those yet to recover amongst the humans and gryphons. Once in the air they all began to wheel around to the south, down towards Xital, far beyond the horizon.

"Why Xital?" Zeena asked me as I turned back around to face my newly formed council. Ilibela glared at me, grinding her teeth but wisely kept her silence.

I was quick to reply. "It's central, has the capacity to support a large population of dragons in terms of shelter and hunting grounds, and has been where dragonkind has been ruled from for generations. It makes sense to go there," I said. I looked around at the small group, but no one offered any dissent, for which I was glad. It would have been a poor start to my leadership.

Hyantl dipped his head, though such was his size that his eyes were still above mine. "We should send for those still in our lairs to meet us in Xital."

"Go and see to it."

"Certainly, Ddraig Ellian." The Axaatl dragon took to wing. Unlike the other dragons, he turned north.

I hopped to address the rest of the council. "The same is asked of you all. Fly to your clans and summon all dragons to Xital. When our future is decided we can determine which of the old lairs will be most suitable for us. Until then, we keep Xital as a beacon for a united species."

Despite his earlier reluctance to cede his lair, Bakucic's eyes were bright. "We will meet you in Xital, Ddraig Ellian."

One by one, the former ddraigs and haeraigs took to wing. Of them all, only Ilibela remained, still under the watchful eye of Prince Kyrus.

I breathed a slow sigh of relief when the last of them were out of sight. Airil pressed close to my side, but I had more to say, more to resolve. I turned to the wyvern and gryphon, doing my best to ignore the snarl on Ilibela's mouth. "Will you be leaving us now, or will you join us in Xital for a short while? You will be free to share our hunting grounds for as long as you like."

Alaron looked up to Kyrus for a moment. Something wordless passed between them. Both nodded. The gryphon chirruped and clicked his beak. "The offer will be graciously accepted, Ddraig Ellian. It will be nice to rest our wings for a short while."

"I'm quite looking forward to doing the same, if I'm to be honest," I said with a smile. My wings were weary and, despite the thrill of the council, my heart was heavy with all those we had lost.

Azlak cautiously approached. The seer gazed at me with eyes shining gold. "You have done an amazing thing today, Ddraig Ellian."

I didn't have anything to say to that. I didn't really want to know what he had Seen in the future, but I was glad that he believed I had made the right choice, echoing the thoughts of Mushussu.

"When will you fly to Xital?" Alaron asked.

I looked down to the dragons still at the bottom of the hill, the wounded and the healers. "When the last of them can fly. Only then will I leave here."

Prince Kyrus chirped. "Then I shall see to my apothecaries and arrange those who can assist."

The gryphon took to wing and soared down to the survivors of his species. I kept my eyes on him for a short while, noticing a distinctive gryphon with blue feathers amongst them. The one who had cared for my brother. I wondered what he would have thought of this.

Mulner had done so much for this new future. I vowed to speak to those gryphons who had helped him. I hoped they would preserve his memory with the same fervour I would hold on to his sacrifice.

I bowed my head as Alaron also took to wing, taking with him Ilibela and Maznar. It was not long before I was alone with Airil.

"I can't believe that just happened," I said quietly, turning to my mate and resting my head on his shoulder.

He rested his paw on mine. "Ddraig of all dragonkind. I'm sure Ddraig Boruc would say otherwise, but I don't think any other dragon has ever claimed that before," he said with a grin. I batted his body with a wing, but his smile was infectious, and I couldn't help but smile back at him. "So. What are you going to do while you wait for the healers to finish?"

I closed my eyes. Excitement warred for control of my emotions with fear and apprehension. There was so much I needed to do. I had to learn how to walk again. I needed to accept the reality that I carried the weight of dragonkind on my wings.

But there was only one thing that I wanted to do first.

I ran my tongue over the new glands in my mouth and felt the heat of magic within me.

"I think I'm going to learn how to breath fire."

# CHAPTER THIRTY-FIVE

**Azlak**

It had been two months already and winter was preparing to give way to spring. This was a future I had never once foreseen, but then my magic was still inconsistent at the best of times. Xital was thriving, the towering mountain overseeing so much activity.

Word had quickly spread through the surviving clans that a new leadership had been set up within the former royal clan's home. Dragons had come from far and wide, abandoning the old clan territories to live within view of the lone mountain. Clan loyalties meant nothing now, and dragons from the north mingled with those from the south, the east, and the west. It wasn't perfect. Fights still broke out as dragons fought for the prime caves that dotted the landscape, and for the best hunting areas, but we as a species were learning.

I sat with Kaz on the summit of the Xital mountain, looking over everything. A flock of gryphons wheeled and soared nearby. They had taken refuge with us for two months now, but Kyrus was talking of flying south soon, taking Alaron with him. We had achieved peace thanks to their efforts, and they had extended the offer of friendship with Ddraig Ellian.

About thirty humans would stay and live in Xital, their houses built close to the slopes of the mountain. James McArthur was not to be amongst them. He, too, would be leaving soon, heading back to Trevena with the other humans who wished to return home. Going with them would be Maznar. My sister had endured many days of trial, explaining her actions to Ddraig Ellian and her council. They had judged that while she had acted of her own free will most of the time, she had been with humans from the egg. From a young age, corruption had set in her thoughts. They could not fault some of her actions against dragons, but nor could they trust her to remain in Xital. She would go back to Trevena to live amongst humans.

Our only fear was that there had been no sign of Rico. The human who had manufactured and created this entire conflict. No one knew anything about him, and nor had Alaron been able to track where he had disappeared to.

There had been little contact with Kernow on the other side of the mountains. What news did reach us told us that Erik Brightwell's power had faded almost overnight. With the defeat of his army and the loss of Rico and George, his control over his own nation had faded. Kernow had a new ddraig now; a new prime minister who had bigger problems to deal with on their side of the mountains than deal with us. Dragonkind had an opportunity to recover. We were not going to waste that chance.

Ddraig Ellian, Three Paw, as she was often now known, was not going to let us.

Magic had touched Ddraig Ellian in our assault of the Hellfire. That magic had changed her, and she was not the only one. My tongue teased at the unfamiliar fire glands in my mouth. Kaz had also taken the blessings of the ancient magic all dragons had once possessed. The gods and magic itself had touched us, changing us in their image.

I rested my head against Kaz's. Everything looked perfect for dragonkind to prosper once more. We had been in danger of extinction, but now we had a new start. A chance to build a new future.

But it was not mine.

I smiled as I felt what I had been waiting for days to feel, what Kaz, Alaron, and Kyrus had all been waiting for. The slate in my paw buzzed.

Esperance called.

# END OF BOOK 3

The saga of Farenar will continue. Follow J.F.R. Coates on social media for more information.

# ABOUT THE AUTHOR

J.F.R. Coates was born and raised in picturesque Somerset, England, but she moved to Brisbane, Australia as a teenager. She grew up reading from a young age, starting with Enid Blyton's *The Famous Five* and *Secret Seven*, before finding her calling with J.R.R. Tolkien's *The Hobbit*. Speculative Fiction has gripped her ever since, and now she calls amongst her favourite authors Maggie Furey, Robin Hobb, and Neil Gaiman.

She still lives in Brisbane, where she lives with her husband and – as seems ubiquitous for authors –two cats.

You can follow her on your social media of choice: Twitter, Facebook, Mastodon, Instagram, and Bluesky. Just search for jfrcoates.

She also has a Patreon, which allows for sneak-previews of what's to come, as well as additional stories that fit in around her novels. All support is always gratefully received.

https://www.patreon.com/jfrcoates

J.F.R. Coates